THE WORKS OF

WILKIE COLLINS

VOLUME FIFTEEN

WITH TWELVE ILLUSTRATIONS

POOR MISS FINCH

A DOMESTIC STORY

NEW YORK
PETER FENELON COLLIER, PUBLISHER

LIST OF ILLUSTRATIONS.

VOLUME FIFTEEN.

POOR MISS FINCH.

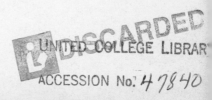

TO

MRS. ELLIOT,

(OF THE DEANERY, BRISTOL).

————

WILL you honor me by accepting the Dedication of this book, in remembrance of an uninterrupted friendship of many years.

More than one charming blind girl, in fiction and in the drama, has preceded "Poor Miss Finch." But, so far as I know, blindness in these cases has been always exhibited, more or less exclusively, from the ideal and the sentimental point of view. The attempt here made is to appeal to an interest of another kind, by exhibiting blindness as it really is. I have carefully gathered the information necessary to the execution of this purpose from competent authorities of all sorts. Whenever "Lucilla" acts or speaks in these pages, with reference to her blindness, she is doing or saying what persons afflicted as she is have done or said before her. Of the other features which I have added to produce and sustain interest in this central person-

(5)

age of my story, it does not become me to speak.
It is for my readers to say if "Lucilla" has
found her way to their sympathies. In this
character, and more especially again in the
characters of "Nugent Dubourg" and "Madame Pratolungo," I have tried to present human nature in its inherent inconsistencies and
self-contradictions—in its intricate mixture of
good and evil, of great and small—as I see it in
the world about me. But the faculty of observing character is so rare, the curiously mistaken
tendency to look for logical consistency in human motives and human actions is so general,
that I may possibly find the execution of this
part of my task misunderstood—sometimes even
resented—in certain quarters. However, Time
has stood my friend in relation to other characters of mine in other books—and who can say
that Time may not help me again here? Perhaps, one of these days, I may be able to make
use of some of the many interesting stories of
events that have really happened, which have
been placed in my hands by persons who could
speak as witnesses to the truth of the narrative.
Thus far, I have not ventured to disturb the repose of these manuscripts in the locked drawer
allotted to them. The true incidents are so "far-
fetched"; and the conduct of the real people is
so "grossly improbable"!

As for the object which I have had in view in
writing this story, it is, I hope, plain enough to
speak for itself. I subscribe to the article of belief which declares, that the conditions of human

happiness are independent of bodily affliction, and that it is even possible for bodily affliction itself to take its place among the ingredients of happiness. These are the views which "Poor Miss Finch" is intended to advocate—and this is the impression which I hope to leave on the mind of the reader when the book is closed.

W. C.

January 16, 1872.

NOTE TO THE PRESENT EDITION.

In expressing my acknowledgments for the favorable reception accorded to the previous editions of this story, I may take the present opportunity of adverting to one of the characters, not alluded to in the Letter of Dedication. The German oculist—"Herr Grosse"—has impressed himself so strongly as a real personage on the minds of some of my readers afflicted with blindness, or suffering from diseases of the eye, that I have received several written applications requesting me to communicate his present address to patients desirous of consulting him! Sincerely appreciating the testimony thus rendered to the truth of this little study of character, I have been obliged to acknowledge to my correspondents—and I may as well repeat it here—that Herr Grosse has no (individual) living prototype. Like the other Persons of the Drama, in this book and in the books which have preceded it, he is drawn from my general observation of humanity. I have always considered it to be a mistake in Art to limit the delineation of character in fiction to a literary portrait taken from any one "sitter." The result of this process is generally (to my mind) to produce a caricature instead of a character.

November 27, 1872.

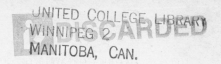

POOR MISS FINCH.

PART THE FIRST.

CHAPTER THE FIRST.

MADAME PRATOLUNGO PRESENTS HERSELF.

You are here invited to read the story of an
Event which occurred some years since in an
out-of-the-way corner of England.

The persons principally concerned in the Event
are—a blind girl, two (twin) brothers, a skilled
surgeon, and a curious foreign woman. I am
the curious foreign woman. And I take it on
myself—for reasons which will presently appear
—to tell the story.

So far we understand each other. Good. I
may make myself known to you as briefly as
I can.

I am Madame Pratolungo—widow of that celebrated South American patriot, Doctor Pratolungo. I am French by birth. Before I married the doctor I went through many vicissitudes
in my own country. They ended in leaving me
(at an age which is of no consequence to anybody) with some experience of the world, with a

(9)

cultivated musical talent on the pianoforte, and
with a comfortable little fortune unexpectedly
bequeathed to me by a relative of my dear dead
mother (which fortune I shared with good Papa
and with my younger sisters).   To these qualifi-
cations I added another, the most precious of all
when I married the Doctor—namely, a strong
infusion of ultra-liberal principles. *Vive la
Republique!*

Some people do one thing, and some do another, in the way of celebrating the event of
their marriage.   Having become man and wife,
Doctor Pratolungo and I took ship to Central
America, and devoted our honeymoon, in those
disturbed districts, to the sacred duty of destroying tyrants.

Ah! the vital air of my noble husband was
the air of revolutions.   From his youth upward
he had followed the glorious profession of Patriot.   Wherever the people of the Southern New
World rose and declared their independence—
and, in my time, that fervent population did
nothing else—there was the Doctor self-devoted
on the altar of his adopted country.   He had
been fifteen times exiled, and condemned to death
in his absence, when I met with him in Paris—
the picture of heroic poverty, with a brown complexion and one lame leg.   Who could avoid falling in love with such a man?   I was proud when
he proposed to devote me on the altar of his
adopted country, as well as himself—me and my
money.   For, alas! everything is expensive in
this world, including the destruction of tyrants

and the saving of Freedom. All my money went in helping the sacred cause of the people. Dictators and filibusters flourished in spite of us. Before we had been a year married the Doctor had to fly (for the sixteenth time) to escape being tried for his life. My husband condemned to death in his absence; and I with my pockets empty. This is how the Republic rewarded us. And yet I love the Republic. Ah, you monarchy people, sitting fat and contented under tyrants, respect that!

This time we took refuge in England. The affairs of Central America went on without us.

I thought of giving lessons in music. But my glorious husband could not spare me away from him. I suppose we should have starved, and made a sad little paragraph in the English newspapers, if the end had not come in another way. My poor Pratolungo was, in truth, worn out. He sank under his sixteenth exile. I was left a widow—with nothing but the inheritance of my husband's noble sentiments to console me.

I went back for a while to good Papa and my sisters in Paris. But it was not in my nature to remain and be a burden on them at home. I returned again to London, with recommendations, and encountered inconceivable disasters in the effort to earn a living honorably. Of all the wealth about me—the prodigal, insolent, ostentatious wealth—none fell to my share. What right has anybody to be rich? I defy you, whoever you may be, to prove that anybody has a right to be rich.

Without dwelling on my disasters, let it be enough to say that I got up one morning with three pounds, seven shillings, and fourpence in my purse, with my excellent temper, and my republican principles, and with absolutely nothing in prospect—that is to say, with not a half-penny more to come to me, unless I could earn it for myself.

In this sad case what does an honest woman, who is bent on winning her own independence by her own work, do? She takes three and sixpence out of her little humble store, and she advertises herself in a newspaper.

One always advertises the best side of one's self. (Ah, poor humanity!) My best side was my musical side. In the days of my vicissitudes (before my marriage) I had at one time had a share in a millinery establishment in Lyons. At another time I had been bed-chamber woman to a great lady in Paris. But in my present situation these sides of myself were, for various reasons, not so presentable as the pianoforte side. I was not a great player—far from it; but I had been soundly instructed, and I had what you call a competent skill on the instrument. Brief, I made the best of myself, I promise you, in my advertisement.

The next day I borrowed the newspaper to enjoy the pride of seeing my composition in print. Ah, Heaven! what did I discover? I discovered what other wretched advertising people have found out before me. Above my own advertisement the very thing I wanted was advertised for by somebody else. Look in any news-paper and you will see strangers who (if I may so express myself) exactly fit each other advertis-ing for each other without knowing it. I had advertised myself as "accomplished musical companion for a lady. With cheerful temper to match." And there, above me, was my un-known necessitous fellow-creature crying out in printers' types: "Wanted, a companion for a lady. Must be an accomplished musician, and have a cheerful temper. Testimonials to capac-ity and first-rate references required." Exactly what I had offered. "Apply by letter only in the first instance." Exactly what I had said. Fie upon me! I had spent three and sixpence for nothing. I threw down the newspaper in a transport of anger (like a fool), and then took it up again (like a sensible woman), and applied by letter for the offered place.

My letter brought me into contact with a law-yer. The lawyer enveloped himself in mystery. It seemed to be a professional habit with him to tell nobody anything if he could possibly help it.

Drop by drop this wearisome man let the cir-cumstances out. The lady was a young lady. She was the daughter of a clergyman. She lived in a retired part of the country. More even than that, she lived in a retired part of the house. Her father had married a second time. Having only the young lady as child by his first marriage, he had (I suppose by way of a change) a large family by his second marriage. Circum-stances rendered it necessary for the young lady to live as much apart as she could from the tumult of a houseful of children. So he went on, until there was no keeping it in any longer, and then he let it out—the young lady was blind!

Young—lonely—blind. I had a sudden inspiration. I felt I should love her.

The question of my musical capacity was in this sad case a serious one. The poor young lady had one great pleasure to illumine her dark life—music. Her companion was wanted to play from the book, and play worthily, the works of the great masters (whom this young creature adored); and she, listening, would take her place next at the piano and reproduce the music, morsel by morsel, by ear. A professor was appointed to pronounce sentence on me, and declare if I could be trusted not to misinterpret Mozart, Beethoven, and the other masters who have written for the piano. Through this ordeal I passed with success. As for my references, they spoke for themselves. Not even the lawyer (though he tried hard) could pick holes in them. It was arranged on both sides that I should, in the first instance, go on a month's visit to the young lady. If we both wished it at the end of that time, I was to stay, on terms arranged to my perfect satisfaction. There was our treaty!

The next day I started for my visit by the railway.

My instructions directed me to travel to the town of Lewes, in Sussex. Arrived there, I was to ask for the pony-chaise of my young lady's father—described on his card as Reverend Tertius

Finch. The chaise was to take me to the rectory house in the village of Dimchurch. And the village of Dimchurch was situated among the South Down Hills, three or four miles from the coast.

When I stepped into the railway carriage this was all I knew. After my adventurous life—after the volcanic agitations of my republican career in the Doctor's time—was I about to bury myself in a remote English village, and live a life as monotonous as the life of a sheep on a hill? Ah! with all my experience, I had yet to learn that the narrowest human limits are wide enough to contain the grandest human emotions. I had seen the Drama of Life amid the turmoil of tropical revolutions. I was to see it again, with all its palpitating interest, in the breezy solitudes of the South Down Hills.

CHAPTER THE SECOND.

MADAME PRATOLUNGO MAKES A VOYAGE ON LAND.

A WELL-FED boy, with yellow Saxon hair, a little shabby green chaise, and a rough brown pony—these objects confronted me at the Lewes station. I said to the boy, "Are you Reverend Finch's servant?" And the boy answered, "I be he."

We drove through the town—a hilly town of desolate, clean houses. No living creatures visible behind the jealously shut windows. No living creatures entering or departing through the sad-colored closed doors. No theater; no place of amusement, except an empty town-hall, with a sad policeman meditating on its spruce white steps. No customers in the shops, and nobody to serve them behind the counter, even if they had turned up. Here and there on the pavement an inhabitant with a capacity for staring, and (apparently) a capacity for nothing else. I said to Reverend Finch's boy, "Is this a rich place?" Reverend Finch's boy brightened, and answered, "That it be!" Good. At any rate, they don't enjoy themselves here—the infamous rich!

Leaving this town of unamused citizens immured in domestic tombs, we got on a fine high-road—still ascending—with a spacious open country on either side of it.

A spacious open country is a country soon exhausted by a sight-seer's eyes. I have learned from my poor Pratolungo the habit of searching for the political convictions of my fellow-creatures when I find myself in contact with them in strange places. Having nothing else to do, I searched Finch's boy. His political programme I found to be: As much meat and beer as I can contain, and as little work to do for it as possible. In return for this, to touch my hat when I meet the Squire, and to be content with the station to which it has pleased God to call me. Miserable Finch's boy!

We reached the highest point of the road. On

our right hand the ground sloped away gently
into a fertile valley, with a village and a church
in it; and beyond, an abominable privileged inclosure of grass and trees torn from the community by a tyrant, and called a Park, with the
palace in which this enemy of mankind caroused
and fattened standing in the midst. On our left
hand spread the open country—a magnificent
prospect of grand grassy hills rolling away to the
horizon, bounded only by the sky. To my surprise, Finch's boy descended, took the pony by
the head, and deliberately led him off the high
road, and on to the wilderness of grassy hills, on
which not so much as a footpath was discernible
anywhere, far or near. The chaise began to
heave and roll like a ship on the sea. It became
necessary to hold with both hands to keep my
place. I thought first of my luggage—then of
myself.

"How much is there of this?" I asked.

"Three mile on't," answered Finch's boy.

I insisted on stopping the ship—I mean the
chaise—and on getting out. We tied my luggage fast with a rope; and then we went on
again, the boy at the pony's head, and I after
them on foot.

Ah, what a walk it was! What air over my
head, what grass under my feet! The sweetness of the inner land and the crisp saltness of
the distant sea were mixed in that delicious
breeze. The short turf, fragrant with odorous
herbs, rose and fell elastic underfoot. The
mountain piles of white cloud moved in sub-

lime procession along the blue field of heaven
overhead. The wild growth of prickly bushes,
spread in great patches over the grass, was in a
glory of yellow bloom. On we went; now up,
now down; now bending to the right, and now
turning to the left. I looked about me. No
house, no road, no paths, fences, hedges, walls;
no landmarks of any sort. All round us, turn
which way we· might, nothing was to be seen
but the majestic solitude of the hills. No living
creatures appeared but the white dots of sheep
scattered over the soft green distance, and the
sky-lark singing his hymn of happiness, a speck
above my head. Truly a wonderful place! Distant not more than a morning's drive from noisy
and populous Brighton—a stranger to this neighborhood could only have found his way by the
compass, exactly as if he had been sailing on the
sea. The further we penetrated on our land voyage, the more wild and the more beautiful the
solitary landscape grew. The boy picked his
way as he chose—there were no barriers here.
Plodding behind, I saw nothing at one time but
the back of the chaise tilted up in the air, both
boy and pony being invisibly buried in the steep
descent of the hill. At other times the pitch
was all the contrary way; the whole interior of
the ascending chaise was disclosed to my view,
and above the chaise the pony, and above the
pony the boy—and, ah, my luggage swaying
and rocking in the frail embraces of the rope
that held it. Twenty times did I confidently
expect to see baggage, chaise, pony, boy, all

rolling down into the bottom of a valley together. But no! Not the least little accident happened to spoil my enjoyment of the day. Politically contemptible, Finch's boy had his merit—he was master of his subject as guide and pony-leader among the South Down Hills.

Arrived at the top of (as it seemed to me) our fiftieth grassy summit, I began to look about for signs of the village.

Behind me rolled back the long undulations of the hills, with the cloud-shadows moving over the solitudes that we had left. Before me, at a break in the purple distance, I saw the soft white line of the sea. Beneath me, at my feet, opened the deepest valley I had noticed yet—with one first sign of the presence of Man scored hideously on the face of Nature, in the shape of a square brown patch of cleared and plowed land on the grassy slope. I asked if we were getting near the village now. Finch's boy winked, and answered, "Yes, we be."

Astonishing Finch's boy! Ask him what questions I might, the resources of his vocabulary remained invariably the same. Still this youthful Oracle answered always in three monosyllabic words!

We plunged into the valley.

Arrived at the bottom, I discovered another sign of Man. Behold the first road I had seen yet—a rough wagon-road plowed deep in the chalky soil! We crossed this and turned a corner of a hill. More signs of human life. Two small boys started up out of a dry ditch—appar-

ently set as scouts to give notice of our approach. They yelled and set off running before
us by some short-cut known only to themselves.
We turned again, round another winding of the
valley, and crossed a brook. I considered it my
duty to make myself acquainted with the local
names. What was the brook called? It was
called "The Cockshoot!" And the great hill,
here, on my right? It was called "The Over-
blow!" Five minutes more, and we saw our
first house—lonely and little—built of mortar
and flint from the hills. A name to this also?
Certainly! Name of "Browndown." Another
ten minutes of walking, involving us more and
more deeply in the mysterious green windings of
the valley, and the great event of the day happened at last. Finch's boy pointed before him
with his whip, and said (even at this supreme
moment still in three monosyllabic words):

"Here we be!"

So this is Dimchurch! I shake out the chalk-
dust from the skirts of my dress. I long (quite
vainly) for the least bit of looking-glass to see
myself in. Here is the population (to the number of at least five or six) gathered together, informed by the scouts, and it is my woman's
business to produce the best impression of myself
that I can. We advance along the little road.
I smile upon the population; the population
stares at me in return. On one side I remark
three or four cottages and a bit of open ground;
also an inn named "The Cross-Hands," and a
bit more of open ground; also a tiny, tiny,

butcher-shop, with sanguinary insides of sheep on one blue pie-dish in the window, and no other meat than that, and nothing to see beyond but again the open ground, and again the hills, indicating the end of the village on this side. On the other side there appears for some distance nothing but a long flint wall guarding the out-houses of a farm. Beyond this comes another little group of cottages, with the seal of civiliza-tion set upon them in the form of a post-office. The post-office deals in general commodities—in boots and bacon, biscuits and flannel, crinoline petticoats and religious tracts. Further on, be-hold another flint wall, a garden, and a private dwelling-house, proclaiming itself as the rec-tory. Further yet, on rising ground, a little desolate church, with a tiny white circular stee-ple topped by an extinguisher in red tiles. Be-yond this, the hills and the heavens once more. And there is Dimchurch!

As for the inhabitants—what am I to say? I suppose I must tell the truth.

I remarked one born gentleman among the in-habitants, and he was a sheep-dog. He alone did the honors of the place. He had a stump of a tail, which he wagged at me with extreme difficulty, and a good honest white and black face which he poked companionably into my hand. "Welcome, Madame Pratolungo, to Dim-church; and excuse these male and female labor-ers who stand and stare at you. The good God who makes us all has made them too, but has not succeeded so well as with you and me." I happen to be one of the few people who can read dogs' language as written in dogs' faces. I correctly report the language of the gentleman sheep-dog on this occasion.

We opened the gate of the rectory and passed in. So my Land Voyage over the South Down Hills came prosperously to its end.

CHAPTER THE THIRD.

POOR MISS FINCH.

THE rectory resembled, in one respect, this narrative that I am now writing. It was in Two Parts. Part the First, in front, composed of the everlasting flint and mortar of the neighborhood, failed to interes' me. Part the Second, running back at a righ' angle, asserted itself as ancient. It had been in its time, as I afterward heard, a convent of nuns. Here were snug little Gothic windows, and dark ivy-covered walls of venerable stone, repaired in places at some past period with quaint red bricks. I had hoped that I should enter the house by this side of it. But no. The boy—after appearing to be at a loss what to do with me—led the way to a door on the modern side of the building, and rang the bell.

A slovenly young maid-servant admitted me to the house.

Possibly this person was new to the duty of receiving visitors. Possibly she was bewildered by a sudden invasion of children in dirty frocks dart-

ing out on us in the hall, and then darting back
again into invisible back regions, screeching at
the sight of a stranger. At any rate, she too appeared to be at a loss what to do with me. After
staring hard at my foreign face, she suddenly
opened a door in the wall of the passage, and admitted me into a small room. Two more children
in dirty frocks darted, screaming, out of the asylum thus offered to me. I mentioned my name
as soon as I could make myself heard. The maid
appeared to be terrified at the length of it. I
gave her my card. The maid took it between a
dirty finger and thumb, looked at it as if it was
some extraordinary natural curiosity, turned it
round, exhibiting correct black impressions in
various parts of it of her finger and thumb, gave
up understanding it in despair, and left the room.
She was stopped outside (as I gathered from the
sounds) by a returning invasion of children in
the hall. There was whispering, there was gig-
gling, there was, every now and then, a loud
thump on the door. Prompted by the children,
as I suppose—pushed in by them, certainly—the
maid suddenly re-appeared with a jerk. "Oh,
if you please, come this way," she said. The invasion of children retreated again up the stairs,
one of them in possession of my card, and waving it in triumph on the first landing. We penetrated to the other end of the passage. Again a
door was opened. Unannounced, I entered another and a larger room. What did I see?

Fortune had favored me at last. My lucky
star had led me to the mistress of the house.

I made my best courtesy and found myself confronting a large, light-haired, languid, lymphatic lady, who had evidently been amusing herself by walking up and down the room at the moment when I appeared. If there can be such a thing as *a damp woman*, this was one. There was a humid shine on her colorless white face, and an overflow of water in her pale blue eyes. Her hair was not dressed, and her lace cap was all on one side. The upper part of her was clothed in a loose jacket of blue merino; the lower part was robed in a dimity dressing-gown of doubtful white. In one hand she held a dirty dog-eared book, which I at once detected to be a circulating library novel. Her other hand supported a baby enveloped in flannel, sucking at her breast. Such was my first experience of Reverend Finch's wife—destined to be also the experience of all after-time. Never completely dressed, never completely dry; always with a baby in one hand and a novel in the other—such was Finch's wife!

"Oh, Madame Pratolungo? Yes. I hope somebody has told Miss Finch you are here. She has her own establishment, and manages everything herself. Have you had a pleasant journey?" (These words were spoken vacantly, as if her mind was occupied with something else. My first impression of her suggested that she was a weak, good-natured woman, and that she must have originally occupied a station in the humbler ranks of life.)

"Thank you, Mrs. Finch," I said. "I have

enjoyed most heartily my journey among your beautiful hills."

"Oh, you like the hills? Excuse my dress. I was half an hour late this morning. When you lose half an hour in this house you never *can* pick it up again, try how you may." (I soon discovered that Mrs. Finch was always losing half an hour out of her day, and that she never, by any chance, succeeded in finding it again, as she had just told me.) "I understand, madam. The cares of a numerous family—"

"Ah! that's just where it is." (This was a favorite phrase with Mrs. Finch.) "There's Finch, he gets up in the morning, and goes and works in the garden. Then there's the washing of the children, and the dreadful waste that goes on in the kitchen. And Finch, he comes in without any notice, and wants his breakfast. And, of course, I can't leave the baby. And half an hour does slip away so easily that how to overtake it again I do assure you I really don't know." Here the baby began to exhibit symptoms of having taken more maternal nourishment than his infant stomach could comfortably contain. I held the novel while Mrs. Finch searched for her handkerchief — first, in her bed-gown pocket; secondly, here, there, and everywhere in the room.

At this interesting moment there was a knock at the door. An elderly woman appeared, who offered a most refreshing contrast to the members of the household with whom I had made acquaintance thus far. She was neatly dressed;

and she saluted me with the polite composure of a civilized being.

"I beg your pardon, ma'am. My young lady has only this moment heard of your arrival. Will you be so kind as to follow me?"

I turned to Mrs. Finch. She had found her handkerchief, and had put her overflowing baby to rights again. I respectfully handed back the novel. "Thank you," said Mrs. Finch. "I find novels compose my mind. Do you read novels too? Remind me, and I'll lend you this one to-morrow." I expressed my acknowledgments and withdrew. At the door I looked round, saluting the lady of the house. Mrs. Finch was promenading the room, with the baby in one hand and the novel in the other, and the dimity bed-gown trailing behind her.

We ascended the stairs, and entered a bare whitewashed passage, with drab-colored doors in it, leading, as I presumed, into the sleeping-chambers of the house.

Every door opened as we passed; children peeped out at me and banged the door to again. "What family has the present Mrs. Finch?" I asked. The decent elderly woman was obliged to stop and consider. "Including the baby, ma'am, and two sets of twins, and one seven months' child of deficient intellect—fourteen in all." Hearing this, I began—though I consider priests, kings and capitalists to be the enemies of the human race—to feel a certain exceptional interest in Reverend Finch. Did he never wish that he had been a priest of the Roman Catholic

Church, mercifully forbidden to marry at all? While the question passed through my mind my guide took out a key and opened a heavy oaken door at the further end of the passage.

"We are obliged to keep the door locked, ma'am," she explained, "or the children would be in and out of our part of the house all day long."

After my experience of the children, I own I looked at the oaken door with mingled sentiments of gratitude and respect.

We turned a corner, and found ourselves in the vaulted corridor of the ancient portion of the house.

The casement windows on one side—sunk deep in recesses—looked into the garden. Each recess was filled with groups of flowers in pots. On the other side the old wall was gayly decorated with hangings of bright chintz. The doors were colored of a creamy white, with gilt moldings. The brightly ornamented matting under our feet I at once recognized as of South American origin. The ceiling above was decorated in delicate pale blue, with borderings of flowers. Nowhere down the whole extent of the place was so much as a single morsel of dark color to be seen anywhere.

At the lower end of the corridor a solitary figure in a pure white robe was bending over the flowers in the window. This was the blind girl whose dark hours I had come to cheer. In the scattered villages of the South Downs the simple people added their word of pity to her name, and called her, compassionately, "Poor Miss

Finch." As for me, I can only think of her by her pretty Christian name. She is "Lucilla" when my memory dwells on her. Let me call her "Lucilla" here.

When my eyes first rested on her she was picking off the dead leaves from her flowers. Her delicate ear detected the sound of my strange footstep long before I reached the place at which she was standing. She lifted her head and advanced quickly to meet me, with a faint flush on her face, which came and died away again in a moment. I happen to have visited the picture-gallery at Dresden in former years. As she approached me, nearer and nearer, I was irresistibly reminded of the gem of that superb collection—the matchless Virgin of Raphael, called "The Madonna di San Sisto." The fair broad forehead; the peculiar fullness of the flesh between the eyebrow and the eyelid; the delicate outline of the lower face; the tender, sensitive lips; the color of the complexion and the hair—all reflected with a startling fidelity the lovely creature of the Dresden picture. The one fatal point at which the resemblance ceased was in the eyes. The divinely beautiful eyes of Raphael's Virgin were lost in the living likeness of her that confronted me now. There was no deformity, there was nothing to recoil from, in my blind Lucilla. The poor, dim, sightless eyes had a faded, changeless, inexpressive look—and that was all. Above them, below them, round them to the very edges of her eyelids, there was beauty, movement, life. *In* them—death. A more charming creature—with

that one sad drawback—I never saw. There was
no other personal defect in her. She had the fine
height, the well-balanced figure and the length
of the lower limbs which make all a woman's
movements graceful of themselves. Her voice
was delicious — clear, cheerful, sympathetic.
This, and her smile, which added a charm of
its own to the beauty of her mouth, won my
heart before she had got close enough to me to put
her hand in mine. "Ah, my dear!" I said, in
my headlong way, "I am so glad to see you!"
The instant the words passed my lips I could
have cut my tongue out for reminding her in
that brutal manner that she was blind.

To my relief, she showed no sign of feeling it
as I did.

"May I see you in *my* way?" she asked,
gently, and held up her pretty white hand.
"May I touch your face?"

I sat down at once on the window-seat. The
soft, rosy tips of her fingers seemed to cover my
whole face in an instant. Three separate times
she passed her hand rapidly over me, her own
face absorbed all the while in breathless attention to what she was about. "Speak again!"
she said, suddenly, holding her hand over me
in suspense. I said a few words. She stopped
me by a kiss. "No more!" she exclaimed, joyously. "Your voice says to my ears what your
face says to my fingers. I know I shall like you.
Come in and see the rooms we are going to live
in together."

As I rose she put her arm round my waist—

then instantly drew it away again, and shook her fingers impatiently, as if something had hurt them.

"A pin?" I asked.

"No! no! What colored dress have you got on?"

"Purple."

"Ah! I knew it! Pray don't wear dark colors. I have my own blind horror of anything that is dark. Dear Madame Pratolungo, wear pretty bright colors, to please *me!*" She put her arm caressingly round me again—round my neck, however, this time, where her hand could rest on my linen collar. "You will change your dress before dinner—won't you?" she whispered. "Let me unpack for you, and choose which dress I like."

The brilliant decorations of the corridor were explained to me now.

We entered the rooms; her bedroom, my bedroom, and our sitting-room between the two. I was prepared to find them—what they proved to be—as bright as looking-glasses and gilding and gayly colored ornaments and cheerful knick-knacks of all sorts could make them. They were more like rooms in my lively native country than rooms in sober, colorless England. The one thing which, I own, did still astonish me was that all this sparkling beauty of adornment in Lucilla's habitation should have been provided for the express gratification of a young lady who could not see. Experience was yet to show me that the blind can live in their imaginations, and have their favorite fancies and illusions like the rest of us.

To satisfy Lucilla by changing my dark purple dress, it was necessary that I should first have my boxes. So far as I knew, Finch's boy had taken my luggage, along with the pony, to the stables Before Lucilla could ring the bell to make inquiries, my elderly guide (who had silently left us while we were talking together in the corridor) re-appeared, followed by the boy and a groom, carrying my things. These servants also brought with them certain parcels for their young mistress, purchased in the town, together with a bottle, wrapped in fair white paper, which looked like a bottle of medicine—and which had a part of its own to play in our proceedings later in the day.

"This is my old nurse," said Lucilla, presenting her attendant to me. "Zillah can do a little of everything—cooking included. She has had lessons at a London club. You must like Zillah, Madame Pratolungo, for my sake. Are your boxes open?"

She went down on her knees before the boxes as she asked the question. No girl with the full use of her eyes could have enjoyed more thoroughly than she did the trivial amusement of unpacking my clothes. This time, however, her wonderful delicacy of touch proved to be at fault. Of two dresses of mine which happened to be exactly the same in texture, though widely different in color, she picked out the dark dress as being the light one. I saw that I disappointed her sadly when I told her of her mistake. The next guess she made, however, restored the tips of her fingers to their place in her estimation: she discovered the stripes in a smart pair of stockings of mine, and brightened up directly. "Don't be long dressing," she said, on leaving me. "We shall have dinner in half an hour— French dishes, in honor of your arrival. I like a nice dinner; I am what you call in your country *gourmande*. See the sad consequences!" She put one finger to her pretty chin. "I am getting fat; I am threatened with a double chin —at two-and-twenty. Shocking! shocking!"

So she left me. And such was the first impression produced on my mind by "Poor Miss Finch."

CHAPTER THE FOURTH.

TWILIGHT VIEW OF THE MAN.

OUR nice dinner had long since come to an end. We had chattered, chattered, chattered— as usual with women—all about ourselves. The day had declined, the setting sun was pouring its last red luster into our pretty sitting-room, when Lucilla started as if she had suddenly remembered something, and rang the bell.

Zillah came in. "The bottle from the chemist's," said Lucilla. "I ought to have remembered it hours ago."

"Are you going to take it to Susan yourself, my dear?"

I was glad to hear the old nurse address her

young lady in that familiar way. It was so
thoroughly un-English. Down with the devilish system of separation between the classes in
this country—that is what I say.

"Yes; I am going to take it to Susan myself."

"Shall I go with you?"

"No, no. Not the least occasion." She turned
to me. "I suppose you are too tired to go out
again after your walk on the hills?" she said.

I had dined; I had rested; I was quite ready
to go out again, and I said so.

Lucilla's face brightened. For some reason
of her own she had apparently attached a certain
importance to persuading me to go out with her.

"It's only a visit to a poor rheumatic woman
in the village," she said. "I have got an embrocation for her; and I can't very well send it.
She is old and obstinate. If I take it to her, she
will believe in the remedy. If anybody else
takes it, she will throw it away. I had utterly
forgotten her in the interest of our nice long talk.
Shall we get ready?"

I had hardly closed the door of my bedroom
when there was a knock at it. Lucilla; No:
the old nurse entering on tiptoe, with a face of
mystery, and a finger confidentially placed on
her lips.

"I beg your pardon, ma'am," she began in a
whisper. "I think you ought to know that my
young lady has a purpose in taking you out with
her this evening. She is burning with curiosity
—like all the rest of us, for that matter. She
took *me* out and used *my* eyes to see with yes-

terday evening, and they have not satisfied her.
She is going to try your eyes now."

"What is Miss Lucilla so curious about?" I
inquired.

"It's natural enough, poor dear," pursued the
old woman, following her own train of thought,
without the slightest reference to my question.
"We none of us can find out anything about
him. He usually takes his walk at twilight.
You are pretty sure to meet him to-night; and
you will judge for yourself, ma'am—with an innocent young creature like Miss Lucilla—what
it may be best to do."

This extraordinary answer set *my* curiosity in
a flame.

"My good creature," I said, "you forget that
I am a stranger. I know nothing about it. Has
this mysterious man got a name? Who is 'He'?"

As I said that there was another knock at the
door. Zillah whispered, eagerly: "Don't tell
upon me, ma'am! You will see for yourself. I
only speak for my young lady's good." She
hobbled away and opened the door—and there
was Lucilla, with her smart garden-hat on,
waiting for me.

We went out by our own door into the garden,
and, passing through a gate in the wall, entered
the village.

After the caution which the nurse had given
me, it was impossible to ask any questions, except at the risk of making mischief in our little
household on the first day of my joining it. I
kept my eyes wide open, and waited for events.

I also committed a blunder at starting—I offered
Lucilla my hand to lead her. She burst out
laughing.

"My dear Madame Pratolungo, I know my
way better than you do. I roam all over the
neighborhood with nothing to help me but this."

She held up a smart ivory walking-cane, with
a bright silk tassel attached. With her cane in
one hand, and her chemical bottle in the other—
and her roguish little hat on the top of her head
—she made the quaintest and prettiest picture
I had seen for many a long day. "*You* shall
guide *me*, my dear," I said, and took her arm.
We went on down the village.

Nothing in the least like a mysterious figure
passed us in the twilight. The few scattered
laboring people whom I had already seen I saw
again, and that was all. Lucilla was silent—
suspiciously silent, as I thought, after what Zillah had told me. She had, as I fancied, the look
of a person who was listening intently. Arrived
at the cottage of the rheumatic woman, she
stopped and went in, while I waited outside.
The affair of the embrocation was not long. She
was out again in a minute, and this time she
took my arm of her own accord.

"Shall we go a little further?" she said. "It
is so nice and cool at this hour of the evening."

Her object in view, whatever it might be, was
evidently an object that lay beyond the village.
In the solemn, peaceful twilight we followed the
lonely windings of the valley along which I had
passed in the morning. When we came opposite

the little solitary house which I had already
learned to know as "Browndown," I felt her
hand unconsciously tighten on my arm. "Aha!"
I said to myself. "Has Browndown anything
to do with this?"

"Does the view look very lonely to-night?"
she asked, waving her cane over the scene before
us.

The true meaning of that question I took to
be: "Do you see anybody walking out to-night?"
It was not my business to interpret her meaning
before she had thought fit to confide her secret to
me. "To my mind, dear," was all I said, "it is
a very beautiful view."

She fell silent again, and absorbed herself in
her own thoughts. We turned into a new winding of the valley, and there, walking toward us
from the opposite direction, was a human figure
at last—the figure of a solitary man!

As we got nearer to each other I perceived that
he was a gentleman; dressed in a light shooting-
jacket, and wearing a felt hat of the conical Italian shape. A little nearer, and I saw that he
was young. Nearer still, and I discovered that
he was handsome, though in rather an effeminate
way. At the same moment Lucilla heard his
footstep. Her color instantly rose, and once
again I felt her hand tighten involuntarily round
my arm. (Good! Here was the mysterious object of Zillah's warning to me found at last!)

I have, and I don't mind acknowledging it,
an eye for a handsome man. I looked at him as
he passed us. Now, I solemnly assure you, I

am not an ugly woman. Nevertheless, as our
eyes met, I saw the strange gentleman's face
suddenly contract, with an expression which
told me plainly that I had produced a disagreeable impression on him. With some difficulty
—for my companion was holding my arm, and
seemed disposed to stop altogether—I quickened
my pace so as to get by him rapidly; showing
him, I dare say, that I thought the change in
his face when I looked at him an impertinence
on his part. However that may be, after a momentary interval I heard his step behind. The
man had turned, and had followed us.

He came close to me, on the opposite side to
Lucilla, and took off his hat.

"I beg your pardon, ma'am," he said. "You
looked at me just now."

At the first sound of his voice I felt Lucilla
start. Her hand began to tremble on my arm
with some sudden agitation inconceivable to me.
In the double surprise of discovering this and of
finding myself charged so abruptly with the
offense of looking at a gentleman, I suffered the
most exceptional of all losses (where woman is
concerned)—the loss of my tongue.

He gave me no time to recover myself. He
proceeded with what he had to say—speaking,
mind, in the tone of a perfectly well-bred man,
with nothing wild in his look and nothing odd
in his manner.

"Excuse me if I venture on asking you a very
strange question," he went on. "Did you happen to be at Exeter on the third of last month?"

(I must have been more or less than a woman if I had not recovered the use of my tongue now.)

"I never was at Exeter in my life, sir," I answered. "May I ask, on my side, why you put the question to me?"

Instead of replying, he looked at Lucilla.

"Pardon me once more. Perhaps this young lady—"

He was plainly on the point of inquiring next whether Lucilla had been at Exeter, when he checked himself. In the breathless interest which she felt in what was going on she had turned her full face upon him. There was still light enough left for her eyes to tell their own sad story, in their own mute way. As he read the truth in them the man's face changed from the keen look of scrutiny which it had worn thus far to an expression of compassion—I had almost said of distress. He again took off his hat, and bowed to me with the deepest respect.

"I beg your pardon," he said, very earnestly; "I beg the young lady's pardon. Pray forgive me. My strange behavior has its excuse—if I could bring myself to explain it. You distressed me when you looked at me. I can't explain why. Good-evening."

He turned away hastily, like a man confused and ashamed of himself, and left us. I can only repeat that there was nothing strange or flighty in his manner. A perfect gentleman, in full possession of his senses—there is the unexaggerated and the just description of him.

I looked at Lucilla. She was standing with

her blind face raised to the sky, lost in herself,
like a person rapt in ecstasy.

"Who is that man?" I asked.

My question brought her down suddenly from
heaven to earth. "Oh!" she said, reproachfully,
"I had his voice still in my ears, and now I have
lost it! Who is he!" she added, after a moment, repeating my question; "nobody knows.
Tell me—what is he like? Is he beautiful? He
must be beautiful, with that voice!"

"Is this the first time you have heard his
voice?" I inquired.

"Yes. He passed us yesterday, when I was
out with Zillah; but he never spoke. What is
he like? Do, pray, tell me—what is he like?"

There was a passionate impatience in her tone
which warned me not to trifle with her. The
darkness was coming. I thought it wise to propose returning to the house. She consented to
do anything I liked, as long as I consented, on
my side, to describe the unknown man.

All the way back I was questioned and cross-
questioned, till I felt like a witness under skillful examination in a court of law. Lucilla appeared to be satisfied so far with the results.

"Ah!" she exclaimed, letting out the secret
which her old nurse had confided to me. "*You*
can use your own eyes. Zillah could tell me
nothing."

When we got home again her curiosity took
another turn. "Exeter?" she said, considering
with herself. "He mentioned Exeter. I am
like you—I never was there. What will books

tell us about Exeter?"   She dispatched Zillah to the other side of the house for a gazetteer."

I followed the old woman into the corridor, and set her mind at ease in a whisper. "I have kept what you told me a secret," I said. "The man was out in the twilight, as you foretold. I have spoken to him; and I am quite as curious as the rest of you. Get the book."

Lucilla had, to confess the truth, infected me with her idea that the gazetteer might help us in interpreting the stranger's remarkable question relating to the third of last month, and his extraordinary assertion that I had distressed him when I looked at him. With the nurse breathless on one side of me, and Lucilla breathless on the other, I opened the book at the letter "E," and found the place, and read aloud these lines, as follows:

"Exeter. A city and sea-port in Devonshire. Formerly the seat of the West Saxon Kings. It has a large foreign and home commerce. Population 33,738. The Assizes for Devonshire are held at Exeter in the spring and summer."

"Is that all?" asked Lucilla.

I shut the book, and answered, like Finch's boy, in three monosyllabic words:

"That is all."

CHAPTER THE FIFTH.

CANDLE-LIGHT VIEW OF THE MAN.

THERE had been barely light enough left for me to read by. Zillah lighted the candles and

drew the curtains. The silence which betokens
a profound disappointment reigned in the room.

"Who *can* he be?" repeated Lucilla, for the
hundredth time. "And why should your looking at him have distressed him? Guess, Madame Pratolungo!"

The last sentence in the gazetteer's description
of Exeter hung a little on my mind, in consequence of there being one word in it which I did
not quite understand—the word "Assizes." I
have, I hope, shown that I possess a competent
knowledge of the English language by this time.
But my experience fails a little on the side of
phrases consecrated to the use of the law. I inquired into the meaning of "Assizes," and was
informed that it signified movable courts, for trying prisoners at given times in various parts of
England. Hearing this, I had another of my
inspirations. I guessed immediately that the
interesting stranger was a criminal escaped from
the Assizes.

Worthy old Zillah started to her feet, convinced that I had hit him off (as the English
saying is) to a T. "Mercy preserve us!" cried
the nurse, "I haven't bolted the garden door!"

She hurried out of the room to rescue us from
robbery and murder before it was too late. I
looked at Lucilla. She was leaning back in her
chair, with a smile of quiet contempt on her
pretty face. "Madame Pratolungo," she remarked, "that is the first foolish thing you
have said since you have been here."

"Wait a little, my dear," I rejoined. "You

have declared that nothing is known of this man. Now you mean by that—nothing which satisfies *you*. He has not dropped down from heaven, I suppose? The time when he came here must be known. Also, whether he came alone or not. Also, how and where he has found a lodging in the village. Before I admit that my guess is completely wrong, I want to hear what general observation in Dimchurch has discovered on the subject of this gentleman. How long has he been here?"

Lucilla did not, at first, appear to be much interested in the purely practical view of the question which I had just placed before her.

"He has been here a week," she answered, carelessly.

"Did he come as I came, over the hills?"

"Yes."

"With a guide, of course?"

Lucilla suddenly sat up in her chair.

"With his brother," she said. "His *twin* brother, Madame Pratolungo."

I sat up in *my* chair. The appearance of his twin brother in the story was a complication in itself. Two criminals escaped from the Assizes, instead of one!

"How did they find their way here?" I asked next.

"Nobody knows."

"Where did they go to when they got here?"

"To the Cross-Hands—the little public-house in the village. The landlord told Zillah he was perfectly astonished at the resemblance between them. It was impossible to know which was which—it was wonderful,-even for twins. They arrived early in the day, when the tap-room was empty; and they had a long talk together in private. At the end of it they rang for the landlord, and asked if he had a bed-room to let in the house. You must have seen for yourself that the Cross Hands is a mere beer-shop. The landlord had a room that he could spare—a wretched place, not fit for a gentleman to sleep in. One of the brothers took the room, for all that."

"What became of the other brother?"

"He went away the same day—very unwillingly. The parting between them was most affecting. The brother who spoke to us to-night insisted on it, or the other would have refused to leave him. They both shed tears—"

"They did worse than that," said old Zillah, re-entering the room at the moment. "I have made all the doors and windows fast downstairs; he can't get in now, my dear, if he tries."

"What did they do that was worse than crying?" I inquired.

"Kissed each other!" said Zillah, with a look of profound disgust. "Two men!"

"Perhaps they are foreigners," I suggested. "Did they give themselves a name?"

"The landlord asked the one who stayed behind for his name," replied Lucilla. "He said it was 'Dubourg.'"

This confirmed me in my belief that I had guessed right. "Dubourg" is as common a name in my country as "Jones" or "Thomp-

son" is in England—just the sort of feigned
name that any man in difficulties would give
among *us*. Was he a criminal countryman of
mine? No! There had been nothing foreign in
his accent when he spoke. Pure English—there
could be no doubt of that. And yet he had
given a French name. Had he deliberately insulted my nation? Yes! Not content with being
stained by innumerable crimes, he had added to the
list of his atrocities—he had insulted my nation!

"Well?" I resumed. "We have left this un-
detected ruffian deserted in the public-house. Is
he there still?"

"Bless your heart!" cried the old nurse, "he
is settled in the neighborhood. He has taken
Browndown."

I turned to Lucilla. "Browndown belongs to
Somebody," I said, hazarding another guess.
"Did Somebody let it without a reference?"

"Browndown belongs to a gentleman at
Brighton," answered Lucilla. "And the gentleman was referred to a well known name in
London—one of the great City merchants. Here
is the most provoking part of the whole mystery. The merchant said, 'I have known Mr.
Dubourg from his childhood. He has reasons
for wishing to live in the strictest retirement. I
answer for his being an honorable man, to whom
you can safely let your house. More than this I
am not authorized to tell you.' My father knows
the landlord of Browndown; and that is what
the reference said to him, word for word! Isn't
it provoking? The house was let for six months,

certain, the next day. It is wretchedly furnished. Mr. Dubourg has had several things that he wanted sent from Brighton. Besides the furniture, a packing-case from London arrived at the house to-day. It was so strongly nailed up that the carpenter had to be sent for to open it. He reports that the case was full of thin plates of gold and silver; and it was accompanied by a box of extraordinary tools, the use of which was a mystery to the carpenter himself. Mr. Dubourg locked up these things in a room at the back of the house, and put the key in his pocket. He seemed to be pleased—he whistled a tune, and said, 'Now we shall do!' The landlady at the Cross Hands is our authority for this. She does what little cooking he requires; and her daughter makes his bed, and so on. They go to him in the morning, and return to the inn in the evening. He has no servants with him. He is all by himself at night. Isn't it interesting? A mystery in real life. It baffles everybody."

"You must be very strange people, my dear," I said, "to make a mystery of such a plain case as this."

"Plain!" repeated Lucilla, in amazement.

"Certainly! The gold and silver plates, and the strange tools, and the living in retirement, and the sending the servants away at night—all point to the same conclusion. My guess is the right one. The man is an escaped criminal; and his form of crime is coining false money. He has been discovered at Exeter, he has escaped

the officers of justice, and he is now going to begin again here. You can do as you please. If
I happen to want change, I won't get it in this
neighborhood."

Lucilla laid herself back in her chair again. I
could see that she gave me up, in the matter of
Mr. Dubourg, as a person willfully and incor-
rigibly wrong.

"A coiner of false money recommended as an
honorable man by one of the first merchants in
London!" she exclaimed. "We do some very
eccentric things in England occasionally; but
there is a limit to our national madness, Madame Pratolungo, and you have reached it.
Shall we have some music?"

She spoke a little sharply. Mr. Dubourg was
the hero of her romance. She resented—seriously resented—any attempt on my part to lower
him in her estimation.

I persisted in my unfavorable opinion of him,
nevertheless. The question between us (as I
might have told her), was a question of believing or not believing in the merchant of London.
To her mind it was a sufficient guarantee of his
integrity that he was a rich man. To my mind
(speaking as a good Socialist), that very circumstance told dead against him. A capitalist is a
robber of one sort, and a coiner is a robber of
another sort. Whether the capitalist recommends the coiner, or the coiner the capitalist, is
all one to me. In either case (to quote the language of an excellent English play), the honest
people are the soft, easy cushions on which these

knaves repose and fatten. It was on the tip of
my tongue to put this large and liberal view of
the subject to Lucilla. But (alas!) it was easy
to see that the poor child was infected by the
narrow prejudices of the class amid which she
lived. How could I find it in my heart to run
the risk of a disagreement between us on the
first day? No—it was not to be done. I gave
the nice pretty blind girl a kiss. And we went
to the piano together. And I put off making a
good Socialist of Lucilla till a more convenient
opportunity.

We might as well have left the piano un-
opened. The music was a failure.

I played my best. From Mozart to Beethoven.
From Beethoven to Schubert. From Schubert
to Chopin. She listened with all the will in the
world to be pleased. She thanked me again and
again. She tried, at my invitation, to play herself, choosing the familiar compositions which
she knew by ear. No! The abominable Dubourg, having got the uppermost place in her
mind, kept it. She tried and tried and tried,
and could do nothing. His voice was still in
her ears—the only music which could possess
itself of her attention that night. I took her
place, and began to play again. She suddenly
snatched my hands off the keys. "Is Zillah
here?" she whispered. I told her Zillah had
left the room. She laid her charming head on
my shoulder, and sighed hysterically. "I can't
help thinking of him," she burst out. "I am
miserable for the first time in my life—no! I am

happy for the first time in my life. Oh, what must you think of me! I don't know what I am talking about. Why did you encourage him to speak to us? I might never have heard his voice but for you." She lifted her head again, with a little shiver, and composed herself. One of her hands wandered here and there over the keys of the piano, playing softly. "His charming voice!" she whispered, dreamily, while she played. "Oh, his charming voice!" She paused again. Her hand dropped from the piano and took mine. "Is this love?" she said, half to herself, half to me.

My duty as a respectable woman lay clearly before me—my duty was to tell her a lie.

"It is nothing, my dear, but too much excitement, and too much fatigue," I said. "To-morrow you shall be my young lady again. To-night you must be only my child. Come and let me put you to bed."

She yielded with a weary sigh. Ah, how lovely she looked in her pretty night-dress, on her knees at the bedside—the innocent, afflicted creature—saying her prayers!

I am, let me own, an equally headlong woman at loving and hating. When I had left her for the night, I could hardly have felt more tenderly interested in her if she had been really a child of my own. You have met with people of my sort —unless you are a very forbidding person indeed —who have talked to you in the most confidential manner of all their private affairs on meeting you in a railway carriage, or sitting next to you at a table d'hote. For myself, I believe I shall go on running up sudden friendships with strangers to my dying day. Infamous Dubourg! If I could have got into Browndown that night, I should have liked to have done to him what a Mexican maid of mine (at the Central American period of my career) did to her drunken husband, who was a kind of peddler dealing in whips and sticks. She sewed him strongly up one night in the sheet while he lay snoring off his liquor in bed; and then she took his whole stock in trade out of the corner of the room and broke it on him, to the last article on sale, until he was beaten to a jelly from head to foot.

Not having this resource open to me, I sat myself down in my bedroom to consider—if the matter of Dubourg went any further—what it was my business to do next.

I have already mentioned that Lucilla and I had idled away the whole afternoon, womanlike, in talking of ourselves. You will best understand what course my reflections took if I here relate the chief particulars which Lucilla communicated to me concerning her own singular position in her father's house.

CHAPTER THE SIXTH.

A CAGE OF FINCHES.

LARGE families are—as my experience goes— of two sorts. There are the families whose

members all admire each other. And there are
the families whose members all detest each other.
For myself I prefer the second sort. Their quar-
rels are their own affair; and they have a merit
which the first sort are never known to possess—
the merit of being sometimes able to see the good
qualities of persons who do not possess the advantage of being related to them by blood. The
families whose members all admire each other
are families saturated with insufferable conceit.
You happen to speak of Shakespeare among these
people as a type of supreme intellectual capacity.
A female member of the family will not fail to
convey to you that you would have illustrated
your meaning far more completely if you had
referred to her "dear papa." You are walking
out with a male member of the household, and
you say of a woman who passes, "What a charming creature!" Your companion smiles at your
simplicity, and wonders whether you have ever
seen his sister when she is dressed for a ball.
These are the families who can not be separated
without corresponding with each other every day.
They read you extracts from their letters, and
say, "Where is the professional writer who can
equal this?" They talk of their private affairs
in your presence, and appear to think that you
ought to be interested too. They enjoy their
own jokes across you at table, and wonder how
it is that you are not amused. In domestic cir-
cles of this sort the sisters sit habitually on the
brothers' knees; and the husbands inquire into
the wives' ailments in public as unconcernedly

as if they were closeted in their own room.
When we arrive at a more advanced stage of
civilization, the State will supply cages for these
intolerable people; and notices will be posted at
the corners of streets, "Beware of number twelve:
a family in a state of mutual admiration is hung
up there!"

I gathered from Lucilla that the Finches were
of the second order of large families, as mentioned above. Hardly one of the members of
this domestic group was on speaking terms
with the other. And some of them had been
separated for years without once troubling Her
Majesty's Post-office to convey even the slightest
expression of sentiment from one to the other.

The first wife of Reverend Finch was a Miss
Batchford. The members of her family (limited
at the time of the marriage to her brother and
her sister) strongly disapproved of her choice of
a husband. The rank of a Finch (I laugh at
these contemptible distinctions!) was decided, in
this case, to be not equal to the rank of a Batchford. Nevertheless, miss married. Her brother
and sister declined to be present at the ceremony.
First quarrel.

Lucilla was born. Reverend Finch's elder
brother (on speaking terms with no other member of the family) interfered with a Christian
proposal—namely, to shake hands across the
baby's cradle. Adopted by the magnanimous
Batchfords. First reconciliation.

Time passed. Reverend Finch—then offici-
ating in a poor curacy near a great manufactur-

ing town—felt a want (the want of money), and took a liberty (the liberty of attempting to borrow of his brother-in-law). Mr. Batchford, being a rich man, regarded this overture, it is needless to say, in the light of an insult. Miss Batchford sided with her brother. Second quarrel.

Time passed, as before. Mrs. Finch the first died. Reverend Finch's elder brother (still at daggers drawn with the other members of the family) made a second Christian proposal— namely, to shake hands across the wife's grave. Adopted once more by the bereaved Batchfords. Second reconciliation.

Another lapse of time. Reverend Finch, left a widower with one daughter, became personally acquainted with an inhabitant of the great city near which he ministered, who was also a widower with one daughter. The status of the parent in this case—social-political-religious—was Shoemaker-Radical-Baptist. Reverend Finch, still wanting money, swallowed it all, and married the daughter, with a dowry of three thousand pounds. This proceeding alienated from him forever, not the Batchfords only, but the peace-making elder brother as well. This excellent Christian ceased to be on speaking terms now with his brother the clergyman as well as with all the rest of the family. The complete isolation of Reverend Finch followed. Regularly every year did the second Mrs. Finch afford opportunities of shaking hands, not only over one cradle, but sometimes over two. Vain and meritorious fertility! Nothing came of it but a kind of compromise. Lucilla, quite overlooked among the rector's rapidly increasing second family, was allowed to visit her maternal uncle and aunt at stated periods in every year. Born, to all appearance, with the full possession of her sight, the poor child had become incurably blind before she was a year old. In all other respects she presented a striking resemblance to her mother. Bachelor Uncle Batchford and his old maiden sister both conceived the strongest affection for the child. "Our niece, Lucilla," they said, "has justified our fondest hopes—she is a Batchford, not a Finch!" Lucilla's father (promoted by this time to the rectory of Dimchurch) let them talk. "Wait a bit, and money will come of it," was all *he* said. Truly, money was wanted!—with fruitful Mrs. Finch multiplying cradles year after year, till the doctor himself (employed on contract) got tired of it, and said one day, "It is not true that there is an end to everything; there is no end to the multiplying capacity of Mr. Finch."

Lucilla grew up from childhood to womanhood. She was twenty years old before her father's expectations were realized, and the money came of it at last.

Uncle Batchford died a single man. He divided his fortune between his maiden sister and his niece. When she came of age Lucilla was to have an income of fifteen hundred pounds a year —on certain conditions, which the will set forth at great length. The effect of these conditions

was (first) to render it absolutely impossible for
Reverend Finch, under any circumstances whatever, to legally inherit a single farthing of the
money, and (secondly) to detach Lucilla from
her father's household, and to place her under
the care of her maiden aunt, so long as she remained unmarried, for a period of three months
in every year.

The will avowed the object of this last condition
in the plainest words. "I die as I have lived"
(wrote Uncle Batchford), "a High-Churchman
and a Tory. My legacy to my niece shall only
take effect on these terms — namely, that she
shall be removed at certain stated periods from
the Dissenting and Radical influences to which
she is subjected under her father's roof, and shall
be placed under the care of an English gentlewoman who unites to the advantages of birth
and breeding the possession of high and honorable principles," et cætera, et cætera. Can you
conceive Reverend Finch's feelings, sitting, with
his daughter by his side, among the company,
while the will was read, and hearing this? He
got up, like a true Englishman, and made them
a speech. "Ladies and gentlemen," he said, "I
admit that I am a Liberal in politics, and that
my wife's family are Dissenters. As an example
of the principles thus engendered in my household, I beg to inform you that my daughter ac-
cepts this legacy with my full permission, and
that I forgive Mr. Batchford." With that, he
walked out, with his daughter on his arm. He
had heard enough, please to observe, to satisfy

him that Lucilla (while she lived unmarried) could do what she liked with her income. Before they had got back to Dimchurch, Reverend Finch had completed a domestic arrangement which permitted his daughter to occupy a perfectly independent position in the rectory, and which placed in her father's pockets—as Miss Finch's contribution to the housekeeping—five hundred a year.

(Do you know what I felt when I heard this? I felt the deepest regret that Finch of the liberal principles had not made a third with my poor Pratolungo and me in Central America. With him to advise us, we should have saved the sacred cause of Freedom without spending a single farthing on it!)

The old side of the rectory, hitherto uninhabited, was put in order and furnished—of course at Lucilla's expense. On her twenty-first birthday the repairs were completed; the first installment of the housekeeping money was paid; and the daughter was established as an independent lodger in her own father's house!

In order to thoroughly appreciate Finch's ingenuity, it is necessary to add here that Lucilla had shown, as she grew up, an increasing dislike of living at home. In her blind state, the endless turmoil of the children distracted her. She and the stepmother did not possess a single sympathy in common. Her relations with her father were in much the same condition. She could compassionate his poverty, and she could treat him with the forbearance and respect due to him

from his child. As to really venerating and
loving him—the less said about that the better.
Her happiest days had been the days she spent
with her uncle and aunt; her visits to the Batchfords had grown to be longer and longer visits
with every succeeding year. If the father, in
appealing to the daughter's sympathies, had not
dexterously contrived to unite the preservation
of her independence with the continuance of her
residence under his roof, she would, on coming
of age, either have lived altogether with her
aunt, or have set up an establishment of her
own. As it was, the rector had secured his five
hundred a year on terms acceptable to both sides
—and, more than that, he had got her safe under
his own eye. For, remark, there was one terrible possibility threatening him in the future—
the possibility of Lucilla's marriage!

Such was the strange domestic position of this
interesting creature at the time when I entered
the house.

You will now understand how completely puzzled I was when I recalled what had happened
on the evening of my arrival, and when I asked
myself—in the matter of the mysterious stranger
—what course I was to take next. I had found
Lucilla a solitary being, helplessly dependent,
in her blindness, on others; and in that sad condition—without a mother, without a sister, without a friend even in whose sympathies she could
take refuge, in whose advice she could trust—I
had produced a first favorable impression on her:
I had won her liking at once, as she had won

mine. I had accompanied her on an evening walk, innocent of all suspicion of what was going on in her mind. I had by pure accident enabled a stranger to intensify the imaginary interest which she felt in him, by provoking him to speak in her hearing for the first time. In a moment of hysterical agitation—and in sheer despair of knowing who else to confide in—the poor, foolish, blind, lonely girl had opened her heart to *me*. What was I to do?

If the case had been an ordinary one, the whole affair would have been simply ridiculous.

But the case of Lucilla was not the case of girls in general.

The minds of the blind are, by cruel necessity, forced inward on themselves. They live apart from us—ah, how hopelessly far apart!—in their own dark sphere, of which we know nothing. What relief could come to Lucilla from the world outside? None! It was part of her desolate liberty to be free to dwell unremittingly on the ideal creature of her own dream. Within the narrow limit of the one impression that it had been possible for her to derive of this man— the impression of the beauty of his voice—her fancy was left to work unrestrained in the changeless darkness of her life. What a picture! I shudder as I draw it. Oh yes, it is easy, I know, to look at it the other way; to laugh at the folly of a girl who first excites her imagination about a total stranger, and then, when she hears him speak, falls in love with his voice! But add that the girl is blind; that the girl lives habitually in the world of her own imagination; that the girl has nobody at home who can exercise a wholesome influence over her. Is there nothing pitiable in such a state of things as this? For myself—though I come of a light-hearted nation that laughs at everything—I saw my own face looking horribly grave and old as I sat before the glass that night brushing my hair.

I looked at my bed. Bah! what was the use of going to bed?

She was her own mistress. She was perfectly free to take her next walk to Browndown alone, and to place herself, for all I knew to the contrary, at the mercy of a dishonorable and designing man. What was I? Only her companion. I had no right to interfere—and yet, if anything happened, I should be blamed. It is so easy to say, "You ought to have done something." Who could I consult? The worthy old nurse only held the position of servant. Could I address myself to the lymphatic lady with the baby in one hand and the novel in the other? Absurd! Her stepmother was not to be thought of. Her father? Judging by hearsay, I had not derived a favorable impression of the capacity of Reverend Finch for interfering successfully in a matter of this sort. However, he *was* her father; and I could feel my way cautiously with him at first. Hearing Zillah moving about the corridor, I went out to her. In the course of a little gossip I introduced the name of the master of the house. How was it I had not seen him yet? For an excellent reason. He had gone to

visit a friend at Brighton. It was then Tuesday. He was expected back on "sermon-day"—
that is to say, on Saturday in the same week.

I returned to my room a little out of temper.
In this state my mind works with wonderful
freedom. I had another of my inspirations.
Mr. Dubourg had taken the liberty of speaking
to me that evening. Good. I determined to go
alone to Browndown the next morning, and take
the liberty of speaking to Mr. Dubourg.

Was this resolution inspired solely by my interest in Lucilla? Or had my own curiosity
been all the time working under the surface, and
influencing the course of my reflections unknown
to myself? I went to bed without inquiring. I
recommend you to go to bed without inquiring
too.

CHAPTER THE SEVENTH.

DAYLIGHT VIEW OF THE MAN.

WHEN I put out my candle that night I made
a mistake—I trusted entirely to myself to wake
in good time in the morning. I ought to have
told Zillah to call me.

Hours passed before I could close my eyes. It
was broken rest when it came until the day
dawned. Then I fell asleep at last in good earnest. When I awoke, and looked at my watch, I
was amazed to find that it was ten o'clock.

I jumped out of bed and rang for the old nurse.

Was Lucilla at home? No. She had gone out for a little walk. By herself? Yes—by herself. In what direction? Up the valley, toward Browndown.

I instantly arrived at my own conclusion.

She had got the start of me—thanks to my laziness in sleeping away the precious hours of the morning in bed. The one thing to do was to follow her as speedily as possible. In half an hour more *I* was out for a little walk by myself—and (what do you think?) *my* direction also was up the valley, toward Browndown.

A pastoral solitude reigned round the lonely little house. I went on beyond it into the next winding of the valley. Not a human creature was to be seen. I returned to Browndown to reconnoiter. Ascending the rising ground on which the house was built, I approached it from the back. The windows were all open. I listened. (Do you suppose I felt scruples in such an emergency as this? Oh, pooh! pooh! who but a fool would have felt anything of the sort!) I listened with both my ears. Through a window at the side of the house I heard the sound of voices. Advancing noiselessly on the turf, I heard the voice of Dubourg. He was answered by a woman. Aha, I had caught her! Lucilla herself!

"Wonderful!" I heard him say. "I believe you have eyes in the ends of your fingers. Take this, now, and try if you can tell me what it is."

"A little vase," she answered, speaking, I give you my word of honor, as composedly as if she had known him for years. "Wait! what metal is it? Silver? No. Gold. Did you really make this yourself, as well as the box?"

"Yes. It is an odd taste of mine, isn't it? to be fond of chasing in gold and silver. Years ago I met with a man in Italy who taught me. It amused me then, and it amuses me now. When I was recovering from an illness last spring I shaped that vase out of the plain metal, and made the ornaments on it."

"Another mystery revealed!" she exclaimed. "Now I know what you wanted with those gold and silver plates that came to you from London. Are you aware of what a character you have got here? There are some of us who suspect you of coining false money!"

They both burst out laughing as gayly as a couple of children. I declare I wished myself one of the party! But no. I had my duty to do as a respectable woman. My duty was to steal a little nearer, and see if any familiarities were passing between these two merry young people. One half of the open window was sheltered, on the outer side, by a Venetian blind. I stood behind the blind and peeped in. (Duty! oh, dear me, painful but necessary duty!) Dubourg was sitting with his back to the window. Lucilla faced me opposite to him. Her cheeks were flushed with pleasure. She held in her lap a pretty little golden vase. Her clever fingers were passing over it rapidly, exactly as they had passed, the previous evening, over my face.

"Shall I tell you what the pattern is on your vase?" she went on.

"Can you really do that?"

"You shall judge for yourself. The pattern is made of leaves, with birds placed among them, at intervals. Stop! I think I have felt leaves like these on the old side of the rectory, against the wall. Ivy?"

"Amazing! it *is* ivy."

"The birds," she resumed. "I shan't be satisfied till I have told you what the birds are. Haven't I got silver birds like them—only much larger—for holding pepper and mustard and sugar and so on? Owls!" she exclaimed, with a cry of triumph. "Little owls, sitting in ivy nests. What a delightful pattern! I never heard of anything like it before."

"Keep the vase," he said. "You will honor me, you will delight me, if you will keep the vase."

She rose and shook her head—without giving back the vase, however.

"I might take it, if you were not a stranger," she said. "Why don't you tell us who you are, and what your reason is for living all by yourself in this dull place?"

He stood before her, with his head down, and sighed bitterly.

"I know I ought to explain myself," he answered. "I can't be surprised if people are suspicious of me." He paused, and added, very earnestly, "I can't tell it to *you*. Oh, no, not to *you!*"

"Why not?"

"Don't ask me."

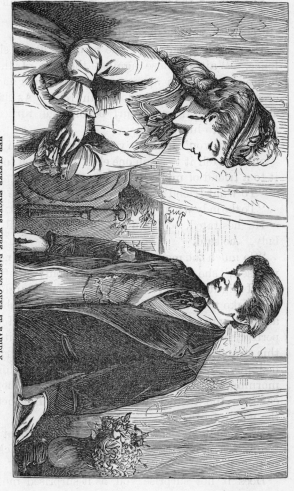

HER CLEVER FINGERS WERE PASSING OVER IT RAPIDLY.
—POOR MISS FINCH, VOL. XV., page 6.

She felt for the table with her ivory cane, and put the vase down on it very unwillingly.

"Good-morning, Mr. Dubourg," she said.

He opened the door of the room for her in silence. Waiting close against the side of the house, I saw them appear under the porch and cross the little walled inclosure in front. As she stepped out on the open turf beyond she turned and spoke to him again.

"If you won't tell *me* your secret," she said, "will you tell it to some one else? Will you tell it to a friend of mine?"

"To what friend?" he asked.

"To the lady whom you met with me last night."

He hesitated. "I am afraid I offended the lady," he said.

"So much the more reason for your explaining yourself," she rejoined. "If you will only satisfy *her*, I might ask you to come and see us—I might even take the vase." With that strong hint she actually gave him her hand at parting. Her perfect self-possession, her easy familiarity with this stranger—so bold and yet so innocent—petrified me. "I shall send my friend to you this morning," she said, imperiously, striking her cane on the turf. "I insist on your telling her the whole truth."

With that she signed to him that he was to follow her no further, and went her way back to the village.

Does it not surprise you, as it surprised me? Instead of her blindness making her nervous in the presence of a man unknown to her, it appeared to have exactly the contrary effect. It made her fearless.

He stood on the spot where she had left him, watching her as she receded in the distance. His manner toward her, in the house and out of the house, had exhibited, it is only fair to say, the utmost consideration and respect. Whatever shyness there had been between them was shyness entirely on his side. I had a short stuff dress on, which made no noise over the grass. I skirted the wall of the inclosure, and approached him unsuspected from behind. "The charming creature!" he said to himself, still following her with his eyes. As the words passed his lips I touched him smartly on the shoulder with my parasol.

"Mr. Dubourg," I said, "I am waiting to hear the truth."

He started violently, and confronted me in speechless dismay, his color coming and going like the color of a young girl. Anybody who understands women will understand that this behavior on his part, far from softening me toward him, only encouraged me to bully him.

"In your present position in this place, sir," I went on, "do you think it honorable conduct on your part to decoy a young lady, to whom you are a perfect stranger, into your house—a young lady who claims, in right of her sad affliction, even more than the usual forbearance and respect which a gentleman owes to her sex?"

His shifting color settled for the time into an angry red.

"You are doing me a great injustice, ma'am," he answered. "It is a shame to say that I have failed in respect to the young lady. I feel the sincerest admiration and compassion for her. Circumstances justify me in what I have done. I could not have acted otherwise. I refer you to the young lady herself."

His voice rose higher and higher. He was thoroughly offended with me. Need I add (seeing the prospect not far off of *his* bullying *me*) that I unblushingly shifted my ground, and tried a little civility next?

"If I have done you an injustice, sir, I ask your pardon," I answered. "Having said so much, I have only to add that I shall be satisfied if I hear what the circumstances are from yourself."

This soothed his offended dignity. His gentle manner began to show itself again.

"The truth is," he said, "that I owe my introduction to the young lady to an ill-tempered little dog belonging to the people at the inn. The dog had followed the person here who attends on me; and it startled the lady by flying out and barking at her as she passed this house. After I had driven away the dog I begged her to come in and sit down until she had recovered herself. Am I to blame for doing that? I don't deny that I felt the deepest interest in her, and that I did my best to amuse her while she honored me by remaining in my house. May I ask if I have satisfied you?"

With the best will in the world to maintain

my unfavorable opinion of him, I was, by this time, fairly forced to acknowledge to myself that the opinion was wrong. His explanation was, in tone and manner, as well as in language, the explanation of a gentleman.

And, besides—though he was a little too effeminate for my taste—he really was such a handsome young man! His hair was of a fine bright chestnut color, with a natural curl in it. His eyes were of the lightest brown I had ever seen—with a singularly winning, gentle, modest expression in them. As for his complexion—so creamy and spotless and fair—he had no right to it: it ought to have been a woman's complexion, or at least a boy's. He looked, indeed, more like a boy than a man; his smooth face was quite uncovered, either by beard, whisker, or mustache. If he had asked me, I should have guessed him (though he was really three years older) to have been younger than Lucilla.

"Our acquaintance has begun rather oddly, sir," I said. "You spoke strangely to me last night; and I have spoken hastily to you this morning. Accept my excuses—and let us try if we can't do each other justice in the end. I have something more to say to you before we part. Will you think me a very extraordinary woman if I suggest that you may as well invite *me* next to take a chair in your house?"

He laughed with the pleasantest good temper, and led the way in.

We entered the room in which he had received Lucilla, and sat down together on the two chairs near the window—with this difference, that I contrived to possess myself of the seat which he had occupied, and so to place him with his face to the light.

"Mr. Dubourg," I began, "you will already have guessed that I overheard what Miss Finch said to you at parting?"

He bowed in silent acknowledgment that it was so, and began to toy nervously with the gold vase which Lucilla had left on the table.

"What do you propose to do?" I went on. "You have spoken of the interest you feel in my young friend. If it is a true interest, it will lead you to merit her good opinion by complying with her request. Tell me plainly, if you please. Will you come and see us, in the character of a gentleman who has satisfied two ladies that they can receive him as a neighbor and a friend? Or will you oblige me to warn the rector of Dimchurch that his daughter is in danger of permitting a doubtful character to force his acquaintance on her?"

He put the vase back on the table and turned deadly pale.

"If you knew what I have suffered," he said; "if you had gone through what I have been compelled to endure—" His voice failed him; his soft brown eyes moistened; his head drooped. He said no more.

In common with all women, I like a man to *be* a man. There was, to my mind, something weak and womanish in the manner in which this Dubourg met the advance which I had made to him. He not only failed to move my pity—he was in danger of stirring up my contempt.

"I too have suffered," I answered. "I too have been compelled to endure. But there is this difference between us. *My* courage is not worn out. In your place, if I knew myself to be an honorable man, I would not allow the breath of suspicion to rest on me for an instant. Cost what it might, I would vindicate myself. I should be ashamed to cry. I should speak."

That stung him. He started up on his feet.

"Have *you* been stared at by hundreds of cruel eyes?" he burst out, passionately. "Have *you* been pointed at without mercy wherever you go? Have *you* been put in the pillory of the newspapers? Has the photograph proclaimed *your* infamous notoriety in all the shop windows?" He dropped back into his chair, and wrung his hands in a frenzy. "Oh, the public!" he exclaimed—"the horrible public! I can't get away from them. I can't hide myself even here. You have had your stare at me like the rest," he cried, turning on me fiercely. "I knew it when you passed me last night."

"I never saw you out of this place," I answered. "As for the portraits of you, whoever you may be, I know nothing about them. I was far too anxious and too wretched to amuse myself by looking into shop windows before I came here. You and your name are equally strange to me. If you have any respect for yourself, tell me who you are. Out with the truth, sir. You

know as well as I do that you have gone too far
to stop.''

I seized him by the hand.   I was wrought up
by the extraordinary outburst that had escaped
him to the highest pitch of excitement.   I was
hardly conscious of what I said or did.   At that
supreme moment we enraged, we maddened each
other.   His hand closed convulsively on my hand.
His eyes looked wildly into mine.

"Do you read the newspapers?'' he asked.

"Yes.''

"Have you seen—''

"I have *not* seen the name of Dubourg.''

"My name is not 'Dubourg.' ''

"What is it?''

He suddenly stooped over me and whispered
his name in my ear.

In my turn I started, thunderstruck, to my
feet.

"Good God!'' I cried.   "You are the man
who was tried for murder last month, and who
was all but hanged on the false testimony of a
clock!''

_____

CHAPTER THE EIGHTH.

THE PERJURY OF THE CLOCK.

WE looked at one another in silence.   Both
alike, we were obliged to wait a little and recover ourselves.

I may occupy the interval by answering two

questions which will arise in your minds in this place. How did Dubourg come to be tried for his life? And what was the connection between this serious matter and the false testimony of a clock?

The reply to both these inquiries is to be found in the story which I call the Perjury of the Clock.

In briefly relating this curious incidental narrative (which I take from a statement of the circumstances placed in my possession) I shall speak of our new acquaintance at Browndown— and shall continue to speak ot him throughout these pages—by his assumed name. In the first place, it was the maiden name of his mother, and he had a right to take it if he pleased. In the second place, the date of our domestic drama at Dimchurch goes back as far as the years 'fifty -eight and 'fifty-nine; and real names are (now that it is all over) of no consequence to anybody. With "Dubourg" we have begun. With "Dubourg" let us go on to the end.

On a summer evening, some years ago, a man was found murdered in a field near a certain town in the west of England. The name of the field was "Pardon's Piece."

The man was a small carpenter and builder in the town, who bore an indifferent character. On the evening in question, a distant relative of his, employed as farm bailiff by a gentleman in the neighborhood, happened to be passing a stile which led from the field into a road, and saw a gentleman leaving the field by way of this stile

rather in a hurry.   He recognized the gentleman
(whom he knew by sight only) as Mr. Dubourg.

The two passed each other on the road in opposite directions.   After a certain lapse of time—
estimated as being half an hour—the farm bailiff
had occasion to pass back along the same road.
On reaching the stile he heard an alarm raised,
and entered the field to see what was the matter.
He found several persons running from the further
side of Pardon's Piece toward a boy who was
standing at the back of a cattle-shed, in a remote
part of the inclosure, screaming with terror.   At
the boy's feet lay, face downward, the dead body
of a man, with his head horribly beaten in.   His
watch was under him, hanging out of his pocket
by the chain.   It had stopped—evidently in consequence of the concussion of its owner's fall on
it—at half-past eight.   The body was still warm.
All the other valuables, like the watch, were left ·
on it.   The farm bailiff instantly recognized the
man as the carpenter and builder mentioned
above.

At the preliminary inquiry the stoppage of
the watch at half-past eight was taken as offering good circumstantial evidence that the blow
which had killed the man had been struck at that
time.

The next question was—if any one had been
seen near the body at half-past eight?   The farm
bailiff declared that he had met Mr. Dubourg
hastily leaving the field by the stile at that very
time.   Asked if he had looked at his watch, he
owned that he had not done so.   Certain pre-

vious circumstances, which he mentioned as hav-
ng impressed themselves on his memory, enabled
him to feel sure of the truth of this assertion without having consulted his watch. He was pressed
on this important point, but he held to his decla-
ration. At half-past eight he had seen Mr. Dubourg hurriedly leave the field. At half-past
eight the watch of the murdered man had stopped.

Had any other person been observed in or near
the field at that time?

No witness could be discovered who had seen
anybody else near the place. Had the weapon
turned up with which the blow had been struck?
It had not been found. Was any one known
(robbery having plainly not been the motive of
the crime) to have entertained a grudge against
the murdered man? It was no secret that he
associated with doubtful characters, male and
female; but suspicion failed to point to any one
of them in particular.

In this state of things there was no alternative
but to request Mr. Dubourg—well known, in and
out of the town, as a young gentleman of independent fortune, bearing an excellent character
—to give some account of himself.

He immediately admitted that he had passed
through the field. But, in contradiction to the
farm bailiff, he declared that *he* had looked at
his watch at the moment before he crossed the
stile, and that the time by it was exactly a quarter past eight. Five minutes later—that is to
say, ten minutes before the murder had been
committed, on the evidence of the dead man's

watch—he had paid a visit to a lady living near
Pardon's Piece, and had remained with her until
his watch, consulted once more on leaving the
lady's house, informed him that it was a quarter
to nine.

Here was the defense called an "alibi." It
entirely satisfied Mr. Dubourg's friends. To
satisfy justice, also, it was necessary to call the
lady as a witness. In the meantime, another
purely formal question was put to Mr. Dubourg.
Did he know anything of the murdered man?

With some appearance of confusion, Mr. Dubourg admitted that he had been induced (by a
friend) to employ the man on some work. Further
interrogation extracted from him the following
statement of facts:

That the work had been very badly done; that
an exorbitant price had been charged for it; that
the man, on being remonstrated with, had behaved in a grossly impertinent manner; that an
altercation had taken place between them; that
Mr. Dubourg had seized the man by the collar of
his coat, and had turned him out of the house;
that he had called the man an infernal scoundrel
(being in a passion at the time), and had threatened to "thrash him within an inch of his life"
(or words to that effect) if he ever presumed to
come near the house again; that he had sincerely
regretted his own violence the moment he recovered his self-possession; and lastly, that, on his
oath (the altercation having occurred six weeks
ago), he had never spoken to the man, or set eyes
on the man, since.

As the matter then stood, these circumstances
were considered as being unfortunate circumstances for Mr. Dubourg—nothing more. He
had his "alibi" to appeal to, and his character
to appeal to; and nobody doubted the result.

The lady appeared as witness.

Confronted with Mr. Dubourg on the question
of time, and forced to answer, she absolutely contradicted him, on the testimony of the clock on
her own mantel-piece. In substance her evidence
was simply this: She had looked at her clock
when Mr. Dubourg entered the room, thinking
it rather a late hour for a visitor to call on her.
The clock (regulated by the maker only the day
before) pointed to twenty-five minutes to nine.
Practical experiment showed that the time required to walk the distance, at a rapid pace,
from the stile to the lady's house, was just five
minutes. Here, then, was the statement of the
farm bailiff (himself a respectable witness) cor-
roborated by another witness of excellent position
and character. The clock, on being examined
next, was found to be right. The evidence of
the clock-maker proved that he kept the key, and
that there had been no necessity to set the clock
and wind it up again since he had performed both
those acts on the day preceding Mr. Dubourg's
visit. The accuracy of the clock thus vouched
for, the conclusion on the evidence was irresistible. Mr. Dubourg stood convicted of having
been in the field at the time when the murder
was committed; of having, by his own admission, had a quarrel with the murdered man not

long before, terminating in an assault and a
threat on his side; and, lastly, of having attempted to set up an alibi by a false statement
of the question of time. There was no alternative but to commit him to take his trial at the
Assizes, charged with the murder of the builder
in Pardon's Piece.

The trial occupied two days.

No new facts of importance were discovered in
the interval. The evidence followed the course
which it had taken at the preliminary examina-
tions—with this difference only, that it was more
carefully sifted. Mr. Dubourg had the double
advantage of securing the services of the leading
barrister in the circuit, and of moving the irrepressible sympathies of the jury, shocked at his
position, and eager for proof of his innocence.
By the end of the first day the evidence had told
against him with such irresistible force that his
own counsel despaired of the result. When the
prisoner took his place in the dock on the second
day, there was but one conviction in the minds
of the people in court—everybody said: "The
clock will hang him."

It was nearly two in the afternoon; and the
proceedings were on the point of being adjourned
for half an hour, when the attorney for the prisoner
was seen to hand a paper to the counsel for the
defense.

The counsel rose, showing signs of agitation
which roused the curiosity of the audience. He
demanded the immediate hearing of a new witness, whose evidence in the prisoner's favor he

declared to be too important to be delayed for a single moment. After a short colloquy between the judge and the barristers on either side, the Court decided to continue the sitting.

The witness, appearing in the box, proved to be a young woman in delicate health. On the evening when the prisoner had paid his visit to the lady she was in that lady's service as housemaid. The day after she had been permitted (by previous arrangement with her mistress) to take a week's holiday, and to go on a visit to her parents in the west of Cornwall. While there she had fallen ill, and had not been strong enough since to return to her employment. Having given this preliminary account of herself, the housemaid then stated the following extraordinary particulars in relation to her mistress's clock.

On the morning of the day when Mr. Dubourg had called at the house she had been cleaning the mantel-piece. She had rubbed the part of it which was under the clock with her duster, had accidentally struck the pendulum, and had stopped it. Having once before done this, she had been severely reproved. Fearing that a repetition of the offense, only the day after the clock had been regulated by the maker, might lead perhaps to the withdrawal of her leave of absence, she had determined to put matters right again, if possible, by herself.

After poking under the clock in the dark and failing to set the pendulum going again properly in that way, she next attempted to lift the clock, and give it a shake. It was set in a marble case, with a bronze figure on the top, and it was so heavy that she was obliged to hunt for something which sne could use as a lever. The thing proved to be not easy to find on the spur of the moment. Having at last laid her hand on what she wanted, she contrived so to lift the clock a few inches and drop it again on the mantel-piece as to set it going once more.

The next necessity was, of course, to move the hands on. Here again she was met by an obstacle. There was a difficulty in opening the glass case which protected the dial. After uselessly searching for some instrument to help her, she got from the footman (without telling him what she wanted it for) a small chisel. With this she opened the case — after accidentally scratching the brass frame of it—and set the hands of the clock *by guess.* She was flurried at the time, fearing that her mistress would discover her. Later in the day she found that she had overestimated the interval of time that had passed while she was trying to put the clock right. She had, in fact, set it exactly *a quarter of an hour too fast.*

No safe opportunity of secretly putting the clock right again had occurred until the last thing at night. She had then moved the hands back to the right time. At the hour of the evening when Mr. Dubourg had called on her mistress she positively swore that the clock was a quarter of an hour too fast. It had pointed, as her mistress had declared, to twenty-five minutes to

nine—the right time then being, as Mr. Dubourg
had asserted, twenty minutes past eight.

Questioned as to why she had refrained from
giving this extraordinary evidence at the inquiry
before the magistrate, she declared that in the
remote Cornish village to which she had gone
the next day, and in which her illness had de-
tained her from that time, nobody had heard of
the inquiry or the trial. She would not have
been then present to state the vitally important
circumstances to which she had just sworn if the
prisoner's twin brother had not found her out on
the previous day, had not questioned her if she
knew anything about the clock, and had not
(hearing what she had to tell) insisted on her
taking the journey with him to the court the
next morning.

This evidence virtually decided the trial.
There was a great burst of relief in the crowded
assembly when the woman's statement had come
to an end.

She was closely cross-examined, as a matter of
course. Her character was inquired into; cor-
roborative evidence (relating to the chisel and
the scratches on the frame) was sought for, and
was obtained. The end of it was that, at a late
hour on the second evening, the jury acquitted
the prisoner without leaving their box. It was
not too much to say that his life had been saved
by his brother. His brother alone had persisted,
from first to last, in obstinately disbelieving the
clock—for no better reason than that the clock
was the witness which asserted the prisoner's

guilt! He had worried everybody with incessant inquiries; he had discovered the absence of the housemaid after the trial had begun; and he had started off to interrogate the girl, knowing nothing and suspecting nothing—simply determined to persist in the one everlasting question with which he persecuted everybody: "The clock is going to hang my brother; can you tell me anything about the clock?"

Four months later the mystery of the crime was cleared up. One of the disreputable companions of the murdered man confessed on his death-bed that he had done the deed. There was nothing interesting or remarkable in the circumstances. Chance, which had put innocence in peril, had offered impunity to guilt. An infamous woman, a jealous quarrel, and an absence at the moment of witnesses on the spot—these were really the commonplace materials which had composed the tragedy of Pardon's Piece.

CHAPTER THE NINTH.

THE HERO OF THE TRIAL.

"You have forced it out of me. Now you have had your way, never mind my feelings. Go!"

Those were the first words the Hero of the Trial said to me, when he was able to speak again. He withdrew, with a curious sullen resignation, to the further end of the room. There he stood looking at me as a man might have looked who carried some contagion about him, and who wished to preserve a healthy fellow-creature from the peril of touching him.

"Why should I go?" I asked.

"You are a bold woman," he said, "to remain in the same room with a man who has been pointed at as a murderer, and who has been tried for his life."

The same unhealthy state of mind which had brought him to Dimchurch, and which had led him to speak to me as he had spoken on the previous evening, was, as I understood it, now irritating him against me as a person who had made his own quick temper the means of entrapping him into letting out the truth. How was I to deal with a man in this condition? I decided to perform the feat which you call in England "taking the bull by the horns."

"I see but one man here," I said: "a man honorably acquitted of a crime which he was incapable of committing—a man who deserves my interest and claims my sympathy. Shake hands, Mr. Dubourg."

I spoke to him in a good hearty voice, and I gave him a good hearty squeeze. The poor, weak, lonely, persecuted young fellow dropped his head on my shoulder like a child, and burst out crying.

"Don't despise me," he said, as soon as he had got his breath again. "It breaks a man down to have stood in the dock, and to have had hundreds of hard-hearted people staring at him in

horror, without his deserving it.   Besides, I have
been very lonely, ma'am, since my brother left
me."

We sat down again side by side.   He was the
strangest compound of anomalies I had ever met
with.   Throw him into one of those passions in
which he flamed out so easily, and you would
have said, This is a tiger.   Wait till he had
cooled down again to his customary mild temperature, and you would have said, with equal
truth, This is a lamb.

"One thing rather surprises me, Mr. Dubourg,"
I went on.   "I can't quite understand—"

"Don't call me 'Mr. Dubourg,'" he interposed.   "You remind me of the disgrace which
has forced me to change my name.   Call me by
my Christian name.   It's a foreign name.   You
are a foreigner by your accent—you will like me
all the better for having a foreign name.   I was
christened 'Oscar,' after my mother's brother—
my mother was a Jersey woman.   Call me 'Oscar.'
What is it you don't understand?"

"In your present situation," I resumed, "I
don't understand your brother leaving you here
all by yourself."

He was on the point of flaming out again at that.

"Not a word against my brother!" he exclaimed, fiercely.   "My brother is the noblest
creature that God ever created!   You must own
that yourself; you know what he did at the trial.
I should have died on the scaffold but for that
angel.   I insist on it that he is not a man.   He
is an angel!"

(I admitted that his brother was an angel. The concession instantly pacified him.)

"People say there is no difference between us," he went on, drawing his chair companionably close to mine. "Ah, people are so shallow! Personally, I grant you, we are exactly alike. (You have heard that we are twins?) But there it ends, unfortunately for *me*. Nugent (my brother was christened Nugent, after my father) —Nugent is a hero! Nugent is a genius! I should have died if he hadn't taken care of me after the trial. I had nobody but him. We are orphans; we have no brothers or sisters. Nugent felt the disgrace even more than I felt it, but *he* could control himself. It fell more heavily on him than it did on me. I'll tell you why. Nugent was in a fair way to make our family name—the name that we have been obliged to drop—famous all over the world. He is a painter—a landscape painter. Have you never heard of him? Ah! you soon will! Where do you think he has gone to? He has gone to the wilds of America in search of new subjects. He is going to found a school of landscape painting. On an immense scale! A scale that has never been attempted yet! Dear fellow! Shall I tell you what he said when he left me here? Noble words—I call them noble words. 'Oscar, I go to make our assumed name famous. You shall be honorably known—you shall be illustrious— as the brother of Nugent Dubourg.' Do you think I could stand in the way of such a career as that? After what he has sacrificed for *me*,

could I let Such a Man stagnate here—for no better purpose than to keep me company? What
does it matter about *my* feeling lonely? Who
am I? Oh, if you had seen how he bore with
the horrible notoriety that followed us after the
trial! He was constantly stared at and pointed
at, for *me*. Not a word of complaint escaped
him. He snapped his fingers at it. '*That* for
public opinion!' he said. What strength of mind
—eh? From one place after another we moved
and moved, and still there were the photographs
and the newspapers and the whole infamous story
('romance in real life,' they called it) known beforehand to everybody. *He* never lost heart.
'We shall find a place yet' (that was the cheerful way he put it). 'You have nothing to do
with it, Oscar; you are safe in my hands; I
promise you exactly the place of refuge you
want.' It was he who got all the information,
and found out this lonely part of England where
you live. *I* thought it pretty as we wandered
about the hills; it wasn't half grand enough for
him. We lost ourselves. I began to feel nervous. He didn't mind it a bit. 'You have Me
with you,' he said. 'My luck is always to be
depended on. Mark what I say! We shall
stumble on a village!' You will hardly believe me—in ten minutes more we stumbled,
exactly as he had foretold, on this place. He
didn't leave me—when I had prevailed on him
to go—without a recommendation. He recommended me to the landlord of the inn here. He
said: 'My brother is delicate; my brother wishes

to live in retirement; you will oblige me by looking after my brother.' Wasn't it kind? The
landlord seemed to be quite affected by it. Nugent cried when he took leave of me. Ah, what
would I not give to have a heart like his, and
a mind like his! It's something—isn't it?—to
have a face like him. I often say that to myself
when I look in the glass. Excuse my running
on in this way. When I once begin to talk of
Nugent, I don't know when to leave off."

One thing, at any rate, was plainly discernible
in this otherwise inscrutable young man. He
adored his twin brother.

It would have been equally clear to me that
Mr. Nugent Dubourg deserved to be worshiped
if I could have reconciled to my mind his leaving his brother to shift for himself in such a place
as Dimchurch. I was obliged to remind myself
of the admirable service which he had rendered
at the trial before I could decide to do him the
justice of suspending my opinion of him in his
absence. Having accomplished this act of magnanimity, I took advantage of the first opportunity to change the subject. The most tiresome
information that I am acquainted with is the
information which tells us of the virtues of an
absent person—when that absent person happens
to be a stranger.

"Is it true that you have taken Browndown
for six months?" I asked. "Are you really
going to settle at Dimchurch?"

"Yes—if you keep my secret," he answered.
"The people here know nothing about me. Don't,

pray don't, tell them who I am! You will drive
me away if you do."

"I must tell Miss Finch who you are," I said.

"No! no! no!" he exclaimed, eagerly. "I
can't bear the idea of her knowing it. I have
been so horribly degraded. What will she think
of me?" He burst into another explosion of
rhapsodies on the subject of Lucilla—mixed up
with renewed petitions to me to keep his story
concealed from everybody. I lost all patience
with his want of common fortitude and common
sense.

"Young Oscar, I should like to box your ears!"
I said. "You are in a villainously unwholesome
state about this matter. Have you nothing else
to think of? Have you no profession? Are you
not obliged to work for your living?"

I spoke, as you perceive, with some force of
expression, aided by a corresponding asperity of
voice and manner.

Mr. Oscar Dubourg looked at me with the puzzled air of a man who feels an overflow of new
ideas forcing itself into his mind. He modestly
admitted the degrading truth. From his childhood upward he had only to put his hand in his
pocket to find the money there, without any preliminary necessity of earning it first. His father
had been a fashionable portrait painter, and had
married one of his sitters, an heiress. Oscar and
Nugent had been left in the detestable position
of independent gentlemen. The dignity of labor
was a dignity unknown to these degraded young
men. "I despise a wealthy idler," I said to

Oscar, with my republican severity. "You want the ennobling influences of labor to make a man of you. Nobody has a right to be idle; nobody has a right to be rich. You would be in a more wholesome state of mind about yourself, my young gentleman, if you had to earn your bread and cheese before you ate it."

He stared at me piteously. The noble sentiments which I had inherited from Doctor Pratolungo completely bewildered Mr. Oscar Dubourg.

"Don't be angry with me," he said, in his innocent way. "I couldn't eat my cheese if I did earn it. I can't digest cheese. Besides, I employ myself as much as I can." He took his little golden vase from the table behind him, and told me what I had already heard him tell Lucilla while I was listening at the window. "You would have found me at work this morning," he went on, "if the stupid people who send me my metal plates had not made a mistake. The alloy, in the gold and silver both, is all wrong this time. I must return the plates to be melted again before I can do anything with them. They are all ready to go back to-day when the cart comes. If there are any laboring people here who want money, I'm sure I will give them some of mine with the greatest pleasure. It isn't my fault, ma'am, that my father married my mother. And how could I help it if he left two thousand a year each to my brother and me?"

Two thousand a year each to his brother and him! And the illustrious Pratolungo had never known what it was to have five pounds sterling at his disposal before his union with Me!

I lifted my eyes to the ceiling. In my righteous indignation I forgot Lucilla and her curiosity about Oscar; I forgot Oscar and his horror of Lucilla discovering who he was. I opened my lips to speak. In another moment I should have launched my thunderbolts against the whole infamous system of modern society, when I was silenced by the most extraordinary and unexpected interruption that ever closed a woman's lips.

CHAPTER THE TENTH.

FIRST APPEARANCE OF JICKS.

THERE walked in at the open door of the room —softly, suddenly, composedly—a chubby female child who could not possibly have been more than three years old. She had no hat or cap on her head. A dirty pinafore covered her from her chin to her feet. This amazing apparition advanced into the middle of the room, holding hugged under one arm a ragged and disreputable-looking doll; stared hard, first at Oscar, then at me; advanced to my knees, laid the disreputable doll on my lap, and pointing to a vacant chair at my side, claimed the rights of hospitality in these words:

"Jicks will sit down."

How was it possible, under these circumstances, to attack the infamous system of modern society? It was only possible to kiss "Jicks."

"Do you know who this is?" I inquired, as I lifted our visitor on to the chair.

Oscar burst out laughing. Like me, he now saw this mysterious young lady for the first time. Like me, he wondered what the extraordinary nickname under which she had presented herself could possibly mean.

We looked at the child. The child—with its legs stretched out straight before it, terminating in a pair of little dusty boots with holes in them —lifted its large round eyes, overshadowed by a penthouse of unbrushed flaxen hair, looked gravely at us in return, and made a second call on our hospitality as follows:

"Jicks will have something to drink."

While Oscar ran into the kitchen for some milk, I succeeded in discovering the identity of "Jicks."

Something—I cannot well explain what—in the manner in which the child had drifted into the room with her doll reminded me of the lymphatic lady of the rectory, drifting backward and forward with the baby in one hand and the novel in the other. I took the liberty of examining "Jicks's" pinafore, and discovered the mark in one corner "Selina Finch." Exactly as I had supposed, here was a member of Mrs. Finch's numerous family. Rather a young member, it struck me, to be wandering hatless round the environs of Dimchurch all by herself.

Oscar returned with the milk in a mug. The

child, insisting on taking the mug into her own hands, steadily emptied it to the last drop, recovered her breath with a gasp, looked at me with a white mustache of milk on her upper lip, and announced the conclusion of her visit in these terms:

"Jicks will get down again."

I deposited our young friend on the floor. She took her doll, and stood for a moment deep in thought. What was she going to do next? We were not kept long in suspense. She suddenly put her little, hot, fat hand into mine, and tried to pull me after her out of the room.

"What do you want?" I asked.

Jicks answered in one untranslatable compound word:

"Man-Gee-gee."

I suffered myself to be pulled out of the room to see "Man-Gee-gee," to play "Man-Gee-gee," or to eat "Man-Gee-gee," it was impossible to tell which. I was pulled along the passage; I was pulled out to the front-door. There—having approached the house inaudibly to us over the grass—stood the horse, cart, and man waiting to take the case of gold and silver plates back to London. I looked at Oscar, who had followed me. We now understood not only the masterly compound word of Jicks (signifying man and horse, and passing over cart as unimportant), but the polite attention of Jicks in entering the house to inform us, after a rest and a drink, of a circumstance which had escaped our notice. The driver of the cart had, on his own ac-

knowledgment, been investigated and questioned by this extraordinary child, strolling up
to the door of Browndown to see what he was
doing there. Jicks was a public character at
Dimchurch. The driver knew all about her.
She had been nicknamed "Gypsy" from her
wandering habits, and had shortened the name
in her own dialect into "Jicks." There was no
keeping her in at the rectory, try how you might.
They had long since abandoned the effort in despair. Sooner or later she turned up again, or
somebody brought her back, or one of the sheep-
dogs found her asleep under a bush and gave the
alarm. "What goes on in that child's head,"
said the driver, regarding Jicks with a sort of
superstitious admiration, "the Lord only knows.
She has a will of her own and a way of her own.
She *is* a child, and she *ain't* a child. At three
years of age she's a riddle none of us can guess.
And that's the long and the short of what I
know about her."

While this explanation was in progress the
carpenter who had nailed up the case, and the
carpenter's son, accompanying him, joined us in
front of the house. They followed Oscar in, and
came out again bearing the heavy burden of
precious metal—more than one man could con-
veniently lift—between them.

The case deposited in the cart, carpenter senior
and carpenter junior got in after it, wanting "a
lift" to Brighton. Carpenter senior—a big burly
man—made a joke. "It's a lonely country between this and Brighton, sir," he said to Oscar.

"Three of us will be none too many to see your precious packing-case safe into the railway station." Oscar took it seriously. "Are there any robbers in this neighborhood?" he asked. "Lord love you, sir!" said the driver, "robbers would starve in these parts; we have got nothing worth thieving here." Jicks, still watching the proceedings with an interest which allowed no detail to escape her notice, assumed the responsibility of starting the men on their journey. The odd child waved her chubby hand imperiously to her friend the driver, and cried in her loudest voice, "Away!" The driver touched his hat with comic respect. "All right, miss; time's money, ain't it?" He cracked his whip, and the cart rolled off noiselessly over the thick, close turf of the South Downs.

It was time for me to go back to the rectory, and to restore the wandering Jicks, for the time being, to the protection of home. I turned to Oscar to say good-by.

"I wish I was going back with you," he said.

"You will be as free as I am to come and to go at the rectory," I answered, "when they know what has passed this morning between you and me. In your own interests I am determined to tell them who you are. You have nothing to fear, and everything to gain, by my speaking out. Clear your mind of fancies and suspicions that are unworthy of you. By tomorrow we shall be good neighbors; by the end of the week we shall be good friends. For the present, as we say in France, *au revoir!*"

I turned to take Jicks by the hand. While I had been speaking to Oscar the child had slipped away from me. Not a sign of her was to be seen.

Before we could stir a step to search for our lost Gypsy, her voice reached us, raised shrill and angry, in the regions behind us, at the side of the house.

"Go away!" we heard the child cry out impatiently. "Ugly men, go away!"

We turned the corner, and discovered two shabby strangers resting themselves against the side wall of the house. Their cadaverous faces, their brutish expressions, and their frowsy clothes proclaimed them, to my eye, as belonging to the vilest blackguard type that the civilized earth has yet produced—the blackguard of London growth. There they lounged, with their hands in their pockets and their backs against the wall, as if they were airing themselves on the outer side of a public-house, and there stood Jicks, with her legs planted wide apart on the turf, asserting the rights of property (even at that early age!), and ordering the rascals off.

"What are you doing there?" asked Oscar, sharply.

One of the men appeared to be on the point of making an insolent answer. The other—the younger and the viler looking villain of the two —checked him, and spoke first.

"We've had a longish walk, sir," said the fellow, with an impudent assumption of humility; "and we've took the liberty of resting our

backs against your wall, and feastin' our eyes
on the beauty of your young lady here."

He pointed to the child. Jicks shook her fist
at him, and ordered him off more fiercely than
ever.

"There's an inn in the village," said Oscar.
"Rest there, if you please—my house is not an
inn."

The elder man made a second effort to speak,
beginning with an oath. The younger checked
him again.

"Shut up, Jim!" said the superior blackguard
of the two. "The gentleman recommends the
tap at the inn. Come and drink the gentleman's
health." He turned to the child, and took off
his hat to her with a low bow. "Wish you
good-morning, miss! You're just the style, you
are, that I admire. Please don't engage yourself to be married till I come back."

His savage companion was so tickled by this
delicate pleasantry that he burst suddenly into a
roar of laughter. Arm in arm the two ruffians
walked off together in the direction of the village. Our funny little Jicks became a tragic
and terrible Jicks all on a sudden. The child
resented the insolence of the two men as if she
really understood it. I never saw so young a
creature in such a furious passion before. She
picked up a stone and threw it at them before I
could stop her. She screamed, and stamped her
tiny feet alternately on the ground, till she was
purple in the face. She threw herself down and
rolled in fury on the grass. Nothing pacified

her but a rash promise of Oscar's (which he was destined to hear of for many a long day afterward) to send for the police, and to have the two men soundly beaten for daring to laugh at Jicks. She got up from the ground, and dried her eyes with her knuckles, and fixed a warning look on Oscar. "Mind!" said this curious child, with her bosom still heaving under the dirty pinafore, "the men are to be beaten. And Jicks is to see it."

I said nothing to Oscar at the time, but I felt some secret uneasiness on the way home—an uneasiness inspired by the appearance of the two men in the neighborhood of Browndown.

It was impossible to say how long they might have been lurking about the outside of the house before the child discovered them. They might have heard, through the open window, what Oscar had said to me on the subject of his plates of precious metal; and they might have seen the heavy packing-case placed in the cart. I felt no apprehension about the safe arrival of the case at Brighton; the three men in the cart were men enough to take good care of it. My fears were for the future. Oscar was living, entirely by himself, in a lonely house more than half a mile distant from the village. His fancy for chasing in the precious metals might have its dangers, as well as its attractions, if it became known beyond the pastoral limits of Dimchurch. Advancing from one suspicion to another, I asked myself if the two men had roamed by mere accident into our remote part of the world, or whether they had deliberately found their way to Brown-down with a purpose in view. Having this doubt in my mind, and happening to encounter the old nurse, Zillah, in the garden as I entered the rectory gates with my little charge, I put the question to her plainly, "Do you see many strangers at Dimchurch?"

"Strangers?" repeated the old woman. "Excepting yourself, ma'am, we see no such thing as a stranger here from one year's end to another."

I determined to say a warning word to Oscar at the first convenient opportunity.

CHAPTER THE ELEVENTH.

BLIND LOVE.

LUCILLA was at the piano when I entered the sitting-room.

"I wanted you of all things," she said. "I have sent all over the house in search of you. Where have you been?"

I told her.

She sprang to her feet with a cry of delight.

"You have persuaded him to trust you—you have discovered everything. You only said, 'I have been at Browndown'—and I heard it in your voice. Out with it! out with it!"

She never moved—she seemed hardly to breathe —while I was telling her all that had passed at the interview between Oscar and me. As soon as I had done she got up in a violent hurry, flushed and eager, and made straight for her bedroom door.

"What are you going to do?" I asked.

"I want my hat and my stick," she answered.

"You are going out?"

"Yes."

"Where?"

"Can you ask the question? To Browndown, of course!"

I begged her to wait a moment, and hear a word or two that I had to say. It is, I suppose, almost needless to add that my object in speaking to her was to protest against the glaring impropriety of her paying a second visit, in one day, to a man who was a stranger to her. I declared, in the plainest terms, that such a proceeding would be sufficient, in the estimation of any civilized community, to put her reputation in peril. The result of my interference was curious and interesting in the extreme. It showed me that the virtue called Modesty (I am not speaking of Decency, mind) is a virtue of purely artificial growth; and that the successful cultivation of it depends, in the first instance, not on the influence of the tongue, but on the influence of the eye.

Suppose the case of an average young lady (conscious of feeling a first love) to whom I might have spoken in the sense that I have just mentioned—what would she have done?

She would assuredly have shown some natural and pretty confusion, and would, in all human probability, have changed color more or less while she was listening to me.   Lucilla's charming face revealed but one expression—an expression of disappointment, slightly mixed, perhaps, with surprise.   I believed her to be then, what I knew her to be afterward, as pure a creature as ever walked the earth.   And yet of the natural and becoming confusion, of the little inevitable feminine changes of color which I had expected to see, not so much as a vestige appeared—and this, remember, in the case of a person of unusually sensitive and impulsive nature; quick, on the most trifling occasions, to feel and to express its feelings in no ordinary degree.

What did it mean?

It meant that here was one strange side shown to me of the terrible affliction that darkened her life.   It meant that modesty is essentially the growth of our own consciousness of the eyes of others judging us, and that blindness is never bashful, for the one simple reason that blindness cannot see.   The most modest girl in existence is bolder with her lover in the dark than in the light.   The female model who "sits" for the first time in a drawing academy, and who shrinks from the ordeal, is persuaded, in the last resort, to enter the students' room by having a bandage bound over her eyes.   My poor Lucilla had always the bandage over her eyes.   My poor Lucilla was never to meet her lover in the light.   She had grown up with the passions of a woman, and yet she had never advanced beyond the fearless and primitive innocence of a child. Ah, if ever there was a sacred charge confided

to any mortal creature, here surely was a sacred
charge confided to Me! I could not endure to
see the poor pretty blind face turned so insensibly toward mine, after such words as I had just
said to her. She was standing within my reach.
I took her by the arm, and made her sit on my
knee. "My dear," I said, very earnestly, "you
must *not* go to him again to-day."

"I have got so much to say to him!" she answered, impatiently. "I want to tell him how
deeply I feel for him, and how anxious I am to
make his life a happier one if I can."

"My dear Lucilla! you can't say this to a
young man. It is as good as telling him, in
plain words, that you are fond of him!"

"I *am* fond of him."

"Hush! hush! Keep it to yourself until you
are sure that *he* is fond of *you*. It's the man's
place, my love, not the woman's, to own the
truth first in matters of this sort."

"This is very hard on the women. If they
feel it first, they ought to own it first." She
paused for a moment, considering with herself,
and abruptly got off my knee. "I *must* speak
to him!" she burst out; "I *must* tell him that
I have heard his story, and that I think all the
better of him after it, instead of the worse!"

She was again on her way to get her hat. My
only chance of stopping her was to invent a
compromise.

"Write him a note," I said, and then suddenly
remembered that she was blind. "You shall
dictate," I added, "and I will hold the pen. Be

content with that for to-day. For my sake,
Lucilla!"

She yielded, not very willingly, poor thing.
But she jealously declined to let me hold the pen.

"My first note to him must be all written by
me," she said. "I can write in my own round-
about way. It's long and tiresome; but still I
can do it. Come and see."

She led the way to a writing-table in the corner of the room, and sat for a while, with the
pen in her hand, thinking. Her irresistible
smile broke suddenly like a glow of light over
her face. "Ah!" she exclaimed, "I know how
to tell him what I think!"

Guiding the pen in her right hand with the
fingers of her left hand, she wrote slowly, in
large childish characters, these words:

"DEAR MR. OSCAR—I have heard all about
you. Please send me the little gold vase.
                    "Your friend,   LUCILLA."

She inclosed and directed the letter, and clapped
her hands for joy. "He will know what *that*
means!" she said, gayly.

It was useless to attempt making a second remonstrance. I rang the bell, under protest (imagine her receiving a present from a gentleman
to whom she had spoken for the first time that
morning!), and the groom was sent off to Browndown with the letter. In making this concession
I privately said to myself, "I shall keep a tight
hand over Oscar; he is the most manageable
person of the two!"

The interval before the return of the nurse was
not an easy interval to fill up. I proposed some
music. Lucilla was still too full of her new
interest to be able to give her attention to anything else. She suddenly remembered that her
father and her stepmother ought both to be informed that Mr. Dubourg was a perfectly presentable person at the rectory. She decided on
writing to her father.

On this occasion she made no difficulty about
permitting me to hold the pen while she told me
what to write. We produced between us rather
a flighty, enthusiastic, high-flown sort of letter.
I felt by no means sure that we should raise a
favorable impression of our new neighbor in the
mind of Reverend Finch. That was, however,
not my affair. I appeared to excellent advantage in the matter as the judicious foreign lady
who had insisted on making inquiries. For the
rest, it was a point of honor with me—writing
for a person who was blind—not to change a single word in the sentences which Lucilla dictated
to me. The letter completed, I wrote the address
of the house in Brighton at which Mr. Finch
then happened to be staying; and I was next
about to close the envelope in due course—when
Lucilla stopped me.

"Wait a little," she said. "Don't close the
letter yet."

I wondered why the envelope was to be left
open, and why Lucilla looked a little confused
when she forbade me to close it. Another unexpected revelation of the influence of their afflic-

tion on the natures of the blind was waiting to enlighten me on those two points.

After consultation between us it had been decided, at Lucilla's express request, that I should inform Mrs. Finch that the mystery at Browndown was now cleared up. Lucilla openly owned to having no great relish for the society of her step-mother, or for the duty invariably devolving on anybody who was long in the company of that fertile lady of either finding her handkerchief or holding her baby. A duplicate key of the door of communication between the two sides of the house was given to me, and I left the room.

Before performing my errand I went for a minute into my bed-chamber to put away my hat and my parasol. Returning into the corridor, and passing the door of the sitting-room, I found that it had been left ajar by some one who had entered after I had left, and I heard Lucilla's voice say, "Take that letter out of the envelope, and read it to me."

I pursued my way along the passage—very slowly, I own—and I heard the first sentences of the letter which I had written under Lucilla's dictation read aloud to her in the old nurse's voice. The incurable suspicion of the blind— always abandoned to the same melancholy distrust of the persons about them, always doubting whether some deceit is not being practiced on them by the happy people who can see—had urged Lucilla, even in the trifling matter of the letter, to put me to the test behind my back.

She was using Zillah's eyes to make sure that I had really written all that she had dictated to me, exactly as, on many an after occasion, she used my eyes to make sure of Zillah's complete performance of tasks allotted to her in the house. No experience of the faithful devotion of those who live with them ever thoroughly satisfies the blind. Ah, poor things, always in the dark! always in the dark!

In opening the door of communication it appeared as if I had also opened all the doors of all the bed-chambers in the rectory. The moment I stepped into the passage out popped the children from one room after another, like rabbits out of their burrows.

"Where is your mamma?" I asked.

The rabbits answered by one universal shriek, and popped back again into their burrows.

I went down the stairs to try my luck on the ground-floor. The window on the landing had a view over the front garden. I looked out, and saw the irrepressible Arab of the family, our small, chubby Jicks, wandering in the garden all by herself, evidently on the watch for her next opportunity of escaping from the house. This curious little creature cared nothing for the society of the other children. Indoors, she sat gravely retired in corners, taking her meals (whenever she could) on the floor. Out-of-doors, she roamed till she could walk no longer, and then lay down anywhere, like a little animal, to sleep. She happened to look up as I stood at the window. Seeing me, she waved her hands in-

dicatively in the direction of the rectory gate.
"What is it?" I asked. The Arab answered,
"Jicks wants to get out."

At the same moment the screaming of a baby
below informed me that I was in the near neighborhood of Mrs. Finch.

I advanced toward the noise, and found myself standing before the open door of a large
storeroom at the extreme end of the passage. In
the middle of the room (issuing household commodities to the cook) sat Mrs. Finch. She was
robed this time in a petticoat and a shawl; and
she had the baby and the novel laid together flat
on their backs in her lap.

"Eight pounds of soap? Where does it all
go to, I wonder?" groaned Mrs. Finch, to the
accompaniment of the baby's screams. "Five
pounds of soda for the laundry? One would
think we did the washing for the whole village.
Six pounds of candles? You must eat candles
like the Russians. Who ever heard of burning
six pounds of candles in a week? Ten pounds of
sugar? Who gets it all? I never taste sugar
from one year's end to another. Waste, nothing
but waste!" Here Mrs. Finch looked my way,
and saw me at the door. "Oh, Madame Pratolungo? How d'ye do? Don't go away. I've
just done.—A bottle of blacking? My shoes are
a disgrace to the house. Five pounds of rice?
If I had Indian servants, five pounds of rice
would last them for a year. There! take the
things away into the kitchen.—Excuse my dress,
Madame Pratolungo. How *am* I to dress, with

all I have got to do? What do you say? My
time must, indeed, be fully occupied? Ah,
that's just where it is! When you have lost
half an hour in the morning, and can't pick it
up again—to say nothing of having the storeroom on your mind, and the children's dinner
late, and the baby fractious—one slips on a petticoat and a shawl, and gives it up in despair.
What *can* I have done with my handkerchief?
Would you mind looking among those bottles
behind you? Oh, here it is under the baby.
Might I trouble you to hold my book for one
moment? I think the baby will be quieter if
I put him the other way." Here Mrs. Finch
turned the baby over on his stomach and patted
him briskly on the back. At this change in his
circumstances the unappeasable infant only roared
louder than ever. His mother appeared to be
perfectly unaffected by the noise. This resigned
domestic martyr looked placidly up at me as I
stood before her, bewildered, with the novel in
my hand. "Ah, that's a very interesting story,"
she went on. "Plenty of love in it, you know.
You have come for it, haven't you? I remember I promised to lend it to you yesterday." Before I could answer the cook appeared again in
search of more household commodities. Mrs.
Finch repeated the woman's demands, one by
one as she made them, in tones of despair. "Another bottle of vinegar? I believe you water the
garden with vinegar! More starch? The Queen's
washing, I'm firmly persuaded, doesn't come to
as much as ours. Sand-paper? Sand-paper means

waste-paper in this profligate house. I shall tell
your master. I really *can* NOT make the housekeeping money last at this rate. — Don't go,
Madame Pratolungo! I shall have done directly. What? You must go? Oh, then, put the
book back on my lap, please, and look behind
that sack of flour. The first volume slipped
down there this morning, and I haven't had time
to pick it up since.—Sand-paper! Do you think
I'm made of sand-paper?—Have you found the
first volume? Ah, that's it. All over flour.
There's a hole in the sack, I suppose.—Twelve
sheets of sand-paper used in a week! What for?
I defy any of you to tell me what for. Waste!
waste! shameful, sinful waste!" At this point
in Mrs. Finch's lamentations I made my escape
with the book, and left the subject of Oscar Dubourg to be introduced at a fitter opportunity.
The last words I heard, through the screams of
the baby, as I ascended the stairs, were words
still relating to the week's prodigal consumption
of sand-paper. Let us drop a tear, if you please,
over the woes of Mrs. Finch, and leave the
British matron apostrophizing domestic econ-
omy in the odorous seclusion of her own storeroom.

I had just related to Lucilla the failure of my
expedition to the other side of the house, when
the groom returned, bringing with him the gold
vase and a letter.

Oscar's answer was judiciously modeled to
imitate the brevity of Lucilla's note. "You
have made me a happy man again. When may

I follow the vase?" There, in two sentences, was the whole letter.

I had another discussion with Lucilla relating to the propriety of our receiving Oscar in Reverend Finch's absence. It was only possible to persuade her to wait until she had at least heard from her father by consenting to take another walk toward Browndown the next morning. This new concession satisfied her. She had received his present; she had exchanged letters with him —that was enough to content her for the time.

"Do you think he is getting fond of me?" she asked, the last thing at night, taking her gold vase to bed with her, poor dear—exactly as she might have taken a new toy to bed with her when she was a child. "Give him time, my love," I answered. "It isn't everybody who can travel at your pace in such a serious matter as this." My banter had no effect upon her. "Go away with your candle," she said. "The darkness makes no difference to *me*. I can see him in my thoughts." She nestled her head comfortably on the pillows, and tapped me saucily on the cheek as I bent over her. "Own the advantage I have over you now," she said. "*You* can't see at night without your candle. *I* could go all over the house at this moment without making a false step anywhere."

When I left her that night I sincerely believe "poor Miss Finch" was the happiest woman in England.

CHAPTER THE TWELFTH.

MR. FINCH SMELLS MONEY.

A DOMESTIC alarm deferred for some hours our proposed walk to Browndown.

The old nurse, Zillah, was taken ill in the night. She was so little relieved by such remedies as we were able to apply that it became necessary to summon the doctor in the morning. He lived at some distance from Dimchurch; and he had to send back to his own house for the medicines required. As a necessary result of these delays, it was close on one o'clock in the afternoon before the medical remedies had their effect, and the nurse was sufficiently recovered to permit of our leaving her in the servants' care.

We had dressed for our walk (Lucilla being ready long before I was), and had got as far as the garden gate on our way to Browndown, when we heard, on the other side of the wall, a man's voice, pitched in superbly deep bass tones, pronouncing these words:

"Believe me, my dear sir, there is not the least difficulty. I have only to send the check to my bankers at Brighton."

Lucilla started, and caught hold of me by the arm.

"My father!" she exclaimed, in the utmost astonishment. "Who is he talking to?"

The key of the gate was in my possession.

"What a grand voice your father has got!" I said, as I took the key out of my pocket. I opened the gate. There, confronting us on the threshold, arm in arm as if they had known each other from childhood, stood Lucilla's father and —Oscar Dubourg!

Reverend Finch opened the proceedings by folding his daughter affectionately in his arms.

"My dear child!" he said, "I received your letter—your most interesting letter—this morning. The moment I read it I felt that I owed a duty to Mr. Dubourg. As pastor of Dimchurch, it was clearly incumbent on me to comfort a brother in affliction. I really felt, so to speak, a longing to hold out the right hand of friendship to this sorely tried man. I borrowed my friend's carriage and drove straight to Browndown. We have had a long and cordial talk. I have brought Mr. Dubourg home with me. He must be one of us. My dear child, Mr. Dubourg must be one of us. Let me introduce you. My eldest daughter—Mr. Dubourg."

He performed the ceremony of presentation with the most impenetrable gravity, as if he really believed that Oscar and his daughter now met each other for the first time!

Never had I set my eyes on a meaner-looking man than this rector. In height he barely reached up to my shoulder. In substance he was so miserably lean that he looked the living picture of starvation. He would have made his fortune in the streets of London if he had only gone out and shown himself to the public in ragged clothes.

His face was deeply pitted with the small-pox. His short grizzly hair stood up stiff and straight on his head like hair fixed in a broom. His small whitish-gray eyes had a restless, inquisitive, hungry look in them indescribably irritating and uncomfortable to see. The one personal distinction he possessed consisted in his magnificent bass voice—a voice which had no sort of right to exist in the person who used it. Until one became accustomed to the contrast, there was something perfectly unbearable in hearing those superb big tones come out of that contemptible little body. The famous Latin phrase conveys, after all, the best description I can give of Reverend Finch. He was in very truth—Voice, and nothing else.

"Madame Pratolungo, no doubt?" he went on, turning to me. "Delighted to make the acquaintance of my daughter's judicious companion and friend. You must be one of us—like Mr. Dubourg. Let me introduce you. Madame Pratolungo—Mr. Dubourg.—This is the old side of the rectory, my dear sir. We had it put in repair—let me see; how long since?—we had it put in repair just after Mrs. Finch's last confinement but one." (I soon discovered that Mr. Finch reckoned time by his wife's confinements.) "You will find it very curious and interesting inside. Lucilla, my child!—(It has pleased Providence, Mr. Dubourg, to afflict my daughter with blindness. Inscrutable Providence!)—Lucilla, this is your side of the house. Take Mr. Dubourg's arm, and lead the way. Do the honors, my child.—Madame Pratolungo, let me offer you my arm. I regret that I was not present when you arrived, to welcome you at the rectory. Consider yourself—do pray consider yourself—one of us." He stopped, and lowered his prodigious voice to a confidential growl. "Delightful person, Mr. Dubourg. I can't tell you how pleased I am with him. And what a sad story! Cultivate Mr. Dubourg, my dear madam. As a favor to Me—cultivate Mr. Dubourg!"

He said this with an appearance of the deepest anxiety—and more, he emphasized it by affectionately squeezing my hand.

I have met with a great many audacious people in my time. But the audacity of Reverend Finch —persisting to our faces in the assumption that he had been the first to discover our neighbor, and that Lucilla and I were perfectly incapable of understanding and appreciating Oscar unassisted by *him*—was entirely without a parallel in my experience. I asked myself what his conduct in this matter—so entirely unexpected by Lucilla, as well as by me—could possibly mean. My knowledge of his character, obtained through his daughter, and my memory of what we had heard him say on the other side of the wall, suggested that his conduct might mean—Money.

We assembled in the sitting-room.

The only person among us who was quite at his ease was Mr. Finch. He never let his daughter and his guest alone for a single moment. "My child, show Mr. Dubourg this; show Mr. Dubourg that.—Mr. Dubourg, my daughter possesses this; my daughter possesses that." So he

went on all round the room.   Oscar appeared to
feel a little daunted by the overwhelming attentions of his new friend.   Lucilla was, as I could
see, secretly irritated at finding herself authorized by her father to pay those attentions to
Oscar which she would have preferred offering
to him of her own accord.   As for me, I was already beginning to weary of the patronizing
politeness of the little priest with the big voice.
It was a relief to us all when a message on domestic affairs arrived in the midst of the proceedings from Mrs. Finch, requesting to see her
husband immediately on the rectory side of the
house.

Forced to leave us, Reverend Finch made his
farewell speech.   Taking Oscar's hand into a
kind of paternal custody in both his own hands,
he spoke with such sonorous cordiality that the
china and glass ornaments on Lucilla's chiffon-
nier actually jingled an accompaniment to his
booming bass notes.

"Come to tea, my dear sir.   Without ceremony.   To - night at six.   We must keep up
your spirits, Mr. Dubourg.   Cheerful society
and a little music.—Lucilla, my dear child, you
will play for Mr. Dubourg, won't you?   Madame
Pratolungo will do the same—at My request—I
am sure.   We shall make even dull Dimchurch
agreeable to our new neighbor before we have
done.   What does the poet say?   'Fixed to no
spot is happiness sincere; 'tis nowhere to be
found, or everywhere.'   How cheering!   how
true!   Good-day; good-day."

The glasses left off jingling. Mr. Finch's wizen little legs took him out of the room. The moment his back was turned we both assailed Oscar with the same question. What had passed at the interview between the rector and himself?

Men are all alike incompetent to satisfy women when the question between the sexes is a question of small details. A woman in Oscar's position would have been able to relate to us not only the whole conversation with the rector, but every little trifling incident which had noticeably illustrated it. As things were, we could only extract from our unsatisfactory man the barest outline of the interview. The coloring and the filling in we were left to do for ourselves.

Oscar had, on his own confession, acknowledged his visitor's kindness by opening his whole heart to the sympathizing rector, and placing that wary priest and excellent man of business in possession of the completest knowledge of all his affairs. In return, Reverend Finch had spoken in the frankest manner on his side. He had drawn a sad picture of the poverty-stricken condition of Dimchurch, viewed as an ecclesiastical endowment; and he had spoken in such feeling terms of the neglected condition of the ancient and interesting church that poor simple Oscar, smitten with pity, had produced his checkbook, and had subscribed on the spot toward the fund for repairing the ancient round tower. They had been still occupied with the subject of the tower and the subscription when we had opened

the garden gate and had let them in. Hearing
this, I now understood the motives under which
our reverend friend was acting as well as if they
had been my own. It was plain to my mind
that the rector had taken his financial measure
of Oscar, and had privately satisfied himself that
if he encouraged the two young people in culti-
vating each other's society, money (to use his
own phrase) might come of it. He had, as I believed, put forward "the round tower," in the
first instance, as a feeler; and he would follow
it up in due time by an appeal of a more personal
nature to Oscar's well-filled purse. Brief, he
was, in my opinion, quite sharp enough (after
having studied his young friend's character) to
foresee an addition to his income rather than a
subtraction from it, if the relations between Oscar
and his daughter ended in a marriage.

Whether Lucilla arrived, on her side, at the
same conclusion as mine is what I cannot venture
positively to declare. I can only relate that she
looked ill at ease as the facts came out, and that
she took the first opportunity of extinguishing
her father, viewed as a topic of conversation.

As for Oscar, it was enough for him that he
had already secured his place as friend of the
house. He took leave of us in the highest spirits.
I had my eye on them when he and Lucilla said
good-by. She squeezed his hand. I saw her do
it. At the rate at which things were now going
on I began to ask myself whether Reverend Finch
would not appear at tea-time in his robes of
office, and celebrate the marriage of his "sorely

tried" young friend between the first cup and the
second.

At our little social assembly in the evening
nothing passed worthy of much remark.

Lucilla and I (I cannot resist recording this)
were both beautifully dressed in honor of the occasion, Mrs. Finch serving us to perfection by
way of contrast. She had made an immense
effort—she was half dressed. Her evening costume was an ancient green silk skirt (with traces
of past babies visible on it to an experienced eye),
topped by the everlasting blue merino jacket.
"I lose everything belonging to me," Mrs. Finch
whispered in my ear. "I have got a body to this
dress, and it can't be found anywhere." The
rector's prodigious voice was never silent: the
pompous and plausible little man talked, talked,
talked in deeper and deeper bass, until the very
teacups on the table shuddered under the influence of him. The elder children, admitted to
the family festival, ate till they could eat no
more, stared till they could stare no more, yawned
till they could yawn no more—and then went to
bed. Oscar got on well with everybody. Mrs.
Finch was naturally interested in him as one of
twins, though she was also surprised and disappointed at hearing that his mother had begun
and ended with his brother and himself. As for
Lucilla, she sat in silent happiness, absorbed in
the inexhaustible delight of hearing Oscar's voice.
She found as many varieties of expression in listening to her beloved tones as the rest of us find
in looking at our beloved face. We had music

later in the evening, and I then heard for the
first time how charmingly Lucilla played. She
was a born musician, with a delicacy and sub-
tlety of touch such as few even of the greatest
virtuosi possess. Oscar was enchanted. In a
word, the evening was a success.

I contrived when our guest took his departure
to say my contemplated word to him in private
on the subject of his solitary position at Browndown.

Those doubts of Oscar's security in his lonely
house, which I have described as having been
suggested to me by the discovery of the two
ruffians lurking under the wall, still maintained
their place in my mind, and still urged me to
warn him to take precautions of some sort before
the precious metals which he had sent to London
to be melted came back to him again. He gave
me the opportunity I wanted by looking at his
watch and apologizing for protracting his visit
to a terribly late hour for the country—the hour
of midnight.

"Is your servant sitting up for you?" I asked,
assuming to be ignorant of his domestic arrangements.

He pulled out of his pocket a great clumsy
key. "This is my only servant at Browndown,"
he said. "By four or five in the afternoon the
people at the inn have done all for me that I
want. After that time there is nobody in the
house but myself."

He shook hands with us. The rector escorted
him as far as the front door. I slipped out while

they were saying their last words, and joined Oscar when he advanced alone into the garden.

"I want a breath of fresh air," I said. "I'll go with you as far as the gate."

He began to talk of Lucilla directly. I surprised him by returning abruptly to the subject of his position at Browndown.

"Do you think it's wise?" I asked, "to be all by yourself at night in such a lonely house as yours? Why don't you have a man-servant?"

"I detest strange servants," he answered. "I infinitely prefer being by myself."

"When do you expect your gold and silver plates to be returned to you?"

"In about a week."

"What would be the value of them in money, at a rough guess?"

"At a rough guess, about seventy or eighty pounds."

"In a week's time, then," I said, "you will have seventy or eighty pounds' worth of property at Browndown—property which a thief need only put into the melting-pot to have no fear of its being traced into his hands."

Oscar stopped and looked at me.

"What *can* you be thinking of?" he asked. "There are no thieves in this primitive place."

"There are thieves in other places," I answered, "and they may come here. Have you forgotten those two men whom we caught hanging about Browndown yesterday?"

He smiled. I had recalled to him a humorous association—nothing more.

"It was not we who caught them," he said. "It was that strange child. What do you say to my having Jicks to sleep in the house and take care of me?"

"I am not joking," I rejoined. "I never met with two more ill-looking villains in all my life. The window was open when you were telling me about the necessity for melting the plates again. They may know as well as we do that your gold and silver will be returned after a time."

"What an imagination you have got!" he exclaimed. "You see a couple of shabby excursionists from Brighton who have wandered to Dimchurch, and you instantly transform them into a pair of housebreakers in a conspiracy to rob and murder me. You and my brother Nugent would just suit each other. His imagination runs away with him exactly like yours."

"Take my advice," I answered, gravely. "Don't persist in sleeping at Browndown without a living creature in the house with you."

He was in wild good spirits. He kissed my hand, and thanked me in his voluble, exaggerated way for the interest that I took in him. "All right!" he said, as he opened the gate. "I'll have a living creature in the house with me. I'll get a dog."

We parted. I had told him what was on my mind. I could do no more. After all, it might be quite possible that his view was the right one, and mine the wrong.

CHAPTER THE THIRTEENTH.

SECOND APPEARANCE OF JICKS.

FIVE more days passed.

During that interval we saw our neighbor constantly. Either Oscar came to the rectory or we went to Browndown. Reverend Finch waited, with a masterly assumption of suspecting nothing, until the relations between the two young people were ripe enough to develop into relations of acknowledged love. They were already (under Lucilla's influence) advancing rapidly to that point. You are not to blame my poor blind girl, if you please, for frankly encouraging the man she loved. He was the most backward man—viewed as a suitor—whom I ever met with. The fonder he grew of her the more timid and self-distrustful he became. I own I don't like a modest man; and I cannot honestly say that Mr. Oscar Dubourg, on closer acquaintance, advanced himself much in my estimation. However, Lucilla understood him, and that was enough. She was determined to have the completest possible image of him in her mind. Everybody in the house who had seen him (the children included) she examined and cross-examined on the subject of his personal appearance, as she had already examined and cross-examined me. His features and his color, his height and his breadth, his ornaments and his clothes—on all these points she collected evidence in every direction and in the smallest detail. It was an especial relief and delight to her to hear on all sides that his complexion was fair. There was no reasoning with her against her blind horror of dark shades of color, whether seen in men, women, or things. She was quite unable to account for it; she could only declare it.

"I have the strangest instincts of my own about some things," she said to me one day. "For instance, I knew that Oscar was bright and fair—I mean I felt it in myself—on that delightful evening when I first heard the sound of his voice. It went straight from my ear to my heart, and it described him just as the rest of you have described him to me since. Mrs. Finch tells me his complexion is lighter than mine. Do you think so too? I am so glad to hear that he is fairer than I am! Did you ever meet before with a person like me? I have the oddest ideas in this blind head of mine. I associate life and beauty with light colors, and death and crime with dark colors. If I married a man with a dark complexion, and if I recovered my sight afterward, I should run away from him."

This singular prejudice of hers against dark people was a little annoying to me on personal grounds. It was a sort of reflection on my own taste. Between ourselves, the late Doctor Pratolungo was of a fine mahogany brown all over.

As for affairs in general at Dimchurch, my chronicle of the five days finds little to dwell on that is worth recording.

We were not startled by any second appearance of the two ruffians at Browndown; neither
was any change made by Oscar in his domestic
establishment. He was favored with more than
one visit from our little wandering Jicks. On
each occasion the child gravely reminded him of
his rash promise to appeal to the police, and visit
with corporal punishment the two ugly strangers
who had laughed at her. When were the men
to be beaten? and when was Jicks to see it?
Such were the serious questions with which this
young lady regularly opened the proceedings on
each occasion when she favored Oscar with a
morning call.

On the sixth day the gold and silver plates
were returned to Browndown from the manufac-
tory in London.

The next morning a note arrived for me from
Oscar. It ran thus:

"DEAR MADAME PRATOLUNGO—I regret to
inform you that nothing happened to me last
night. My locks and bolts are in their usual
good order, my gold and silver plates are safe in
the workshop, and I myself am now eating my
breakfast with an uncut throat.

'Yours ever, OSCAR."

After this there was no more to be said. Jicks
might persist in remembering the two ill-looking strangers. Older and wiser people dismissed
them from all further consideration.

Saturday came—making the tenth day since

the memorable morning when I had forced Oscar to disclose himself to me in the little side room at Browndown.

In the forenoon we had a visit from him at the rectory. In the afternoon we went to Browndown to see him begin a new piece of chasing in gold—a casket for holding gloves—destined to take its place on Lucilla's toilet-table when it was done. We left him industriously at work, determined to go on as long as the daylight lasted.

Early in the evening Lucilla sat down at her pianoforte, and I paid a visit by appointment to the rectory side of the house.

Unhappy Mrs. Finch had determined to institute a complete reform of her wardrobe. She had entreated me to give her the benefit of "my French taste" in the capacity of confidential critic and adviser. "I can't afford to buy any new things," said the poor lady. "But a deal might be done in altering what I have got by me if a clever person took the matter up." Who could resist that piteous appeal? I resigned myself to the baby, the novel, and the children in general; and (Reverend Finch being out of the way, writing his sermon) I presented myself in Mrs. Finch's parlor, full of ideas, with my scissors and my pattern-paper ready in my hand.

We had only begun our operations when one of the elder children arrived with a message from the nursery.

It was tea-time; and, as usual, Jicks was missing. She was searched for, first, in the lower regions of the house; secondly, in the garden. Not a trace of her was to be discovered in either quarter. Nobody was surprised or alarmed. We said, "Oh, dear! she has gone to Browndown again!" and immersed ourselves once more in the shabby recesses of Mrs. Finch's wardrobe.

I had just decided that the blue merino jacket was an article of wearing apparel which had done its duty, and earned its right to a final retirement from the scene, when a plaintive cry reached my ear through the open door which led into the back garden.

I stopped and looked at Mrs. Finch.

The cry was repeated, louder and nearer—recognizable this time as a cry in a child's voice. The door of the room had been left ajar when we sent the messenger back to the nursery. I threw it open, and found myself face to face with Jicks in the passage.

I felt every nerve in my body shudder at the sight of the child.

The poor little thing was white and wild with terror. She was incapable of uttering a word. When I knelt down to fondle and soothe her she caught convulsively at my hand, and attempted to raise me. I got on my feet again. She repeated her dumb cry more loudly, and tried to drag me out of the house. She was so weak that she staggered under the effort. I took her up in my arms. One of my hands, as I embraced her, touched the top of her frock, just below the back of her neck. I felt something on my fingers. I looked at them. Gracious God! I was stained with blood!

I turned the child round. My own blood froze. Her mother, standing behind me, screamed with horror.

The dear little thing's white frock was spotted and splashed with wet blood. Not her own blood. There was not a scratch on her. I looked closer at the horrid marks. They had been drawn purposely on her—drawn, as it seemed, with a finger. I took her out into the light. It was writing! A word had been feebly traced on the back of her frock. I made out something like the letter "H." Then a letter which it was impossible to read. Then another next to it, which might have been "L," or might have been "J." Then a last letter, which I guessed to be "P."

Was the word—"Help"?

Yes!—traced on the back of the child's frock, with a finger dipped in blood—"HELP."

CHAPTER THE FOURTEENTH.

DISCOVERIES AT BROWNDOWN.

It is needless to tell you at what conclusion I arrived as soon as I was sufficiently myself to think at all.

Thanks to my adventurous past life, I have got the habit of deciding quickly in serious emergencies of all sorts. In the present emergency—as

I saw it—there were two things to be done. One, to go instantly with help to Browndown; the other, to keep the knowledge of what had happened from Lucilla until I could get back again and prepare her for the discovery.

I looked at Mrs. Finch. She had dropped helplessly into a chair. "Rouse yourself!" I said, and shook her. It was no time for sympathizing with swoons and hysterics. The child was still in my arms, fast yielding, poor little thing, to the exhaustion of fatigue and terror. I could do nothing until I had relieved myself of the charge of her. Mrs. Finch looked up at me, trembling and sobbing. I put the child in her lap. Jicks feebly resisted being parted from me; but soon gave up, and dropped her weary little head on her mother's bosom. "Can you take off her frock?" I asked, with another shake —a good one this time.

The prospect of a domestic occupation (of any sort) appeared to rouse Mrs. Finch. She looked at the baby, in its cradle in one corner of the room, and at the novel, reposing on a chair in another corner of the room. The presence of these two familiar objects appeared to encourage her. She shivered, she swallowed a sob, she recovered her breath, she began to undo the frock.

"Put it away carefully," I said, "and say nothing to anybody of what has happened until I come back. You can see for yourself that the child is not hurt. Soothe her, and wait here. Is Mr. Finch in the study?"

Mrs. Finch swallowed another sob, and said, Yes. The child made a last effort. "Jicks will go with you," said the indomitable little Arab, faintly. I ran out of the room, and left the three babies—big, little, and least—together.

After knocking at the study door without getting any reply, I opened it and went in. Reverend Finch, comfortably prostrate in a large armchair (with his sermon-paper spread out in fair white sheets by his side), started up, and confronted me in the character of a clergyman that moment awakened from a sound sleep.

The rector of Dimchurch instantly recovered his dignity.

"I beg your pardon, Madame Pratolungo, I was deep in thought. Please state your business briefly." Saying those words, he waved his hand magnificently over his empty sheets of paper, and added in his deepest bass: "Sermon day!"

I told him in the plainest words what I had seen on his child's frock, and what I feared had happened at Browndown. He turned deadly pale. If I ever yet set my two eyes on a man thoroughly frightened, Reverend Finch was that man.

"Do you anticipate danger?" he inquired. "Is it your opinion that criminal persons are in or near the house?"

"It is my opinion that there is not a moment to be lost," I answered. "We must go to Browndown; and we must get what help we can on the way."

I opened the door, and waited for him to come out with me. Mr. Finch (still apparently pre-occupied with the question of the criminal persons) looked as if he wished himself a hundred miles from his own rectory at that particular moment. But he was the master of the house; he was the principal man in the place—he had no other alternative, as matters now stood, than to take his hat and go.

We went out together into the village. My reverend companion was silent for the first time in my limited experience of him. We inquired for the one policeman who patrolled the district. He was away on his rounds. We asked if anybody had seen the doctor. No; it was not the doctor's day for visiting Dimchurch. I had heard the landlord of the Cross Hands described as a capable and respectable man; and I suggested stopping at the inn and taking him with us. Mr. Finch instantly brightened at that proposal. His sense of his own importance rose again, like the mercury in a thermometer when you put it into a warm bath.

"Exactly what I was about to suggest," he said. "Gootheridge, of the Cross Hands, is a very worthy person—for his station in life. Let us have Gootheridge, by all means. Don't be alarmed, Madame Pratolungo. We are all in the hands of Providence. It is most fortunate for you that I was at home. What would you have done without me? Now don't, pray don't be alarmed. In case of criminal persons—I have my stick, as you see. I am not tall, but I possess immense physical strength. I am, so to speak, all muscle. Feel!"

He held out one of his wizen little arms. It was about half the size of my arm. If I had not been far too anxious to think of playing tricks, I should certainly have declared that it was needless, with such a tower of strength by my side, to disturb the landlord. I dare not assert that Mr. Finch actually detected the turn my thoughts were taking—I can only declare that he did certainly shout for Gootheridge in a violent hurry the moment we were in sight of the inn.

The landlord came out; and, hearing what our errand was, instantly consented to join us.

"Take your gun," said Mr. Finch.

Gootheridge took his gun. We hastened on to the house.

"Were Mrs. Gootheridge or your daughter at Browndown to-day?" I asked.

"Yes, ma'am; they were both at Browndown. They finished up their work as usual, and left the house more than an hour since."

"Did anything out of the common happen while they were there?"

"Nothing that I heard of, ma'am."

I considered with myself for a minute, and ventured on putting a few more questions to Mr. Gootheridge.

"Have any strangers been seen here this evening?" I inquired.

"Yes, ma'am. Nearly an hour ago two strangers drove by my house in a chaise."

"In what direction?"

"Coming from Brighton way, and going toward Browndown."

"Did you notice the men?"

"Not particularly, ma'am. I was busy at the time."

A sickening suspicion that the two strangers in the chaise might be the two men whom I had seen lurking under the wall forced its way into my mind. I said no more until we reached the house.

All was quiet. The one sign of anything unusual was in the plain traces of the passage of wheels over the turf in front of Browndown. The landlord was the first to see them. "The chaise must have stopped at the house, sir," he said, addressing himself to the rector.

Reverend Finch was suffering under a second suspension of speech. All he could say as we approached the door of the silent and solitary building—and he said *that* with extreme difficulty—was "Pray let us be careful!"

The landlord was the first to reach the door. I was behind him. The rector—at some little distance—acted as rearguard, with the South Downs behind him to retreat upon. Gootheridge rapped smartly on the door, and called out, "Mr. Dubourg!" There was no answer. There was only a dreadful silence. The suspense was more than I could endure. I pushed by the landlord, and turned the handle of the unlocked door.

"Let me go first, ma'am," said Gootheridge. He pushed by me in his turn. I followed him close. We entered the house, and called again.

Again there was no answer. We looked into
the little sitting-room on one side of the passage,
and into the dining-room on the other. Both
were empty. We went on to the back of the
house, where the room was situated which Oscar
called his workshop. When we tried the door
of the workshop it was locked.

We knocked, and called again. The horrid
silence was all that followed, as before.

I tried the keyhole with my finger. The key
was not in the lock. I knelt down and looked
through the keyhole. The next instant I was up
again on my feet, wild and giddy with horror.

"Burst open the door!" I screamed. "I can
just see his hand lying on the floor!"

The landlord, like the rector, was a little man;
and the door, like everything else at Browndown, was of the clumsiest and heaviest con-
struction. Unaided by instruments, we should
all three together have been too weak to burst it
open. In this difficulty, Reverend Finch proved
to be—for the first time, and also for the last—
of some use.

"Stay!" he said. "My friends, if the back garden gate is open, we can get in by the window."

Neither the landlord nor I had thought of the
window. We ran round to the back of the
house, seeing the marks of the chaise wheels
leading in the same direction. The gate in the
wall was wide open. We crossed the little garden. The window of the workshop—opening to
the ground—gave us admission, as the rector
had foretold. We entered the room.

There he lay—poor, harmless, unlucky Oscar
—senseless, in a pool of his own blood. A blow
on the left side of his head had, to all appearance, felled him on the spot. The wound had
split the scalp. Whether it had also split the
skull was more than I was surgeon enough to be
able to say. I had gathered some experience of
how to deal with wounded men when I served
the sacred cause of Freedom with my glorious
Pratolungo. Cold water, vinegar and linen for
bandages—these were all in the house, and these
I called for. Gootheridge found the key of the
door flung aside in a corner of the room. He
got the water and the vinegar, while I ran upstairs to Oscar's bedroom and provided myself
with some of his handkerchiefs. In a few minutes I had a cold-water bandage over the wound,
and was bathing his face in vinegar and water.
He was still insensible; but he lived. Reverend
Finch—not of the slightest help to anybody—
assumed the duty of feeling Oscar's pulse. He
did it as if, under the circumstances, this was
the one meritorious action that could be performed. He looked as if nobody could feel a
pulse but himself. "Most fortunate," he said,
counting the slow, faint, throbbing at the poor
fellow's wrist—"most fortunate that I was at
home. What would you have done without
me?"

The next necessity was, of course, to send for
the doctor, and to get help in the meantime to
carry Oscar upstairs to his bed.

Gootheridge volunteered to borrow a horse and

to ride off for the doctor. We arranged that he
was to send his wife and his wife's brother to
help me. This settled, the one last embarrassment left to deal with was the embarrassment of
Mr. Finch. Now that we were free from all
fear of encountering bad characters in the house,
the *boom-boom* of the little man's big voice
went on unintermittingly, like a machine at
work in the neighborhood. I had another of
my inspirations—sitting on the floor with Oscar's head on my lap. I gave my reverend companion something to do. "Look about the
room," I said: "see if the packing-case with
the gold and silver plates is here or not."

Mr. Finch did not quite relish being treated
like an ordinary mortal, and being told what he
was to do.

"Compose yourself, Madame Pratolungo," he
said. "No hysterical activity, if you please.
This business is in My hands. Quite needless,
ma'am, to tell Me to look for the packing-case."

"Quite needless," I agreed. "I know beforehand the packing-case is gone."

That answer instantly set him fussing about
the room. Not a sign of a case was to be seen.

All doubt in my mind was at an end now.
The two ruffians lounging against the wall had
justified — horribly justified — my worst suspicions of them.

On the arrival of Mrs. Gootheridge and her
brother we carried him up to his room. We laid
him on the bed, with his necktie off and his
throat free, and the air blowing over him from

the open window. He showed no sign yet of coming to his senses. But still the pulse went faintly on. No change was discernible for the worse.

It was useless to hope for the doctor's arrival before another hour at least. I felt the necessity of getting back at once to the rectory, so as to be able to tell Lucilla (with all needful preparation) the melancholy truth. Otherwise, the news of what had happened would get abroad in the village, and might come to her ears, in the worst possible way, through one of the servants. To my infinite relief, Mr. Finch, when I rose to go, excused himself from accompanying me. He had discovered that it was his duty, as rector, to give the earliest information of the outrage at Browndown to the legal authorities. He went his way to the nearest magistrate. And I went mine—leaving Oscar under the care of Mrs. Gootheridge and her brother—back to the house. Mr. Finch's last words at parting reminded me once more that we had one thing at least to be thankful for under the circumstances, sad as they otherwise were.

"Most fortunate, Madame Pratolungo, that I was at home. What would you have done without me?"

CHAPTER THE FIFTEENTH.

EVENTS AT THE BEDSIDE.

I AM, if you will be so good as to remember, constitutionally French, and, therefore, consti-

tutionally averse to distressing myself, if I can
possibly help it. For this reason, I really cannot summon courage to describe what passed between my blind Lucilla and me when I returned
to our pretty sitting-room. She made me cry at
the time; and she would make me (and perhaps
you) cry again now, if I wrote the little melancholy story of what this tender young creature
suffered when I told her my miserable news. I
won't write it! I am dead against tears. They
affect the nose; and my nose is my best feature.
Let us use our eyes, my fair friends, to conquer
—not to cry.

Be it enough to say that when I went back to
Browndown Lucilla went with me.

I now observed her, for the first time, to be
jealous of the eyes of us happy people who could
see. The instant she entered she insisted on being near enough to the bed to hear us or to touch
us as we waited on the injured man. This was
at once followed by her taking the place occupied by Mrs. Gootheridge at the bed-head, and
herself bathing Oscar's face and forehead. She
was even jealous of *me*, when she discovered
that I was moistening the bandages on the
wound. I irritated her into boldly kissing the
poor insensible face in our presence! The landlady of the Cross Hands was one of my sort—she
took cheerful views of things. "Sweet on him,
eh, ma'am?" she whispered in my ear; "we
shall have a wedding in Dimchurch." In presence of these kissings and whisperings Mrs.
Gootheridge's brother, as the only man present,

"SWEET ON HIM, EH, MA'AM?"—POOR MISS FINCH, Vol. XV., page 134.

began to look very uncomfortable. This worthy
creature belonged to that large and respectable
order of Englishmen who don't know what to do
with their hands, or how to get out of a room.
I took pity on him; he was, I assure you, a fine
man. "Smoke your pipe, sir, in the garden,"
I said; "we will call to you from the window
if we want you up here." Mrs. Gootheridge's
brother cast on me one look of unutterable gratitude, and escaped as if he had been let out of a
trap.

At last the doctor arrived.

His first words were an indescribable relief to
us. The skull of our poor Oscar was not injured.
There was concussion of the brain, and there was
a scalp wound—inflicted evidently with a blunt
instrument. As to the wound, I had done all
that was necessary in the doctor's absence. As
to the injury to the brain, time and care would
put everything right again. "Make your minds
easy, ladies," said this angel of a man. "There
is no reason for feeling the slightest alarm about
him."

He came to his senses—that is to say, he opened
his eyes and looked vacantly about him—between
four and five hours after the time when we had
found him on the floor of the workshop.

His mind, poor fellow, was still all astray. He
recognized nobody. He imitated the action of
writing with his finger, and said, very earnestly,
over and over again, "Go home, Jicks; go home,
go home!"—fancying himself (as I suppose) lying helpless on the floor, and sending the child

back to us to give the alarm. Later in the night
he fell asleep. All through the next day he still
wandered in his mind when he spoke. It was
not till the day after that he began feebly to recover his reason. The first person he recognized
was Lucilla. She was engaged at the moment
in brushing his beautiful chestnut hair. To her
unutterable joy he patted her hand and murmured her name. She bent over him; and, under cover of the hair-brush, whispered something
in his ear which made the young fellow's pale
face flush, and his dull eyes brighten with pleasure. A day or two afterward she owned to me
that she had said, "Get well, for my sake."

She was not in the least ashamed of having
spoken to that plain purpose. On the contrary,
she triumphed in it. "Leave him to me," said
Lucilla, in the most positive manner. "I mean
first to cure him, and then I mean to be his
wife."

In a week more he was in complete possession
of his faculties, but still wretchedly weak, and
only gaining ground very slowly after the shock
that he had suffered.

He was now able to tell us, by a little at a
time, of what had happened in the workshop.

After Mrs. Gootheridge and her daughter had
quitted the house at their usual hour, he had
gone up to his room, had remained there some
little time, and had then gone downstairs again.
On approaching the workshop he heard voices
talking in whispers in the room. The idea in-

stantly occurred to him that something was
wrong. He softly tried the door, and found it
locked—the robbers having no doubt taken that
precaution to prevent their being surprised at
their thieving work by any person in the house.
The one other way of getting into the room was
the way that we had tried. He went round to
the back garden, and found an empty chaise
drawn up outside the door. The circumstance
thoroughly puzzled him. But for the mysterious
locking of the workshop door it would have suggested to him nothing more alarming than the
arrival of some unexpected visitors. Eager to
solve the mystery, he crossed the garden; and,
entering the room, found himself face to face
with the same two men whom Jicks had discovered ten days previously lounging against the
garden wall.

As he approached the window they were both
busily engaged, with their backs toward him, in
cording up the packing-case which contained the
metal plates.

They rose and faced him as he stepped into the
room. The act of robbery which he found them
coolly perpetrating in broad daylight instantly
set his irritable temper in a flame. He rushed
at the younger of the two men—being the one
nearest to him. The ruffian sprang aside out of
his reach, snatched up from the table on which
it was lying ready a short loaded staff of leather,
called "a life-preserver," and struck him with it
on the head before he had recovered himself and
could face his man once more.

From that moment he remembered nothing until he had regained his consciousness after the first shock of the blow.

He found himself lying, giddy and bleeding, on the floor; and he saw the child (who must have strayed into the room while he was senseless) standing, petrified with fear, looking at him. The idea of making use of her—as the only living being near—to give the alarm, came to him instinctively the moment he recognized her. He coaxed the little creature to venture within reach of his hand, and, dipping his finger in the blood that was flowing from him, sent us the terrible message which I had spelled out on the back of her frock. That done, he exerted his last remains of strength to push her gently toward the open window, and direct her to go home. He fainted from loss of blood while he was still repeating the words, "Go home! go home!" and still seeing, or fancying that he saw, the child stopping obstinately in the room, stupefied with terror. Of the time at which she found the courage and the sense to run home, and of all that had happened after that, he was necessarily ignorant. His next conscious impression was the impression, already recorded, of seeing Lucilla sitting by his bedside.

The account of the matter thus given by Oscar was followed by a supplementary statement provided by the police.

The machinery of the law was put in action, and the village was kept in a fever of excitement for days together. Never was there a more com-

plete investigation—and never was a poorer result achieved. Substantially, nothing was discovered beyond what I had already found out for
myself. The robbery was declared to have been
(as I had supposed) a planned thing. Though
we had none of us noticed them at the rectory,
it was ascertained that the thieves had been at
Dimchurch on the day when the unlucky plates
were first delivered at Browndown. Having
taken their time to examine the house, and to
make themselves acquainted with the domestic
habits of the persons in it, the rogues had paid
their second visit to the village—no doubt to commit the robbery—on the occasion when we had
discovered them. Foiled by the unexpected return of the gold and silver to London, they had
waited again, had followed the plates back to
Browndown, and had effected their object—
thanks to the lonely situation of the house, and
to the murderous blow which had stretched Oscar
insensible on the floor.

More than one witness had met them on the
road back to Brighton, with the packing-case in
the chaise. But when they returned to the liv-
ery stables from which they had hired the vehicle
the case was not to be seen. Accomplices in
Brighton had, in all probability, assisted them
in getting rid of it, and in shifting the plates
into ordinary articles of luggage which would
attract no special attention at the railway station.
This was the explanation given by the police.
Right or wrong, the one fact remains that the
villains were not caught, and that the assault

and robbery at Oscar's house may be added to the long list of crimes cleverly enough committed to defy the vengeance of the law.

For ourselves, we all agreed—led by Lucilla—to indulge in no useless lamentations, and to be grateful that Oscar had escaped without serious injury. The mischief was done; and there was an end of it.

In this philosophical spirit we looked at the affair while our invalid was recovering. We all plumed ourselves on our excellent good sense—and (ah, poor stupid human wretches!) we were all fatally wrong. So far from the mischief being at an end, the mischief had only begun. The true results of the robbery at Browndown were yet to show themselves, and were yet to be felt in the strangest and the saddest way by every member of the little circle assembled at Dimchurch.

CHAPTER THE SIXTEENTH.

THE RESULT OF THE ROBBERY.

BETWEEN five and six weeks passed. Oscar was out of his bedroom, and was well of his wound.

During this lapse of time Lucilla steadily pursued that process of her own of curing him which was to end in marrying him. Never had I seen such nursing before—never do I expect to see such nursing again. From morning to night, she interested him and kept him in good spirits.

The charming creature actually made her blindness a means of lightening the weary hours of the man she loved.

Sometimes she would sit before Oscar's looking-glass, and imitate all the innumerable tricks, artifices, and vanities of a coquette arraying herself for conquest, with such wonderful truth and humor of mimicry that you would have sworn she possessed the use of her eyes. Sometimes she would show him her extraordinary power of calculating, by the sound of a person's voice, the exact position which that person occupied toward her in a room. Selecting me as the victim, she would first provide herself with one of the nosegays always placed by her own hands at Oscar's bedside, and would then tell me to take up my position noiselessly in any part of the room that I pleased, and to say "Lucilla." The instant the words were out of my mouth the nosegay flew from her hand and hit me on the face. She never once missed her aim on any one of the occasions when this experiment was tried, and she never once flagged in her childish enjoyment of the exhibition of her own skill.

Nobody was allowed to pour out Oscar's medicine but herself. She knew when the spoon into which it was to be measured was full by the sound which the liquid made in falling into it. When he was able to sit up in his bed, and when she was standing by the pillow-side, she could tell him how near his head was to hers by the change which he produced, when he bent forward or when he drew back, in the action of the

air on her face. In the same way she knew as
well as he knew when the sun was out, and when
it was behind a cloud, judging by the differing
effect of the air at such times on her forehead
and on her cheeks.

All the litter of little objects accumulating in
a sick-room she kept in perfect order on a system
of her own. She delighted in putting the room
tidy late in the evening, when we helpless people
who could see were beginning to think of light-
ing the candles. The time when we could just
discern her flitting to and fro in the dusk in her
bright summer dress—now visible as she passed
the window, now lost in the shadows at the end
of the room—was the time when she began to
clear the tables of the things that had been
wanted in the day, and to replace them by the
things which would be wanted at night. We
were only allowed to light the candles when
they showed us the room magically put in order
during the darkness, as if the fairies had done it.
She laughed scornfully at our surprise, and said
she sincerely pitied the poor useless people who
could only see.

The same pleasure which she had in arranging
the room in the dark she also felt in wandering
all over the house in the dark, and in making
herself thoroughly acquainted with every inch
of it from top to bottom. As soon as Oscar was
well enough to go downstairs, she insisted on
leading him.

"You have been so long up in your bedroom,"
she said, "that you must have forgotten the rest

of the house. Take my arm, and come along. Now we are out in the passage. Mind! there is a step down just at this place. And now a step up again. Here is a sharp corner to turn at the top of the staircase. And there is a rod out of the stair-carpet, and an awkward fold in it that might throw you down." So she took him into his own drawing-room, as if it was he that was blind and she who had the use of her eyes. Who could resist such a nurse as this? Is it wonderful that I heard a sound suspiciously like the sound of a kiss, on that first day of convalescence, when I happened for a moment to be out of the room? I strongly suspected her of leading the way in that also. She was so wonderfully composed when I came back, and he was so wonderfully flurried.

In a week from his convalescence Lucilla completed the cure of the patient. In other words, she received from Oscar an offer of marriage. I have not the slightest doubt in my mind that he required assistance in bringing this delicate matter to a climax—and that Lucilla helped him.

I may be right or I may be wrong about this. But I can at least certify that Lucilla was in such mad high spirits when she told me the news, out in the garden, on a lovely autumn morning, that she actually danced for joy; and, more improper still, she made me, at my discreet time of life, dance too. She took me round the waist, and we waltzed on the grass, Mrs. Finch standing by in the condemned blue merino jacket (with the baby in one hand and the novel in the other), and warning us both that if we lost half

an hour out of our day in whirling each other
round the lawn, we should never succeed in
picking it up again in that house. We went on
whirling, for all that, until we were both out of
breath. Nothing short of downright exhaustion
could tame Lucilla. As for me, I am, I sincerely believe, the rashest person of my age now in
existence. (What is my age? Ah! I am always discreet about that; it is the one exception.)
Set down my rashness to my French nationality,
my easy conscience, and my excellent stomach—
and let us go on with our story.

There was a private interview at Browndown,
later on that day, between Oscar and Reverend
Finch.

Of what passed on this occasion I was not informed. The rector came back among us, with
his head high in the air, strutting magnificently
on his wizen little legs. He embraced his daughter in pathetic silence, and gave me his hand
with a serene smile of condescension worthy of
the greatest humbug (say Louis the Fourteenth)
that ever sat on a throne. When he got the better of his paternal emotion and began to speak,
his voice was so big that I really thought it must
have burst him. The vapor of words in which
he enveloped himself (condensed on paper)
amounted to these two statements. First, that
he hailed in Oscar—not having, I suppose, children enough already of his own—the advent of
another son. Secondly, that he saw the finger
of Providence in everything that had happened.
Alas for me! my irreverent French nature saw

nothing but the finger of Finch — in Oscar's pocket.

The wedding-day was not then actually fixed. It was only generally arranged that the marriage should take place in about six weeks.

This interval was intended to serve a double purpose. It was to give the lawyers time to prepare the marriage-settlements, and to give Oscar time to completely recover his health. Some anxiety was felt by all of us on this latter subject. His wound was well, and his mind was itself again. But still there was something wrong with him, for all that.

Those curious contradictions in his character which I have already mentioned showed themselves more strangely than ever. The man who had found the courage (when his blood was up) to measure himself, alone and unarmed, against two robbers, was now unable to enter the room in which the struggle had taken place without trembling from head to foot. He who had laughed at me when I begged him not to sleep in the house by himself, now had *two* men (a gardener and an indoor servant) domiciled at Browndown to protect him, and felt no sense of security even in that. He was constantly dreaming that the ruffian with the "life-preserver" was attacking him again, or that he was lying bleeding on the floor, and coaxing Jicks to venture within reach of his hand. If any of us hinted at his occupying himself once more with his favorite art, he stopped his ears and entreated us not to renew his horrible associations with

the past. He could not even look at his box
of chasing tools. The doctor—summoned to say
what was the matter with him—told us that his
nervous system had been shaken, and frankly
acknowledged that there was nothing to be done
but to wait until time set it right again.

I am afraid I must confess that I myself took
no very indulgent view of the patient's case.

It was his duty to exert himself, as I thought.
He appeared to me to be too indolent to make a
proper effort to better his own condition. Lucilla
and I had more than one animated discussion
about him. On a certain evening when we were
at the piano gossiping, and playing in the intervals, she was downright angry with me for not
sympathizing with her darling as unreservedly
as she did. "I have noticed one thing, Madame
Pratolungo," she said to me, with a flushed face
and a heightened tone: "you have never done
Oscar justice from the first."

(Mark those trifling words. The time is coming when you will hear of them again.) The
preparations for the contemplated marriage went
on. The lawyers produced their sketch of the
settlement, and Oscar wrote (to an address in
New York given to him by Nugent) to tell his
brother of the approaching change in his life, and
of the circumstances which had brought it about.

The marriage-settlement was not shown to me,
but from certain signs and tokens I guessed that
Oscar's perfect disinterestedness on the question
of money had been turned to profitable account
by Oscar's future father-in-law. Reverend Finch

was reported to have shed tears when he first read
the document. And Lucilla came out of the study,
after an interview with her father, more thoroughly and vehemently indignant than I had ever seen
her yet. "Don't ask what is the matter!" she
said to me between her teeth. "I am ashamed
to tell you." When Oscar came in, a little later,
she fell on her knees—literally fell on her knees
—before him. Some overmastering agitation
was in possession of her whole being, which
made her, for the moment, reckless of what she
said or did. "I worship you!" she burst out,
hysterically, kissing his hand. "You are the
noblest of living men. I can never, never be
worthy of you!" The interpretation of these
high-flown sayings and doings was, to my mind,
briefly this: Oscar's money in the rector's pocket,
and the rector's daughter used as the means.

The interval expired; the weeks succeeded each
other. All had been long since ready for the
marriage, and still the marriage did not take place.

Far from becoming himself again, with time
to help him, as the doctor had foretold, Oscar
steadily grew worse. All the nervous symptoms
(to use the medical phrase) which I have already
described strengthened instead of loosening their
hold on him. He grew thinner and thinner, and
paler and paler. Early in the month of November we sent for the doctor again. The question
to be put to him this time was the question (suggested by Lucilla) of trying as a last remedy
change of air.

Something—I forget what—delayed the arrival

of our medical man. Oscar had given up all idea of seeing him that day, and had come to us at the rectory, when the doctor drove into Dimchurch. He was stopped before he went on to Browndown, and he and his patient saw each other alone in Lucilla's sitting-room.

They were a long time together. Lucilla, waiting with me in my bed-chamber, grew impatient. She begged me to knock at the sitting-room door, and inquire when she might be permitted to assist at the consultation.

I found doctor and patient standing together at the window, talking quietly. Evidently nothing had passed to excite either of them in the smallest degree. Oscar looked a little pale and weary, but he, like his medical adviser, was perfectly composed.

"There is a young lady in the next room," I said, "who is getting anxious to hear what your consultation has ended in."

The doctor looked at Oscar and smiled.

"There is really nothing to tell Miss Finch," he said. "Mr. Dubourg and I have gone all over the case again, and nothing new has come of it. His nervous system has not recovered its balance so soon as I expected. I am sorry, but I am not in the least alarmed. At his age things are sure to come right in the end. He must be patient, and the young lady must be patient. I can say no more."

"Do you see any objection to his trying change of air?" I inquired.

"None whatever. Let him go where he likes,

and amuse himself as he likes. You are all of you a little disposed to take Mr. Dubourg's case too seriously. Except the nervous derangement (unpleasant enough in itself, I grant), there is really nothing the matter with him. He has not a trace of organic disease anywhere. The pulse," continued the doctor, laying his fingers lightly on Oscar's wrist, "is perfectly satisfactory. I never felt a quieter pulse in my life."

As the words passed his lips a frightful contortion fastened itself on Oscar's face.

His eyes turned up hideously.

From head to foot his whole body was wrenched round, as if giant hands had twisted it, toward the right.

Before I could speak he was in convulsions on the floor at his doctor's feet.

"Good God! what is this?" I cried out.

The doctor loosened his cravat, and moved away the furniture that was near him. That done, he waited, looking at the writhing figure on the floor.

"Can you do nothing more?" I asked.

He shook his head gravely. "Nothing more."

"What is it?"

"An epileptic fit."

CHAPTER THE SEVENTEENTH.

WHAT DOES THE DOCTOR SAY?

BEFORE another word had been exchanged between us Lucilla entered the room. We looked at each other. If we could have spoken at that moment, I believe we should both have said: "Thank God, she is blind!"

"Have you all forgotten me?" she asked. "Oscar! where are you? What does the doctor say?"

She advanced into the room. In a moment more she would have stumbled against the prostrate man still writhing on the floor. I laid my hand on her arm and stopped her.

She suddenly caught my hand in hers. "Why did you tremble," she asked, "when you took me by the arm? Why are you trembling now?" Her delicate sense of touch was not to be deceived. I vainly denied that anything had happened: my hand had betrayed me. "There is something wrong!" she exclaimed. "Oscar has not answered me."

The doctor came to my assistance.

"There is nothing to be alarmed about," he said. "Mr. Dubourg is not very well to-day."

She turned on the doctor with a sudden burst of anger.

"You are deceiving me!" she cried. "Something serious has happened to him. The truth! tell me the truth! Oh, it's shameful, it's heartless of both of you, to deceive a wretched blind creature like me!"

The doctor still hesitated. I told her the truth.

"Where is he?" she asked, seizing me by the two shoulders and shaking me in the violence of her agitation.

I entreated her to wait a little; I tried to place

her in a chair. She pushed me contemptuously
away, and went down on the floor on her hands
and knees. "I shall find him," she muttered;
"I shall find him in spite of you!" She began
to crawl over the floor, feeling the empty space
before her with her hand. It was horrible. I
followed her, and raised her again by main force.

"Don't struggle with her," said the doctor.
"Let her come here. He is quiet now."

I looked at Oscar. The worst of it was over.
He was exhausted—he was quite still now. The
doctor's voice guided her to the place. She sat
down by Oscar on the floor, and laid his head on
her lap. The moment she touched him the same
effect was produced on her which would be produced (if our eyes were bandaged) on you or me
when the bandage was taken off. An instant
sense of relief diffused itself through her whole
being. She became her gentler and sweeter self
again. "I am sorry I lost my temper," she said,
with the simplicity of a child. "But you don't
know how hard it is to be deceived when you are
blind." She stooped as she said those words,
and passed her handkerchief lightly over his
forehead. "Doctor," she asked, "will this happen again?"

"I hope not."

"Are you sure not?"

"I can't say that."

"What has brought it on?"

"I am afraid the blow he received on the head
has brought it on."

She asked no more questions: her eager face

passed suddenly into a state of repose. Something seemed to have come into her mind—after
the doctor's answer to her last question—which
absorbed her in herself. When Oscar recovered
his consciousness she left it to me to answer the
first natural questions which he put. When he
personally addressed her she spoke to him kindly
but briefly. Something in her at that moment
seemed to keep her apart even from *him*. When
the doctor proposed taking him back to Browndown she did not insist, as I had anticipated, on
going with them. She took leave of him tenderly—but still she let him go. While he yet
lingered near the door, looking back at her, she
moved away slowly to the further end of the
room; self-withdrawn into her own dark world
—shut up in her thoughts from him and from us.

The doctor tried to rouse her.

"You must not think too seriously of this," he
said, following her to the window at which she
stood, and dropping his voice so that Oscar could
not hear him. "He has himself told you that he
feels lighter and better than he felt before the fit.
It has relieved instead of injuring him. There
is no danger. I assure you, on my honor, there
is nothing to fear."

"Can you assure me, on your honor, of one
other thing," she asked, lowering her voice on
her side: "can you honestly tell me that this is
not the first of other fits that are to come?"

The doctor parried the question.

"We will have another medical opinion," he
answered, "before we decide. The next time I

go to see him a physician from Brighton shall go with me."

Oscar, who had thus far waited, wondering at the change in her, now opened the door. The doctor returned to him. They left us.

She sat down on the window-seat, with her elbows on her knees and her hands grasping her forehead. A long moaning cry burst from her. She said to herself bitterly the one word—"Farewell!"

I approached her, feeling the necessity of reminding her that I was in the room.

"Farewell to what?" I asked, taking my place by her side.

"To his happiness and to mine," she answered, without lifting her head from her hands. "The dark days are coming for Oscar and for me."

"Why should you think that? You heard what the doctor said."

"The doctor doesn't know what I know."

"What you know?"

She paused before she answered me. "Do you believe in Fate?" she said, suddenly breaking the silence.

"I believe in nothing which encourages people to despair of themselves," I replied.

She went on without heeding me.

"What caused the fit which seized him in this room? The blow that struck him on the head. How did he receive the blow? In trying to defend what was his and what was mine. What had he been doing on the day when the thieves entered the house? He had been working on the casket which was meant for me. Do you see those events linked together in one chain? I believe the fit will be followed by some next event springing out of it. Something else is coming to darken his life and to darken mine. There is no wedding-day near for *us*. The obstacles are rising in front of him and in front of me. The next misfortune is very near us. You will see! you will see!" She shivered as she said those words; and, shrinking away from me, huddled herself up in a corner of the window-seat.

It was useless to dispute with her, and worse than useless to sit there and encourage her to say more. I got up on my feet.

"There is one thing I believe in," I said, cheerfully. "I believe in the breeze on the hills. Come for a walk!"

She shrank closer into her corner and shook her head.

"Let me be!" she broke out, impatiently. "Leave me by myself!" She rose, repenting the words the moment they were uttered; she put her arm round my neck and kissed me. "I didn't mean to speak so harshly," said the gentle, affectionate creature. "Sister! my heart is heavy. My life to come never looked so dark to my blind eyes as it looks now." A tear dropped from those poor sightless eyes on my cheek. She turned her head aside abruptly. "Forgive me," she murmured, "and let me go." Before I could answer she turned away to hide herself in her room. The sweet girl! How you would have pitied her—how you would have loved her!

I went out alone for my walk. She had not infected me with her superstitious forebodings of ill things to come. But there was one sad word that she had said in which I could not but agree. After what I had witnessed in that room, the wedding-day did, indeed, look further off than ever.

CHAPTER THE EIGHTEENTH.

FAMILY TROUBLES.

IN four or five days more Lucilla's melancholy doubts about Oscar were confirmed. He was attacked by a second fit.

The promised consultation with the physician from Brighton took place. Our new doctor did not encourage us to hope. The second fit following so close on the first was, in his opinion, a bad sign. He gave general directions for the treatment of Oscar, and left him to decide for himself whether he would or would not try change of scene. No change, the physician appeared to think, would exert any immediate influence on the recurrence of the epileptic attacks. The patient's general health might be benefited, and that was all. As for the question of the marriage, he declared without hesitation that we must for the present dismiss all consideration of it from our minds.

Lucilla received the account of what passed at the visit of the doctors with a stubborn resignation which it distressed me to see. "Remember

what I told you when the first attack seized him,"
she said. "Our summer-time is ended; our winter is come."

Her manner, while she spoke, was the manner
of a person who is waiting without hope—who
feels deliberately that calamity is near. She only
roused herself when Oscar came in. He was,
naturally enough, in miserable spirits under the
sudden alteration in all his prospects. Lucilla
did her best to cheer him, and succeeded. On
my side, I tried vainly to persuade him to leave
Browndown, and amuse himself in some gayer
place. He shrank from new faces and new scenes.
Between these two unelastic young people, I felt
even my native good spirits beginning to sink.
If we had been all three down in the bottom of a
dry well in a wilderness, we could hardly have
surveyed a more dismal prospect than the prospect we were contemplating now. By good luck
Oscar, like Lucilla, was passionately fond of
music. We turned to the piano as our best resource in those days of our adversity. Lucilla
and I took it in turns to play, and Oscar listened.
I have to report that we got through a great
deal of music. I have also to acknowledge
that we were very dull.

As for Reverend Finch, he talked his way
through his share of the troubles that were trying us now at the full compass of his voice.

If you had heard the little priest in those days
you would have supposed that nobody could feel
our domestic misfortunes as *he* felt them, and

grieve over them as *he* grieved.   He was a sight
to see on the day of the medical consultation,
strutting up and down his wife's sitting-room,
and haranguing his audience—composed of his
wife and myself. Mrs. Finch sat in one corner,
with the baby and the novel, and the petticoat
and the shawl.   I occupied the other corner, summoned to "consult with the rector."   In plain
words, summoned to hear Mr. Finch declare that
he was the person principally overshadowed by
the cloud which hung over the household.

"I despair, Madame Pratolungo—I assure
you, I despair of conveying any idea of how *I*
feel under this most melancholy state of things.
You have been very good; you have shown the
sympathy of a true friend. But you cannot possibly understand how this blow has fallen on
Me. I am crushed. Madame Pratolungo" (he
appealed to me in my corner), "Mrs. Finch" (he
appealed to his wife, in *her* corner), "I am
crushed. There is no other word to express it
but the word I have used. Crushed." He
stopped in the middle of the room. He looked
expectantly at me—he looked expectantly at his
wife. His face and manner said, plainly, "If
both these women faint, I shall consider it a natural and becoming proceeding on their parts,
after what I have just told them." I waited
for the lead of the lady of the house. Mrs.
Finch did *not* roll prostrate, with the baby
and the novel, on the floor. Thus encouraged,
I presumed to keep my seat. The rector still
waited for us. I looked as miserable as I could.

Mrs. Finch cast her eyes up reverentially at her husband, as if she thought him the noblest of created beings, and silently put her handkerchief to her eyes. Mr. Finch was satisfied; Mr. Finch went on: "My health has suffered—I assure you, Madame Pratolungo, My health has suffered. Since this sad occurrence my stomach has given way. My balance is lost; my usual regularity is gone. I am subject—entirely through this miserable business—to fits of morbid appetite. I want things at wrong times — breakfast in the middle of the night; dinner at four in the morning. I want something now." Mr. Finch stopped, horrorstruck at his condition, pondering with his eyebrows fiercely knit, and his hand pressed convulsively on the lower buttons of his rusty black waistcoat. Mrs. Finch's watery blue eyes looked across the room at me in a moist melancholy of conjugal distress. The rector, suddenly enlightened after his consultation with his stomach, strutted to the door, flung it wide open, and called down the kitchen stairs with a voice of thunder, "Poach me an egg!" He came back into the room, held another consultation, keeping his eyes severely fixed on me, strutted back in a furious hurry to the door, and bellowed a counter-order down the kitchen stairs, "No egg! Do me a red herring!" He came back for the second time, with his eyes closed and his hand laid distractedly on his head. He appealed alternately to Mrs. Finch and to me, "See for yourselves. Mrs. Finch! Madame Pratolungo! see for yourselves what a state I am in. It's simply pitiable. I hesitate about the most trifling things. First I think I want a poached egg; then I think I want a red herring: now I don't know what I want. Upon my word of honor as a clergyman and a gentleman, I don't know what I want. Morbid appetite all day; morbid wakefulness all night: what a condition! I can't rest. I disturb my wife at night. Mrs. Finch! I disturb you at night. How many times —since this misfortune fell upon us—do I turn in bed before I fall off to sleep? Eight times? Are you certain of it? Don't exaggerate! Are you certain you counted? Very well: good creature! I never remember—I assure you, Madame Pratolungo, I never remember such a complete upset as this before. The nearest approach to it was some years since—at my wife's last confinement but four. Mrs. Finch! was it at your last confinement but four? or your last but five? Your last but four? Are you sure? Are you certain you are not misleading our friend here? Very well: good creature! Pecuniary difficulties, Madame Pratolungo, were at the bottom of it on that last occasion. I got over the pecuniary difficulties. How am I to get over this? My plans for Oscar and Lucilla were completely arranged. My relations with my wedded children were pleasantly laid out. I saw my own future; I saw the future of my family. What do I see now? All, so to speak, annihilated at a blow. Inscrutable Providence!" He paused, and lifted his eyes and hands devotionally to the ceiling. The cook appeared with the red

herring. "Inscrutable Providence," proceeded
Mr. Finch, a tone lower. "Eat it, dear," said
Mrs. Finch, "while it's hot." The rector paused
again. His unresting tongue urged him to
proceed; his undisciplined stomach clamored
for the herring. The cook uncovered the dish.
Mr. Finch's nose instantly sided with Mr.
Finch's stomach. He stopped at "Inscrutable
Providence," and peppered his herring.

Having reported how the rector spoke in the
presence of the disaster which had fallen on the
family, I have only to complete the picture by
stating next what he did. He borrowed two
hundred pounds of Oscar, and left off commanding red herrings in the day and disturbing Mrs.
Finch at night immediately afterward.

The dull autumn days ended, and the long
nights of winter began.

No change for the better appeared in our prospects. The doctors did their best for Oscar—
without avail. The horrible fits came back,
again and again. Day after day our dull lives
went monotonously on. I almost began now to
believe, with Lucilla, that a crisis of some sort
must be at hand. "This cannot last," I used to
say to myself—generally when I was very hungry. "Something will happen before the year
comes to its end."

The month of December began; and something happened at last. The family troubles at
the rectory were matched by family troubles of
my own. A letter arrived for me from one of

my younger sisters at Paris. It contained alarming news of a person very dear to me—already mentioned in the first of these pages as my good Papa.

Was the venerable author of my being dangerously ill of a mortal disease? Alas! he was not exactly that, but the next worst thing to it. He was dangerously in love with a disreputable young woman. At what age? At the age of seventy-five! What can we say of my surviving parent? We can only say, This is a vigorous nature; Papa has an ever green heart.

I am grieved to trouble you with my family concerns. But they mix themselves up intimately, as you will see in due time, with the concerns of Oscar and Lucilla. It is my unhappy destiny that I cannot possibly take you through the present narrative without sooner or later disclosing the one weakness (amiable weakness) of the gayest and brightest and best-preserved man of his time.

Ah, I am now treading on egg-shells, I know! The English specter called Propriety springs up rampant on my writing-table, and whispers furiously in my ear, "Madame Pratolungo, raise a blush on the Cheek of Innocence, and it is all over from that moment with you and your story." Oh, inflammable Cheek of Innocence, be good-natured for once, and I will rack my brains to try if I can put it to you without offense! May I picture good Papa as an elder in the Temple of Venus, burning incense inexhaustibly on the altar of love? No: Temple of

Venus is Pagan; altar of love is not proper—
take them out. Let me only say of my ever
green parent that his life from youth to age had
been one unintermitting recognition of the
charms of the sex, and that my sisters and I (being of the sex) could not find it in our hearts to
abandon him on that account. So handsome, so
affectionate, so sweet-tempered; with only one
fault, and that a compliment to the women, who
naturally adored him in return! We accepted
our destiny. For years past (since the death of
Mamma) we accustomed ourselves to live in perpetual dread of his marrying some one of the
hundreds of unscrupulous hussies who took possession of him; and, worse if possible than that,
of his fighting duels about them with men young
enough to be his grandsons. Papa was so susceptible! Papa was so brave! Over and over
again I had been summoned to interfere, as the
daughter who had the strongest influence over
him, and had succeeded in effecting his rescue,
now by one means and now by another; ending
always, however, in the same sad way, by the
sacrifice of money for damages—on which damages, when the woman is shameless enough to
claim them, my verdict is, "Serve her right!"

On the present occasion it was the old story
over again. My sisters had done their best to
stop it, and had failed. I had no choice but to
appear on the scene—to begin, perhaps, by boxing
her ears; to end, certainly, by filling her pockets.

My absence at this time was something more
than an annoyance—it was a downright grief to

my blind Lucilla. On the morning of my departure she clung to me as if she was determined not to let me go.

"What shall I do without you?" she said. "It is hard, in these dreary days, to lose the comfort of hearing your voice. I shall feel all my security gone when I feel you no longer near me. How many days shall you be away?"

"A day to get to Paris," I answered; "and a day to get back—two. Five days (if I can do it in the time) to thunderstrike the hussy and to rescue Papa—seven. Let us say, if possible, a week."

"You must be back, no matter what happens, before the new year."

"Why?"

"I have my yearly visit to pay to my aunt. It has been twice put off. I must absolutely go to London on the last day of the old year, and stay there my allotted three months in Miss Batchford's house. I had hoped to be Oscar's wife before the time came round again—" (she waited a moment to steady her voice). "That is all over now. We must be parted. If I can't leave you here to console him and to take care of him, come what may of it—I shall stay at Dimchurch."

Her staying at Dimchurch while she was still unmarried meant, under the terms of her uncle's will, sacrificing her fortune. If Reverend Finch had heard her, he would not even have been able to say "Inscrutable Providence"; he would have lost his senses on the spot.

"Don't be afraid," I said; "I shall be back, Lucilla, before you go. Besides, Oscar may get better. He may be able to follow you to London, and visit you at your aunt's."

She shook her head with such a sad, sad doubt of it that the tears came into my eyes. I gave her a last kiss, and hurried away.

My route was to Newhaven, and then across the Channel to Dieppe. I don't think I really knew how fond I had grown of Lucilla until I lost sight of the rectory at the turn in the road to Brighton. My natural firmness deserted me; I felt torturing presentiments that some great misfortune would happen in my absence; I astonished myself—I, the widow of the Spartan Pratolungo!—by having a good cry, like any other woman. Sooner or later we susceptible people pay with the heartache for the privilege of loving. No matter; heartache or not, one must have something to love in this world as long as one lives in it. I have lived in it—never mind how many years—and I have got Lucilla. Before Lucilla I had the Doctor. Before the Doctor—ah, my friends, we won't look back beyond the Doctor!

CHAPTER THE NINETEENTH.

SECOND RESULT OF THE ROBBERY.

THE history of my proceedings in Paris can be dismissed in very few words. It is only necessary to dwell in detail on one among the many particulars which connect themselves in my memory with the rescue of good Papa.

The affair this time assumed the gravest possible aspect. The venerable victim had gone the length of renewing his youth in respect of his teeth, his hair, his complexion, and his figure (this last involving the purchase of a pair of stays). I declare I hardly knew him again, he was so outrageously and unnaturally young. The utmost stretch of my influence was exerted over him in vain. He embraced me with the most touching fervor; he expressed the noblest sentiments; but in the matter of his contemplated marriage he was immovable. Life was only tolerable to him on one condition. The beloved object, or death: such was the programme of this volcanic old man.

To make the prospect more hopeless still, the beloved object proved, on this occasion, to be a bold enough woman to play her trump card at starting.

I give the jade her due. She assumed a perfectly unassailable attitude: we had her full permission to break off the match—if we could. "I refer you to your father. Pray understand that *I* don't wish to marry him if his daughters object to it. He has only to say, 'Release me'; from that moment he is free." There was no contending against such a system of defense as this. We knew as well as she did that our fascinated parent would *not* say the word. Our one chance was to spend money in investigating the antecedent indiscretions of this lady's life, and to produce against her proof so indisputable that not even an old man's infatuation could say, This is a lie.

We disbursed; we investigated; we secured our proof. It took a fortnight. At the end of that time we had the necessary materials in hand for opening the eyes of good Papa.

In the course of the inquiry I was brought into contact with many strange people—among others with a man who startled me, at our first interview, by presenting a personal deformity which, with all my experience of the world, I now saw, oddly enough, for the first time.

The man's face, instead of exhibiting any of the usual shades of complexion, was hideously distinguished by a superhuman—I had almost said a devilish—coloring of livid blackish-*blue!* He proved to be a most kind, intelligent, and serviceable person. But when we first confronted each other his horrible color so startled me that I could not repress a cry of alarm. He not only passed over my involuntary act of rudeness in the most indulgent manner—he explained to me the cause which had produced his peculiarity of complexion, so as to put me at my ease before we entered on the delicate private inquiry which had brought us together.

"I beg your pardon," said this unfortunate man, "for not having warned you of my disfigurement before I entered the room. There are hundreds of people discolored as I am in the various parts of the civilized world; and I supposed that you had met in the course of your ex-

perience with other examples of my case. The
blue tinge in my complexion is produced by the
effect on the blood of Nitrate of Silver—taken
internally. It is the only medicine which relieves sufferers like me from an otherwise incurable malady. We have no alternative but to
accept the consequences for the sake of the cure."

He did not mention what his malady had
been; and I abstained, it is needless to say, from
questioning him further. I got used to his disfigurement in the course of my relations with
him; and I should no doubt have forgotten my
blue man in attending to more absorbing matters of interest if the effects of Nitrate of Silver
as a medicine had not been once more unexpectedly forced on my attention in another quarter,
and under circumstances which surprised me in
no ordinary degree.

Having saved Papa on the brink of—let us
say, his twentieth precipice, it was next necessary to stay a few days longer and reconcile him
to the hardship of being rescued in spite of himself. You would have been greatly shocked if
you had seen how he suffered. He gnashed his
expensive teeth; he tore his beautifully manu-
factured hair. In the fervor of his emotions I
have no doubt he would have burst his new
stays—if I had not taken them away and sold
them half price, and made (to that small extent) a profit out of our calamity to set against
the loss. Do what one may in the detestable
system of modern society, the pivot on which it
all turns is Money. Money, when you are sav-

ing Freedom! Money, when you are saving Papa! Is there no remedy for this? A word in your ear. Wait till the next revolution!

During the time of my absence I had, of course, corresponded with Lucilla.

Her letters to me—very sad and very short—reported a melancholy state of things at Dimchurch. While I had been away the dreadful epileptic seizures had attacked Oscar with increasing frequency and increasing severity. The moment I could see my way to getting back to England I wrote to Lucilla to cheer her with the intimation of my return. Two days only before my departure from Paris I received another letter from her. I was weak enough to be almost afraid to open it. Her writing to me again, when she knew that we should be reunited at such an early date, suggested that she must have some very startling news to communicate. My mind misgave me that it would prove to be news of the worst sort.

I summoned courage to open the envelope. Ah, what fools we are! For once that our presentiments come right, they prove a hundred times to be wrong. Instead of distressing me, the letter delighted me. Our gloomy prospect was brightening at last.

Thus, feeling her way over the paper in her large childish characters, Lucilla wrote:

"DEAREST FRIEND AND SISTER — I cannot wait until we meet to tell you my good news. The Brighton doctor has been dismissed, and a

doctor from London has been tried instead. My
dear, for intellect there is nothing like London.
The new man sees, thinks, and makes up his
mind on the spot. He has a way of his own of
treating Oscar's case; and he answers for curing
him of the horrible fits. There is news for you!
Come back, and let us jump for joy together.
How wrong I was to doubt the future! Never,
never, never will I doubt it again. This is the
longest letter I have ever written.

"Your affectionate   LUCILLA."

To this a postscript was added, in Oscar's
handwriting, as follows:

"Lucilla has told you that there is some hope
for me at last. What I write in this place is
written without her knowledge—for your private
ear only. Take the first opportunity you can
find of coming to see me at Browndown, without allowing Lucilla to hear of it. I have a
great favor to ask of you. My happiness depends on your granting it. You shall know
what it is when we meet.   OSCAR."

This postscript puzzled me.

It was not in harmony with the implicit confidence which I had observed Oscar to place habitually in Lucilla. It jarred on my experience of
his character, which presented him to me as the
reverse of a reserved, secretive man. His concealment of his identity when he first came
among us had been a forced concealment—due
entirely to his horror of being identified with
the hero of the trial. In all the ordinary rela-

tions of life he was open and unreserved to a fault. That he could have a secret to keep from Lucilla, and to confide to me, was something perfectly unintelligible to my mind. It highly excited my curiosity; it gave me a new reason for longing to get back.

I was able to make all my arrangements, and to bid adieu to my father and my sisters on the evening of the twenty-third. Early on the morning of the twenty-fourth I left Paris, and reached Dimchurch in time for the final festivities in celebration of Christmas-eve.

The first hour of Christmas-day had struck on the clock in our own pretty sitting-room before I could prevail upon Lucilla to let me rest, after my journey, in bed. She was now once more the joyous, light-hearted creature of our happier time; and she had so much to say to me that not even her father himself (on this occasion) could have talked her down. The next morning she paid the penalty of exciting herself over night. When I went into her room she was suffering from a nervous headache, and was not able to rise at her usual hour. She proposed of her own accord that I should go alone to Browndown to see Oscar on my return. It is only doing common justice to myself to say that this was a relief to me. If she had had the use of her eyes, my conscience would have been easy enough; but I shrank from deceiving my dear blind girl even in the slightest things.

So, with Lucilla's knowledge and approval, I went to Oscar alone.

I found him fretful and anxious, ready to flame out into one of his sudden passions on the smallest provocation. Not the slightest reflection of Lucilla's recovered cheerfulness appeared in Lucilla's lover.

"Has she said anything to you about the new doctor?" were the first words he addressed to me.

"She has told me that she feels the greatest faith in him," I answered. "She firmly believes that he speaks the truth in saying he can cure you."

"Did she show any curiosity to know *how* he is curing me?"

"Not the slightest curiosity that I could see. It is enough for her that you are to be cured. The rest she leaves to the doctor."

My last answer appeared to relieve him. He sighed, and leaned back in his chair. "That's right!" he said to himself. "I am glad to hear that."

"Is the doctor's treatment of you a secret?" I asked.

"It must be a secret from Lucilla," he said, speaking very earnestly. "If she attempts to find it out, she must be kept—for the present, at least—from all knowledge of it. Nobody has any influence over her but you. I look to you to help me."

"Is this the favor you had to ask me?"

"Yes."

"Am I to know the secret of the medical treatment?"

"Certainly! How can I expect you to help

me unless you know what a serious reason there is for keeping Lucilla in the dark?"

He laid a strong emphasis on the two words "serious reason." I began to feel a little uneasy. I had never yet taken the slightest advantage of my poor Lucilla's blindness. And here was her promised husband—of all the people in the world —proposing to me to keep her in the dark!

"Is the new doctor's treatment dangerous?" I inquired.

"Not in the least."

"Is it not so certain as he has led Lucilla to believe?"

"It is quite certain."

"Did the other doctors know of it?"

"Yes."

"Why did they not try it?"

"They were afraid."

"Afraid? What *is* the treatment?"

"Medicine."

"Many medicines? or one?'

"Only one."

"What is the name of it?"

"Nitrate of Silver."

I started to my feet, looked at him, and dropped back into my chair.

My mind reverted, the instant I recovered myself, to the effect produced on me when the blue man in Paris first entered my presence. In informing me of the effect of the medicine he had (you will remember) concealed from me the malady for which he had taken it. It had been left to Oscar, of all the people in the world, to enlighten me—and that by a reference to his own case! I was so shocked that I sat speechless.

With his quick sensibilities, there was no need for me to express myself in words. My face revealed to him what was passing in my mind.

"You have seen a person who has taken Nitrate of Silver!" he exclaimed.

"Have *you?*" I asked.

"I know the price I pay for being cured," he answered, quietly.

His composure staggered me. "How long have you been taking this horrible drug?" I inquired.

"A little more than a week."

"I see no change in you yet."

"The doctor tells me there will be no visible change for weeks and weeks to come."

Those words roused a momentary hope in me.

"There is time to alter your mind," I said. "For Heaven's sake reconsider your resolution before it is too late!"

He smiled bitterly. "Weak as I am," he answered, "for once my mind is made up."

I suppose I took a woman's view of the matter. I lost my temper when I looked at his beautiful complexion, and thought of the future.

"Are you in your right senses?" I burst out. "Do you mean to tell me that you are deliberately bent on making yourself an object of horror to everybody who sees you."

"The one person whose opinion I care for." he replied, "will never see me."

I understood him at last. That was the consideration which had reconciled him to it!

Lucilla's horror of dark people and dark shades of color of all kinds was, it is needless to say, recalled to my memory by the turn the conversation was taking now. Had she confessed it to him, as she had confessed it to me? No! I remembered that she had expressly warned me not to admit him into our confidence in this matter. At an early period of their acquaintance she had asked him which of his parents he resembled. This led him into telling her that his father had been a dark man. Lucilla's delicacy had at once taken the alarm. He speaks very tenderly of his dead father," she said to me. "It may hurt him if he finds out the antipathy I have to dark people. Let us keep it to ourselves." As things now were, it was on the tip of my tongue to remind him that Lucilla would hear of his disfigurement from other people; and then to warn him of the unpleasant result that might follow. On reflection, however, I thought it wiser to wait a little and sound his motives first.

"Before you tell me how I can help you," I said, "I want to know one thing more. Have you decided in this serious matter entirely by yourself? Have you taken no advice?"

"I don't want advice," he answered, sharply. "My case admits of no choice. Even such a nervous, undecided creature as I am can judge for himself where there is no alternative."

"Did the doctors tell you there was no alternative?" I asked.

"The doctors hesitated to tell me. I had to force it out of them. I said, 'I appeal to your honor to answer a plain question plainly. Is there any certain prospect of my getting the better of the fits?' They only said, 'At your time of life, we may reasonably hope so.' I pressed them closer. 'Can you fix a date to which I may look forward as the date of my deliverance?' They could neither of them do it. All they could say was, 'Our experience justifies us in believing that you will grow out of it; but it does *not* justify us in saying when.' 'Then I may be years growing out of it?' They were obliged to own that it might be so. 'Or I may never grow out of it at all?' They tried to turn the conversation. I wouldn't have it. I said, 'Tell me honestly, is that one of the possibilities in my case?' The Dimchurch doctor looked at the London doctor. The London man said, 'If you will have it, it *is* one of the possibilities.' Just consider the prospect which his answer placed before me! Day after day, week after week, month after month, always in danger, go where I may, of falling down in a fit—is that a miserable position? or is it not?"

How could I answer him? What could I say? He went on:

"Add to that wretched state of things that I am engaged to be married. The hardest disappointment which can fall on a man falls on me. The happiness of my life is within my reach and I am forbidden to enjoy it. It is not only my health that is broken up; my prospects in life

are ruined as well. The woman I love is a woman forbidden to me while I suffer as I suffer
now. Realize that, and then fancy you see a
man sitting at this table here, with pen, ink and
paper before him, who has only to scribble a line
or two, and to begin the cure of you from that
moment. Deliverance in a few months from
the horror of the fits; marriage in a few months
to the woman you love. That heavenly prospect
in exchange for the hellish existence that you
are enduring now. And the one price to pay for
it, a discolored face for the rest of your life—
which the one person who is dearest to you will
never see! Would you have hesitated? When
the doctor took up the pen to write the prescrip-
tion—tell me, if you had been in my place, would
you have said No?"

I still sat silent. My obstinacy—women are
such mules!—declined to give way, even when
my conscience told me that he was right.

He sprang to his feet in the same fever of excitement which I remembered so well when I
had irritated him at Browndown into telling me
who he really was.

"Would you have said No?" he reiterated,
stoping over me, flushed and heated, as he
had stopped on that first occasion, when he had
whispered his name in my ear. "Would you?"
he repeated, louder and louder—"would you?"

At the third reiteration of the words the frightful contortion that I knew so well seized on his
face. The wrench to the right twisted his body.
He dropped at my feet. Good God! who could

have declared that he was wrong, with such an argument in his favor as I saw at that moment? Who would not have said that any disfigurement would be welcome as a refuge from *this?*

The servant ran in, and helped me to move the furniture to a safe distance from him. "There won't be much more of it, ma'am," said the man, noticing my agitation, and trying to compose me. "In a month or two, the doctor says, the medicine will get hold of him." I could say nothing on my side—I could only reproach myself bitterly for disputing with him and exciting him, and leading perhaps to the hideous seizure which had attacked him in my presence for the second time.

The fit, on this occasion, was a short one. Perhaps the drug was already beginning to have some influence over him. In twenty minutes he was able to resume his chair and to go on talking to me.

"You think I shall horrify you when my face has turned blue," he said, with a faint smile. "Don't I horrify you now when you see me in convulsions on the floor?"

I entreated him to dwell on it no more.

"God knows," I said, "you have convinced me—obstinate as I am. Let us try to think of nothing now but of the prospect of your being cured. What do you wish me to do?"

"You have a great influence over Lucilla," he said. "If she expresses any curiosity, in future conversations with you, about the effect of the medicine, check her at once. Keep her as ignorant of it as she is now."

"Why?"

"Why! If she knows what you know, how will she feel? Shocked and horrified, as you felt. What will she do? She will come straight here, and try, as you have tried, to persuade me to give it up. Is that true, or not?"

(Impossible to deny that it was true.)

"I am so fond of her," he went on, "that I can refuse her nothing. She would end in making me give it up. The instant her back was turned I should repent my own weakness, and return to the medicine. Here is a perpetual struggle in prospect for a man who is already worn out. Is it desirable, after what you have just seen, to expose me to that?"

It would have been useless cruelty to expose him to it. How could I do otherwise than consent to make his sacrifice of himself—his *necessary* sacrifice—as easy as I could? At the same time I implored him to remember one thing.

"Mind," I said, "we can never hope to keep her in ignorance of the change in you when the change comes. Sooner or later, some one will let the secret out."

"I only want it to be concealed from her while the disfigurement of me is in progress," he answered. "When nothing she can say or do will alter it, I will tell her myself. She is so happy in the hope of my recovery! What good *can* be gained by telling her beforehand of the penalty that I pay for my deliverance? My ugly color will never terrify my poor darling. As for other persons, I shall not force myself on the view of the world. It is my one wish to live out of the world. The few people about me will soon get reconciled to my face. Lucilla will set them the example. She won't trouble herself long about a change in me that she can neither feel nor see."

Ought I to have warned him here of Lucilla's inveterate prejudice, and of the difficulty there might be in reconciling her to the change in him when she heard of it? I dare say I ought. I dare say I was to blame in shrinking from inflicting new anxieties and new distresses on a man who had already suffered so much. The simple truth is—I could not do it. Would you have done it? Ah, if you would, I hope I may never come in contact with you. What a horrid wretch you must be!

The end of it was that I left the house—pledged to keep Lucilla in ignorance of the cost at which Oscar had determined to purchase his cure.

CHAPTER THE TWENTIETH.

GOOD PAPA AGAIN!

THE promise I had given did not expose me to the annoyance of being kept long on the watch against accidents. If we could pass safely over the next five days, we might feel pretty sure of the future. On the last day of the old year Lucilla was bound by the terms of the will to go to

London, and live her allotted three months under the roof of her aunt.

In the short interval that elapsed before her departure she twice approached the dangerous subject.

On the first occasion she asked me if I knew what medicine Oscar was taking. I pleaded ignorance, and passed at once to other matters. On the second occasion she advanced still further on the way to discovery of the truth. She now inquired if I had heard how the physic worked the cure. Having been already informed that the fits proceeded from a certain disordered condition of the brain, she was anxious to know whether the medical treatment was likely to affect the patient's head. This question (which I was, of course, unable to answer) she put to both the doctors. Already warned by Oscar, they quieted her by declaring that the process of cure acted by general means, and did *not* attack the head. From that moment her curiosity was satisfied. Her mind had other objects of interest to dwell on before she left Dimchurch. She touched on the perilous topic no more.

It was arranged that I was to accompany Lucilla to London.

Oscar was to follow us when the state of his health permitted him to take the journey. As betrothed husband of Lucilla, he had his right of entry during her residence in her aunt's house. As for me, I was admitted at Lucilla's intercession. She declined to be separated from me for three months. Miss Batchford wrote, most politely, to offer me a hospitable welcome during the day. She had no second spare room at her disposal; so we settled that I was to sleep at a lodging-house in the neighborhood. In this same house Oscar was also to be accommodated when the doctors sanctioned his removal to London. It was now thought likely—if all went well— that the marriage might be celebrated, at the end of the three months, from Miss Batchford's residence in town.

Three days before the date of Lucilla's departure these plans—so far as I was concerned in them—were all overthrown.

A letter from Paris reached me, with more bad news. My absence had produced the worst possible effect on good Papa. The moment my influence had been removed he had become perfectly unmanageable. My sisters assured me that the abominable woman from whom I had rescued him would most certainly end in marrying him, after all, unless I re-appeared immediately on the scene. What was to be done? Nothing was to be done but to fly into a rage, to grind my teeth, and throw down all my things, in the solitude of my own room, and then to go back to Paris.

Lucilla behaved charmingly. When she saw how angry and how distressed I was she suppressed all exhibition of disappointment on her side, with the truest and kindest consideration for my feelings. "Write to me often," said the charming creature; "and come back to me as soon as you can." Her father took her to Lon-

don. Two days before they left I said good-by
at the rectory and at Browndown, and started—
once more by the Newhaven and Dieppe route
—for Paris.

I was in no humor (as your English saying is)
to mince matters in controlling this new outbreak
on the part of my ever green parent. I insisted
on instantly removing him from Paris, and taking him on a Continental tour. I was proof
against his paternal embraces; I was deaf to
his noble sentiments. He declared he should
die on the road. When I look back at it now,
I am amused at my own cruelty. I said, "En
route, Papa!" and packed him up, and took him
to Italy.

He became enamored at intervals, now of one
fair traveler and now of another, all through the
journey from Paris to Rome. (Wonderful old
man!) Arrived at Rome—that hot-bed of the
enemies of mankind—I saw my way to putting
a moral extinguisher on the author of my being.
The Eternal City contains three hundred and
sixty-five churches and (say) three million and
sixty-five pictures. I insisted on his seeing them
all—at the advanced age of seventy-five years!
The sedative result followed exactly as I had
anticipated. I stupefied good Papa with churches
and pictures, and then I tried him with a marble
woman to begin with. He fell asleep before the
Venus of the Capitol. When I saw that I said
to myself, Now he will do; Don Juan is reformed at last.

Lucilla's correspondence with me — at first

cheerful — gradually assumed a desponding tone.

Six weeks had passed since her departure from Dimchurch; and still Oscar's letters held out no hope of his being able to join her in London. His recovery was advancing, but not so rapidly as his medical adviser had anticipated. It was possible—to look the worst in the face boldly— that he might not get the doctor's permission to leave Browndown before the time arrived for Lucilla's return to the rectory. In this event he could only entreat her to be patient, and to remember that though he was gaining ground but slowly, he was still getting on. Under these circumstances Lucilla was naturally vexed and dejected. She had never (she wrote), from her girlhood upward, spent such a miserable time with her aunt as she was spending now.

On reading this letter I instantly smelled something wrong.

I corresponded with Oscar almost as frequently as with Lucilla. His last letter to me flatly contradicted his last letter to his promised wife. In writing to my address he declared himself to be rapidly advancing toward recovery. Under the new treatment, the fits succeeded each other at longer and longer intervals, and endured a shorter and shorter time. Here, then, was plainly a depressing report sent to Lucilla, and an encouraging report sent to me.

What did it mean?

Oscar's next letter to me answered the question.

"I told you in my last" (he wrote) "that the

discoloration of my skin had begun. The complexion which you were once so good as to admire has disappeared forever. I am now of a
livid ashen color—so like death that I sometimes
startle myself when I look in the glass. In about
six weeks more, as the doctor calculates, this will
deepen to a blackish-blue; and then 'the satura-
tion' (as he calls it) will be complete.

"So far from feeling any useless regrets at
having taken the medicine which is producing
these ugly effects, I am more grateful to my
Nitrate of Silver than words can say. If you
ask for the secret of this extraordinary exhibition of philosophy on my part, I can give it in
one line. For the last ten days I have not had
a fit. In other words, for the last ten days I
have lived in Paradise. I declare I would have
cheerfully lost an arm or a leg to gain the blessed
peace of mind, the intoxicating confidence in the
future—it is nothing less—that I feel now.

"Still, there is a drawback which prevents
me from enjoying perfect tranquillity even yet.
When was there ever a pleasure in the world
without a lurking possibility of pain hidden away
in it somewhere?

"I have lately discovered a peculiarity in
Lucilla which is new to me, and which has
produced a very unpleasant impression on my
mind. My proposed avowal to her of the change
in my personal appearance has now become a
matter of far more serious difficulty than I had
anticipated when the question was discussed between you and me at Browndown.

"Have you ever found out that the strongest antipathy she has is her purely imaginary antipathy to dark people and to dark shades of color of all kinds? This strange prejudice is the result, as I suppose, of some morbid growth of her blindness, quite as inexplicable to herself as to other people. Explicable, or not, there it is in her. Read the extract that follows from one of her letters to her father, which her father showed to me, and you will not be surprised to hear that I tremble for myself when the time comes for telling her what I have done.

"Thus she writes to Mr. Finch:

" 'I am sorry to say I have had a little quarrel with my aunt. It is all made up now, but it has hardly left us such good friends as we were before. Last week there was a dinner-party here; and among the guests was a Hindoo gentleman (converted to Christianity) to whom my aunt has taken a great fancy. While the maid was dressing me I unluckily inquired if she had seen the Hindoo—and hearing that she had, I still more unfortunately asked her to tell me what he was like. She described him as being very tall and lean, with a dark-brown complexion and glittering black eyes. My mischievous fancy instantly set to work on this horrid combination of darkness. Try as I might to resist it, my mind drew a dreadful picture of the Hindoo, as a kind of monster in human form. I would have given worlds to have been excused from going down into the drawing-room. At

the last moment I was sent for, and the Hindoo
was introduced to me. The instant I felt him
approaching my darkness was peopled with brown
demons. He took my hand. I tried hard to
control myself—but I really could not help shuddering and starting back when he touched me.
To make matters worse, he sat next to me at
dinner. In five minutes I had long, lean, black-
eyed beings all round me; perpetually growing
in numbers, and pressing closer and closer on me
as they grew. It ended in my being obliged to
leave the table. When the guests were all gone
my aunt was furious. I admitted my conduct
was unreasonable in the last degree. At the same
time I begged her to make allowance for me. I
reminded her that I was blind at a year old, and
that I had really no idea of what any person was
like, except by drawing pictures of them in my
imagination, from description, and from my own
knowledge obtained by touch. I appealed to her
to remember that, situated as I am, my fancy is
peculiarly liable to play me tricks, and that *I*
have no sight to see with and to show me—as
other people's eyes show *them*—when they have
taken a false view of persons and things. It was
all in vain. My aunt would admit of no excuse
for me. I was so irritated by her injustice that
I reminded her of an antipathy of her own, quite
as ridiculous as mine—an antipathy to cats. She,
who can *see* that cats are harmless, shudders and
turns pale, for all that, if a cat is in the same
room with her. Set my senseless horror of dark
people against her senseless horror of cats—and

say which of us has the right to be angry with
the other?' ''

Such was the quotation from Lucilla's letter
to her father. At the end of it Oscar resumed,
as follows:

"I wonder whether you will now understand
me, if I own to you that I have made the worst
of my case in writing to Lucilla? It is the only
excuse I can produce for not joining her in London. Weary as I am of our long separation, I
cannot prevail on myself to run the risk of meeting her in the presence of strangers, who would
instantly notice my frightful color and betray it
to her. Think of her shuddering and starting
back from *my* hand when it took hers! No! no!
I must choose my own opportunity, in this quiet
place, of telling her what (I suppose) must be
told—with time before me to prepare her mind
for the disclosure (if it must come) and with nobody but you near to see the first mortifying effect
of the shock which I shall inflict on her.

"I have only to add, before I release you, that
I write these lines in the strictest confidence.
You have promised not to mention my disfigurement to Lucilla, unless I first give you leave. I
now, more than ever, hold you to that promise.
The few people about me here are all pledged to
secrecy as you are. If it is really inevitable that
she should know the truth—I alone must tell it;
in my own way, and at my own time."

"If it must come," "if it is really inevitable"
—these phrases in Oscar's letter satisfied me that

he was already beginning to comfort himself with
an insanely delusive idea—the idea that it might
be possible permanently to conceal the ugly personal change in him from Lucilla's knowledge.

If I had been at Dimchurch, I have no doubt
I should have begun to feel seriously uneasy at
the turn which things appeared to be taking
now.

But distance has a very strange effect in altering one's customary way of thinking of affairs
at home. Being in Italy instead of in England,
I dismissed Lucilla's antipathies and Oscar's
scruples, as both alike unworthy of serious consideration. Sooner or later, time (I considered)
would bring these two troublesome young people
to their senses. Their marriage would follow,
and there would be an end of it! In the meanwhile, I continued to feast good Papa on holy
families and churches. Ah, poor dear, how he
yawned over Caraccis and cupolas! and how fervently he promised never to fall in love again, if
I would only take him back to Paris!

We set our faces homeward a day or two after
the receipt of Oscar's letter. I left my reformed
father resting his aching old bones in his own
easy-chair; capable perhaps, even yet, of con-
tracting a Platonic attachment to a lady of his
own time of life, but capable (as I firmly believe)
of nothing more. "Oh, my child, let me rest!"
he said, when I wished him good-by, "and never
show me a church or a picture again as long as
I live!"

CHAPTER THE TWENTY-FIRST.

MADAME PRATOLUNGO RETURNS TO DIMCHURCH.

I REACHED London in the last week of Lucilla's residence under her aunt's roof, and waited in town until it was time to take her back to Dimchurch.

As soon as it had become obviously too late for Oscar to risk the dreaded meeting with Lucilla, before strangers, his correspondence had, as a matter of course, assumed a brighter tone. She was in high spirits once more, poor thing, when we met, and full of delight at having me near her again. We thoroughly enjoyed our few days in London, and took our fill of music at operas and concerts. I got on excellently well with the aunt until the last day, when something happened which betrayed me into an avowal of my political convictions.

The old lady's consternation, when she discovered that I looked hopefully forward to a coming extermination of kings and priests, and a general redistribution of property all over the civilized globe, is unutterable in words. On that occasion I made one more aristocrat tremble. I also closed Miss Batchford's door on me for the rest of my life. No matter! The day is coming when the Batchford branch of humanity will not possess a door to close. All Europe is drifting nearer and nearer to the Pratolungo programme. Cheer up, my brothers without land, and my sisters without money in the Funds! We will have it out with the infamous rich yet. Long live the Republic!

Early in the month of April Lucilla and I took leave of the metropolis and went back to Dimchurch.

As we drew nearer and nearer to the rectory, as Lucilla began to flush and fidget in eager anticipation of her reunion with Oscar, that uneasiness of mind which I had so readily dismissed while I was in Italy began to find its way back to me again. *My* imagination now set to work at drawing pictures—startling pictures of Oscar as a changed being, as a Medusa's head too terrible to be contemplated by mortal eyes. Where would he meet us? At the entrance to the village? No. At the rectory gate? No. In the quieter part of the garden which was at the back of the house? Yes! There he stood, waiting for us—alone.

Lucilla flew into his arms with a cry of delight. I stood behind and looked at them.

Ah, how vividly I remember—at the moment when she embraced him—the first shock of seeing the two faces together! The drug had done its work. I saw her fair cheek laid innocently against the livid blackish-blue of *his* discolored skin. Heavens! how cruelly that first embrace marked the contrast between what he had been when I left him and what he had changed to when I saw him now! His eyes turned from her face to mine, in silent appeal to me while he held

her in his arms. Their look told me the thought
in him, as eloquently as if he had put it into
words. "You, who love her, say—can we ever
be cruel enough to tell her of *this?*"

I approached to take his hand. At the same
moment Lucilla suddenly drew back from him,
laid her left hand on his shoulder, and passed her
right hand rapidly over his face.

For an instant I felt my heart stand still. Her
miraculous sensitiveness of touch had detected
the dark color of my dress on the day when we
first met. Would it serve her this time as truly
as it had served her then?

She paused after the first passage of her fingers over his face, with breathless attention to
what she was about which, in my own case, I
remembered so well. A second time she passed
her hand over him—considered again—and turned
my way next.

"What does his face tell *you?*" she asked.
"It tells *me* that he has something on his mind.
What is it?"

We were safe—so far! The hateful medicine,
in altering the color, had not affected the texture
of his skin. As her touch had left it on her departure, so her touch found it again on her return.

Before I could reply to Lucilla, Oscar answered
for himself.

"Nothing is wrong, my darling," he said.
"My nerves are a little out of order to-day; and
the joy of seeing you has overcome me for the
moment—that is all."

She shook her head impatiently.

I SAW HER FAIR CHEEK LAID INNOCENTLY AGAINST THE LIVID BLACKISH-BLUE OF HIS DISCOLORED SKIN.
—POOR MISS FINCH, VOL. XV., page 191.

"No," she said, "it is not all." She touched his heart. "Why is it beating so fast?" She took his hand in hers. "Why has it turned so cold? I must know. I *will* know! Come indoors."

At that awkward moment the most wearisome of all living men suddenly proved himself to be the most welcome of living men. The rector appeared in the garden to receive his daughter on her return. Infolded in Reverend Finch's paternal embraces, harangued by Reverend Finch's prodigious voice, Lucilla was effectually silenced —the subject was inevitably changed. Oscar drew me aside out of hearing, while her attention was diverted from him.

"I saw you!" he said. "*You* were horrified at the first sight of me. *You* were relieved when you found that her touch told her nothing. Help me to keep her from suspecting it for two months more—and you will be the best friend that man ever had."

"Two months?" I repeated.

"Yes. If there is no return of the fits in two months, the doctor will consider my recovery complete. Lucilla and I may be married at the end of that time."

"My friend Oscar, are you contemplating a fraud on Lucilla?"

"What do you mean?"

"Come! come! you know what I mean! Is it honorable first to entrap her into marrying you—and then to confess to her the color of your face?"

He sighed bitterly.

"I shall fill her with horror of me if I confess it. Look at me! look at me!" he said, lifting his ghastly hands in despair to his blue face.

I was determined not to give way—even to that.

"Be a man!" I said. "Own it boldly. What is she going to marry you for? For your face that she can never see? No! For your heart that is one with her own. Trust to her natural good sense—and, better than that, to the devoted love that you have inspired in her. She will see her stupid prejudice in its true light when she feels it trying to part her from *you*."

"No! no! no! Remember her letter to her father. I shall lose her forever, if I tell her now."

I took his arm and tried to lead him to Lucilla. She was already trying to escape from her father; she was already longing to hear the sound of Oscar's voice again.

He obstinately shrank back. I began to feel angry with him. In another moment I should have said or done something that I might have repented of afterward if a new interruption had not happened before I could open my lips.

Another person appeared in the garden—the man-servant from Browndown, with a letter for his master in his hand.

"This has just come, sir," said the man, "by the afternoon post. It is marked 'Immediate.' I thought I had better bring it to you here."

Oscar took the letter and looked at the address.

"My brother's writing!" he exclaimed. "A letter from Nugent!"

He opened the letter and burst out with a cry of joy which brought Lucilla instantly to his side.

"What is it?" she asked, eagerly.

"Nugent is coming back! Nugent will be here in a week! Oh, Lucilla, my brother is coming to stay with me at Browndown!"

He caught her in his arms and kissed her, in the first rapture of receiving that welcome news. She forced herself away from him without answering a word. She turned her poor blind face round and round, in search for me.

"Here I am!" I said.

She roughly and angrily put her arm in mine. I saw the jealous misery in her face as she dragged me away with her to the house. Never yet had Oscar's voice, in *her* experience of him, sounded the note of happiness that she heard in it now! Never yet had she felt Oscar's heart on Oscar's lips as she felt it when he kissed her in the first joy of anticipating Nugent's return!

"Can he hear me?" she whispered, when we had left the lawn, and she felt the gravel under her feet.

"No. What is it?"

"I hate his brother!"

CHAPTER THE TWENTY-SECOND.

THE TWIN BROTHER'S LETTER.

LITTLE thinking what a storm he had raised, poor innocent Oscar—paternally escorted by the rector—followed us into the house, with his open letter in his hand.

Judging by certain signs visible in my reverend friend, I concluded that the announcement of Nugent Dubourg's coming visit to Dimchurch —regarded by the rest of us as heralding the appearance of a twin brother—was regarded by Mr. Finch as promising the arrival of a twin fortune. Oscar and Nugent shared the comfortable paternal inheritance. Finch smelled money.

"Compose yourself," I whispered to Lucilla as the two gentlemen followed us into the sitting-room. "Your jealousy of his brother is a childish jealousy. There is room enough in his heart for his brother as well as for you."

She only repeated, obstinately, with a vicious pinch on my arm: "I hate his brother!"

"Come and sit down by me," said Oscar, approaching her on the other side. "I want to run over Nugent's letter. It's so interesting! There is a message in it to you." Too deeply absorbed in his subjcet to notice the sullen submission with which she listened to him, he placed her on a chair and began reading "The first lines," he explained, "relate to Nugent's return to England,

and to his delightful idea of coming to stay with
me at Browndown. Then he goes on: 'I found
all your letters waiting for me on my return
to New York. Need I tell you, my dearest
brother—'"

Lucilla stopped him at those words by rising
abruptly from her seat.

"What is the matter?" he asked.

"I don't like this chair!"

Oscar got her another—an easy-chair this time
—and returned to the letter.

"'Need I tell you, my dearest brother, how
deeply you have interested me by the announcement of your contemplated marriage? Your
happiness is my happiness. I feel with you; I
congratulate you; I long to see my future sister-
in-law—'"

Lucilla got up again. Oscar, in astonishment, asked what was wrong now.

"I am not comfortable at this end of the room."

She walked to the other end of the room. Patient Oscar walked after her, with his precious
letter in his hand. He offered her a third chair.
She petulantly declined to take it, and selected
another chair for herself. Oscar returned to the
letter:

"'How melancholy, and yet how interesting
it is, to hear that she is blind! My sketches of
American scenery happened to be lying about
in the room when I read your letter. The first
thought that came to me on hearing of Miss
Finch's affliction was suggested by my sketches.
I said to myself: "Sad! sad! my sister-in-law

will never see my Works." The true artist, Oscar, is always thinking of his Works. I shall bring back, let me tell you, some very remarkable studies for future pictures. They will not be so numerous, perhaps, as you may expect. I prefer to trust to my intellectual perception of beauty rather than to mere laborious transcripts from Nature. In certain moods of mine (speaking as an artist) Nature puts me out.' " There Oscar paused, and appealed to me. "What writing!—eh? I always told you, Madame Pratolungo, that Nugent was a genius. You see it now. Don't get up, Lucilla. I am going on. There is a message to you in this part of the letter. So neatly expressed!"

Lucilla persisted in getting up; the announcement of the neatly expressed message to be read next produced no effect on her. She walked to the window, and trifled impatiently with the flowers placed in it. Oscar looked in mild astonishment, first at me, then at the rector. Reverend Finch—listening thus far with the complimentary attention due to the correspondence of one young man of fortune with another young man of fortune—interfered in Oscar's interests to secure him a patient hearing.

"My dear Lucilla, endeavor to control your restlessness. You interfere with our enjoyment of this interesting letter. I could wish to see fewer changes of place, my child, and a more undivided attention to what Oscar is reading to you."

"I am not interested in what he is reading to

me." In the nervous irritation which produced
this ungracious answer she overthrew one of the
flower-pots. Oscar set it up again for her with
undiminished good temper.

"Not interested!" he exclaimed. "Wait a
little. You haven't heard Nugent's message
yet. Listen to this! 'Present my best and
kindest regards to the future Mrs. Oscar' (dear
fellow!), 'and say that she has given me a new
interest in hastening my return to England.'
There! Isn't that prettily put? Come, Lucilla!
own that Nugent is worth listening to when he
writes about *you!*"

She turned toward him for the first time. The
charm of the tone in which he spoke those words
subdued her in spite of herself.

"I am much obliged to your brother," she answered, gently, "and very much ashamed of
myself for what I said just now." She stole
her hand into his, and whispered, "You are so
fond of Nugent, I begin to be almost afraid
there will be no love left for me."

Oscar was enchanted. "Wait till you see
him, and you will be as fond of him as I am,"
he said. "Nugent is not like me. He fasci-
nates people the moment they come in contact
with him. Nobody can resist Nugent."

She still held his hand, with a perplexed and
saddened face. The admirable absence of any
jealousy on his side—his large and generous confidence in *her* love for *him*—was just the rebuke
to her that she could feel; just the rebuke, also
(in my opinion), that she had deserved.

"Go on, Oscar," said the rector, in his deepest notes of encouragement. "What next, dear boy? what next?"

"Another interesting bit, of quite a new kind," Oscar replied. "There is a little mystery to stir us up on the last page of the letter. Nugent says: 'I have become acquainted (here in New York) with a very remarkable man, a German who has made a great deal of money in the United States. He proposes to visit England early in the present year; and he will write and let me know when he has arrived. I shall feel particular pleasure in presenting him to you and your future wife. It is quite possible that you may have special reason to congratulate yourselves on making his acquaintance. For the present no more of my new friend until we meet at Browndown.'—'Special reason to congratulate ourselves on making his acquaintance'!" repeated Oscar, folding up the letter. "Nugent never writes in that way without a reason for it. Who can the German gentleman be?"

Mr. Finch suddenly lifted his head, and looked at Oscar with a certain appearance of alarm.

"Your brother mentions that he has made his fortune in America," said the reverend gentleman. "I hope he is not connected with the money market! He might infect Mr. Nugent with the spirit of reckless speculation which is, so to speak, the national sin of the United States. Your brother, having no doubt the same generous disposition as yours—"

"A far finer disposition than mine, Mr. Finch," interposed Oscar.

"Possessed, like you, of the gifts of fortune," proceeded the rector, with mounting enthusiasm.

"Once possessed of them," said Oscar. "Far from being overburdened with the gifts of fortune now!"

"What!!!" cried Mr. Finch, with a start of consternation.

"Nugent has run through his fortune," proceeded Oscar, quite composedly. "I lent him the money to go to America. My brother is a genius, Mr. Finch. When did you ever hear of a genius who could keep within limits? Nugent is not content to live in my humble way. He has the tastes of a prince—money is nothing to him. It doesn't matter. He will make a new fortune out of his pictures; and, in the meantime, you know, I can always lend him something to go on with."

Mr. Finch rose from his seat with the air of a man whose just anticipations have not been realized—whose innocent confidence has been scandalously betrayed. Here was a prospect! Another person in perpetual want of money going to settle under the shadow of the rectory? Another man likely to borrow of Oscar—and that man his brother!

"I fail to take your light view of your brother's extravagance," said the rector, addressing Oscar with his loftiest severity of manner, at the door. "I deplore and reprehend Mr. Nugent's misuse of the bounty bestowed on him by an all-

wise Providence. You will do well to consider
before you encourage your brother's extravagance by lending him money. What does the
great poet of humanity say of lenders? The
Bard of Avon tells us that 'loan oft loses both
itself and friend.' Lay that noble line to heart,
Oscar! Lucilla, be on your guard against that
restlessness which I have already had occasion
to reprove. I find I must leave you, Madame
Pratolungo. I had forgotten my parish duties.
My parish duties are waiting for me. Good-
day! good-day!"

He looked round on us all three, in turn, with
a very sour face, and walked out. "Surely," I
thought to myself, "this brother of Oscar's is
not beginning well! First the daughter takes
offense at him, and now the father follows her
example. Even on the other side of the Atlantic,
Mr. Nugent Dubourg exercises a malignant influence, and disturbs the family tranquillity before he has shown his nose in the house!"

Nothing more that is worth recording happened on that day. We had a very dull evening. Lucilla was out of spirits. As for me, I
had not yet had time to accustom myself to the
shocking spectacle of Oscar's discolored face. I
was serious and silent. You would never have
guessed me to be a Frenchwoman, if you had
seen me for the first time on the occasion of my
return to the rectory.

The next day a small domestic event happened
which must be chronicled in this place.

Our Dimchurch doctor, always dissatisfied with his position in an obscure country place, had obtained an appointment in India which offered great professional advantages to an ambitious man. He called to take leave of us on his departure. I found an opportunity of speaking to him about Oscar. He entirely agreed with me that the attempt to keep the change produced in his former patient by the Nitrate of Silver from Lucilla's knowledge was simply absurd. It would come to her ears, he said, before many days were over our heads. With that prediction, addressed to my private ear, he left us. The removal of him from the scene was, you will please to bear in mind, the removal of an important local witness to the medical treatment of Oscar, and was, as such, an incident with a bearing of its own on the future, which claims a place for it in the present narrative.

Two more days passed, and nothing happened. On the morning of the third day the doctor's prophecy was all but fulfilled through the medium of the wandering Arab of the family, our funny little Jicks.

While Lucilla and I were strolling about the garden with Oscar, the child suddenly darted out on us from behind a tree, and, seizing Oscar round the legs, hailed him affectionately at the top of her voice as "The Blue Man!" Lucilla instantly stopped, and said, "Who do you call 'The Blue Man'?" Jicks answered, boldly, "Oscar." Lucilla caught the child up in her arms. "Why do you call Oscar 'The Blue

Man'?" she asked. Jicks pointed to Oscar's face, and then, remembering Lucilla's blindness, appealed to me. "You tell her," said Jicks, in high glee. Oscar seized my hand, and looked at me imploringly. I determined not to interfere. It was bad enough to remain passive, and to let her be kept in the dark. Actively, I was resolved to take no part in deceiving her. Her color rose; she put Jicks down on the ground. "Are you both dumb?" she asked. "Oscar, I insist on knowing it—how have you got the nickname of 'The Blue Man'?" Left helpless, Oscar (to my disgust) took refuge in a lie—and, worse still, a clumsy lie. He declared that he had got his nickname in the nursery, at the time of Lucilla's absence in London, by one day painting his face in the character of Bluebeard to amuse the children! If Lucilla had felt the faintest suspicion of the truth, blind as she was, she must now have discovered it. As things were, Oscar annoyed and irritated her. I could see that it cost her a struggle to suppress something like a feeling of contempt for him. "Amuse the children, the next time, in some other way," she said. "Though I can't see you, still I don't like to hear of your disfiguring your face by painting it blue." With that answer she walked away a little by herself, evidently disappointed in her betrothed husband for the first time in her experience of him. He cast another imploring look at me. "Did you hear what she said about my face?" he whispered.

"You have lost an excellent opportunity of

speaking out," I answered. "I believe you will bitterly regret the folly and the cruelty of deceiving her."

He shook his head, with the immovable obstinacy of a weak man.

"Nugent doesn't think as you do," he said, handing me the letter. "Read that bit there— now Lucilla is out of hearing."

I paused for a moment before I could read. The resemblance between the twins extended even to their handwritings! If I had picked Nugent's letter up, I should have handed it to Oscar as a letter of Oscar's own writing.

The paragraph to which he pointed only contained these lines: "Your last relieves my anxiety about your health. I entirely agree with you that any personal sacrifice which cures you of those horrible attacks is a sacrifice wisely made. As to your keeping the change a secret from the young lady. I can only say I suppose you know best how to act in this emergency. I will abstain from forming any opinion of my own until we meet."

I handed Oscar back the letter.

"There is no very warm approval there of the course you are taking," I said. "The only difference between your brother and me is that he suspends his opinion, and that I express mine."

"I have no fear of my brother," Oscar answered. "Nugent will feel for me and understand me when he comes to Browndown. In the meantime this shall not happen again."

He stooped over Jicks. The child, while we

were talking, had laid herself down luxuriously on the grass, and was singing to herself little snatches of a nursery song. Oscar pulled her up on her legs rather roughly. He was out of temper with her, as well as with himself.

"What are you going to do?" I asked.

"I am going to see Mr. Finch," he answered, "and to have Jicks kept for the future out of Lucilla's garden."

"Does Mr. Finch approve of your silence?"

"Mr. Finch, Madame Pratolungo, leaves me to decide on a matter which concerns nobody but Lucilla and myself."

After that reply there was an end of all further remonstrance from me, as a matter of course. Oscar walked off with his prisoner to the house. Jicks trotted along by his side, unconscious of the mischief she had done, singing another verse of the nursery song. I rejoined Lucilla, with my mind made up as to the line of conduct I should adopt in the future. If Oscar did succeed in keeping the truth concealed from her, I was positively resolved, come what might of it, to enlighten her, before they were married, with my own lips. What! after pledging myself to keep the secret? Yes. Perish the promise that makes me false to a person whom I love! I despise such promises from the bottom of my heart.

Two more days slipped by—and then a telegram found its way to Browndown. Oscar came running to us, at the rectory, with his news. Nugent had landed at Liverpool. Oscar was to expect him at Dimchurch on the next day.

CHAPTER THE TWENTY-THIRD.

HE SETS US ALL RIGHT.

I HAVE thus far quite inadvertently omitted to mention one of the prominent virtues of Reverend Finch. He was an accomplished master of that particular form of human persecution which is called reading aloud; and he inflicted his accomplishment on his family circle at every available opportunity. Of what we suffered on these occasions I shall say nothing. Let it be enough to mention that the rector thoroughly enjoyed the pleasure of hearing his own magnificent voice.

There was no escaping Mr. Finch when the rage for "reading" seized on him. Now on one pretense, and now on another, he descended on us unfortunate women, book in hand, seated us at one end of the room, placed himself at the other, opened his dreadful mouth, and fired words at us, like shots at a target, by the hour together. Sometimes he gave us poetical readings from Shakespeare or Milton; and sometimes Parliamentary speeches by Burke or Sheridan. Read what he might, he made such a noise and such a fuss over it—he put his own individuality so prominently in the foremost place, and he kept the poets or the orators whom he was supposed to be interpreting so far in the background —that they lost every trace of character of their own, and became one and all perfectly intolera-

ble reflections of Mr. Finch. I date my first unhappy doubts of the supreme excellence of Shakespeare's poetry from the rector's readings; and I
attribute to the same exasperating cause my im-
placable hostility (on every question of the time)
to the policy of Mr. Burke.

On the evening when Nugent Dubourg was
expected at Browndown—and when we particularly wanted to be left alone to dress ourselves,
and to gossip by anticipation about the expected
visitor—Mr. Finch was seized with one of his
periodical rages for firing off words at his family
after tea. He selected "Hamlet" as the medium
for exhibiting his voice on this occasion; and he
declared, as the principal motive for taking his
elocutionary exercise, that the object he especially had in view was the benefit of poor Me.

"My good creature, I accidentally heard you
reading to Lucilla the other day. It was very
nice, as far as it went—very nice indeed. But
you will allow me—as a person, Madame Pratolungo, possessing considerable practice in the art
of reading aloud—to observe that you might be
benefited by a hint or two. I will give you a
few ideas. (Mrs. Finch! I propose giving Madame Pratolungo a few ideas.) Pay particular
attention, if you please, to the Pauses, and to the
management of the Voice at the end of the lines.
Lucilla, my child, you are interested in this.
The perfecting of Madame Pratolungo is a matter of considerable importance to *you*. Don't go
away."

Lucilla and I happened, on that evening, to

be guests at the rectory table.   It was one of the regular occasions on which we left our own side of the house, and joined the family at (what Mr. Finch called) "the pastor's evening meal."   He had got his wife; he had got his eldest daughter; he had got your humble servant.   A horrid smile of enjoyment overspread the reverend gentleman's face as he surveyed us from the opposite end of the room and opened his vocal fire on his audience of three.

"'Hamlet:' Act the First; Scene the First. Elsinore.   A Platform before the Castle.   Francisco on his post" (Mr. Finch).   "Enter to him Bernardo" (Mr. Finch).   "Who's there?" "Nay, answer me: stand, and unfold yourself." (Mrs. Finch unfolds herself—she suckles the baby, and tries to look as if she was having an intellectual treat.)   Francisco and Bernardo converse in bass—Boom-boom-boom.   "Enter Horatio and Marcellus" (Mr. Finch and Mr. Finch). "Stand, ho!   Who is there?"   "Friends to this ground."   "And liegemen to the Dane."   (Madame Pratolungo begins to feel the elocutionary exposition of Shakespeare, where she always feels it, in her legs.   She tries to sit still on her chair.   Useless!   She is suffering under the malady known to her, by bitter experience of Mr. Finch, as the Hamlet-Fidgets.)   Bernardo and Francisco, Horatio and Marcellus, converse —Boom-boom-boom.   "Enter Ghost of Hamlet's Father."   Mr. Finch makes an awful pause.   In the supernatural silence we can hear the baby sucking.   Mrs. Finch enjoys her intellectual treat. Madame Pratolungo fidgets. Lucilla catches the infection, and fidgets too. Marcellus-Finch goes on. "Thou art a scholar, speak to it, Horatio." Bernardo-Finch backs him: "Looks it not like the King? Mark it, Horatio." Lucilla-Finch inserts herself in the dialogue: "Papa, I am very sorry; I have had a nervous headache all day; please excuse me if I take a turn in the garden." The rector makes another awful pause, and glares at his daughter. (Exit Lucilla.) Horatio looks at the Ghost, and takes up the dialogue: "Most like; it harrows me"—Boom-boom-boom. The baby is satiated. Mrs. Finch wants her handkerchief. Madame Pratolungo seizes the opportunity of moving her distracted legs, and finds the handkerchief. Mr. Finch pauses—glares—goes on again—reaches the second scene. "Enter the King, Queen, Hamlet, Polonius, Laertes, Voltimand, Cornelius, and Lords Attendant." All Mr. Finch! Oh, my legs! my legs! all Mr. Finch, and Boom-boom-boom. Third scene. "Enter Laertes and Ophelia." (Both Rectors of Dimchurch; both with deep bass voices; both about five feet high, pitted with the small-pox, and adorned around the neck with dingy white cravats.) Mr. Finch goes on and on and on. Mrs. Finch and the baby simultaneously close their eyes in slumber. Madame Pratolungo suffers such tortures of restlessness in her lower limbs that she longs for a skilled surgeon to take out his knife and deliver her from her own legs. Mr. Finch advances in deeper and deeper bass, in keener and keener enjoyment, to the Fourth Scene. ("Enter Hamlet, Horatio, and Marcellus.") Mercy! what do I hear! Is relief approaching to us from the world outside? Are there footsteps in the hall? Yes! Mrs. Finch opens her eyes; Mrs. Finch hears the footsteps, and rejoices in them as I do. Reverend Hamlet hears nothing but his own voice. He begins the scene: "The air bites shrewdly; it is very cold." The door opens. The rector feels a gust of air, dramatically appropriate, just at the right moment. He looks round. If it is a servant, let that domestic person tremble! No—not a servant. Guests—heavens be praised, guests. Welcome, gentlemen—welcome! No more "Hamlet" to-night, thanks to You. Enter two Characters who must be instantly attended to—Mr. Oscar Dubourg, introducing his twin brother from America, Mr. Nugent Dubourg.

Astonishment at the extraordinary resemblance between them was the one impression felt by all three of us as the brothers entered the room.

Exactly alike in their height, in their walk, in their features, and in their voices. Both with the same colored hair and the same beardless faces. Oscar's smile exactly reflected on Nugent's lips. Oscar's odd little semi-foreign tricks of gesticulation with his hands, exactly reproduced in the hands of Nugent. And, to crown it all, there was the complexion which Oscar had lost forever (just a shade darker perhaps, found again on Nugent's cheeks! The one dif-

ference which made it possible to distinguish
between them, at the moment when they first
appeared together in the room, was also the one
difference which Lucilla was physically incapable of detecting—the terrible contrast of color
between the brother who bore the blue disfigurement of the drug, and the brother who was left
as Nature had made him.

"Delighted to make your acquaintance, Mrs.
Finch. I have long wished for this pleasure.
Thank you, Mr. Finch, for all your kindness to
my brother. Madame Pratolungo, I presume?
Permit me to shake hands. It is needless to say
I have heard of your illustrious husband. Aha!
here's a baby. Yours, Mrs. Finch? Girl or
boy, ma'am? A fine child—if a bachelor may
be allowed to pronounce an opinion. *Tweet—
tweet—tweet!*"

He chirruped to the baby as if he had been
a family man, and snapped his fingers gayly.
Poor Oscar's blue face turned in silent triumph
toward me. "What did I tell you?" his look
asked. "Did I not say Nugent fascinated everybody at first sight?" Most true. An irresistible man. So utterly different in his manner
from Oscar, except when he was in repose, and
yet so like Oscar in other respects. I can only
describe him as his brother completed. He had
the pleasant, lively flow of spirits, the easy,
winning, gentleman-like confidence in himself
which Oscar wanted; and then what excellent
taste he possessed! He liked children; he respected the memory of my glorious Pratolungo!

In half a minute from the time when he entered the room, Nugent Dubourg had won Mrs. Finch's heart and mine.

He turned from the baby to Mr. Finch and pointed to the open Shakespeare on the table.

"You were reading to the ladies?" he said. "I am afraid we have interrupted you."

"Don't mention it," said the rector, with his loftiest politeness. "Another time will do. It is a habit of mine, Mr. Nugent, to read aloud in my family circle. As a clergyman and a lover of poetry (in both capacities) I have long culti-vated the art of elocution--"

"My dear sir, excuse me: you have cultivated it all wrong!"

Mr. Finch paused, thunderstruck. A man in his presence presuming to have an opinion of his own! a man in the rectory parlor capable of in-terrupting the rector in the middle of a sentence! guilty of the insane audacity of telling him, as a reader, with Shakespeare open before them, that he read wrong!

"Oh, we heard you as we came in!" proceeded Nugent, with the most undiminished confidence, expressed in the most gentleman-like manner. "You read it like this." He took up "Ham-let," and read the opening line of the Fourth Scene ("The air bites shrewdly; it is very cold") with an irresistibly accurate imitation of Mr. Finch. "That's not the way Hamlet would speak. No man in his position would remark that it was very cold in that bow-wow manner. What is Shakespeare before all things? True to nature—always true to nature. What condition is Hamlet in when he is expecting to see the Ghost? He is nervous, and he feels the cold. Let him show it naturally; let him speak as any other man would speak under the circumstances. Look here! Quick and quiet—like this: 'The air bites shrewdly'—there Hamlet stops and shivers—pur-rer-rer! 'it is very cold.' There! That's the way to read Shakespeare."

Mr. Finch lifted his head into the air as high as it could possibly go, and brought the flat of his hand down with a solemn and sounding smack on the open book.

"Allow me to say, sir—" he began.

Nugent stopped him again, more good-humoredly than ever.

"You don't agree with me? All right. Quite useless to dispute about it. I don't know what *you* may be. *I* am the most opinionated man in existence. Sheer waste of time, my dear sir, to attempt convincing Me. Now just look at that child!" Here Mr. Nugent Dubourg's attention was suddenly attracted by the baby. He twisted round on his heel, and addressed Mrs Finch. "I take the liberty of saying, ma'am, that a more senseless dress doesn't exist than the dress that is put in this country on infants of tender years. What are the three main functions which that child—that charming child of yours—performs? He sucks, he sleeps and he grows. At the present moment he isn't sucking, he isn't sleeping—he is growing with all his might. Under those interesting circumstances what does he want to do? To move his limbs freely in every direction. You let him swing his arms to his heart's content, and you deny him freedom to kick his legs. You clothe him in a dress three times as long as himself. He tries to throw his legs up in the air as he throws his arms, and he can't do it. There is his senseless long dress entangling itself in his toes, and making an effort of what Nature intended to be a luxury. Can anything be more absurd? What are mothers about? Why don't they think for themselves? Take my advice—short petticoats, Mrs. Finch. Liberty, glorious liberty, for my young friend's legs! Room, heaps of room, for that infant martyr's toes!"

Mrs. Finch listened helplessly; lifted the baby's long petticoats, and looked at them; stared piteously at Nugent Dubourg; opened her lips to speak; and, thinking better of it, turned her watery eyes on her husband, appealing to *him* to take the matter up. Mr. Finch made another attempt to assert his dignity—a ponderously satirical attempt this time.

"In offering your advice to my wife, Mr. Nugent," said the rector, "you must permit me to remark that it would have had more practical force if it had been the advice of a married man. I beg to remind you—"

"You beg to remind me that it is the advice of a bachelor? Oh, come! that really won't do at this time of day. Dr. Johnson settled that argument at once and forever a century since. 'Sir,' he said to somebody of your way of thinking, 'you may scold your carpenter when he has made a bad table, though you can't make a table yourself.' I say to you: 'Mr. Finch, you may point out a defect in a baby's petticoats, though you haven't got a baby yourself!' Doesn't that satisfy you? All right. Take another illustration. Look at your room here. I can see in the twinkling of an eye that it's badly lit. You have only got one window; you ought to have two. Is it necessary to be a practical builder to discover that? Absurd! Are you satisfied now? No! Take another illustration. What's this printed paper here on the chimney-piece? Assessed taxes. Ha! Assessed taxes will do. You're not in the House of Commons; you're not Chancellor of the Exchequer; but haven't you an opinion of your own about taxation in spite of that? Must you and I be in Parliament before we can presume to see that the feeble old British Constitution is at its last gasp?"

"And the vigorous young Republic drawing its first breath of life!" I burst in, introducing the Pratolungo programme (as my way is) at every available opportunity.

Nugent Dubourg instantly wheeled round in my direction, and set *me* right on *my* subject, just as he had set the rector right on reading "Hamlet," and Mrs. Finch right on clothing babies.

"Not a bit of it!" he pronounced, positively. "The 'young Republic' is the rickety child of the political family. Give him up, ma'am. You will never make a man of him."

I tried to assert myself as the rector had tried
before me—with precisely the same result. I
appealed indignantly to the authority of my illustrious husband.

"Doctor Pratolungo—" I began.

"Was an honest man," interposed Nugent
Dubourg. "I am an advanced Liberal myself;
I respect him. But he was quite wrong. All
sincere republicans make the same mistake.
They believe in the existence of public spirit
in Europe. Amiable delusion! Public spirit is
dead in Europe. Public spirit is the generous
emotion of young nations, of new peoples. In
selfish old Europe private interest has taken its
place. When your husband preached the republic, on what ground did he put it? On the
ground that the republic was going to elevate
the nation. Pooh! Ask me to accept the republic on the ground that I elevate Myself—and,
supposing you can prove it, I will listen to you.
If you are ever to set republican institutions going in the Old World—*there* is the only motive
power that will do it!"

I was indignant at such sentiments. "My
glorious husband—" I began again.

"Would have died rather than appeal to the
meanest instincts of his fellow-creatures. Just
so! There was his mistake. That's why he
never could make anything of the republic.
That's why the republic is the rickety child of
the political family. *Quod erat demonstran-
dum*," said Nugent Dubourg, finishing me off
with a pleasant smile, and an easy indicative

gesture of the hand which said: "Now I have settled these three people in succession, I am equally well satisfied with myself—and with them!"

His smile was irresistible. Bent as I was on disputing the degrading conclusions at which he had arrived, I really had not fire enough in me at the moment to feed my own indignation. As to Reverend Finch, he sat silently swelling in a corner; digesting as he best might the discovery that there was another man in the world, besides the Rector of Dimchurch, with an excellent opinion of himself, and with perfectly unassailable confidence and fluency in expressing it. In the momentary silence that now followed, Oscar got his first opportunity of speaking. He had, thus far, been quite content to admire his clever brother. He now advanced to me, and asked what had become of Lucilla.

"The servant told me she was here," he said. "I am so anxious to introduce her to Nugent."

Nugent put his arm affectionately round his brother's neck and gave him a hug. "Dear old boy! I am just as anxious as you are."

"Lucilla went out a little while since," I said, "to take a turn in the garden."

"I'll go and find her," said Oscar. "Wait here, Nugent. I'll bring her in."

He left the room. Before he could close the door one of the servants appeared, to claim Mrs. Finch's private ear on some mysterious domestic emergency. Nugent facetiously entreated her, as she passed him, to clear her mind of prejudice and consider the question of infant petticoats on its own merits. Mr. Finch took offense at this second reference to the subject. He rose to follow his wife. . .

"When you are a married man, Mr. Dubourg," said the rector, severely, "you will learn to leave the management of an infant in its mother's hands."

"There's another mistake!" remarked Nugent, following him, with unabated good-humor, to the door. "A married man's idea of another man as a husband, always begins and ends with his idea of himself." He turned to me as the door closed on Mr. Finch. "Now we are alone, Madame Pratolungo," he said, "I want to speak to you about Miss Finch. There is an opportunity before she comes in. Oscar's letter only told me that she was blind. I am naturally interested in everything that relates to my brother's future wife. I am particularly interested about this affliction of hers. May I ask how long she has been blind?"

"Since she was a year old," I replied.

"Through an accident?"

"No."

"After a fever? or a disease of any other sort?"

I began to feel a little surprised at his entering into these medical details.

"I never heard that it was through a fever or other illness," I said. "So far as I know, the blindness came on unexpectedly, from some cause that did not express itself to the people about her at the time."

He drew his chair confidentially nearer to mine. "How old is she?" he asked.

I began to feel more than a little surprised, and I showed it, I suppose, on telling him Lucilla's age.

"As things are now," he explained, "there are reasons which make me hesitate to enter on the question of Miss Finch's blindness either with my brother or with any members of the family. I must wait to speak about it to *them* until I can speak to good practical purpose. There is no harm in my starting the subject with *you*. When she first lost her sight, no means of restoring it were left untried, of course?"

"I should suppose not," I replied. "It's so long since, I have never asked."

"So long since," he repeated; and then considered for a moment.

His reflections ended in a last question:

"She is resigned, I suppose—and everybody about her is resigned—to the idea of her being hopelessly blind for life?"

Instead of answering him, I put a question on my side. My heart was beginning to beat rapidly, without my knowing why.

"Mr. Nugent Dubourg," I said, "what have you got in your mind about Lucilla?"

"Madame Pratolungo," he replied, "I have got something in my mind which was put into it by a friend of mine whom I met in America."

"The friend you mentioned in your letter to your brother?"

"The same."

"The German gentleman whom you propose to introduce to Oscar and Lucilla?"

"Yes."

"May I ask who he is?"

Nugent Dubourg looked at me attentively, considered with himself for the second time, and answered in these words:

"He is the greatest living authority and the greatest living operator in diseases of the eye."

The idea in his mind burst its way into my mind in a moment.

"Gracious God!" I exclaimed; "are you mad enough to suppose that Lucilla's sight can be restored, after a blindness of one and-twenty years?"

He suddenly held up his hand, in sign to me to be silent.

At the same moment the door opened and Lucilla (followed by Oscar) entered the room.

CHAPTER THE TWENTY-FOURTH.

HE SEES LUCILLA.

THE first impression which Poor Miss Finch produced on Nugent Dubourg was precisely the same as the first impression which she had produced on me.

"Good heavens!" he cried. "The Dresden Madonna! The Virgin of San Sisto!"

Lucilla had already heard from me of her extraordinary resemblance to the chief figure in

Raphael's renowned picture. Nugent's blunt
outburst of recognition passed unnoticed by her.
She stopped short in the middle of the room—
startled, the instant he spoke, by the extraordinary similarity of his tone and accent to the tone
and accent of his brother's voice.

"Oscar," she asked, nervously, "are you behind me? or in front of me?" Oscar laughed,
and answered "Here!"—speaking behind her.
She turned her head toward the place in front
of her, from which Nugent had spoken. "Your
voice is wonderfully like Oscar's," she said, addressing him timidly. "Is your face exactly
like his face, too? May I judge for myself of
the likeness between you? I can only do it in
one way—by my touch."

Oscar advanced, and placed a chair for his
brother by Lucilla's side.

"She has eyes in the tips of her fingers," he
said. "Sit down, Nugent, and let her pass her
hand over your face."

Nugent obeyed him in silence. Now that the
first impression of surprise had passed away, I
observed that a marked change was beginning
to assert itself in his manner.

Little by little, an unnatural constraint got
possession of him. His fluent tongue found
nothing to talk about. His easy movements
altered in the strangest way until they almost
became the movements of a slow, awkward man.
He was more like his brother than ever, as he
sat down in the chair to submit himself to Lucilla's investigation. She had produced, at first

sight—as well as I could judge—some impression on him for which he had not been prepared; causing some mental disturbance in him which he was for the moment quite unable to control. His eyes looked up at her, spell-bound; his color came and went; his breath quickened audibly when her fingers touched his face.

"What's the matter?" said Oscar, looking at him in surprise.

"Nothing is the matter," he answered, in the low absent tone of a man whose mind was secretly pursuing its own train of thought.

Oscar said no more. Once, twice, three times Lucilla's hand passed slowly over Nugent's face. He submitted to it silently, gravely, immovably —a perfect contrast to the talkative, lively young man of half an hour since. Lucilla employed a much longer time in examining him than she had occupied in examining me.

While the investigation was proceeding, I had leisure to think again over what had passed between Nugent and me on the subject of Lucilla's blindness before she entered the room. My mind had by this time recovered its balance. I was able to ask myself what this young fellow's daring idea was really worth. Was it within the range of possibility that a sense so delicate as the sense of sight, lost for one-and-twenty years, could be restored by any means short of a miracle? It was monstrous to suppose it: the thing could not be. If there had been the faintest chance of giving my poor dear back the blessing of sight, that chance would have been tried by competent per-

sons years and years since. I was ashamed of
myself for having been violently excited at the
moment by the new thought which Nugent had
started in my mind; I was honestly indignant at
his uselessly disturbing me with the vainest of
all vain hopes. The one wise thing to do in the
future was to caution this flighty and inconse-
quent young man to keep his mad notion about
Lucilla to himself—and to dismiss it from my
own thoughts at once and forever.

Just as I arrived at that sensible resolution, I
was recalled to what was going on in the room
by Lucilla's voice, addressing me by my name.

"The likeness is wonderful," she said. "Still,
I think I can find a difference between them."

(The only difference between them was in the
contrast of complexion and in the contrast of
manner—both these being dissimilarities which
appealed more or less directly to the eye.)

"What difference do you find?" I asked.

She slowly came toward me, with an anxious,
perplexed face, pondering as she advanced.

"I can't explain it," she answered, after a
long silence.

When Lucilla left him, Nugent rose from his
chair. He abruptly—almost roughly—took his
brother's hand. He spoke to his brother in a
strangely excited, feverish, headlong way.

"My dear fellow, now I have seen her, I congratulate you more heartily than ever. She is
charming; she is unique. Oscar! I could almost
envy you, if you were any one else!"

Oscar was radiant with delight. His brother's

opinion ranked above all human opinions in his
estimation. Before he could say a word in return, Nugent left him as abruptly as he had approached him; walking away by himself to the
window—and standing there, looking out.

Lucilla had not heard him. She was still pondering, with the same perplexed face. The likeness between the twins was apparently weighing
on her mind—an unsolved problem that vexed
and irritated it. Without anything said by me
to lead to resuming the subject, she returned obstinately to the assertion that she had just made.

"I tell you again I am sensible of a difference
between them," she repeated—"though you don't
seem to believe me."

I interpreted this uneasy reiteration as meaning that she was rather trying to convince herself than to convince me. In her blind condition
it was doubly and trebly embarrassing not to
know one brother from the other. I understood
her unwillingness to acknowledge this—I felt (in
her position) how it would have irritated *me*.
She was waiting—impatiently waiting—for me
to say something on my side. I am, as you
know already, an indiscreet woman. I innocently said one of my rash things.

"I believe whatever you tell me, my dear," I
answered. "You can find out a difference between them, I have no doubt. Still, I own I
should like to see it put to the proof."

Her color rose. "How?" she asked, abruptly.

"Try your touch alternately on ·both their
faces," I suggested, "without knowing before-

hand which position they each of them occupy.
Make three trials—leaving them to change their
places or not, between each trial, just as they
please. If you guess which is which correctly
three times following, there will be the proof
that you can really lay your hand on a difference
between them."

Lucilla shrank from accepting the challenge.
She drew back a step, and silently shook her
head. Nugent, who had overheard me, turned
round suddenly from the window and supported
my proposal.

"A capital notion!" he burst out. "Let's try
it! You don't object, Oscar—do you?"

"I object?" cried Oscar, amazed at the bare
idea of his opposing any assertion of his will to
the assertion of his brother's will. "If Lucilla
is willing, I say Yes with all my heart."

The two brothers approached us, arm in arm.
Lucilla, very reluctantly, allowed herself to be
persuaded into trying the experiment. Two
chairs, exactly alike, were placed in front of
her. At a sign from Nugent, Oscar silently
took the chair on her right. By this arrangement the hand which she had used in touching
Nugent's face would be now the hand that she
would employ in touching Oscar's face. When
they were both seated I announced that we were
ready. Lucilla placed her hands on their faces,
right and left, without the faintest idea in her
mind of the positions which the two relatively
occupied.

After first touching them with both hands, and

both together, she tried them separately next, beginning with Oscar, and using her right hand only. She left him for Nugent; again using her right hand—then came back to him again—then returned to Nugent—hesitated—decided—tapped Nugent lightly on the head.

"Oscar!' she said.

Nugent burst out laughing. The laugh told her, before any of us could speak, that she had made a mistake at the first attempt.

"Try again, Lucilla," said Oscar, kindly.

"Never," she answered angrily, stepping back from both of them. "One mystification is enough."

Nugent tried next to persuade her to renew the experiment. She checked him sternly at the first word.

"Do you think, if I won't do it for Oscar," she said, "that I would do it for you? You laughed at me. What was there to laugh at? Your brother's features are your features; your brother's hair is your hair; your brother's height is your height. What is there so very ridiculous —with such a resemblance as that—in a poor blind girl like me mistaking you one for the other? I wish to preserve a good opinion of you, for Oscar's sake. Don't turn me into ridicule again, or I shall be forced to think that your brother's good heart is not yours also!"

Nugent and Oscar looked at each other, petrified by this sudden outbreak; Nugent, of the two, being the most completely overwhelmed by it.

I attempted to interfere and put things right. My easy philosophy and my volatile French nature failed to see any adequate cause for this vehement exhibition of resentment on Lucilla's part. Something in my tone, as I suppose, only added to her irritation. I, in my turn, was checked sternly at the first word. "You proposed it," she said; "you are the most to blame." I hastened to make my apologies (inwardly remarking that the habit of raising a storm in a tea-cup is a growing habit with the rising generation in England). Nugent followed me with more apologies on his side. Oscar supported us with his superior influence. He took Lucilla's hand, kissed it, and whispered something in her ear. The kiss and the whisper acted like a charm. She held out her hand to Nugent; she put her arm round my neck and embraced me, with all her own grace and sweetness. "Forgive me," she said to us, gently. "I wish I could learn to be patient. But oh, Mr. Nugent, it is sometimes *so* hard to be blind!" I can repeat the words; but I can give no idea of the touching simplicity with which they were spoken—of her innocently earnest anxiety to win her pardon. She so affected Nugent that he, too—after a look at Oscar which said: "May I?"—kissed the hand that she offered to him. As his lips touched her she started. The bright flush which always indicated the sudden rising of a thought in her mind flew over her face. She unconsciously held Nugent's hand in her own, absorbed in the interest of realizing the new thought. For a moment she stood, still as a statue, consulting with herself. The moment passed, she dropped Nugent's hand and turned brightly to me.

"Will you think me very obstinate?" she asked.

"Why, my love?"

"I am not satisfied yet. I want to try again."

"No! no! At any rate, not to-day."

"I want to try again," she repeated. "Not in your way. In a way of my own that has just come into my head." She turned to Oscar. "Will you humor me in this?" It is needless to set down Oscar's reply. She turned to Nugent. "Will you?"

"Only say what you wish me to do!" he answered.

"Go with your brother," she said, "to the other end of the room. I know where you are each of you standing at this end. Madame Pratolungo will lead me to the place, and will put me just within reach of both your hands. I want each of you in turn (arrange by a sign between yourselves which is to begin) to take my hand, and hold it for a moment, and then drop it. I have an idea that I can distinguish between you in that way—and I want very much to try it."

The brothers went silently to the other end of the room. I led Lucilla, after them, to the place in which they stood. At my suggestion Nugent was the first to take her hand, as she had requested, to hold it for a moment, and then to drop it.

"Nugent!" she said, without the slightest hesitation.

"Quite right," I answered.

She laughed gayly. "Go on! Puzzle me if you possibly can."

The brothers noiselessly changed places. Oscar took her hand, standing exactly where Nugent had stood.

"Oscar!" she said.

"Right again," I told her.

At a sign from Nugent, Oscar took her hand for the second time. She repeated his name. At a sign from me the brothers noiselessly placed themselves one on either side of her— Oscar on the left, Nugent on the right. I gave them the signal, and they each took one of her hands at the same moment. This time she waited a little longer before she spoke. When she did speak she was right once more. She turned, smiling, toward the left side, pointed to him as he stood by her, and said, "Oscar!"

We were all three equally surprised. I examined Oscar's hand and Nugent's hand alternately. Except the fatal difference in the color, they were, to all intents and purposes, the same hands —the same size, the same shape, the same texture of skin; no scar or mark on the hand of one to distinguish it from the hand of the other. By what mysterious process of divination had she succeeded in discovering which was which?

She was unwilling, or unable, to reply to that question plainly.

"Something in me answers to one of them and not to the other," she said.

"What is it?" I asked.

"I don't know. It answers to Oscar. It doesn't answer to Nugent—that's all."

She stopped any further inquiries by proposing that we should finish the evening with some music in her own sitting-room, on the other side of the house. When we were seated together at the pianoforte—with the twin brothers established as our audience at the other end of the room—she whispered in my ear:

"I'll tell *you!*"

"Tell me what?"

"How I know which is which, when they both of them take my hand. When Oscar takes it, a delicious tingle runs from his hand into mine, and steals all over me. I can't describe it any better than that."

"I understand. And when Nugent takes your hand, what do you feel?"

"Nothing!"

"And that is how you found out the difference between them downstairs?"

"That is how I shall always find out the difference between them. If Oscar's brother ever attempts to play tricks upon my blindness (he is quite capable of it—he laughed at my blindness!), that is how I shall find him out. I told you before I saw him that I hated him. I hate him still."

"My dear Lucilla!"

"I hate him still!"

She struck the first chords on the piano with an obstinate frown on her pretty brow. Our little evening concert began.

———

CHAPTER THE TWENTY-FIFTH.

HE PUZZLES MADAME PRATOLUNGO.

I WAS far from sharing Lucilla's opinion of Nugent Dubourg.

His enormous self-confidence was, to my mind, too amusing to be in the least offensive. I liked the spirit and gayety of the young fellow. He came much nearer than his brother did to my ideal of the dash and resolution which ought to distinguish a man on the right side of thirty. So far as my experience of them went, Nugent was (in the popular English phrase) good company, and Oscar was not. My nationality leads me to attach great importance to social qualities. The higher virtues of a man only show themselves occasionally on compulsion. His social qualities come familiarly in contact with us every day of our lives. I like to be cheerful; I am all for the social qualities.

There was one little obstacle in those early days which set itself up between my sympathies and Nugent.

I was thoroughly at a loss to understand the impression which Lucilla had produced on him.

The same constraint which had, in such a marked manner, subdued him at his first inter-

view with her, still fettered him in the time
when they became better acquainted with one
another. He was never in high spirits in her
presence. Mr. Finch could talk him down without difficulty if Mr. Finch's daughter happened
to be by. Even when he was vaporing about
himself, and telling us of the wonderful things
he meant to do in Painting, Lucilla's appearance was enough to check him, if she happened
to come into the room. On the first day when
he showed me his American sketches (I define
them, if you ask my private opinion, as false
pretenses of Art, by a dashing amateur)—on
that day he was in full flow, marching up and
down the room, smacking his forehead, and announcing himself quite gravely as "the coming
man" in landscape painting. "My mission,
Madame Pratolungo, is to reconcile Humanity
and Nature. I propose to show (on an immense
scale) how Nature (in her grandest aspects) can
adapt herself to the spiritual wants of mankind.
In your joy or your sorrow Nature has subtle
sympathies with you, if you only know where to
look for them. My pictures—no! my poems in
color—will show you. Multiply my works, as
they certainly will be multiplied, by means of
prints, and what does Art become in my hands?
A Priesthood! In what aspect do I present myself
to the public? As a mere landscape painter?
No! As Grand Consoler!" In the midst of this
rhapsody (how wonderfully he resembled Oscar
in *his* bursts of excitement while he was talking!)—in the full torrent of his predictions of his

own coming greatness—Lucilla quietly entered the room. The "Grand Consoler" shut up his portfolios, dropped Painting on the spot, asked for Music, and sat down, a model of conventional propriety, in a corner of the room. I inquired afterward why he had checked himself when she came in. "Did I?" he said. "I don't know why." The thing was really inexplicable. He honestly admired her; one had only to notice him when he was looking at her to see it. He had not the faintest suspicion of her dislike for him; she carefully concealed it for Oscar's sake. He felt genuine sympathy for her in her affliction: his mad idea that her sight might yet be restored was the natural offspring of a true feeling for her. He was not unfavorable to his brother's marriage—on the contrary, he ruffled the rector's dignity (he was always giving offense to Mr. Finch) by suggesting that the marriage might be hastened. I heard him say the words myself: "The church is close by. Why can't you put on your surplice and make Oscar happy to-morrow after breakfast?" More even than this, he showed the most vivid interest—like a woman's interest rather than a man's —in learning how the love-affair between Oscar and Lucilla had begun. I referred him, so far as Oscar was concerned, to his brother as the fountain-head of information. He did not decline to consult his brother. He did not own to me that he felt any difficulty in doing so. He simply dropped Oscar in silence, and asked about Lucilla. How had it begun on her side? I reminded him of his brother's romantic position at Dimchurch, and told him to judge for himself of the effect it would produce on the excitable imagination of a young girl. He declined to judge for himself; he persisted in appealing to me. When I told the little love-story of the two young people, one event in it appeared to make a very strong impression on him. The effect produced on Lucilla (when she first heard it) by the sound of his brother's voice dwelt strangely on his mind. He failed to understand it; he ridiculed it; he declined to believe it. I was obliged to remind him that Lucilla was blind, and that love, which, in other cases, first finds its way to the heart through the eyes, could only, in her case, first find its way through the ears. My explanation, thus offered, had its effect: it set him thinking. "The sound of his voice!" he said to himself, still turning the problem over and over in his mind. "People say my voice is exactly like Oscar's," he added, suddenly addressing himself to me: "do you think so too?" I answered that there could be no doubt of it. He got up from his chair with a quick little shudder, like a man who feels a chill, and changed the subject. On the next occasion when he and Lucilla met, so far from being more familiar with her, he was more constrained than ever. As it had begun between these two, so it seemed likely to continue to the end. In my society he was always at his ease; in Lucilla's society, never!

What was the obvious conclusion which a person with my experience ought to have drawn from all this?

I know well enough what it was, now. On my oath, as an honest woman, I failed to see it at the time. We are not always (suffer me to remind you) consistent with ourselves. The cleverest people commit occasional lapses into stupidity—just as the stupid people light up with gleams of intelligence at certain times. You may have shown your usual good sense in conducting your affairs on Monday, Tuesday, and Wednesday in the week; but it doesn't at all follow from this that you may not make a fool of yourself on Thursday. Account for it as you may, for a much longer time than it suits my self-esteem to reckon up I suspected nothing and discovered nothing. I noted his behavior in Lucilla's presence as odd behavior and unaccountable behavior—and that was all.

During the first fortnight just mentioned the London doctor came to see Oscar.

He left again, perfectly satisfied with the results of his treatment. The dreadful epileptic malady would torture the patient and shock the friends about him no more; the marriage might safely be celebrated at the time agreed on. Oscar was cured.

The doctor's visit—reviving our interest in observing the effect of the medicine—also revived the subject of Oscar's false position toward Lucilla. Nugent and I held a debate about it between ourselves. I opened the interview by suggesting that we should unite our forces to persuade his brother into taking the frank and manly course. Nugent neither said Yes nor No to that proposal at the outset. He, who made up his mind at a moment's notice about everything else, took time to decide on this one occasion.

"There is something that I want to know first," he said. "I want to understand this curious antipathy of Lucilla's, which my brother regards with so much alarm. Can you explain it?"

"Has Oscar attempted to explain it?" I inquired on my side.

"He mentioned it in one of his letters to me; and he tried to explain it, when I asked (on my arrival at Browndown) if Lucilla had discovered the change in his complexion. But he failed entirely to meet my difficulty in understanding the case."

"What is your difficulty?"

"This. So far as I can see, she fails to discover intuitively the presence of dark people in a room, or of dark colors in the ornaments of a room. It is only when *she is told* that such persons or such things are present that her prejudice declares itself. In what state of mind does such a strange feeling as this take its rise? It seems impossible that she can have any conscious associations with colors, pleasant or painful—if it is true that she was blind at a year old. How do you account for it? Can there be such a thing as a purely instinctive antipathy, remaining passive until external influences rouse it, and resting on no sort of practical experience whatever?"

"I think there may be," I replied. "Why, when I was a child just able to walk, did I shrink away from the first dog I saw who barked at me? I could not have known at that age, either by experience or teaching, that a dog's bark is sometimes the prelude to a dog's bite. My terror, on that occasion, was purely instinctive, surely?"

"Ingeniously put," he said. "But I am not satisfied yet."

"You must also remember," I continued, "that she has a positively painful association with dark colors on certain occasions. They sometimes produce a disagreeable impression on the nerves through her sense of touch. She discovered in that way that I had a dark gown on on the day when I first saw her."

"And yet she touches my brother's face, and fails to discover any alteration in it."

I met that objection also—to my own satisfaction, though not to his.

"I am far from sure that she might not have made the discovery," I said, "if she had touched him for the first time since the discoloration of his face. But she examines him now with a settled impression in her mind, derived from previous experience of what she has felt in touching his skin. Allow for the modifying influence of that impression on her sense of touch—and remember, at the same time, that it is the color and not the texture of the skin that is changed —and his escape from discovery becomes, to my mind, intelligible."

He shook his head; he owned he could not dispute my view. But he was not content, for all that.

"Have you made any inquiries," he asked, "about the period of her infancy before she was blind? She may be still feeling, indirectly and unconsciously, the effect of some shock to her nervous system in the time when she could see."

"I have never thought of making inquiries."

"Is there anybody within our reach who was familiarly associated with her in the first year of her life? It is hardly likely, I am afraid, at this distance of time."

"There is a person now in the house," I said. "Her old nurse is still living."

"Send for her directly."

Zillah appeared. After first explaining what he wanted with her, Nugent went straight to the inquiry which he had in view.

"Was your young lady ever frightened when she was a baby by any dark person, or any dark thing, suddenly appearing before her?"

"Never, sir! I took good care to let nothing come near her that could frighten her—so long, poor little thing, as she could see."

"Are you quite sure you can depend on your memory?"

"Quite sure, sir—when it's a long time ago."

Zillah was dismissed. Nugent—thus far unusually grave and unusually anxious—turned to me with an air of relief.

"When you proposed to me to join you in forcing Oscar to speak out," he said, "I was not quite easy in my mind about the consequences. After what I have just heard, my fear is removed."

"What fear?" I asked.

"The fear of Oscar's confession producing an estrangement between them which might delay the marriage. I am against all delay. I am especially anxious that Oscar's marriage should not be put off. When we began our conversation I own to you I was of Oscar's opinion that he would do wisely to let marriage make him sure of his position in her affections before he risked the disclosure. Now—after what the nurse has told us—I see no risk worth considering."

"In short," I said, "you agree with me."

"I agree with you—though I *am* the most opinionated man living. The chances now seem to me to be all in Oscar's favor. Lucilla's antipathy is not what I feared it was—an antipathy firmly rooted in a constitutional malady. It is nothing more serious," said Nugent, deciding the question, at once and forever, with the air of a man profoundly versed in physiology—"it is nothing more serious than a fanciful growth, a morbid accident of her blindness. She may live to get over it—she would, I believe, certainly get over it if she could see. In two words, after what I have found out this morning, I say as you say—Oscar is making a mountain out of a mole-hill. He ought to have put himself right with Lucilla long since. I have unbounded influence over him. It shall back your influence. Oscar shall make a clean breast of it before the week is out."

We shook hands on that bargain. As I looked at him—bright and dashing and resolute—Oscar, as I had always wished Oscar to be—I own, to my shame, I privately regretted that we had not met Nugent in the twilight on that evening walk of ours which had opened to Lucilla the gates of a new life.

Having said to each other all that we had to say—our two lovers being away together, at the time, for a walk on the hills—we separated, as I then supposed, for the rest of the day. Nugent went to the inn to look at a stable which he proposed converting into a studio; no room at Browndown being half large enough for the first prodigious picture with which the "Grand Consoler" in Art proposed to astonish the world. As for me, having nothing particular to do, I went out to see if I could meet Oscar and Lucilla on their return from their walk.

Failing to find them, I strolled back by way of Browndown. Nugent was sitting alone on the low wall in front of the house, smoking a cigar. He rose and came to meet me, with his finger placed mysteriously on his lips.

"You mustn't come in," he said; "and you mustn't speak loud enough to be heard." He pointed round the corner of the house to the little room at the side, already familiar to you in these pages. "Oscar and Lucilla are shut up together there. And Oscar is making his confession to her at this moment."

I lifted my hands and eyes in astonishment. Nugent went on:

"I see you want to know how it has all come about. You shall know. While I was looking at the stable (it isn't half big enough for a studio for Me!) Oscar's servant brought me a little pencil note, entreating me, in Oscar's name, to go to him directly at Browndown. I found him waiting out here, dreadfully agitated. He cautioned me (just as I have cautioned you) not to speak loud. For the same reason too. Lucilla was in the house—"

"I thought they had gone out for a walk," I interposed.

"They did go out for a walk. But Lucilla complained of fatigue; and Oscar brought her back to Browndown to rest. Well, I inquired what was the matter. The answer informed me that the secret of Oscar's complexion had forced its way out, for the second time, in Lucilla's hearing."

"Jicks again!" I exclaimed.

"No—not Jicks. Oscar's own man-servant this time."

"How did it happen?"

"It happened through one of the boys in the village. Oscar and Lucilla found the little imp howling outside the house. They asked what was the matter. The imp told them that the servant at Browndown had beaten him. Lucilla

was indignant. She insisted on having the thing
inquired into. Oscar left her in the drawing-
room (unluckily, as it turned out, without shutting the door), called the man up into the passage, and asked what he meant by ill-using the
boy. The man answered, 'I boxed his ears, sir,
as an example to the rest of them.' 'What did
he do?' 'Rapped at the door, sir, with a stick
(he is not the first who has done it when you are
out), and asked if Blue Face was at home.' Lucilla heard every word of it through the open
door. Need I tell you what happened next?"

It was quite needless to relate that part of the
story. I remembered too well what had happened on the former occasion in the garden. I
saw too plainly that Lucilla must have connected
the two occurrences in her mind, and must have
had her ready suspicion roused to serious action
on the necessary result.

"I understand," I said. "Of course she insisted on an explanation. Of course Oscar com-
promised himself by a clumsy excuse, and
wanted you to help him. What did you do?"

"What I told you I should do this morning.
He had counted confidently on my taking his
side—it was pitiable to see him, poor fellow!
Still, for his own sake, I refused to yield. I
left him the choice of giving her the true explanation himself, or of leaving me to do it. There
wasn't a moment to lose; she was in no humor
to be trifled with, I can tell you! Oscar behaved
very well about it—he always behaves well when
I drive him into a corner. In one word, he was

man enough to feel that he was the right person
to make a clean breast of it—not I. I gave the
poor old boy a hug to encourage him, pushed
him into the room, shut the door on him, and
came out here. He ought to have done it by
this time. He *has* done it! Here he comes!"

Oscar ran out, bareheaded, from the house.
There were signs of disturbance in him as he
approached us, which warned me that something
had gone wrong before he opened his lips.

Nugent spoke first.

"What's amiss now?" he asked. "Have you
told her the truth?"

"I have tried to tell her the truth."

"Tried? What do you mean?"

Oscar put his arm round his brother's neck,
and laid his head on his brother's shoulder, without answering a word.

I put a question to him on my side.

"Did Lucilla refuse to listen to you?" I asked.
"No."

"Has she said anything, or done anything—"

He lifted his head from his brother's shoulder,
and stopped me before I could finish the sentence.

"You need feel no anxiety about Lucilla. Lucilla's curiosity is satisfied."

"Is she satisfied with *you?*"

He dropped his head back on his brother's
shoulder, and answered, faintly: "Perfectly
satisfied."

Nugent and I gazed at one another in complete
bewilderment. Lucilla had heard it all; Lucilla
was on the same good terms with him as ever.

He had that incredibly happy result to communicate to us, and he announced it with a look
of humiliation, in a tone of despair! Nugent's
patience gave way.

"Let us have an end of this mystification," he
said, putting Oscar back from him, sharply, at
arms-length. "I want a plain answer to a plain
question. She knows that the boy knocked at
the door and asked if Blue Face was at home.
Does she know what the boy's impudence meant?
Yes or no?"

"Yes."

"Does she know that it is you who are Blue
Face?"

"No."

"No!!! Who else does she think it is?"

As he asked the question Lucilla appeared at
the door of the house. She moved her blind face
inquiringly first one way, then the other. "Oscar!" she called out, "why have you left me
alone? where are you?"

Oscar turned, trembling, to his brother.

"For God's sake, forgive me, Nugent!" he
said. "She thinks it's You."

CHAPTER THE TWENTY-SIXTH.

HE PROVES EQUAL TO THE OCCASION.

At that astounding confession, abruptly revealed in those plain words, even resolute Nugent lost all power of self-control. He burst out

with a cry which reached Lucilla's ears. She instantly turned toward us, and instantly assumed that the cry had come from Oscar's lips.

"Ah! there you are!" she exclaimed. "Oscar! Oscar! what *is* the matter with you to-day?"

Oscar was incapable of answering her. He had cast one glance of entreaty at his brother as Lucilla came nearer to us. The mute reproach which had answered him, in Nugent's eyes, had broken down his last reserves of endurance. He was crying silently—crying like a woman—on Nugent's breast.

It was necessary that somebody should break the silence. I spoke first.

"Nothing is the matter, my dear," I said, advancing to meet Lucilla. "We were passing the house, and Oscar ran out to stop us and bring us in."

My excuse roused a new alarm in her.

"Us?" she replied. "Who is with you?"

"Nugent is with me."

The result of the deplorable misunderstanding which had taken place instantly declared itself. She turned deadly pale under the horror of feeling blindly that she was in the presence of the man with the blue face.

"Take me near enough to speak to him, but not to touch him," she whispered. "I have heard what he is like. (Oh, if you saw him, as I see him, *in the dark!*) I must control myself. I must speak to Oscar's brother, for Oscar's sake."

She seized my arm and held me close to her.

What ought I to have said? What ought I to have done? I neither knew what to say nor what to do. I looked from Lucilla to the twin brothers. There was Oscar the Weak, over-whelmed by the humiliating position in which he had placed himself toward the woman whom he was to marry, toward the brother whom he loved! And there was Nugent the Strong, mas-ter of himself—with his arm around his brother, with his head erect, with his hand signing to me to keep silence. He was right. I had only to look back at Lucilla's face to see that the deli-cate and perilous work of undeceiving her was not work to be done at a moment's notice, on the spot.

"You are not yourself to-day," I said to her. "Let us go home."

"No!" she answered. "I must accustom my-self to speak to him. I will begin to-day. Take me to him—but don't let him touch me!"

Nugent disengaged himself from Oscar—whose unfitness to help us through our difficulties was too manifest to be mistaken—as he saw us ap-proaching. He pointed to the low wall in front of the house, and motioned to his brother to wait there out of the way before Lucilla could speak to him again. The wisdom of this proceeding was not long in asserting itself. Lucilla asked for Oscar the moment after he had left us. Nu-gent answered that Oscar had gone back to the house to get his hat.

The sound of Nugent's voice helped her to cal-culate her distance from him without assistance

SIGNING TO ME TO KEEP SILENCE.—Poor Miss Finch, Vol. XV., page 248.

from me.   Still holding my arm, she stopped and
spoke to him.

"Nugent," she said, "I have made Oscar tell
me—what he ought to have told me long since."
(She paused between each sentence, painfully controlling herself, painfully catching her breath.)
"He has discovered a foolish antipathy of mine.
I don't know how; I tried to keep it a secret from
him.   I need not tell you what it is."

She made a longer pause at those words, holding me closer and closer to her; struggling more
and more painfully against the irresistible nervous loathing that had got possession of her.   He
listened, on his side, with the constraint which
always fell upon him in her presence more marked
than ever.   His eyes were on the ground.   He
seemed reluctant even to look at her.

"I think I understand," she went on, "why
Oscar was unwilling to tell me"—she stopped,
at a loss how to express herself without running
the risk of hurting his feelings—"to tell me,"
she resumed, "what it is in you which is not like
other people.   He was afraid my stupid weakness might prejudice me against you.   I wish
to say that I won't let it do that.   I never was
more ashamed of it than now.   I, too, have my
misfortune.   I ought to sympathize with you,
instead of—" .

Her voice had been growing fainter and fainter
as she proceeded.   She leaned against me heavily.   One glance at her told me that if I let it
go on any longer she would fall into a swoon.
"Tell your brother that we have gone back to

the rectory," I said to Nugent. He looked up at Lucilla for the first time. "You are right," he answered. "Take her home." He repeated the sign by which he had already hinted to me to be silent, and joined Oscar at the wall in front of the house.

"Has he gone?" she asked.

"He has gone."

The moisture stood thick on her forehead. I passed my handkerchief over her face and turned her toward the wind.

"Are you better now?"

"Yes."

"Can you walk home?"

"Easily."

I put her arm in mine. After advancing with me a few steps she suddenly stopped—with a blind apprehension, as it seemed, of something in front of her. She lifted her little walking-cane, and moved it slowly backward and forward in the empty air, with the action of some one who is clearing away an incumbrance to a free advance—say the action of a person walking in a thick wood, and pushing aside the lower twigs and branches that intercept the way.

"What are you about?" I asked.

"Clearing the air," she answered. "The air is full of him. I am in a forest of hovering figures, with faces of black-blue. Give me your arm. Come through!"

"Lucilla!"

"Don't be angry with me. I am coming to my senses again. Nobody knows what folly,

what madness it is, better than I do. I have a
will of my own: suffer as I may, I promise to
break myself of it this time. I can't and won't
let Oscar's brother see that he is an object of horror to me.'' She stopped once more, and gave
me a little propitiatory kiss. ''Blame my blindness, dear, don't blame *me*. If I could only see—
Ah, how can I make you understand me, you
who don't live in the dark?'' She went on a
few paces, silent and thoughtful, and then spoke
again. ''You won't laugh at me if I say something?''

''You know I won't.''

''Suppose yourself to be in bed at night.''

''Yes?''

''I have heard people say that they have sometimes woke in the middle of the night, on a sudden, without any noise to disturb them. And
they have fancied (without anything particular
to justify it) that there was something, or somebody, in the dark room. Has that ever happened
to you?''

''Certainly, my love. It has happened to most
people to fancy what you say when their nerves
are a little out of order.''

''Very well. There is *my* fancy, and there
are *my* nerves. When it happened to you what
did you do?''

''I struck a light, and satisfied myself that I
was wrong.''

''Suppose yourself without candle or matches,
in a night without end, left alone with your fancy
in the dark. There you have Me! It would not

be easy, would it, to satisfy yourself if you were in that helpless condition? You might suffer under it, very unreasonably, and yet very keenly for all that." She lifted her little cane with a sad smile. "You might be almost as great a fool as poor Lucilla, and clear the air before you with this!"

The charm of her voice and the manner added to the touching simplicity, the pathetic truth, of those words. She made me realize, as I had never realized before, what it is to have, at one and the same time, the blessing of imagination and the curse of blindness. For a moment, I was absorbed in my admiration and my love for her. For a moment, I forgot the terrible position in which we were all placed. She unconsciously recalled it to me when she spoke next.

"Perhaps I was wrong to force the truth out of Oscar," she said, putting her arm again in mine, and walking on. "I might have reconciled myself to his brother, if I had never known what his brother was like. And yet I felt there was something strange in him, without being told, and without knowing what it was. There must have been a reason in me for the dislike that I felt for him from the first."

Those words appeared to me to indicate the state of mind which had led to Lucilla's deplorable mistake. I cautiously put some questions to her to test the correctness of my own idea.

"You spoke just now of forcing the truth out of Oscar," I said. "What made you suspect that he was concealing the truth from you?"

"He was so strangely embarrassed and confused," she answered. "Anybody in my place would have suspected him of concealing the truth."

So far the answer was conclusive. "And how came you to find out what the truth really was?" I asked next.

"I guessed at it," she replied, "from something he said in referring to his brother. You know that I took a fanciful dislike to Nugent Dubourg before he came to Dimchurch?"

"Yes."

"And you remember that my prejudice against him was confirmed, on the first day when I passed my hand over his face to compare it with his brother's?"

"I remember."

"Well—while Oscar was rambling and contradicting himself—he said something (a mere trifle) which suggested to me that the person with the blue face must be his brother. There was the explanation that I had sought for in vain—the explanation of my persistent dislike to Nugent! That horrid dark face of his must have produced some influence on me when I first touched it, like the influence which your horrid purple dress produced on me when I first touched *that*. Don't you see?"

I saw but too plainly. Oscar had been indebted for his escape from discovery entirely to Lucilla's misinterpretation of his language. And Lucilla's misinterpretation now stood revealed as the natural product of her anxiety to account for her prejudice against Nugent Dubourg. Although the mischief had been done—still, for the quieting of my own conscience, I made an attempt to shake her faith in the false conclusion at which she had arrived.

"There is one thing I don't see yet," I said. "I don't understand Oscar's embarrassment in speaking to you. As you interpret him, he had nothing to be afraid of, and nothing to make him doubt how you would receive what he said. Why should he be embarrassed?"

She smiled satirically.

"What has become of your memory, my dear?" she asked. "You forget that in speaking to Me of his brother, Oscar was placed between a choice of difficulties. On one side, my dislike of dark colors and dark people warned him to hold his tongue. On the other, my hatred of having advantage taken of my blindness to keep things secret from me, pressed him to speak out. Isn't that enough—with his shy disposition, poor fellow—to account for his being embarrassed? Besides," she added, speaking more seriously, "I let him see in my manner toward him that he had disappointed and pained me."

"How?" I asked.

"Don't you remember his once acknowledging in the garden that he had painted his face, in the character of Bluebeard, to amuse the children? It was not delicate, it was not affectionate — it was not like *him* — to show such insensibility as that to his brother's shocking disfigurement. He ought to have remembered it. he ought to have respected it. There! we will say no more. We will go indoors and open the piano and try to forget."

Even Oscar's clumsy excuse in the garden—instead of arousing her suspicion—had lent itself to strengthen the foregone conclusion rooted in her mind! At that critical moment—before I had consulted with the twin brothers as to what was to be done next—it was impossible to say more. I own I felt alarmed when I thought of the future. When she was told — as told she must be—of the dreadful delusion into which she had fallen, what would be the result to Oscar? what would be the effect on herself? I own I shrank from pursuing the inquiry.

When we reached the turn in the valley I looked back at Browndown for the last time. The twin brothers were still in the place at which we had left them. Though the faces were indistinguishable, I could still see the figures plainly—Oscar sitting crouched upon the wall; Nugent erect at his side, with one hand laid on his shoulder. Even at that distance the types of the two characters were expressed in the attitudes of the two men. As we entered the new winding of the valley which shut them out from view I felt (so easy is it to comfort a woman!) that the commanding position of Nugent had produced its encouraging impression on my mind. "He will find a way out of it," I said to myself. "Nugent will help us through!"

CHAPTER THE TWENTY-SEVENTH.

HE FINDS A WAY OUT OF IT.

WE sat down at the piano, as Lucilla had proposed. She wished me to play first, and to play alone. I was teaching her at the time, one of the *Sonatas* of Mozart, and I now tried to go on with the lesson. Never, before or since, have I played so badly as on that day. The divine serenity and completeness by which Mozart's music is, to my mind, raised above all other music that ever was written, can only be worthily interpreted by a player whose whole mind is given undividedly to the work. Devoured as I then was by my own anxieties, I might profane those heavenly melodies—I could not play them. Lucilla accepted my excuses, and took my place.

Half an hour passed without news from Browndown.

Calculated by reference to itself, half an hour is, no doubt, a short space of time. Calculated by reference to your own suspense, while your own interests are at stake, half an hour is an eternity. Every minute that passed, leaving Lucilla still undisturbed in her delusion, was a minute that pricked me in the conscience. The longer we left her in ignorance the more painful to all of us the hard duty of enlightening her would become. I began to get restless. Lucilla, on her side, began to complain of fatigue. After the agitation that she had gone through the inevitable reaction had come. I recommended her to go to her room and rest. She took my advice. In the state of my mind at that time it was an inexpressible relief to me to be left by myself.

After pacing backward and forward for some little time in the sitting-room, and trying vainly to see my way through the difficulties that now beset us, I made up my mind to wait no longer for the news that never came. The brothers were still at Browndown. To Browndown I determined to return.

I peeped quietly into Lucilla's room. She was asleep. After a word to Zillah, recommending her young mistress to her care, I slipped out. As I crossed the lawn I heard the garden gate opened. In a minute more the man of all others whom I most wanted to see presented himself before me in the person of Nugent Dubourg. He had borrowed Oscar's key, and had set off alone for the rectory to tell me what had passed between his brother and himself.

"This is the first stroke of luck that has fallen to me to-day," he said. "I was wondering how I should contrive to speak to you privately. And here you are—accessible and alone. Where is Lucilla? Can we depend on having the garden to ourselves?"

I satisfied him on both those points. He looked sadly pale and worn. Before he opened his lips I saw that he too had had his mind disturbed and his patience tried since I had left him. There was a summer-house at the end of the garden, with a view over the breezy solitude of the Downs. Here we established ourselves; and here, in my headlong way, I opened the interview with the one formidable question: "Who is to tell her of the mistake that she has made?"

"Nobody is to tell her."

That answer staggered me at the outset. I looked at Nugent in silent astonishment.

"There is nothing to be surprised at," he said. "Let me put my point of view before you in two words. I have had a serious talk with Oscar—"

Women are proverbially bad listeners, and I am no better than the rest of them. I interrupted him before he could get any further.

"Did Oscar tell you how the mistake happened?" I asked.

"He could no more tell me than you can. He owns—when he found himself face to face with her—that his presence of mind completely failed him: he didn't himself know what he was saying at the time. *He* lost his head, and *she* lost her patience. Think of his nervous confusion in collision with her nervous irritability, and the result explains itself: nothing *could* come of it but misapprehension and mistake. I turned the thing over in my mind after you had left us; and the one course to take that *I* could see was to accept the position patiently, and to make the best instead of the worst of it. Having reached this conclusion, I settled the matter (as I settle most other difficulties) by cutting the Gordian knot. I said to Oscar: 'Would it be a relief to your mind to leave her present impression undis-

turbed until you are married?' You know him
—I needn't tell you what his answer was. 'Very
well,' I said. 'Dry your eyes and compose yourself. I have begun as Blue Face. As Blue Face
I will go on till further notice.' I spare you the
description of Oscar's gratitude. I proposed,
and he accepted. There is the way out of the
difficulty as I see it."

"Your way out of the difficulty is an unworthy way and a false way," I answered. "I
protest against taking that cruel advantage of
Lucilla's blindness. I refuse to have anything
to do with it."

He opened his case and took out a cigar.

"Do as you please," he said. "You saw the
pitiable state she was in when she forced herself
to speak to me. You saw how her disgust and
horror overpowered her at the end. Transfer
that disgust and horror to Oscar (with indignation and contempt added in *his* case); expose
him to the result of rousing those feelings in her,
before he is fortified by a husband's influence
over her mind, and a husband's place in her
affections—if you dare. I love the poor fellow,
and *I* daren't. May I smoke?"

I gave him his permission to smoke by a gesture. Before I said anything more to this inscrutable gentleman I felt the necessity of understanding him—if I could.

There was no difficulty in accounting for his
readiness to sacrifice himself in the interests of
Oscar's tranquillity. He never did things by
halves—he liked dashing at difficulties which

would have made other men pause. The same
zeal in his brother's service which had saved
Oscar's life at the Trial, might well be the zeal
that animated him now. The perplexity that I
felt was not roused in me by the course that he
had taken, but by the language in which he
justified himself, and, more still, by his behavior
to me while he was speaking. The well-bred,
brilliant young fellow of my previous experience
had now turned as dogged and as ungracious as
a man could be. He waited to hear what I had to
say to him next with a hard defiance and desperation of manner entirely uncalled for by the circumstances, and entirely out of harmony with his
character so far as I had observed it. That there
was something lurking under the surface, some
inner motive at work in him which he was concealing from his brother and concealing from
me, was as plainly visible as the sunshine and
shade on the view that I was looking at from
the summer-house. But what that something
was, or what that inner motive might be, it
baffled my utmost sagacity to guess. Not the
faintest idea of the terrible secret that he was
hiding from me crossed my mind. Innocent of
all suspicion of the truth, there I sat opposite to
him, the unconscious witness of that unhappy
man's final struggle to be true to the brother
whom he loved, and to master the devouring
passion that consumed him. So long as Lucilla
falsely believed him to be disfigured by the
drug, so long the commonest consideration for
her tranquillity would, in the estimation of oth-

ers, excuse and explain his keeping out of her
presence. In that separation lay his last chance
of raising an insurmountable barrier between
Lucilla and himself. He had already tried uselessly to place another obstacle in the way—he
had vainly attempted to hasten the marriage,
which would have made Lucilla sacred to him
as his brother's wife. That effort having failed,
there was but one honorable alternative left to
him—to keep out of her society until she was
married to Oscar. He had accepted the position
in which Oscar had placed him as the one
means of reaching the end in view without exciting suspicion of the truth, and he had encountered, as his reward for the sacrifice, my
ignorant protest, my stupid opposition, set as
obstacles in his way! There were the motives—
the pure, the noble motives—which animated
him, as I know them now. There is the right
reading of the dogged language that mystified
me, of the defiant manner that offended me, interpreted by the one light that I have to guide
my pen—the light of later events!

"Well?" he said. "Are we allies, or not?
Are you with me, or against me?"

I gave up attempting to understand him and
answered that plain question plainly.

"I don't deny that the consequences of undeceiving her may be serious," I said. "But, for
all that, I will have no share in the cruelty of
keeping her deceived."

Nugent held up his forefinger warningly.

"Pause and reflect, Madame Pratolungo! The

mischief that you may do, as matters stand now, may be mischief that you can never repair. It's useless to ask you to alter your mind. I only ask you to wait a little. There is plenty of time before the wedding-day. Something may happen which will spare you the necessity of enlightening Lucilla with your own lips."

"What can happen?" I asked.

"Lucilla may yet see him as we see him," Nugent answered. "Lucilla's own eyes may discover the truth."

"What! have you not abandoned your mad notion of curing her blindness yet?"

"I will abandon my notion when the German surgeon tells me it is mad. Not before."

"Have you said anything about it to Oscar?"

"Not a word. I shall say nothing about it to anybody but you until the German is safe on the shores of England."

"Do you expect him to arrive before the marrage?"

"Certainly. He would have left New York with me, but for one patient who still required his care. No new patients will tempt him to stay in America. His extraordinary success has made his fortune. The ambition of his life is to see England, and he can afford to gratify it. He may be here by the next steamer that reaches Liverpool."

"And when he does come, you mean to bring him to Dimchurch?"

"Yes—unless Lucilla objects to it."

"Suppose Oscar objects? She is resigned to be blind for life. If you disturb that resignation with no useful result, you may make an unhappy woman of her for the rest of her days. In your brother's place, I should object to running that risk."

"My brother is doubly interested in running the risk. I repeat what I have already told you. The physical result will not be the only result, if her sight can be restored. There will be a new mind put into her as well as a new sense. Oscar has everything to dread from this morbid fancy of hers as long as she is blind. Only let her eyes correct her fancy—only let her see him as we see him, and get used to him, as we have got used him, and Oscar's future with her is safe. Will you leave things as they are for the present, on the chance that the German surgeon may get here before the wedding-day?"

I consented to that; being influenced, in spite of myself, by the remarkable coincidence between what Nugent had just said of Lucilla, and what Lucilla had said to me of herself earlier in the day. It was impossible to deny that Nugent's theory, wild as it sounded, found its confirmation, so far, in Lucilla's view of her own case. Having settled the difference between us in this way, for the time being, I shifted our talk next to the difficult question of Nugent's relations toward Lucilla. "How are you to meet her again," I said, "after the effect you produced on her at the meeting to-day?"

He spoke far more pleasantly in discussing

this side of the subject. His language and his manner both improved together.

"If I could have had my own way," he said, "Lucilla would have been relieved, by this time, of all fear of meeting with me again. She would have heard from you or from Oscar that business had obliged me to leave Dimchurch."

"Does Oscar object to let you go?"

"He won't hear of my going. I did my best to persuade him—I promised to return for the marriage. Quite useless! 'If you leave me here by myself,' he said, 'to think over the mischief I have done, and the sacrifices I have forced on you, you will break my heart. You don't know what an encouragement your presence is to me; you don't know what a blank you will leave in my life if you go!' I am as weak as Oscar is, when Oscar speaks to me in that way. Against my own convictions, against my own wishes, I yielded. I should have been better away—far, far better away."

He said those closing words in a tone which startled me. It was nothing less than a tone of despair. How little I understood him then! how well I understand him now! In those melancholy accents spoke the last of his honor, the last of his truth. Miserable, innocent Lucilla! Miserable, guilty Nugent!

"And now you remain at Dimchurch," I resumed, "what are you to do?"

"I must do my best to spare her the nervous suffering which I unwillingly inflicted on her to-day. The morbid repulsion that she feels in my presence is not to be controlled—I can see that plainly. I shall keep out of her way, gradually withdrawing myself, so as not to force my absence on her attention. I shall pay fewer and fewer visits at the rectory, and remain longer and longer at Browndown every day. After they are married—" He suddenly stopped; the words seemed to stick in his throat. He busied himself in relighting his cigar, and took a long time to do it.

"After they are married," I repeated; "what then?"

"When Oscar is married, Oscar will not find my presence indispensable to his happiness. I shall leave Dimchurch."

"You will have to give a reason."

"I shall give the true reason. I can find no studio here big enough for Me—as I have told you. And even if I could find a studio, I should be doing no good if I remained at Dimchurch. My intellect would contract, my brains would rust, in this remote place. Let Oscar live his quiet married life here. And let me go to the atmosphere that is fitter for me—the atmosphere of London or Paris."

He sighed, and fixed his eyes absently on the open hilly view from the summer-house door.

"It's strange to see *you* depressed," I said. "Your spirits seemed to be quite inexhaustible on that first evening, when you interrupted Mr. Finch over 'Hamlet.' "

He threw away the end of his cigar, and laughed bitterly.

"We artists are always in extremes," he said. "What do you think I was wishing just before you spoke to me?"

"I can't guess."

"I was wishing I had never come to Dimchurch!"

Before I could return a word on my side, Lucilla's voice reached our ears, calling to me from the garden. Nugent instantly sprang to his feet.

"Have we said all we need say?" he asked.

"Yes—for to-day, at any rate."

"For to-day, then—good-by!"

He leaped up, caught the cross-bar of wood over the entrance to the summer-house, and, swinging himself on to the low garden wall beyond, disappeared in the field on the other side. I answered Lucilla's call, and hastened away to find her. We met on the lawn. She looked wild and pale, as if something had frightened her.

"Anything wrong at the rectory?" I asked.

"Nothing wrong," she answered, "except with Me. The next time I complain of fatigue, don't advise me to go and lie down on my bed."

"Why not? I looked in at you before I came out here. You were fast asleep—the picture of repose."

"Repose? You were never more mistaken in your life. I was in the agony of a horrid dream."

"You were perfectly quiet when I saw you."

"It must have been after you saw me, then. Let me come and sleep with you to-night. I daren't be by myself if I dream of it again."

"What did you dream of?"

"I dreamed that I was standing, in my wedding-dress, before the altar of a strange church; and that a clergyman, whose voice I had never heard before, was marrying me—"

She stopped, impatiently waving her hand before her in the air. "Blind as I am," she said, "I see him again now!"

"The bridegroom?"

"Yes."

'Oscar?"

"No."

"Who, then?"

"Oscar's brother. Nugent Dubourg."

(Haven't I mentioned before that I am sometimes a great fool? If I have not, I beg to mention it now. I burst out laughing.)

"What is there to laugh at?" she asked, angrily. "I saw his hideous, discolored face—I am never blind in my dreams. I felt his blue hand put the ring on my finger. Wait! The worst part of it is to come. I married Nugent Dubourg willingly—married him without a thought of my engagement to Oscar. Yes! yes! I know it's only a dream. I can't bear to think of it, for all that. I don't like to be false to Oscar even in a dream. Let us go to him. I want to hear him tell me that he loves me. Come to Browndown. I'm so nervous, I don't like going by myself. Come to Browndown!"

I have another humiliating confession to make —I tried to get off going to Browndown. (So like those unfeeling French people, isn't it?)

But I had my reason, too. If I disapproved of the resolution at which Nugent had arrived, I viewed far more unfavorably the selfish weakness on Oscar's part, which had allowed his brother to sacrifice himself. Lucilla's lover had sunk to something very like a despicable character in my estimation. I felt that I might let him see what I thought of him if I found myself in his company at that moment.

"Considering the object that you have in view, my dear," I said to Lucilla, "do you think you want *me* at Browndown?"

"Haven't I already told you?" she asked, impatiently. "I am so nervous—so completely upset—that I don't feel equal to going out by myself. Have you no sympathy for me? Suppose *you* had dreamed that you were marrying Nugent instead of Oscar?"

"Ah, bah! what of that? I should only have dreamed that I was marrying the most agreeable man of the two."

"The most agreeable man of the two! There you are again—always unjust to Oscar."

"My love! if you could see for yourself, you would learn to appreciate Nugent's good qualities as I do."

"I prefer appreciating Oscar's good qualities."

"You are prejudiced, Lucilla."

"So are you."

"You happen to have met Oscar first."

"That has nothing to do with it."

"Yes! yes! If Nugent had followed us instead of Oscar; if, of those two charming voices which are both the same, one had spoken instead of the other—"

"I won't hear a word more!"

"Tra-la-la-la! It happens to have been Oscar. Turn it the other way, and Nugent might have been the man."

"Madame Pratolungo, I am not accustomed to be insulted! I have no more to say to you."

With that dignified reply, and with the loveliest color in her face that you ever saw in your life, my darling Lucilla turned her pretty back on me, and set off for Browndown by herself.

Ah, my rash tongue! Ah, my nasty foreign temper! Why did I let her irritate me? I, the elder of the two—why did I not set her an example of self-control? Who can tell? When does a woman know why she does anything? Did Eve know, when Mr. Serpent offered her the apple, why she ate it? Not she!

What was to be done now? Two things were to be done. First thing: to cool myself down. Second thing: to follow Lucilla, and kiss and make it up.

Either I took some time to cool—or, in the irritation of the moment, Lucilla walked faster than usual. She had got to Browndown before I could overtake her. On opening the house door I heard them talking. It would hardly do to disturb them—especially now I was in disgrace. While I was hesitating, and wondering what my next proceeding had better be, my eye was attracted by a letter lying on the hall table. I looked (one is always inquisitive in those idle moments when one doesn't know what to do)—I looked at the address. The letter was directed to Nugent, and the postmark was Liverpool.

I drew the inevitable conclusion. The German oculist was in England!

CHAPTER THE TWENTY-EIGHTH.

HE CROSSES THE RUBICON.

I WAS still in doubt whether to enter the room or to wait outside until she left Browndown to return to the rectory, when Lucilla's keen sense of hearing decided the question which I had been unable to settle for myself. The door of the room opened, and Oscar advanced into the hall.

"Lucilla insisted that she heard somebody outside," he said. "Who could have guessed it was you? Why did you wait in the hall? Come in! come in!"

He held open the door for me, and I went in. Oscar announced me to Lucilla. "It was Madame Pratolungo you heard," he said. She took no notice either of him or of me. A heap of flowers from Oscar's garden lay in her lap. With the help of her clever figures she was sorting them to make a nosegay as quickly and as tastefully as if she had possessed the sense of sight. In all my experience of that charming face it had never looked so hard as it looked now. Nobody would have recognized her likeness to the Madonna of Raphael's picture. Offended—mortally offended with me—I saw it at a glance.

"I hope you will forgive my intrusion, Lucilla, when you know my motive," I said. "I have followed you here to make my excuses."

"Oh, don't think of making excuses!" she rejoined, giving three-fourths of her attention to the flowers, and one-fourth to me. "It's a pity you took the trouble of coming here. I quite agree with what you said in the garden. Considering the object I had in view at Browndown, I could not possibly expect you to accompany me. True! quite true!"

I kept my temper. Not that I am a patient woman; not that I possess a meek disposition. Very far from it, I regret to say! Nevertheless, I kept my temper—so far.

"I wish to apologize for what I said in the garden," I resumed. "I spoke thoughtlessly, Lucilla. It is impossible that I could intentionally offend you."

I might as well have spoken to one of the chairs. The whole of her attention became absorbed in the breathless interest of making her nosegay.

"*Was* I offended?" she said, addressing herself to the flowers. "Excessively foolish of me, if I was." She suddenly became conscious of my existence. "You had a perfect right to express your opinion," she said, loftily. "Accept *my* excuses if I appeared to dispute it."

She tossed her pretty head; she showed her

brightest color; she tapped her nice little foot
briskly on the floor. (Oh, Lucilla! Lucilla!) I
still kept my temper. More, by this time (I admit), for Oscar's sake than for her sake. He
looked so distressed, poor fellow—so painfully
anxious to interfere, without exactly knowing
how.

"My dear Lucilla!" he began. "Surely you
might answer Madame Pratolungo—"

She petulantly interrupted him with another
toss of the head—a little higher than the last.

"I don't attempt to answer Madame Pratolungo! I prefer admitting that Madame Pratolungo may have been quite right. I dare say I
am ready to fall in love with the first man who
comes my way. I dare say if I had met your
brother before I met you I should have fallen in
love with *him*. Quite likely!"

"Quite likely—as you say," answered poor
Oscar, humbly. "I am sure I think it very
lucky for *me* that you didn't meet Nugent first."

She threw her lapful of flowers away from her
on the table at which she was sitting. She became perfectly furious with him for taking my
side. I permitted myself (the poor child could
not see it, remember) the harmless indulgence of
a smile.

"You agree with Madame Pratolungo," she
said to him, viciously. "Madame Pratolungo
thinks your brother a much more agreeable man
than you."

Humble Oscar shook his head in melancholy
acknowledgment of this self-evident fact. "There

can be no two opinions about that," he said, resignedly.

She stamped her foot on the carpet and raised quite a little cloud of dust. My lungs are occasionally delicate. I permitted myself another harmless indulgence—indulgence in a slight cough. She heard the second indulgence, and suddenly controlled herself the instant it reached her ears. I am afraid she took my cough as my commentary on what was going on.

"Come here, Oscar," she said, with a complete change of tone and manner. "Come and sit down by me."

Oscar obeyed.

"Put your arm round my waist."

Oscar looked at me. Having the use of his sight he was sensible of the absurd side of the demonstration required of him—in the presence of a third person. *She*, poor soul, strong in her blind insensibility to all shafts of ridicule shot from the eye, cared nothing for the presence of a third person. She repeated her commands, in a tone which said, sharply, "Embrace me—I am not to be trifled with!"

Oscar timidly put his arm round her waist— with an appealing look at me. She issued another command instantly.

"Say you love me."

Oscar hesitated.

"Say you love me!"

Oscar whispered it.

"Out loud!"

Endurance has its limits. I began to lose my

temper. She could not have been more superbly indifferent to my presence if there had been a cat in the room instead of a lady.

"Permit me to inform you," I said, "that I have not (as you appear to suppose) left the room."

She took no notice. She went on with her commands, rising irrepressibly from one amatory climax to another.

"Give me a kiss!"

Unhappy Oscar — sacrificed between us — blushed. Stop! Don't revel prematurely in the greatest enjoyment a reader has—namely, catching a writer out in a mistake. I have not forgotten that his disfigured complexion would prevent his blush from showing on the surface. I beg to say I saw it under the surface—saw it in his expression. I repeat, he blushed.

I felt it necessary to assert myself for the second time.

"I have only one object in remaining in the room, Miss Finch. I merely wish to know whether you refuse to accept my excuses."

"Oscar, give me a kiss!"

He still hesitated. She threw her arm round his neck. My duty to myself was plain—my duty was to go.

"Good-afternoon, Mr. Dubourg," I said, and turned to the door. She heard me cross the room, and called to me to stop. I paused. There was a glass on the wall opposite to me. On the authority of the glass, I beg to mention that I paused in my most becoming manner. Grace tempered with dignity; dignity tempered with grace.

"Madame Pratolungo!"

"Miss Finch?"

"This is the man who is not half so agreeable as his brother. Look!"

She tightened her hold round his neck, and gave him—ostentatiously gave him—the kiss which he was ashamed to give *her*. I advanced, in contemptuous silence, to the door. My attitude expressed disgust accompanied by sorrow; sorrow accompanied by disgust.

"Madame Pratolungo!"

I made no answer.

"This is the man whom I should never have loved if I had happened to meet his brother first. Look!"

She put both arms round his neck, and gave him a shower of kisses all in one. The door had been imperfectly closed when I had entered the room. It was ajar. I pulled it open—walked out into the hall—and found myself face to face with Nugent Dubourg, standing by the table, with his letter from Liverpool in his hand! He must have certainly heard Lucilla cast my own words back in my teeth—if he had heard no more.

I stopped short; looking at him in silent surprise. He smiled, and held out the open letter to me. Before we could speak we heard the door of the room closed. Oscar had followed me out (shutting the door behind him) to apologize for Lucilla's behavior to me. He explained what had happened to his brother. Nugent nodded, and tapped his open letter smartly. "Leave me to manage it. I shall give you something better to do than quarreling among yourselves. You will hear what it is directly. In the meantime, I have got a message for our friend at the inn. Gootheridge in on his way here to speak to me about altering the stable. Run and tell him I have other business on hand, and I can't keep my appointment to-day. Stop! Give him this at the same time, and ask him to leave it at the rectory."

He took one of his visiting cards out of the case, wrote a few lines on it in pencil, and handed it to his brother. Oscar (always ready to go on errands for Nugent) hurried out to meet the landlord. Nugent turned to me.

"The German is in England," he said. "Now I may open my lips."

"At once!" I exclaimed.

"At once. I have put off my own business (as you heard) in favor of this. My friend will be in London to-morrow. I mean to get my authority to consult him to-day, and to start to-morrow for town. Prepare yourself to meet one of the strangest characters you ever set eyes on! You saw me write on my card. It was a message to Mr. Finch, asking him to join us immediately (on important family business) at Browndown. As Lucilla's father, he has a voice in the matter. When Oscar comes back, and when the rector joins us, our domestic privy council will be complete."

He spoke with his customary spirit; he moved with his customary briskness: he had become quite himself again since I had seen him last.

"I am stagnating in this place," he went on, seeing that I noticed the change in him. "It puts me in spirits again, having something to do. I am not like Oscar; I must have action to stir my blood—action to keep me from fretting over my anxieties. How do you think I found the witness to my brother's innocence at the Trial? In that way. I said to myself, 'I shall go mad if I don't do something.' I did something—and saved Oscar. I am going to do something again. Mark my words! Now I am stirring in it, Lucilla will recover her sight."

"This is a serious matter," I said. "Pray give it serious consideration."

"Consideration?" he repeated. "I hate the word. I always decide on the instant. If I am wrong in my view of Lucilla's case, consideration is of no earthly use. If I am right, every day's delay is a day of sight lost to the blind. I'll wait for Oscar and Mr. Finch; and then I'll open the business. Why are we talking in the hall? Come in!"

He led the way to the sitting-room. I had a new interest now in going back. Still Lucilla's behavior hung on my mind. Suppose she treated me with renewed coldness and keener contempt? I remained standing at the table in the hall. Nugent looked back at me over his shoulder.

"Nonsense!" he said. "I'll set things right. It's beneath a woman like you to take notice of what a girl says in a pet. Come in!"

I doubt if I should have yielded to please any other living man. But, there is no denying it, some people have a magnetic attracting power over others. Nugent had that power over me. Against my own will—for I was really hurt and offended by her usage of me—I went back with him into the room.

Lucilla was still sitting in the place which she had occupied when I withdrew. On hearing the door open, and a man's footsteps entering, she, of course, assumed that the man was Oscar. She had penetrated his object in leaving her to follow me out, and it had not improved her temper.

"Oh!" she said. "You have come back at last? I thought you had offered yourself as Madame Pratolungo's escort to the rectory." She stopped, with a sudden frown. Her quick ears had detected my return into the room. "Oscar!" she exclaimed, "what does this mean? Madame Pratolungo and I have nothing more to say to each other. What has she come back for? Why don't you answer? This is infamous! I shall leave the room!"

The utterance of that final threat was followed so rapidly by its execution that before Nugent (standing between her and the door) could get out of her way she came in violent contact with him. She instantly caught him by the arm, and shook him angrily. "What does your silence

mean? Is it at Madame Pratolungo's instigation that you are insulting me?''

I had just opened my lips to make one more
attempt at reconciliation, by saying some pacify-
ing words to her, when she planted that last sting
in me. French flesh and blood (whatever English flesh and blood might have done) could bear
no more. I silently turned my back on her, in
a rage.

At the same moment Nugent's eyes brightened
as if a new idea had struck him. He gave me
one significant look—and answered her in his
brother's character. Whether he was possessed
at the moment by some demon of mischief, or
whether he had the idea of trying to make
Oscar's peace for him before Oscar returned, is
more than I can say. I ought to have stopped
it, I know. But my temper was in a flame. I
was as spiteful as a cat and as fierce as a bear.
I said to myself (in your English idiom), She
wants taking down a peg; quite right, Mr. Nugent; do it. Shocking! shameful! no words
are bad enough for me: give it me well. Ah,
Heaven! what is a human being in a rage? On
my sacred word of honor, nothing but a human
beast! The next time it happens to You, look
at yourself in the glass, and you will find your
soul gone out of you at your face, and nothing
left but an animal—and a bad, a villainous bad
animal too.

"You ask what my silence means?" said Nugent.

He had only to model his articulation on his

brother's slower manner of speaking, as distinguished from his own, to be his brother himself. In saying those few words he did it so dexterously that I could have sworn—if I had not seen him standing before me—Oscar was in the room.

"Yes," she said, "I ask that."

"I am silent," he answered, "because I am waiting."

"What are you waiting for?"

"To hear you make your apologies to Madame Pratolungo."

She started back a step. Submissive Oscar was taking a peremptory tone with her for the first time in his life. Submissive Oscar, instead of giving her time to speak, sternly went on.

"Madame Pratolungo has made her excuses to *you.* You ought to receive them; you ought to reciprocate them. It is distressing to see you and hear you. You are behaving ungratefully to your best friend."

She raised her face, she raised her hands, in blank amazement: she looked as if she distrusted her own ears.

"Oscar!" she exclaimed.

"Here I am," said Oscar, opening the door at the same moment.

She turned like lightning toward the place from which he had spoken. She detected the deception which Nugent had practiced on her with a cry of indignation that rang through the room.

Oscar ran to her in alarm. She thrust him back violently.

"A trick!" she cried. "A mean, vile, cowardly trick played upon my blindness! Oscar!
your brother has been imitating you; your
brother has been speaking to me in your voice.
And that woman who calls herself my friend—
that woman stood by and heard him, and never
told me. She encouraged it; she enjoyed it.
The wretches! Take me away from them. They
are capable of any deceit. She always hated
you, dear, from the first—she took up with your
brother the moment he came here. When you
marry me, it mustn't be at Dimchurch; it must
be in some place they don't know of. There
is a conspiracy between them against you and
against me. Beware of them! beware of them!
She said I should have fallen in love with your
brother if I had met him first. There is a deeper
meaning in that, my love, than you can see. It
means that they will part us if they can. Ha!
I hear somebody moving! Has he changed places
with you? Is it *you* whom I am speaking to
now? Oh, my blindness! my blindness! O God!
of all your creatures the most helpless, the most
miserable, is the creature who can't see."

I never heard anything in all my life so pitiable
and so dreadful as the frantic suspicion and misery which tore their way out from her in those
words. She cut me to the heart. I had spoken
rashly—I had behaved badly; but had I deserved
this? No! no! no! I had *not* deserved it. I
threw myself into a chair and burst out crying.
My tears scalded me; my sobs choked me. If
I had had poison in my hand, I would have

drunk it, I was so furious and so wretched; so
hurt in my honor, so wounded at my heart.

The only voice that answered her was Nugent's. Reckless what the consequences might
be—speaking in his own proper person from the
opposite end of the room—he asked the all-important question which no human being had ever
put to her yet.

"Are you sure, Lucilla, that you are blind for
life?"

A dead silence followed the utterance of those
words.

I brushed away the tears from my eyes, and
looked up.

Oscar had been—as I supposed—holding her
in his arms, silently soothing her, when his
brother spoke. At the moment when I saw
her she had just detached herself from him.
She advanced a step toward the part of the
room in which Nugent stood, and stopped, with
her face turned toward him. Every faculty in
her seemed to be suspended by the silent passage
into her mind of the new idea that he had called
up. Through childhood, girlhood, womanhood,
never once, waking or dreaming, had the prospect of restoration to sight presented itself within
her range of contemplation until now. Not a
trace was left in her countenance of the indignation which Nugent had roused in her hardly
more than a moment since. Not a sign appeared
indicating a return of the nervous suffering
which the sense of his presence had inflicted
on her earlier in the day. The one emotion

in possession of her was astonishment—astonishment that had struck her dumb; astonishment that had waited, helplessly and mechanically, to hear more.

I observed Oscar next. His eyes were fixed on Lucilla — absorbed in watching her. He spoke to Nugent without looking at him; animated, as it seemed, by a vague fear for Lucilla, which was slowly developing into a vague fear for himself.

"Mind what you are doing!" he said. "Look at her, Nugent—look at her!"

Nugent approached his brother circuitously, so as to place Oscar between Lucilla and himself.

"Have I offended you?" he asked.

Oscar looked at him in surprise. "Offended with you," he answered, "after what you have forgiven and what you have suffered for my sake?"

"Still," persisted the other, "there is something wrong."

"I am startled, Nugent."

"Startled—by what?"

"By the question that you have just put to Lucilla."

"You will understand me, and she will understand me, directly."

While those words were passing between the brothers, my attention remained fixed on Lucilla. Her head had turned slowly toward the new position which Nugent occupied when he spoke to Oscar. With this exception, no other movement had escaped her. No sense of what the two men were saying to each other seemed to have entered her mind. To all appearance, she had heard nothing since Nugent had started the first doubt in her whether she was blind for life.

"Speak to her," I said. "For God's sake, don't keep her in suspense *now!*"

Nugent spoke.

"You have had reason to be offended with me, Lucilla. Let me, if I can, give you reason to be grateful to me before I have done. When I was in New York I became acquainted with a German surgeon who had made a reputation and a fortune in America by his skill in treating diseases of the eye. He had been especially successful in curing cases of blindness given up as hopeless by other surgeons. I mentioned your case to him. He could say nothing positively (as a matter of course) without examining you. All he could do was to place his services at my disposal when he came to England. I, for one, Lucilla, decline to consider you blind for life until this skillful man sees no more hope for you than the English surgeons have seen. If there is the faintest chance still left of restoring your sight, his is, I firmly believe, the one hand that can do it. He is now in England. Say the word, and I will bring him to Dimchurch."

She slowly lifted her hands to her head, and held it as if she was holding her reason in its place. Her color changed from pale to red—from red to pale once more. She drew a long, deep, heavy breath, and dropped her hands

again, recovering from the shock. The change
that followed held us all three breathless. It was
beautiful to see her. It was awful to see her.
A mute ecstasy of hope transfigured her face; a
heavenly smile played serenely on her lips. She
was among us, and yet apart from us. In the
still light of evening, shining in on her from
the window, she stood absorbed in her own
rapture—the silent creature of another sphere!
There was a moment when she overcame me
with admiration, and another moment when she
overcame me with fear. Both the men felt it.
Both signed to me to speak to her first.

I advanced a few steps. I tried to consider
with myself what I should say. It was useless.
I could neither think nor speak. I could only
look at her. I could only say, nervously:

"Lucilla."

She came back to the world—she came back
to *us*—with a little start, and a faint flush of
color in her cheeks. She turned herself toward
the place from which I had spoken, and whispered:

"Come."

In a moment my arms were round her. Her
head sank on my bosom. We were reconciled
without a word. We were friends again, sisters
again, in an instant.

"Have I been fainting? have I been sleeping?" she said to me, in faint, bewildered tones.
"Am I just awake? Is this Browndown?" She
suddenly lifted her head. "Nugent! are you
there?"

"Yes."

She gently withdrew herself from me, and approached Nugent.

"Did you speak to me just now? Was it you who put the doubt into my mind whether I am really doomed to be blind for life? Surely I have not fancied it? Surely you said the man was coming, and the time coming?" Her voice suddenly rose. "The man who may cure me! the time when I may see!"

"I said it, Lucilla. I meant it, Lucilla!"

"Oscar! Oscar!! Oscar!!!"

I stepped forward to lead her to him. Nugent touched me, and pointed to Oscar, as I took her hand. He was standing before the glass, with an expression of despair which I see again while I write these lines—he was standing close to the glass, looking in silence at the hideous reflection of his face. In sheer pity, I hesitated to take her to him. She stepped forward, and, stretching out her hand, touched his shoulder. The reflection of *her* charming face appeared above *his* face in the glass. She bent gayly over, with both hands on him, and said, "The time is coming, my darling, when I may see You!"

With a cry of joy, she drew his face up to her and kissed him on the forehead. His head fell on his breast when she released it; he covered his face with his hands, and stifled, for the moment, all outward expression of the pang that wrung him. I drew her rapidly away, before her quick sensibilities had time to warn her that something was wrong. Even as it was, she resisted me. Even as it was, she asked, suspiciously, "Why do you take me away from him?"

What excuse could I make? I was at my wit's end.

She repeated the question. For once Fortune favored us. A timely knock at the door stopped her just as she was trying to release herself from me. "Somebody coming in," I said. The servant entered as I spoke with a letter from the rectory.

CHAPTER THE TWENTY-NINTH.

PARLIAMENTARY SUMMARY.

OH, the welcome interruption. After the agitation that we had suffered we all stood equally in need of some such relief as this. It was absolutely a luxury to fall back again into the commonplace daily routine of life. I asked to whom the letter was addressed. Nugent answered, "The letter is addressed to me; and the writer is Mr. Finch."

Having read the letter, he turned to Lucilla.

"I sent a message to your father, asking him to join us here," he said. "Mr. Finch writes back to say that his duties keep him at home, and to suggest that the rectory is the fitter place for the discussion of family matters. Have you any objection to return to the house? And do you mind going on first with Madame Pratolungo?"

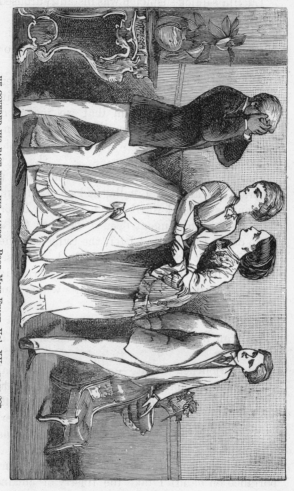

HE COVERED HIS FACE WITH HIS HANDS.—POOR MISS FINCH, Vol. XV., page 287.

Lucilla's quick suspicion was instantly aroused. "Why not with Oscar?" she asked.

"Your father's note suggests to me," replied Nugent, "that he is a little hurt at the short notice I gave him of our discussion here. I thought—if you and Madame Pratolungo went on first—that you might make our peace with the rector, and assure him that we meant no disrespect, before Oscar and I appear. Don't you think yourself you would make it easier for *us* if you did that?"

Having contrived in this dexterous way to separate Oscar and Lucilla, and to gain time for composing and fortifying his brother before they met again, Nugent opened the door for us to go out. Lucilla and I left the twins together in the modest little room which had witnessed a scene alike memorable to all of us for its interest at the time, and for the results which were to come of it in the future.

Half an hour later we were all assembled at the rectory.

Our adjourned debate—excepting one small suggestion emanating from myself—was a debate which led to nothing. It may be truly described as resolving itself into the delivery of an Oration by Mr. Finch. Subject, the assertion of Mr. Finch's dignity.

On this occasion (having matters of more importance on hand) I take the liberty of cutting the reverend gentleman's speech by the pattern of the reverend gentleman's stature. Short in figure, the rector shall be here, for the first time in his life, short in language too.

Reverend Finch rose and said—he objected to everything. To receiving a message on a card instead of a proper note. To being expected to present himself at Browndown at a moment's notice. To being the last person informed (instead of the first) of Mr. Nugent Dubourg's exaggerated and absurd view of the case of his afflicted child. To the German surgeon, as being certainly a foreigner and a stranger, and possibly a quack. To the slur implied on British Surgery by bringing the foreigner to Dimchurch. To the expense involved in the same proceeding. Finally, to the whole scope and object of Mr. Nugent Dubourg's proposal, which had for its origin rebellion against the decrees of an all-wise Providence, and for its result the disturbance of his daughter's mind—"under My influence, sir, a mind in a state of Christian resignation: under Your influence, a mind in a state of infidel revolt." With those concluding remarks, the reverend gentleman sat down—and paused for a reply.

A remarkable result followed, which might be profitably permitted to take place in some other Parliaments. Nobody replied.

Mr. Nugent Dubourg rose—no! sat—and said he declined to take any part in the proceedings. He was quite ready to wait until the end justified the means which he proposed to employ. For the rest, his conscience was at ease; and he was entirely at Miss Finch's service. (Memorandum in parentheses: Mr. Finch might not have got off so easily as this but for one circumstance. I have already mentioned it as part of the strange constraint which Lucilla innocently imposed on Nugent that her father could always talk him down in her presence. She was present on this occasion. And Reverend Finch reaped the benefit.)

Mr. Oscar Dubourg, sitting hidden from notice behind his brother, followed his brother's example. The decision in the matter under discussion rested with Miss Finch alone. He had no opinion of his own to offer in it.

Miss Finch herself, appealed to next: Had but one reply to give. If her whole fortune was involved in testing her chance of recovering her sight, she would cheerfully sacrifice her whole fortune to that one object. With all possible respect to her father, she ventured to think that neither he nor any one possessing the sense of vision could quite enter into her feelings as the circumstances then were. She entreated Mr. Nugent Dubourg not to lose one unnecessary moment in bringing the German surgeon to Dimchurch.

Mrs. Finch, called upon next. Spoke after some little delay, caused by the loss of her pocket - handkerchief. Would not presume to differ in opinion with her husband, whom she had never yet known to be otherwise than perfectly right about everything. But, if the German surgeon *did* come, and if Mr. Finch saw no objection to it, she would much like to consult him (gratis, if possible) on the subject of "baby's

eyes." Mrs. Finch was proceeding to explain
that there was happily nothing the matter, that
she could see, with the infant's eyes at that particular moment, and that she merely wished to
take a skilled medical opinion, in the event of
something happening on some future occasion,
when she was called to order by Mr. Finch. The
reverend gentleman, at the same time, appealed
to Madame Pratolungo to close the debate by
giving frank expression to her own opinion.

Madame Pratolungo, speaking in conclusion,
remarked:

That the question of consulting the German
surgeon appeared (after what had fallen from
Miss Finch) to be a question which had passed
beyond the range of any expression of feeling
on the part of other persons. That she proposed,
accordingly, to look beyond the consultation at
the results which might follow it. That, contemplating these possible results, she held very
strong views of her own, and would proceed to
give frank expression to them as follows. That,
in her opinion, the proposed investigation of the
chances which might exist of restoring Miss
Finch's sight involved consequences far too
serious to be trusted to the decision of any one
man, no matter how skillful or how famous he
might be. That, in pursuance of this view, she
begged to suggest (1) the association of an
eminent English oculist with the eminent German oculist; (2) an examination of Miss Finch's
case by both the professional gentlemen, consulting on it together; and (3) a full statement of the

opinions at which they might respectively arrive
to be laid before the meeting now assembled, and
to become the subject of a renewed discussion,
before any decisive measures were taken. Lastly,
that this proposal be now submitted in the form
of a resolution, and forthwith (if necessary) put
to the vote.

Resolution, as above, put to the vote.

Majority—Ayes.

    Miss Finch.

    Mr. Nugent Dubourg.

    Mr. Oscar Dubourg.

    Madame Pratolungo.

Minority—Noes.

No (on the score of expense), Mr. Finch.

No (because Mr. F. says No), Mrs. Finch.

Resolution carried by a majority of two. Debate adjourned to a day to be hereafter decided
on.

By the first train the next morning Nugent
Dubourg started for London.

At luncheon, the same day, a telegram arrived
reporting his proceedings in the following terms:

"I have seen my friend. He is at our service.
He is also quite willing to consult with any
English oculist whom we may choose. I am
just off to find the man. Expect a second telegram later in the day."

The second telegram reached us in the evening, and ran thus:

"Everything is settled. The German oculist
and the English oculist leave London with

me by the twelve-forty train to-morrow afternoon."

After reading this telegram to Lucilla I sent
it to Oscar at Browndown. Judge for yourself
how *he* slept, and how *we* slept, that night.

CHAPTER THE THIRTIETH.

HERR GROSSE.

SEVERAL circumstances deserving to be mentioned here took place in the early part of the
day on which we expected the visit of the two
oculists. I have all the will to relate them, but
the capacity to do it completely fails me.

When I look back at that eventful morning, I
recall a scene of confusion and suspense, the bare
recollection of which seems to upset my mind
again, even at this distance of time. Things
and persons all blend distractedly one with another. I see the charming figure of my blind
Lucilla, robed in rose-color and white, flitting
hither and thither, in the house and out of the
house—at one time mad with impatience for
the arrival of the surgeons; at another, shuddering with apprehension of the coming ordeal,
and the coming disappointment which might
follow. A moment more, and, just as my mind
has seized it, the fair figure melts and merges
into the miserable apparition of Oscar, hovering
and hesitating between Browndown and the
rectory, painfully conscious of the new com-

plications introduced into his position toward
Lucilla by the new state of things, and yet not
man enough, even yet, to seize the opportunity
and set himself right. Another moment passes,
and a new figure—a little strutting, consequen-
tial figure—forces its way into the foreground
before I am ready for it. I hear a big voice
booming in my ear, with big language to correspond. "No, Madame Pratolungo, nothing will
induce me to sanction by my presence this insane medical consultation, this extravagant and
profane attempt to reverse the decrees of an all-
wise Providence by purely human means. My
foot is down—I use the language of the people,
observe, to impress it the more strongly on your
mind—MY FOOT is down!" Another moment
yet, and Finch and Finch's Foot disappear over
my mental horizon just as my eye has caught
them. Damp Mrs. Finch and the baby, whose
everlasting programme is suction and sleep, take
the vacant place. Mrs. Finch pledges me with
watery earnestness to secrecy, and then confides
her intention of escaping her husband's super-
vision if she can, and bringing British surgery
and German surgery to bear both together (gratis)
on baby's eyes. Conceive these persons all twist-
ing and turning in the convolutions of my brains,
as if those brains were a labyrinth, with the sayings and doings of one confusing themselves with
the sayings and doings of the other—with a thin
stream of my own private anxieties (comprehend-
ing luncheon on a side-table for the doctors) trick-
ling at intervals through it all—and you will not

wonder if I take a jump, like a sheep, over some six hours of precious time, and present my solitary self to your eye, posted alone in the sitting-room to receive the council of surgeons on its arrival at the house.

I had but two consolations to sustain me.

First, a Mayonnaise of chicken of my own making on the luncheon-table, which, as a work of Art, was simply adorable—I say no more. Secondly, my green silk dress, trimmed with my mother's famous lace — another work of Art, equally adorable with the first. Whether I looked at the luncheon - table, or whether I looked in the glass, I could feel that I worthily asserted my nation; I could say to myself, Even in this remote corner of the earth the pilgrim of civilization searching for the elegant luxuries of life looks and sees—France supreme!

The clock chimed the quarter past three. Lucilla, wearying for the hundredth time of waiting in her own room, put her head in at the door, and still repeated the never-changing question:

"No signs of them yet?"

"None, my love."

"Oh, how much longer will they keep us waiting!"

"Patience, Lucilla—patience!"

She disappeared again with a weary sigh. Five minutes more passed, and old Zillah peeped into the room next.

"Here they are, ma'am, in a chaise at the gate!"

I shook out the skirts of my green silk, I cast a last inspiriting glance at the Mayonnaise. Nugent's cheerful voice reached us from the garden, conducting the strangers. "This way, gentlemen — follow me." A pause. Steps outside. The door opened. Nugent brought them in.

Herr Grosse, from America. Mr. Sebright, of London.

The German gave a little start when my name was mentioned. The Englishman remained perfectly unaffected by it. Herr Grosse had heard of my glorious Pratolungo. Mr. Sebright was barbarously ignorant of his existence. I shall describe Herr Grosse first, and shall take the greatest pains with him.

A squat, broad, sturdy body, waddling on a pair of short bandy-legs; slovenly, shabby, unbrushed clothes; a big, square, bilious-yellow face, surmounted by a mop of thick iron-gray hair; dark beetle-brows; a pair of staring, fierce, black, goggle eyes, with huge circular spectacles standing up like fortifications in front of them; a shaggy beard and mustache of mixed black, white and gray; a prodigious cameo ring on the forefinger of one hairy hand; the other hand always in and out of a deep silver snuff-box like a small tea-caddy; a rough, rasping voice; a diabolically humorous smile; a curtly confident way of speaking; resolution, independence, power, expressed all over him from head to foot—there is the portrait of the man who held in his hands (if Nugent was to be trusted) the restoration of Lucilla's sight!

The English oculist was as unlike his German colleague as it is possible for one human being to be to another.

Mr. Sebright was slim and spare, and scrupulously (painfully) clean and neat. His smooth light hair was carefully parted; his well-shaved face exhibited two little crisp morsels of whisker about two inches long, and no hair more. His decent black clothes were perfectly made; he wore no ornaments, not even a watch-chain; he moved deliberately; he spoke gravely and quietly; disciplined attention looked coldly at you out of his light gray eyes, and said, Here I am if you want me, in every movement of his thin, finely cut lips. A thoroughly capable man, beyond all doubt—but defend me from accidentally sitting next to him at dinner, or traveling with him for my only companion on a long journey!

I received these distinguished persons with my best grace. Herr Grosse complimented me in return on my illustrious name, and shook hands. Mr. Sebright said it was a beautiful day, and bowed. The German, the moment he was at liberty to look about him, looked at the luncheon - table. The Englishman looked out of window.

"Will you take some refreshment, gentlemen?"

Herr Grosse nodded his shock head in high approval. His wild eyes glared greedily at the Mayonnaise through his prodigious spectacles. "Aha! I like that," said the illustrious surgeon,

pointing at the dish with his ringed forefinger.
"You know how to make him—you make him
with creams. Is he chickens or lobsters? I like
lobsters best, but chickens is goot too. The gar-
nish is lofely—anchovy, olive, beet-roots; brown,
green, red on the fat white sauce. This I call a
heavenly dish. He is nice-cool in two different
ways—nice-cool to the eye, nice-cool to the taste.
Soh! we will break into his inside. Madame
Pratolungo, you shall begin. Here goes for the
liver-wings!"

In this extraordinary English—turning words
in the singular into words in the plural, and
banishing from the British vocabulary the cop-
ulative conjunction "and"—Herr Grosse announced his readiness to sit down to lunch. He
was politely recalled from the Mayonnaise to the
patient by his discreet English colleague.

"I beg your pardon," said Mr. Sebright.
"Would it not be advisable to see the young
lady before we do anything else? I am obliged
to return to London by the next train."

Herr Grosse—with a fork in one hand and a
spoon in the other, and a napkin tied round his
neck—stared piteously, shook his shock head,
and turned his back on the Mayonnaise, with a
heavy heart at parting.

"Goot. We shall do our works first: then eat
our lunches afterward. Where is the patients?
Come-begin-begin!" He removed the napkin,
blew a sigh (there is no other way of expressing
it), and plunged his finger and thumb into his
tea-caddy snuff-box. "Where is the patients?"

he repeated, irritably. "Why is she not close-handy in here?"

"She is waiting in the next room," I said. "I will bring her in directly. You will make allowances for her, gentlemen, I am sure, if you find her a little nervous?" I added, looking at both the oculists. Silent Mr. Sebright bowed. Herr Grosse grinned diabolically, and said: "Make your mind easy, my goot creature. I am not such a brutes as I look!"

"Where is Oscar?" asked Nugent, as I passed him on my way to Lucilla's room.

"After altering his mind a dozen times at least," I replied, "he has decided on not being present at the examination."

I had barely said the words before the door opened, and Oscar entered the room. He had altered his mind for the thirteenth time—and here he was, as the result of it!

Herr Grosse burst out with an exclamation in his own language at the sight of Oscar's face. "Ach Gott!" he exclaimed, "he has been taking Nitrates of Silvers. His complexions is spoilt. Poor boys! poor boys!" He shook his shaggy head — turned — and spat compassionately into a corner of the room. Oscar looked offended; Mr. Sebright looked disgusted; Nugent thoroughly enjoyed it. I left the room, and closed the door behind me.

I had not taken two steps in the corridor when I heard the door opened again. Looking back directly, I found myself, to my amazement, face to face with Herr Grosse—staring ferociously at

me through his spectacles, and offering me his
arm.

"Hosh!" said the famous oculist, in a heavy
whisper. "Say nothing to nobody. I am come
to help you."

"To help me?" I repeated.

Herr Grosse nodded vehemently — so vehemently that his prodigious spectacles hopped
up and down on his nose.

"What did you tell me just now?" he asked.
"You told me the patients was nervous. Goot!
I am come to go with you to the patients, and
help you to fetch her. Soh! soh! I am not
such a brutes as I look. Come-begin-begin!
Where is she?"

I hesitated for a moment about introducing
this remarkable embassador into Lucilla's bedroom. One look at him decided me. After all,
he was a doctor—and such an ugly one! I took
his arm.

We went together into Lucilla's room. She
started up from the sofa on which she was reclin-
ing when she heard the strange footsteps entering
side by side with mine.

"Who is it?" she cried.

"It is me, my dears," said Herr Grosse.
"Ach Gott! what a pretty girls! Here is jost
the complexions I like—nice-fair! nice-fair! I
am come to see what I can do, my pretty miss,
for this eyes of yours. If I can let the light in
on you—hey? you will lofe me, won't you? You
will kees even an ugly Germans like me. Soh!
Come under my arm. We will go back into the

odder rooms. There is anodder one waiting to
let the light in too—Mr. Sebrights. Two surgeon-optic to one pretty miss—English surgeon-
optic; German surgeon optic —hey! between us
we shall cure this nice girls. Madame Pratolungo, here is my odder arms at your service.
Hey! what? You look at my coat-sleeve. He
is shabby-greasy—I am ashamed of him. No
matter! You have got Mr. Sebright's to look at
in the odder rooms. He is spick-span, beauti-
ful-new. Come! Forwards! Marsch!"

Nugent, waiting in the corridor, threw the
door open for us. "Isn't he delightful?" Nugent whispered behind me, pointing to his friend.
Escorted by Herr Grosse, we made a magnificent
entry into the room. Our German doctor had
done Lucilla good already. The examination
was relieved of all its embarrassments and its ter-
rors at the outset. Herr Grosse had made her
laugh—Herr Grosse had set her completely at
her ease.

Mr. Sebright and Oscar were talking together
in a perfectly friendly way when we returned to
the sitting-room. The reserved Englishman appeared to have his attraction for the shy Oscar.
Even Mr. Sebright was struck by Lucilla. His
cold face lighted up with interest when he was
presented to her. He placed a chair for her in
front of the window. There was a warmth in
his tone which I had not heard yet when he
begged her to be seated in that place. She took
the chair. Mr. Sebright thereupon drew back,
and bowed to Herr Grosse, with a courteous

wave of his hand toward Lucilla which signified: "You first!"

Herr Grosse met this advance with a counter
wave of the hand, and a vehement shake of his
shock head, which signified: "I couldn't think
of such a thing!"

"Pardon me," entreated Mr. Sebright. "As
my senior, as a visitor to England, as a master
in our art."

Herr Grosse responded by regaling himself
with three pinches of snuff in rapid succession—
a pinch as senior, a pinch as visitor to England,
a pinch as master in the art. An awful pause
followed. Neither of the surgeons would take
precedence of the other. Nugent interfered.

"Miss Finch is waiting," he said. "Come,
Grosse, you were first presented to her. You
examine her first."

Herr Grosse took Nugent's ear between his
finger and thumb, and gave it a good-humored
pinch. "You clever boys!" he said. "You
have the right word always at the tips of your
tongue." He waddled to Lucilla's chair and
stopped short with a scandalized look. Oscar
was bending over her, and whispering to her
with her hand in his. "Hey! what?" cried
Herr Grosse. "Is this a third surgeon-optic!
What, sir! you treat young miss's eyes by taking hold of young miss's hand? You are a
Quack. Get out!" Oscar withdrew—not very
graciously. Herr Grosse took a chair in front
of Lucilla and removed his spectacles. As a
short-sighted man, he had necessarily excellent

eyes for all objects which were sufficiently near
to him. He bent forward, with his face close
to Lucilla's, and parted her eyelids alternately,
with his finger and thumb, peering attentively
first into one eye, then into the other.

It was a moment of breathless interest. Who
could say what an influence on her future life
might be exercised by this quaint, kindly, un-
couth little foreign man? How anxiously we
watched those shaggy eyebrows, those piercing
goggle eyes! And, O heavens! how disappointed
we were at the first result! Lucilla suddenly
gave a little irrepressible shudder of disgust.
Herr Grosse drew back from her, and glared at
her benignantly with his diabolical smile.

"Aha!" he said. "I see what it is. I snuff,
I smoke, I reek of tobaccos. The pretty miss
smells me. She says in her inmost heart—Ach
Gott, how he stink!"

Lucilla burst into a fit of laughter. Herr
Grosse, unaffectedly amused on his side, grinned
with delight, and snatched her handkerchief out
of her apron pocket. "Gif me scents," said this
excellent German. "I shall stop up her nose
with her handkerchiefs. So she will not smell
my tobacco-stinks—all will be nice-right again
—we shall go on." I gave him some lavender-
water from a scent-bottle on the table. He
gravely drenched the handkerchief with it, and
popped it suddenly on Lucilla's nose. "Hold
him there, miss. You cannot for the life of
you smell Grosse now. Goot! We may go on
again."

He took a magnifying-glass out of his waist-coat pocket, and waited till Lucilla had fairly exhausted herself with laughing. Then the examination—so cruelly grotesque in itself, so terribly serious in the issues which it involved—resumed its course: Herr Grosse glaring at his patient through his magnifying-glass; Lucilla leaning back in the chair, holding the handkerchief over her nose.

A minute or more passed, and the ordeal of the examination came to an end.

Herr Grosse put back his magnifying-glass with a grunt which sounded like a grunt of relief, and snatched the handkerchief away from Lucilla. "Ach! what a nasty smell!" he said, holding the handkerchief to his nose with a grimace of disgust. "Tobaccos is much better than this." He solaced his nostrils, offended by the lavender-water, with a huge pinch of snuff. ''Now I am going to talk," he went on. "See! I keep my distance. You don't want your hand-kerchiefs—you smell me no more."

"Am I blind for life?" said Lucilla. "Pray, pray, pray tell me, sir. Am I blind for life?"

"Will you kees me if I tell you?"

"Oh, do consider how anxious I am! Pray, pray, pray tell me!"

She tried to go down on her knees before him. He held her back firmly and kindly in her chair.

"Now! now! now! you be nice-goot, and tell me this first. When you are out in the garden, taking your little lazy lady's walks on a shiny-sunny day, is it all the same to your eyes as if

HE HELD HER BACK FIRMLY AND KINDLY IN HER CHAIR.—Poor Miss Finch, Vol. XV., page 306.

you were lying in your bed in the middles of the night?"

"No."

"Hah! You know it is nice-light at one time? you know it is horrid-dark at the odder?"

"Yes."

"Then why you ask me if you are blind for life? If you can see as much as that, you are not properly blind at all!"

She clasped her hands, with a low cry of delight. "Oh, where is Oscar?" she said, softly. "Where is Oscar?" I looked round for him. He was gone. While his brother and I had been hanging spell-bound over the surgeon's questions and the patient's answers, he must have stolen silently out of the room.

Herr Grosse rose and vacated the chair in favor of Mr. Sebright. In the ecstasy of the new hope now confirmed in her, Lucilla seemed to be unconscious of the presence of the English oculist when he took his colleague's place. His grave face looked more serious than ever as he, too, produced a magnifying-glass from his pocket, and, gently parting the patient's eyelids, entered on the examination of her blindness, in his turn.

The investigation by Mr. Sebright lasted a much longer time than the investigation by Herr Grosse. He pursued it in perfect silence. When he had done, he rose without a word and left Lucilla as he had found her, rapt in the trance of her own happiness—thinking, thinking, thinking of the time when she should open her eyes in the morning, and see!

"Well?" said Nugent, impatiently addressing Mr. Sebright. "What do *you* say?"

"I say nothing yet." With that implied reproof to Nugent, he turned to me. "I understand that Miss Finch was blind—or as nearly blind as could be discovered—at a year old?"

"I have always heard so," I replied.

"Is there any person in the house—parent, or relative, or servant—who can speak to the symptoms noticed when she was an infant?"

I rang the bell for Zillah. "Her mother is dead," I said, "and there are reasons which prevent her father from being present to-day. Her old nurse will be able to give you all the information you want."

Zillah appeared. Mr. Sebright put his questions. "Were you in the house when Miss Finch was born?"

"Yes, sir."

"Was there anything wrong with her eyes at her birth, or soon afterward?"

"Nothing, sir."

"How did you know?"

"I knew by seeing her take notice, sir. She used to stare at the candles, and clutch at things that were held before her, as other babies do."

"How did you discover it when she began to get blind?"

"In the same way, sir. There came a time, poor little thing! when her eyes looked glazed-like, and try her as we might, morning or evening, it was all the same—she noticed nothing."

"Did the blindness come on gradually?"

"Yes, sir—bit by bit, as you may say. Slowly worse and worse one week after another. She was a little better than a year old before we clearly made it out that her sight was gone."

"Was her father's sight, or her mother's sight, ever affected in any way?"

"Never, sir, that I heard of."

Mr. Sebright turned to Herr Grosse, sitting at the luncheon-table resignedly contemplating the Mayonnaise. "Do you wish to ask the nurse any questions?" he said.

Herr Grosse shrugged his shoulders, and pointed backward with his thumb at the place in which Lucilla was sitting.

"Her case is as plain to me as twos and twos make fours. Ach Gott! what do I want with the nurse?" He turned again longingly toward the Mayonnaise. "My fine appetites is going! When shall we lonch?"

Mr. Sebright dismissed Zillah with a frigid inclination of the head. His discouraging manner made me begin to feel a little uneasy. I ventured to ask if he had arrived at a conclusion yet. "Permit me to consult with my colleague before I answer you," said the impenetrable man. I roused Lucilla. She again inquired for Oscar. I said I supposed we should find him in the garden—and so took her out. Nugent followed us. I heard Herr Grosse whisper to him, piteously, as we passed the luncheon-table: "For the lofe of Heaven, come back soon, and let us lonch!" We left the ill-assorted pair to their consultation in the sitting-room.

CHAPTER THE THIRTY-FIRST.

"WHO SHALL DECIDE WHEN DOCTORS DISAGREE?"

WE had certainly not been more than ten minutes in the garden when we were startled by an extraordinary outbreak of shouting in broken English proceeding from the window of the sitting-room. "Hi-hi-hoi! hoi-hi! hoi-hi!" We looked up, and discovered Herr Grosse frantically waving a huge red silk handkerchief at the window. "Lonch! lonch!" cried the German surgeon. "The consultations is done. Come-begin-begin!"

Obedient to this peremptory summons, Lucilla, Nugent, and I returned to the sitting-room. We had, as I had foreseen, found Oscar wandering alone in the garden. He had entreated me, by a sign, not to reveal our discovery of him to Lucilla, and had hurried away to hide himself in one of the side walks. His agitation was pitiable to see. He was totally unfit to be trusted in Lucilla's presence at that anxious moment.

When we had left the oculists together I had sent Zillah with a little written message to Reverend Finch, entreating him (if it was only for form's sake) to reconsider his resolution, and be present on the all-important occasion to his daughter of the delivery of the medical opinions on her case. At the bottom of the stairs (on our return) my answer was handed to me on a slip of sermon paper. "Mr. Finch declined to submit a question of principle to any considerations dictated by mere expediency. He desired seriously to remind Madame Pratolungo of what he had already told her. In other words, he would repeat, and he would beg her to remember this time, that his Foot was down."

On re-entering the room we found the eminent oculists seated as far apart as possible one from the other. Both gentlemen were engaged in reading. Mr. Sebright was reading a book. Herr Grosse was reading the Mayonnaise.

I placed Lucilla close by me, and took her hand. It was as cold as ice. My poor dear trembled pitiably. For *her*, what moments of unutterable suffering were those moments of suspense before the surgeons delivered their sentence! I pressed her little cold hand in mine, and whispered: "Courage!" Truly, I can say it (though I am not usually one of the sentimental sort), my heart bled for her.

"Well, gentlemen," said Nugent, "what is the result? Are you both agreed?"

"No," said Mr. Sebright, putting aside his book.

"No," said Herr Grosse, ogling the Mayonnaise.

Lucilla turned her face toward me—her color shifting and changing, her bosom rising and falling more and more rapidly. I whispered to her to compose herself. "One of them, at any rate," I said, "thinks you will recover your sight."

She understood me, and became quieter directly. Nugent went on with his questions, addressed to the two oculists.

"What do you differ about?" he asked. "Will you let us hear your opinions?"

The wearisome contest of courtesy was renewed between our medical advisers. Mr. Sebright bowed to Herr Grosse: "You first." Herr Grosse bowed to Mr. Sebright: "No—you!"

My impatience broke through this cruel and ridiculous professional restraint. "Speak both together, gentlemen, if you like!" I said, sharply. "Do anything, for God's sake, but keep us in suspense! Is it, or is it not, possible to restore her sight?"

"Yes," said Herr Grosse

Lucilla sprang to her feet, with a cry of joy.

"No," said Mr. Sebright.

Lucilla dropped back again into her chair, and silently laid her head on my shoulder.

"Are you agreed about the cause of her blindness?" asked Nugent.

"Cataracts is the cause," answered Herr Grosse.

"So far, I agree," said Mr. Sebright. "Cataract is the cause."

"Cataracts is curable," pursued the German.

"I agree again," continued the Englishman — "with a reservation. Cataract is *sometimes* curable."

"*This* cataracts is curable!" cried Herr Grosse.

"With all possible deference," said Mr. Sebright, "I dispute that conclusion. The cataract in Miss Finch's case is *not* curable."

"Can you give us your reasons, sir, for saying that?" I inquired.

"My reasons are based on surgical considerations which it requires a professional training to understand," Mr. Sebright replied. "I can only tell you that I am convinced—after the most minute and careful examination — that Miss Finch's sight is irrevocably gone. Any attempt to restore it by an operation would be, in my opinion, an unwarrantable proceeding. The young lady would not only have the operation to undergo, she would be kept secluded afterward, for at least six weeks or two months, in a darkened room. During that time, it is needless for me to remind you that she would inevitably form the most confident hope of her restoration to sight. Remembering this, and believing as I do that the sacrifice demanded of her will end in failure, I think it most undesirable to expose our patient to the moral consequences of a disappointment which must seriously try her. She has been resigned from childhood to her blindness. As an honest man, who feels bound to speak out, and to speak strongly, I advise you not further to disturb that resignation. I declare it to be, in my opinion, certainly useless, and possibly dangerous, to allow her to be operated on for the restoration of her sight."

In those uncompromising words the Englishman delivered his opinion.

Lucilla's hand closed fast on mine. "Cruel! cruel!" she whispered to herself, angrily. I gave her a little squeeze, recommending patience, and looked in silent expectation (just as Nugent was looking too) at Herr Grosse. The German rose deliberately to his feet, and waddled to the place in which Lucilla and I were sitting together.

"Has goot Mr. Sebrights done?" he asked.

Mr. Sebright only replied by his everlasting, never-changing bow.

"Goot! I have now my own word to put in," said Herr Grosse. "It shall be one little word— no more. With my best compliments to Mr. Sebrights, I set up against what he only thinks what I—Grosse—with these hands of mine have done. The cataracts of miss there is a cataracts that I have cut into before, a cataracts that I have cured before. Now look!" He suddenly wheeled round to Lucilla, tucked up his cuffs, laid a forefinger of each hand on either side of her forehead, and softly turned down her eyelids with his two big thumbs. "I pledge you my word as surgeon-optic," he resumed, "my knife shall let the light in here. This lofable-nice girls shall be more lofable-nicer than ever. My pretty Feench must be first in her best goot health. She must next gif me my own ways with her—and then one, two, three—ping! my pretty Feench shall see!" He lifted Lucilla's eyelids again as he said the last word—glared fiercely at her through his spectacles—gave her the loudest kiss, on the forehead, that I ever heard given in my life—laughed till the room rang again—and returned to his post as sentinel on guard over the Mayonnaise. "Now," cried Herr Grosse, cheerfully, "the talkings is all done. Gott be thanked, the eatings may begin!"

Lucilla left her chair for the second time.

"Herr Grosse," she said, "where are you?"

"Here, my dears."

She crossed the room to the table at which he was sitting, already occupied in carving his favorite dish.

"Did you say you must use a knife to make me see?" she asked, quite calmly.

"Yes, yes. Don't you be frightened of that. Not much pains to bear—not much pains."

She tapped him smartly on the shoulder with her hand.

"Get up, Herr Grosse," she said. "If you have your knife about you, here am I—do it at once!"

Nugent started. Mr. Sebright started. Her daring amazed them both. As for me, I am the greatest coward living, in the matter of surgical operations performed on myself or on others. Lucilla terrified me. I ran headlong across the room to her. I was even fool enough to scream.

Before I could reach her Herr Grosse had risen, obedient to command, with a choice morsel of chicken on the end of his fork. "You charming little fools," he said, "I don't cut into cataracts in such a hurry as that. I perform but one operations on you to-day. It is this!" He unceremoniously popped the morsel of chicken into Lucilla's mouth. "Aha! Bite him well. He is nice-goot! Now, then! Sit down all of you. Lonch! lonch!"

He was irresistible. We all sat down at table.

The rest of us ate. Herr Grosse gobbled. From Mayonnaise to marmalade tart. From marmalade tart back again to Mayonnaise. From Mayonnaise forward again to ham sandwiches and blanc-mange; and then back once more (on the word of an honest woman) to Mayonnaise! His drinking was on the same scale as his eating. Beer, wine, brandy—nothing came amiss to him: he mixed them all. As for the lighter elements in the feast—the almonds and raisins, the preserved ginger and the crystallized fruits—he ate them as accompaniments to everything. A dish of olives especially won his favor. He plunged both hands into it, and deposited his fistfuls of olives in the pockets of his trousers. "In this ways," he explained, "I shall trouble nobody to pass the dish—I shall have by me continually all the olives that I want." When he could eat and drink no more, he rolled up his napkin into a ball, and became devoutly thankful. "How goot of Gott," he remarked, "when he invented the worlds to invent eatings and drinkings too! Ah!" sighed Herr Grosse, gently laying his outspread fingers on the pit of his stomach, "what immense happiness there is in This!"

Mr. Sebright looked at his watch.

"If there is anything more to be said on the question of the operation," he announced, "it must be said at once. We have barely five minutes more to spare. You have heard my opinion. I hold to it."

Herr Grosse took a pinch of snuff. "I also," he said, "hold to mine."

Lucilla turned toward the place from which Mr. Sebright had spoken.

"I am obliged to you, sir, for your opinion," she said, very quietly and firmly. "I am determined to try the operation. If it does fail, it will only leave me what I am now. If it succeeds, it gives me a new life. I will bear anything and risk anything on the chance that I may see."

So she announced her decision. In those memorable words she cleared the way for the coming Event in her life and in our lives which it is the purpose of these pages to record.

Mr. Sebright answered her, in Mr. Sebright's discreet way.

"I cannot affect to be surprised at your decision," he said. "However sincerely I may regret it, I admit that it is the natural decision in your case."

Lucilla addressed herself next to Herr Grosse.

"Choose your own day," she said. "The sooner the better. To-morrow, if you can."

"Answer me one little thing, miss," rejoined the German, with a sudden gravity of tone and manner, which was quite new in our experience of him. "Do you mean what you say?"

She answered him gravely on her side. "I mean what I say."

"Goot. There is times, my lofe, to be funny. There is also times to be grave. It is grave times now. I have my last word to say to you before I go."

With his wild black eyes staring through his owlish spectacles at Lucilla's face, speaking earnestly in his strange broken English, he now impressed on his patient the necessity of gravely considering and preparing for the operation which he had undertaken to perform. I was greatly relieved by the tone he took with her. He spoke with authority; she would be obliged to listen to *him*.

In the first place, he warned Lucilla, if the operation failed, that there would be no possibility of returning to it and trying it again. Once done, be the results what they might, it was done for good.

In the second place, before he would consent to operate, he must insist on certain conditions, essential to success, being rigidly complied with on the part of the patient and her friends. Mr. Sebright had by no means exaggerated the length of the time of trial which would follow the operation, in the darkened room. Under no circumstances could she hope to have her eyes uncovered, even for a few moments, to the light, after a shorter interval than six weeks. During the whole of that time, and probably during another six weeks to follow, it was absolutely necessary that she should be kept in such a state of health as would assist her, constitutionally, in her gradual progress toward complete restoration of sight. If body and mind both were not preserved in their best and steadiest condition, all that his skill could do might be done in vain. Nothing to excite or to agitate her must be allowed to find its way into the quiet daily routine of her life until her medical attendant was satisfied that her sight was safe. The success of Herr Grosse's professional career had been due, in no small degree, to his rigid enforcement of these rules, founded on his own experience of the influence which a patient's general health, moral as well as physical, exercised on that patient's chance of profiting under an operation—more especially an operation on an organ so delicate as the organ of sight.

Having spoken to this effect, he appealed to Lucilla's own good sense to recognize the necessity of taking time to consider her decision, and to consult on it with her relatives and friends. In plain words, for at least three months the family arrangements must be so shaped as to enable the surgeon in attendance on her to hold the absolute power of regulating her life, and of deciding on any changes introduced into it. When she and the members of her family circle were sure of being able to comply with these conditions, Lucilla had only to write to him at his hotel in London. On the next day he would undertake to be at Dimchurch. And then and there (if he was satisfied with the state of her health at the time) he would perform the operation.

After pledging himself in those terms, Herr Grosse puffed out his remaining breath in one deep guttural "Hah!" and got briskly on his short legs. At the same moment Zillah knocked at the door, and announced that the chaise was waiting for the two gentlemen at the rectory gate.

Mr. Sebright rose—in some doubt, apparently, whether his colleague had done talking. "Don't let me hurry you," he said. "I have business in London; and I must positively catch the next train."

"Soh! I have my business in London too," answered his brother oculist—"the business of pleasure." (Mr. Sebright looked scandalized at the frankness of this confession, coming from a professional man.) "I am so passion-fond of musics," Herr Grosse went on, "I want to be in goot times for the opera. Ach Gott! musics is expensive in England! I climb to the gallery, and pay my five silver shillingses even there. For five copper pences, in my own country, I can get the same thing—only better done. From the deep bottoms of my heart," proceeded this curious man, taking a cordial leave of me, "I thank you, dear madam, for the Mayonnaise. When I come again, I pray you more of that lofely dish." He turned to Lucilla and popped his thumbs on her eyelids for the last time at parting. "My sweet-Feench, remember what your surgeon-optic has said to you. I shall let the light in here—but in my own way, at my own time. Pretty lofe! Ah, how infinitely much prettier she will be when she can see!" He took Lucilla's hand, and put it sentimentally inside the collar of his waistcoat, over the region of the heart, laying his other hand upon it as if he was keeping it warm. In this tender attitude he blew a prodigious sigh, recovered himself with a shake of his shock-head, winked at me through his spectacles, and waddled out after Mr. Sebright, who was already at the bottom of the stairs. Who would have guessed that this man held the key which was to open for my blind Lucilla the gates of a new life!

CHAPTER THE THIRTY-SECOND.

ALAS FOR THE MARRIAGE!

WE were left together: Nugent having accompanied the two oculists to the garden gate.

Now that we were alone, Oscar's absence could hardly fail to attract Lucilla's attention. Just as she was referring to him, in terms which made it no easy task for me to quiet her successfully, we were interrupted by the screams of the baby, ascending from the garden below. I ran to the window and looked out.

Mrs. Finch had actually effected her desperate purpose of waylaying the two surgeons in the interests of "baby's eyes." There she was, in a skirt and a shawl—with her novel dropped in one part of the lawn, and her handkerchief in the other—pursuing the oculists on their way to the chaise. Reckless of appearances, Herr Grosse

had taken to his heels. He was retreating from
the screeching infant (with his fingers stuffed
into his ears) as fast as his short legs would let
him. Nugent was ahead of him, hurrying on
to open the garden gate. Respectable Mr. Sebright (professionally incapable of running)
brought up the rear. At short intervals Mrs.
Finch, close on his heels, held up the baby for
inspection. At short intervals Mr. Sebright
held up his hands in polite protest. Nugent,
roaring with laughter, threw open the garden
gate. Herr Grosse rushed through the opening
and disappeared. Mr. Sebright followed Herr
Grosse; and Mrs. Finch attempted to follow Mr.
Sebright—when a new personage appeared on
the scene. Startled in the sanctuary of his study
by the noise, the rector himself strutted into the
garden, and brought his wife to a sudden standstill, by inquiring in his deepest bass notes,
"What does this unseemly disturbance mean?"

The chaise drove off; and Nugent closed the
garden gate.

Some words, inaudible to my ears, passed between Nugent and the rector—referring, as I
could only suppose, to the visit of the two departing surgeons. After a while Mr. Finch
turned away (to all appearance offended by
something which had been said to him), and
addressed himself to Oscar, who now reappeared
on the lawn, having evidently only waited to
show himself until the chaise drove away. The
rector fraternally took his arm; and, beckoning
to his wife with the other hand, took Mrs.

Finch's arm next.   Majestically marching back
to the house between the two, Reverend Finch
asserted himself and his authority alternately,
now to Oscar and now to his wife. His big
booming voice reached my ears distinctly, accompanied in sharp discord by the last wailings
of the exhausted child.

In these terrible words the Pope of Dimchurch
began:

"Oscar! you are to understand distinctly, if
you please, that I maintain my protest against
this impious attempt to meddle with my afflicted
daughter's sight.—Mrs. Finch! *you* are to understand that I excuse your unseemly pursuit of
two strange surgeons in consideration of the state
that I find you in at this moment. After your
last confinement but eight you became, I remember, hysterically irresponsible. Hold your
tongue. You are hysterically irresponsible now.
—Oscar! I decline, in justice to myself, to be present at any discussion which may follow the visit
of these two professional persons. But I am not
averse to advising you for your own good. My
Foot is down. Put *your* foot down too.—Mrs.
Finch! how long is it since you ate last! Two
hours? Are you sure it is two hours? Very
good. You require a sedative application. I
order you, medically, to get into a warm bath,
and stay there till I come to you.—Oscar! you
are deficient, my good fellow, in moral weight.
Endeavor to oppose yourself resolutely to any
scheme, on the part of my unhappy daughter or
of those who advise her, which involves more

MRS. FINCH HELD UP THE BABY FOR INSPECTION.—POOR MISS FINCH, Vol. XV., page 323.

expenditure of money in fees, and new appearances of professional persons.—Mrs. Finch! the temperature is to be ninety-eight, and the position partially recumbent.—Oscar! I authorize you (if you can't stop it in any other way) to throw My moral weight into the scale. You are free to say 'I oppose This, with Mr. Finch's approval; I am, so to speak, backed by Mr. Finch.' —Mrs Finch! I wish you to understand the object of the bath. Hold your tongue. The object is to produce a gentle action on your skin. One of the women is to keep her eye on your forehead. The instant she perceives an appearance of moisture she is to run for me.—Oscar! you will let me know at what decision they arrive upstairs in my daughter's room. Not after they have merely heard what *you* have to say, but after My Moral Weight has been thrown into the scale. —Mrs. Finch! on leaving the bath, I shall have you only lightly clothed. I forbid, with a view to your head, all compression, whether of stays or strings, round the waist. I forbid garters— with the same object. You will abstain from tea and talking. You will lie, loose, on your back. You will—"

What else this unhappy woman was to do I failed to hear. Mr. Finch disappeared with her round the corner of the house. Oscar waited at the door of our side of the rectory until Nugent joined him on their way back to the sitting-room in which we were expecting their return.

After an interval of a few minutes the brothers appeared.

Throughout the whole of the time during which the surgeons had been in the house I had noticed that Nugent persisted in keeping himself scrupulously in the background. Having assumed the responsibility of putting the serious question of Lucilla's sight scientifically to the test, he appeared to be resolved to pause there, and to interfere no further in the affair after it had passed its first stage. And now again, when we were met in our little committee to discuss, and possibly to combat, Lucilla's resolution to proceed to extremities, he once more refrained from interfering actively with the matter in hand.

"I have brought Oscar back with me," he said to Lucilla, "and I have told him how widely the two oculists differ in opinion on your case. He knows also that you have decided on being guided by the more favorable view taken by Herr Grosse—and he knows no more."

There he stopped abruptly, and seated himself apart from us, at the lower end of the room.

Lucilla instantly appealed to Oscar to explain his conduct.

"Why have you kept out of the way?" she asked. "Why have you not been with me at the most important moment of my life?"

"Because I felt your anxious position too keenly," Oscar answered. "Don't think me inconsiderate toward you, Lucilla. If I had not kept away, I might not have been able to control myself."

I thought that reply far too dexterous to have

come from Oscar on the spur of the moment.
Besides, he looked at his brother when he said
the last words. It seemed more than likely—
short as the interval had been before they appeared in the sitting-room—that Nugent had
been advising Oscar, and had been telling him
what to say.

Lucilla received his excuses with the readiest
grace and kindness.

"Mr. Sebright tells me, Oscar, that my sight
is hopelessly gone," she said. "Herr Grosse answers for it that an operation will make me see.
Need I tell you which of the two I believe in?
If I could have had my own way, Herr Grosse
should have operated on my eyes before he went
back to London."

"Did he refuse?"

"Yes."

"Why?"

Lucilla told him of the reasons which the German oculist had stated as unanswerable reasons
for delay. Oscar listened attentively, and looked
at his brother again before he replied.

"As I understand it," he said, "if you decide
on risking the operation at once, you decide on
undergoing six weeks' imprisonment in a darkened room, and on placing yourself entirely at
the surgeon's disposal for six weeks more after
that. Have you considered, Lucilla, that this
means putting off our marriage *again* for at
least three months?"

"If you were in my place, Oscar, you would
let nothing, not even your marriage, stand in

the way of your restoration to sight. Don't ask me to consider, love. I can consider nothing but the prospect of seeing You!"

That fearlessly frank confession silenced him. He happened to be sitting opposite to the glass, so that he could see his face. The poor wretch abruptly moved his chair, so as to turn his back on it.

I looked at Nugent, and surprised him trying to catch his brother's eye. Prompted by him, as I could now no longer doubt, Oscar had laid his finger on a certain domestic difficulty which I had had in my mind from the moment when the question of the operation had been first agitated among us.

(The marriage of Oscar and Lucilla—it is here necessary to explain—had encountered another obstacle, and undergone a new delay, in consequence of the dangerous illness of Lucilla's aunt. Miss Batchford, invited to the ceremony as a matter of course, had most considerately sent a message begging that the marriage might not be deferred on her account. Lucilla, however, had refused to allow her wedding to be celebrated while the woman who had been a second mother to her lay at the point of death. The rector (with an eye to rich Miss Batchford's money) had supported his daughter's decision, and Oscar had been compelled to submit. These domestic events had taken place about three weeks since; and we were now in receipt of news which not only assured us of the old lady's recovery, but informed us also that she would be well enough to make

one of the wedding-party in a fortnight's time.
The bride's dress was in the house; the bride's
father was ready to officiate—and here, like a
fatality, was the question of the operation unexpectedly starting up, and threatening another
delay yet for a period which could not possibly
be shorter than a period of three months! Add
to this, if you please, a new element of embarrassment as follows. Supposing Lucilla to persist in her resolution, and Oscar to persist in
concealing from her the personal change in him
produced by the medical treatment of the fits,
what would happen? Nothing less than this:
Lucilla, if the operation succeeded, would find
out for herself—before instead of after her marriage—the deception that had been practiced on
her. And how she might resent that deception,
thus discovered, the cleverest person among us
could not pretend to foresee. There was our
situation, as we sat in domestic parliament assembled, when the surgeons had left us!)

Finding it impossible to attract his brother's
attention, Nugent had no alternative but to interfere actively for the first time.

"Let me suggest, Lucilla," he said, "that it
is your duty to look at the other side of the
question before you make up your mind. In
the first place, it is surely hard on Oscar to post-
pone the wedding-day again. In the second
place, clever as he is, Herr Grosse is not infal-
lible. It is just possible that the operation may
fail, and that you may find you have put off your
marriage for three months to no purpose. Do

think of it! If you defer the operation on your
eyes till after your marriage, you conciliate all
interests, and you only delay by a month or so
the time when you may see."

Lucilla impatiently shook her head.

"If you were blind," she answered, "you would
not willingly delay by a single hour the time
when you might see. You ask me to think of
it. I ask *you* to think of the years I have lost.
I ask *you* to think of the exquisite happiness I
shall feel when Oscar and I are standing at the
altar, if I can *see* the husband to whom I am
giving myself for life! Put it off for a month?
You might as well ask me to die for a month.
It is like death to be sitting here blind, and to
know that a man is within a few hours' reach
of me who can give me my sight! I tell you
all plainly, if you go on opposing me in this, I
don't answer for myself. If Herr Grosse is not
recalled to Dimchurch, before the end of the
week—I am my own mistress—I will go to him
in London!"

Both the brothers looked at me.

"Have you nothing to say, Madame Pratolungo?" asked Nugent.

Oscar was too painfully agitated to speak.
He softly crossed to my chair; and, kneeling
by me, put my hand entreatingly to his lips.

You may consider me a heartless woman if
you will. I remained entirely unmoved even
by this. Lucilla's interests and my interests,
you will observe, were now one. I had resolved,
from the first, that she should not be married in

ignorance of which was the man who was disfigured by the blue face. If she took the course
which would enable her to make that discovery
for herself, at the right time, she would spare
me the performance of a very painful and ungracious duty, and she would marry, as I was determined she should marry, with a full knowledge of the truth. In this position of affairs
it was no business of mine to join the twin
brothers in trying to make her alter her resolution. On the contrary, it was my business
to confirm her in it.

"I can't see that I have any right to interfere," I said. "In Lucilla's place—after one-
and-twenty years of blindness — I too should
sacrifice every other consideration to the consideration of recovering my sight."

Oscar instantly rose, offended with me, and
walked away to the window. Lucilla's face
brightened gratefully. "Ah!" she said, "*you*
understand me!" Nugent, in his turn, left his
chair. He had confidently calculated, in his
brother's interests, on Lucilla's marriage preceding the recovery of Lucilla's sight. That
calculation was completely baffled. The marriage would now depend on the state of Lucilla's
feelings after she had penetrated the truth for
herself. I saw Nugent's face darken as he
walked to the door.

"Madame Pratolungo," he said, "you may,
one day, regret the course you have just taken.
Do as you please, Lucilla—I have no more to
say."

He left the room, with a quiet submission to circumstances which became him admirably. Now, as always, it was impossible not to compare him advantageously with his vacillating brother. Oscar turned round at the window, apparently with the idea of following Nugent out. At the first step he checked himself. There was a last effort still left to make. Reverend Finch's "moral weight" had not been thrown into the scale yet.

"There is one thing more, Lucilla," he said, "which you ought to know before you decide. I have seen your father. He desires me to tell you that he is strongly opposed to the experiment which you are determined to try."

Lucilla sighed wearily. "It is not the first time that I find my father failing to sympathize with me," she said. "I am distressed—but not surprised. It is *you* who surprise me!" she added, suddenly raising her voice. "You, who love me, are not one with me, when I am standing on the brink of a new life. Good Heavens! are my interests not your interests in this? Is it not worth your while to wait till I can *look at you* when I vow before God to love, honor, and obey you? Do you understand him?" she asked, appealing abruptly to me. "Why does he try to start difficulties? why is he not as eager about it as I am?"

I turned to Oscar. Now was the time for him to fall at her feet and own it! Here was the golden opportunity that might never come again. I signed to him impatiently to take it. He tried to take it—let me do him the justice now which I failed to do him at the time—he tried to take it. He advanced toward her; he struggled with himself; he said, "There is a motive for my conduct, Lucilla—" and stopped. His breath failed him; he struggled again; he forced out a word or two more: "A motive," he went on, "which I have been afraid to confess—" He paused again, with the perspiration pouring over his livid face.

Lucilla's patience failed her. "What is your motive?" she asked, sharply.

The tone in which she spoke broke down his last reserves of resolution. He turned his head suddenly so as not to see her. At the final moment—miserable, miserable man!—at the final moment he took refuge in an excuse.

"I don't believe in Herr Grosse," he said, faintly, "as you believe in him."

Lucilla rose, bitterly disappointed, and opened the door that led into her own room.

"If it had been you who were blind," she answered, "*your* belief would have been *my* belief, and *your* hope *my* hope. It seems I have expected too much from you. Live and learn! live and learn!"

She went into her room and closed the door on us. I could bear it no longer. I got up, with the firm resolution in me to follow her and say the words he had failed to say for himself. My hand was on the door, when I was suddenly pulled back from it by Oscar. I turned and faced him in silence.

"No!" he said, with his eyes fixed on mine, and his hand still on my arm. "If I don't tell her, nobody shall tell her for me."

"She shall be deceived no longer—she must and shall hear it," I answered. "Let me go!"

"You have given me your promise to wait for my leave before you open your lips. I forbid you to open your lips."

I snapped the fingers of my hand that was free in his face. "*That* for my promise!" I said. "Your contemptible weakness is putting her happiness in peril as well as yours." I turned my head toward the door, and called to her. "Lucilla!"

His hand closed fast on my arm. Some lurking devil in him that I had never seen yet leaped up and looked at me out of his eyes.

"Tell her," he whispered, savagely, between his teeth, "and I will contradict you to your face! If you are desperate, I am desperate too. I don't care what meanness I am guilty of! I will deny it on my honor; I will deny it on my oath. You heard what she said about you at Browndown. She will believe *me* before *you*."

Lucilla opened her door, and stood waiting on the threshold.

"What is it?" she asked, quietly.

A moment's glance at Oscar warned me that he would do what he had threatened if I persisted in my resolution. The desperation of a weak man is, of all desperations, the most unscrupulous and the most unmanageable—when it is once roused. Angry as I was, I shrank from degrading him, as I must now have degraded him if I matched my obstinacy against his. In mercy to both of them, I gave way.

"I may be going out, my dear, before it gets dark," I said to Lucilla. "Can I do anything for you in the village?"

"Yes," she said; "if you will wait a little, you can take a letter for me to the post."

She went back into her room and closed the door.

I neither looked at Oscar nor spoke to him when we were alone again. He was the first who broke the silence.

"You have remembered your promise to me," he said. "You have done well."

"I have nothing more to say to you," I answered. "I shall go to my room."

His eyes followed me uneasily as I walked to the door.

"I shall speak to her," he muttered, doggedly, "at my own time."

A wise woman would not have allowed him to irritate her into saying another word. Alas! I am not a wise woman—that is to say, not always.

"Your own time?" I repeated, with the whole force of my contempt. "If you don't own the truth to her before the German surgeon comes back, your time will have gone by forever. He has told us, in the plainest terms, when once the operation is performed nothing must be said to agitate or distress her for months afterward. The preservation of her tranquillity is the condition of the recovery of her sight. You will soon have an excuse for your silence, Mr. Oscar Dubourg!"

The tone in which I said those last words stung him to some purpose.

"Spare your sneers, you heartless Frenchwoman!" he broke out, angrily. "I don't care how I stand in *your* estimation. Lucilla loves me. Nugent feels for me."

My vile. temper instantly hit on the most merciless answer I could make him in return.

"Ah, poor Lucilla!" I said. "What a much happier prospect hers might have been! What a thousand, thousand pities it is that she is not going to marry your brother instead of marrying *you!*"

He winced under that reply as if I had cut him with a knife. His head dropped on his breast. He started back from me like a beaten dog, and suddenly and silently left the room.

I had not been a minute by myself before my anger cooled. I tried to keep it hot; I tried to remember that he had aspersed my nation in calling me a "heartless Frenchwoman." No! it was not to be done. In spite of myself I repented what I had said to him.

In a moment I was out on the stairs to try if I could overtake him.

I was too late. I heard the garden gate bang before I was out of the house. Twice I approached the gate to follow him. And twice I drew back in the fear of making bad worse. It ended in my return to the sitting-room, very seriously dissatisfied with myself.

The first welcome interruption to my solitude came, not from Lucilla, but from the old nurse. Zillah appeared with a letter for me: left that moment at the rectory by the servant from Browndown. The direction was in Oscar's handwriting. I opened the envelope and read these words:

"MADAME PRATOLUNGO—You have distressed and pained me more than I can say. There are faults, and serious ones, on my side, I know. I heartily beg your pardon for anything that I may have said or done to offend you. I cannot submit to your hard verdict on me. If you knew how I adore Lucilla, you would make allowances for me—you would understand me better than you do. I cannot get your last cruel words out of my ears. I cannot meet you again without some explanation of them. You stabbed me to the heart when you said this evening that it would be a happier prospect for Lucilla if she had been going to marry my brother instead of marrying me. I hope you did not really mean that? Will you please write and tell me whether you did or not?
"OSCAR."

Write and tell him! It was absurd enough— when we were within a few minutes' walk of each other—that Oscar should prefer the cold formality of a letter to the friendly ease of a personal interview. Why could he not have called and spoken to me? We should have made it up together far more comfortably in that way —and in half the time. At any rate, I determined to go to Browndown, and be good friends again, vivâ voce, with this poor, weak, well-meaning, ill-judging boy. Was it not monstrous to have attached serious meaning to what Oscar had said when he was in a panic of nervous terror! His tone of writing so keenly distressed me that I resented his letter on that very account. It was one of the chilly evenings of an English June. A small fire was burning in the grate. I crumpled up the letter, and threw it, as I supposed, into the fire. (After-events showed that I only threw it into a corner of the fender instead.) Then I put on my hat, without stopping to think of Lucilla, or of what she was writing for the post, and ran off to Browndown.

Where do you think I found him? Locked up in his own room! His insane shyness—it was really nothing less—made him shrink from that very personal explanation which (with such a temperament as mine) was the only possible explanation under the circumstances. I had to threaten him with forcing his door before I could get him to show himself and take my hand.

Once face to face with him, I soon set things right. I really believe he had been half mad with his own self-imposed troubles when he had threatened giving me the lie at the door of Lucilla's room.

It is needless to dwell on what took place between us. I shall only say here that I had serious reason, at a later time—as you will soon see —to regret not having humored Oscar's request that I should reconcile myself to him by writing, instead of by word of mouth. If I had only placed on record, in pen and ink, what I actually said in the way of making atonement to him, I might have spared some suffering to myself and to others. As it was, the only proof that I had absolved myself in his estimation consisted in his cordially shaking hands with me at the door when I left him.

"Did you meet Nugent?" he asked, as he walked with me across the inclosure in front of the house.

I had gone to Browndown by a short-cut at the back of the garden, instead of going through the village. Having mentioned this, I asked if Nugent had returned to the rectory.

"He went back to see you," said Oscar.

"Why?"

"Only his usual kindness. He takes your views of things. He laughed when he heard I had sent a letter to you, and he ran off (dear fellow!) to see you on my behalf. You must have met him if you had come here by the village."

On getting back to the rectory I questioned Zillah. Nugent, in my absence, had run up into the sitting-room; had waited there a few minutes alone, on the chance of my return; had got tired of waiting, and had gone away again. I inquired about Lucilla next. A few minutes after Nugent had gone she had left her room, and she too had asked for me. Hearing that I was not to be found in the house, she had given Zillah a letter to post, and had then returned to her bed-chamber.

I happened to be standing by the hearth looking into the dying fire while the nurse was speaking. Not a vestige of Oscar's letter to me (as I now well remember) was to be seen. In my position, the plain conclusion was that I had really done what I supposed myself to have done —that is to say, thrown the letter into the flames.

Entering Lucilla's room, soon afterward, to make my apologies for having forgotten to wait and take her letter to the post, I found her, weary enough after the events of the day, getting ready for bed.

"I don't wonder at your being tired of waiting for me," she said. "Writing is long, long work for *me*. But this was a letter which I felt bound to write myself if I could. Can you guess who I am corresponding with? It is done, my dear! I have written to Herr Grosse!"

"Already!"

"What is there to wait for? What is there left to determine on? I have told Herr Grosse that our family consultation is over, and that I am entirely at his disposal for any length of time he may think right. And I warn him, if he attempts to put it off, that he will be only forcing on me the inconvenience of going to him in London. I have expressed that part of my letter strongly, I can tell you! He will get it to-morrow by the afternoon post. And the next day— if he is a man of his word—he will be here."

"Oh, Lucilla! not to operate on your eyes?"

"Yes—to operate on my eyes!"

CHAPTER THE THIRTY-THIRD.

THE DAY BETWEEN.

THE interval day before the second appearance of Herr Grosse, and the experiment on Lucilla's sight that was to follow it, was marked by two incidents which ought to be noticed in this place. The first incident was the arrival, early in the morning, of another letter addressed to me privately by Oscar Dubourg. Like many other shy people, he had a perfect mania, where any embarrassing circumstances were concerned, for explaining himself, with difficulty, by means of his pen, in preference to explaining himself, with ease, by means of his tongue.

Oscar's present communication informed me that he had left us for London by the first morning train, and that his object in taking this sudden journey was to state his present position toward Lucilla to a gentleman especially conversant with the peculiarities of blind people. In plain words, he had resolved on applying to Mr. Sebright for advice.

"I like Mr. Sebright" (Oscar wrote) "as cordially as I detest Herr Grosse. The short conversation I had with him has left me with the pleasantest impression of his delicacy and his kindness. If I freely reveal to this skillful surgeon the sad situation in which I am placed, I believe his experience will throw an entirely new

light on the present state of Lucilla's mind, and
on the changes which we may expect to see produced in her if she really does recover her sight.
The result may be of incalculable benefit in
teaching me how I may own the truth most
harmlessly to her as well as to myself. Pray
don't suppose I undervalue your advice. I only
want to be doubly fortified, before I risk my confession, by the advice of a scientific man."

All this I took to mean, in plain English, that
vacillating Oscar wanted to quiet his conscience
by gaining time, and that his absurd idea of
consulting Mr. Sebright was nothing less than
a new and plausible excuse for putting off the
evil day. His letter ended by pledging me to
secrecy, and by entreating me so to manage matters as to grant him a private interview on his
return to Dimchurch by the evening train.

I confess I felt some curiosity as to what would
come of the proposed consultation between un-
ready Oscar and precise Mr. Sebright; and I
accordingly arranged to take my walk alone, toward eight o'clock that evening, on the road that
led to the distant railway station.

The second incident of the day may be described as a confidential conversation between
Lucilla and myself on the subject which now
equally absorbed us both—the momentous subject of her restoration to the blessing of sight.

She joined me at the breakfast-table, with her
ready distrust newly excited, poor thing, by Oscar. He had accounted to her for his journey to

London by putting forward the commonplace excuse of "business." She instantly suspected (knowing how he felt about it) that he was secretly bent on interfering with the performance of the operation by Herr Grosse. I contrived to compose the anxiety thus aroused in her mind by informing her, on Oscar's own authority, that he personally disliked and distrusted the German oculist. "Whatever else he may do in London," I said, "make your mind easy, my dear. I answer for his not venturing near Herr Grosse."

After a long silence between us, following on those words, Lucilla raised her head from her second cup of tea, and abruptly referred to Oscar in another way—a way which revealed to me a new peculiarity of feeling belonging exclusively to the strange temperament of the blind.

"Do you know one thing?" she said. "If I had not been going to be married to Oscar, I doubt if I should have cared to put any oculist, native or foreign, to the trouble of coming to Dimchurch."

"I don't think I understand you," I answered. "You cannot surely mean to say that you would not have been glad, under any circumstances, to recover the use of your eyes?"

"That is just what I do mean to say," she rejoined.

"What! you, who have been blind from your infancy, don't care to see?"

"I only care to see Oscar. And what is more, I only care to see *him* because I am in love with him. But for that, I really don't feel as if it would give me any particular pleasure to use my eyes. I have been blind so long, I have learned to do without them."

"Impossible! My dear Lucilla, I really cannot believe you are in earnest in talking in that way!"

She laughed, and finished her tea.

"You people who can see," she said, "attach such an absurd importance to your eyes! I set my touch, my dear, against your eyes, as much the most trustworthy and much the most intelligent sense of the two. If Oscar was not, as I have said, the uppermost feeling with me, shall I tell you what I should have infinitely preferred to recovering my sight—supposing it could have been done?" She shook her head with a comic resignation to circumstances. "Unfortunately, it can't be done."

"What can't be done?"

She suddenly held out both her arms over the breakfast-table.

"The stretching out of *these* to an enormous and unheard-of length. That is what I should have liked!" she answered. "I could find out better what was going on at a distance with my hands than you could with your eyes and your telescopes. What doubts I might set at rest for instance, about the planetary system, among the people who can see, if I could only stretch out far enough to touch the stars!"

"This is talking sheer nonsense, Lucilla."

"Is it? Just tell me which knows best in the

dark—my touch or your eyes? Who has got a
sense that she can always trust to serve her
equally well through the whole four-and-twenty
hours? You or me? But for Oscar—to speak in
sober earnest this time—I tell you I would much
rather perfect the sense in me that I have already got than have a sense given to me that
I have *not* got. Until I knew Oscar I don't
think I ever honestly envied any of you the use
of your eyes."

"You astonish me, Lucilla!"

She rattled her teaspoon impatiently in her
empty cup.

"Can you always trust to your eyes, even in
broad daylight?" she burst out. "How often
do they deceive you in the simplest things! What
did I hear you all disputing about the other day
in the garden? You were looking at some
view?"

"Yes, at the view down the alley of trees at
the other end of the churchyard wall."

"Some object in the alley had attracted general notice—had it not?"

"Yes, an object at the further end of it."

"I heard you up here. You all differed in
opinion, in spite of your wonderful eyes. My
father said it moved. You said it stood still.
Oscar said it was a man. Mrs. Finch said it
was a calf. Nugent ran off and examined this
amazing object at close quarters. And what did
it turn out to be? A stump of an old tree, blown
across the road in the night! Why am I to envy
people the possession of a sense which plays them

such tricks as that? No! no! Herr Grosse is going to 'cut into my cataracts,' as he calls it— because I am going to be married to a man I love; and I fancy, like a fool, I may love him better still if I can see him. I may be quite wrong," she added, archly. "It may end in my not loving him half as well as I do now."

I thought of Oscar's face, and felt a sickening fear that she might be speaking far more seriously than she suspected. I tried to change the subject. No! Her imaginative nature had found its way into a new region of speculation before I could open my lips.

"I associate light," she said, thoughtfully, "with all that is beautiful and heavenly, and dark with all that is vile and horrible and devilish. I wonder how light and dark will look to me when I see?"

"I believe they will astonish you," I answered, "by being entirely unlike what you fancy them to be now."

She started. I had alarmed her without intending it.

"Will Oscar's face be utterly unlike what I fancy it to be now?" she asked, in suddenly altered tones. "Do you mean to say that I have not had the right image of him in my mind all this time?"

I tried again to draw her off to another topic. What more could I do, with my tongue tied by the German's warning to us not to agitate her in the face of the operation to be performed on the next day?

It was quite useless. She went on, as before, without heeding me.

"Have I no means of judging rightly what Oscar is like?" she said. "I touch my own face; I know how long it is, and how broad it is; I know how big the different features are, and where they are. And then I touch Oscar, and compare his face with my knowledge of my own face. Not a single detail escapes me. I see him in my mind as plainly as you see me across this table. Do you mean to say, when I see him with my eyes, that I shall discover something perfectly new to me? I don't believe it!" She started up impatiently, and took a turn in the room. "Oh!" she exclaimed, with a stamp of her foot, "why can't I take laudanum enough or chloroform enough to kill me for the next six weeks, and then come to life again when the German takes the bandage off my eyes!" She sat down once more, and drifted all on a sudden into a question of pure morality. "Tell me this," she said. "Is the gravest virtue the virtue which it is most difficult to practice?"

"I suppose so," I answered.

She drummed with both hands on the table, petulantly, viciously, as hard as she could. "Then, Madame Pratolungo," she said, "the greatest of all the virtues is—Patience. Oh, my friend, how I hate the greatest of all the virtues at this moment!"

That ended it—there the conversation found its way into other topics at last.

Thinking afterward of the strange things which

Lucilla had said to me, I derived one consolation from what had passed at the breakfast-table. If Mr. Sebright proved to be right, and if the operation failed, after all, I had Lucilla's word for it that blindness, of itself, is not the terrible affliction to the blind which the rest of us fancy it to be—because we can see.

Toward half-past seven in the evening I went out alone, as I had planned, to meet Oscar on his return from London.

At a long straight stretch of the road I saw him advancing toward me. He was walking more rapidly than usual, and singing as he walked. Even through its livid discoloration the poor fellow's face looked radiant with happiness as he came nearer. He waved his walking-stick exultingly in the air. "Good news!" he called out at the top of his voice. "Mr. Sebright has made me a happy man again!" I had never before seen him so like Nugent in manner as I now saw him when we met and he shook hands with me.

"Tell me all about it," I said.

He gave me his arm; and, talking all the way, we walked back slowly to Dimchurch.

"In the first place," he began, "Mr. Sebright holds to his own opinion more firmly than ever. He feels absolutely certain that the operation will fail."

"Is that your good news?" I asked, reproachfully.

"No," he said. "Though, mind, I own to my shame there was a time when I almost hoped it would fail. Mr. Sebright has put me in a better frame of mind. I have little or nothing to dread from the success of the operation, if by any extraordinary chance it should succeed. I remind you of Mr. Sebright's opinion merely to give you a right idea of the tone which he took with me at starting. He only consented under protest to contemplate the event which Lucilla and Herr Grosse consider to be a certainty. 'If the statement of your position requires it,' he said, 'I will admit that it is barely possible she may be able to see you two months hence. Now begin.' I began by informing him of my marriage engagement."

"Shall I tell how Mr. Sebright received the information?" I said. "He held his tongue, and made you a bow."

Oscar laughed. "Quite true," he answered. "I told him next of Lucilla's extraordinary antipathy to dark people, and dark shades of color of all kinds. Can you guess what he said to me when I had done?"

I owned that my observation of Mr. Sebright's character did not extend to guessing that.

"He said it was a common antipathy in his experience of the blind. It was one among the many strange influences exercised by blindness on the mind. 'The physical affliction has its mysterious moral influence,' he said. 'We can observe it, but we can't explain it. The special antipathy which you mention is an incurable antipathy, except on one condition—the recovery of the sight.' There he stopped. I entreated

him to go on.   No! He declined to go on until
I had finished what I had to say to him first.   I
had my confession still to make to him—and I
made it."

"You concealed nothing?"

"Nothing.   I laid my weakness bare before
him.   I told him that Lucilla was still firmly
convinced that Nugent's was the discolored face
instead of mine.   And then I put the question—
What am I to do?"

"And how did he reply?"

"In these words: 'If you ask me what you are
to do in the event of her remaining blind (which
I tell you again *will* be the event), I decline to
advise you.   Your own conscience and your own
sense of honor must decide the question.   On the
other hand, if you ask me what you are to do in
the event of her recovering her sight, I can answer you unreservedly in the plainest terms.
Leave things as they are, and wait till she sees.'
Those were his own words.   Oh, the load that
they took off my mind!   I made him repeat them
—I declare I was almost afraid to trust the evidence of my own ears."

I understood the motive of Oscar's good spirits
better than I understood the motive of Mr. Sebright's advice.   "Did he give his reasons?" I
asked.

"You shall hear his reasons directly.   He insisted on first satisfying himself that I thoroughly understood my position at that moment.   'The
prime condition of success, as Herr Grosse has
told you,' he said, 'is the perfect tranquillity of

your patient. If you make your confession to
the young lady when you get back to-night to
Dimchurch, you throw her into a state of excitement which will render it impossible for my
German colleague to operate on her to-morrow.
If you defer your confession, the medical necessities of the case force you to be silent until the
professional attendance of the oculist has ceased.
There is your position! My advice to you is to
adopt the last alternative. Wait (and make the
other persons in the secret wait) until the result
of the operation has declared itself.' There I
stopped him. 'Do you mean that I am to be
present on the first occasion when she is able to
use her eyes?' I asked. 'Am I to let her see
me without a word beforehand to prepare her for
the color of my face?' "

We were now getting to the interesting part
of it. You English people, when you are out
walking and are carrying on a conversation with
your friend, never come to a standstill at the
points of interest. We foreigners, on the other
hand, invariably stop. I surprised Oscar by suddenly pulling him up in the middle of the road.

"What is the matter?" he asked.

"Go on!" I said, impatiently.

"I can't go on," he rejoined. "You're holding me."

I held him tighter than ever, and ordered him
more resolutely than ever to go on. Oscar resigned himself to a halt (foreign fashion) on the
high-road.

"Mr. Sebright met my question by putting a

question on his side," he resumed. "He asked me how I proposed to prepare her for the color of my face."

"And what did you tell him?"

"I said I had planned to make an excuse for leaving Dimchurch, and, once away, to prepare her by writing for what she might expect to see when I returned."

"What did he say to that?"

"He wouldn't hear of it. He said: 'I strongly recommend you to be present on the first occasion when she is capable (if she ever *is* capable) of using her sight. I attach the greatest importance to her being able to correct the hideous and absurd image now in her mind of a face like yours, by seeing you as you really are at the earliest available opportunity.' "

We were just walking on again when certain words in that last sentence startled me. I stopped short once more.

"Hideous and absurd image?" I repeated, thinking instantly of my conversation of that morning with Lucilla. "What did Mr. Sebright mean by using such language as that?"

"Just what I asked him. His reply will interest you. It led him into that explanation of his motives which you inquired for just now. Shall we walk on?"

My petrified foreign feet recovered their activity. We went on again.

"When I had spoken to Mr. Sebright of Lucilla's inveterate prejudice," Oscar continued, "he had surprised me by saying that it was common in his experience, and was only curable by her restoration to sight. In support of those assertions he now told me of two interesting cases which had occurred in his professional practice. The first was the case of the little daughter of an Indian officer—blind from infancy, like Lucilla. After operating successfully, the time came when he could permit his patient to try her sight—that is to say, to try if she could see sufficiently well at first to distinguish dark objects from light. Among the members of the household assembled to witness the removal of the bandage was an Indian nurse who had accompanied the family to England. The first person the child saw was her mother— a fair woman. She clasped her little hands in astonishment, and that was all. At the next turn of her head she saw the dark Indian nurse, and instantly screamed with terror. Mr. Sebright owned to me that he could not explain it. The child could have no possible association with colors. Yet there, nevertheless, was the most violent hatred and horror of a dark object (the hatred and horror peculiar to the blind) expressing itself unmistakably in a child of ten years old! My first thought, while he was telling me this, was of myself, and of my chance with Lucilla. My first question was, 'Did the child get used to the nurse?' I can give you his answer in his own words. 'In a week's time I found the child sitting in the nurse's lap as composedly as I am sitting in this chair.' That is encouraging, isn't it?"

"Most encouraging—nobody can deny it."

"The second instance was more curious still. This time the case was the case of a grown man —and the object was to show me what strange fantastic images (utterly unlike the reality) the blind form of the people about them. The patient was married, and was to see his wife (as Lucilla is one day to see me) for the first time. He had been told before he married her that she was personally disfigured by the scar of a wound on one of her cheeks. The poor woman—ah, how well I can understand her!—trembled for the consequences. The man who had loved her dearly while he was blind might hate her when he saw her scarred face. Her husband had been the first to console her when the operation was determined on. He declared that his sense of touch, and the description given to him by others, had enabled him to form, in his own mind, the most complete and faithful image of his wife's face. Nothing that Mr. Sebright could say would induce him to believe that it was physically impossible for him to form a really correct idea of any object, animate or inanimate, which he had never seen. He wouldn't hear of it. He was so certain of the result that he held his wife's hand in his, to encourage her, when the bandage was removed from him. At his first look at her he uttered a cry of horror, and fell back in his chair in a swoon. His wife, poor thing, was distracted. Mr. Sebright did his best to compose her, and waited till her husband was able to answer the questions put to him. It then appeared that his blind idea of his wife and of her disfigurement had been something so grotesque and horribly unlike the reality that it was hard to know whether to laugh or to tremble at it. She was as beautiful as an angel, by comparison with her husband's favorite idea of her—and yet, because it *was* his idea, he was absolutely disgusted and terrified at the first sight of her! In a few weeks he was able to compare his wife with other women, to look at pictures, to understand what beauty was, and what ugliness was; and from that time they have lived together as happy a married couple as any in the kingdom."

I was not quite sure which way this last example pointed. It alarmed me when I thought of Lucilla. I came to a standstill again.

"How did Mr. Sebright apply this second case to Lucilla and to you?" I asked.

"You shall hear," said Oscar. "He first appealed to the case as supporting his assertion that Lucilla's idea of me must be utterly unlike what I am myself. He asked if I was now satisfied that she could have no correct conception of what faces and colors were really like, and if I agreed with him in believing that the image in her mind of the man with the blue face was in all probability something fantastically and hideously unlike the reality. After what I had heard, I agreed with him as a matter of course. 'Very well,' says Mr. Sebright. 'Now let us remember that there is one important difference between the case of Miss Finch and the case that

I have just mentioned. The husband's blind idea of his wife was the husband's favorite idea. The shock of the first sight of her was plainly a shock to him on that account. Now Miss Finch's blind idea of the blue face is, on the contrary, a hateful idea to her—the image is an image that she loathes. Is it not fair to conclude from this that the first sight of you as you really are is likely to be, in her case, a relief to her instead of a shock? Reasoning from my experience, I reach that conclusion; and I advise you, in your own interests, to be present when the bandage is taken off. Even if I prove to be mistaken—even if she is not immediately reconciled to the sight of you—there is the other example of the child and the Indian nurse to satisfy you that it is only a question of time. Sooner or later she will take the discovery as any other young lady would take it. At first she will be indignant with you for deceiving her; and then, if you are sure of your place in her affections, she will end in forgiving you. There is my view of your position, and there are the grounds on which I form it! In the meantime my own opinion remains unshaken. I firmly believe that you will never have occasion to act on the advice that I have given to you. When the bandage is taken off, the chances are five hundred to one that she is no nearer to seeing you then than she is now.' These were his last words —and on that we parted.''

Oscar and I walked on again for a little way in silence.

I had nothing to say against Mr. Sebright's reasons; it was impossible to question the professional experience from which they were drawn. As to blind people in general, I felt no doubt that his advice was good, and that his conclusions were arrived at correctly. But Lucilla's was no ordinary character. My experience of her was better experience than Mr. Sebright's; and the more I thought of the future, the less inclined I felt to take Oscar's hopeful view. She was just the person to say something or do something, at the critical moment of the experiment, which would take the wisest previous calculation by surprise. Oscar's prospects had never looked darker to me than they looked at that moment. It would have been useless and cruel to have said to him what I have just said here. I put as bright a face on it as I could, and asked if he proposed to follow Mr Sebright's advice.

"Yes," he said. "With a certain reservation of my own, which occurred to me after I had left his house."

"May I ask what it is?"

"Certainly. I mean to beg Nugent to leave Dimchurch before Lucilla tries her sight for the first time. He will do that, I know, to please me."

"And when he has done it, what then?"

"Then I mean to be present—as Mr. Sebright suggested—when the bandage is taken off."

"Previously telling Lucilla," I interposed, "that it is you who are in the room?"

"No. There I take the precaution that I al-

luded to just now. I propose to leave Lucilla
under the impression that it is I who have left
Dimchurch, and that Nugent's face is the face
she sees. If Mr. Sebright proves to be right,
and if her first sensation is a sensation of relief,
I will own the truth to her the same day. If
not, I will wait to make my confession until she
has become reconciled to the sight of me. That
plan meets every possible emergency. It is one
of the few good ideas that my stupid head has
hit on since I have been at Dimchurch."

He said those last words with such an innocent
air of triumph that I really could not find it in
my heart to damp his ardor by telling him what
I thought of his idea. All I said was, "Don't
forget, Oscar, that the cleverest plans are at the
mercy of circumstances. At the last moment,
an accident may happen which will force you to
speak out."

We came in sight of the rectory as I gave him
that final warning. Nugent was strolling up
and down the road on the lookout for us. I left
Oscar to tell his story over again to his brother,
and went into the house.

Lucilla was at her piano when I entered the
sitting-room. She was not only playing, but (a
rare thing with her) singing too. The song was,
poetry and music both, of her own composing.
"I shall see him! I shall see him!" In those
four words the composition began and ended.
She adapted them to all the happy melodies in
her memory. She accompanied them with hands
that seemed to be mad for joy—hands that threat-

ened every moment to snap the chords of the instrument. Never, since my first day at the rectory, had I heard such a noise in our quiet
sitting-room as I heard now. She was in a fever
of exhilaration which, in my foreboding frame
of mind at that moment, it pained and shocked
me to see. I lifted her off the music-stool, and
shut up the piano by main force.

"Compose yourself, for Heaven's sake," I
said. "Do you want to be completely exhausted
when the German comes to-morrow?"

That consideration instantly checked her. She
suddenly became quiet, with the abrupt facility
of a child.

"I forgot that," she said, sitting down in a
corner, with a face of dismay. "He might refuse to perform the operation! Oh, my dear,
quiet me down somehow. Get a book and read
to me."

I got the book. Ah, the poor author! Neither
she nor I paid the slightest attention to him.
Worse still, we abused him for not interesting
us—and then shut him up with a bang, and
pushed him rudely into his place on the book-
shelf, and left him upside down, and went to bed.

She was standing at her window when I went
in to wish her good-night. The mellow moonlight fell tenderly on her lovely face. "Moon
that I have never seen," she murmured, softly,
"I feel you looking at me! Is the time coming
when *I* shall look at You?" She turned from
the window, and eagerly put my fingers on her
pulse. "Am I quite composed again?" she

asked. "Will he find me well to-morrow? Feel
it! feel it! Is it quiet now?" I felt it—throbbing faster and faster. "Sleep will quiet it," I
said, and kissed her and left her.

She slept well. As for me, I passed such a
wretched night, and got up so completely worn
out, that I had to go back to my room after
breakfast, and lie down again. Lucilla persuaded me to do it. "Herr Grosse won't be
here till the afternoon," she said. "Rest till he
comes."

We had reckoned without allowing for the
eccentric character of our German surgeon.
Excepting the business of his profession, Herr
Grosse did everything by impulse, and nothing
by rule. I had not long fallen into a broken,
unrefreshing sleep, when I felt Zillah's hand on
my shoulder, and heard Zillah's voice in my ear.

"Please to get up, ma'am! He's here—he has
come from London by the morning train."

I hurried into the sitting-room.

There, at the table, sat Herr Grosse, with an
open instrument-case before him; his wild black
eyes gloating over a hideous array of scissors,
probes, and knives, and his shabby hat hard by,
with lint and bandages huddled together anyhow
inside it. And there stood Lucilla by his side,
stooping over him—with one hand laid familiarly on his shoulder, and with the other deftly fin-
gering one of his horrid instruments to find out
what it was like!

PART THE SECOND.

CHAPTER THE THIRTY-FOURTH.

NUGENT SHOWS HIS HAND.

I CLOSED the First Part of my narrative on the day of the operation—the twenty-fifth of June.

I open the Second Part, between six and seven weeks later, on the ninth of August.

How did the time pass at Dimchurch in that interval?

Searching backward in my memory, I call to life again the domestic history of the six weeks. It looks, on retrospection, miserably dull and empty of incident. I wonder, when I contemplate it now, how we got through that weary interval—how we bore that forced inaction, that unrelieved oppression of suspense.

Changing from bedroom to sitting-room, from sitting-room back to bedroom, with the daylight always shut out, with the bandages always on except when the surgeon looked at her eyes, Lucilla bore the imprisonment—and, worse than the imprisonment, the uncertainty—of her period of probation with the courage that can endure anything, the courage sustained by Hope.   With books, with music, with talk—above all, with Love to help her—she counted her way calmly through the dull succession of hours and days till the time came which was to decide the question in dispute between the oculists—the terrible question of which of the two, Mr. Sebright or Herr Grosse, was right.

I was not present at the examination which finally decided all doubt. I joined Oscar in the garden—quite as incapable as he was of exerting the slightest self-control. We paced silently backward and forward on the lawn, like two animals in a cage. Zillah was the only witness present when the German examined our poor darling's eyes, Nugent engaging to wait in the next room and announce the result from the window. As the event turned out, Herr Grosse was beforehand with him. Once more we heard his broken English shouting, "Hi-hi-hoi! hoi-hi! hoi-hi!" Once more we beheld his huge silk handkerchief waving at the window. I turned sick and faint under the excitement of the moment—under the rapture (it was nothing less) of hearing those three electrifying words, "She will see!" Mercy! how we did abuse Mr. Sebright, when we were all reunited again in Lucilla's room!

The first excitement over, we had our difficulties to contend with next.

From the moment when she was positively informed that the operation had succeeded, our once patient Lucilla developed into a new being. She now rose in perpetual revolt against the caution which still deferred the day on which she was to be allowed to make the first trial of her sight. It required all my influence, backed by Oscar's entreaties, and strengthened by the furious foreign English of our excellent German surgeon (Herr Grosse had a temper of his own, I can tell you!) to prevent her from breaking through the medical discipline which held her in its grasp. When she became quite unmanageable, and vehemently abused him to his face, our good Grosse used to swear at her, in a compound bad language of his own, with a tremendous aspiration at the beginning of it, which alwise set matters right by making her laugh. I see him again as I write, leaving the room on these occasions, with his eyes blazing through his spectacles, and his shabby hat cocked sidewise on his head. "Soh, you little-spitfire-Feench! If you touch that bandages when I have have put him on—Ho-Damn-Damn! I say no more. Good-by!"

From Lucilla I turn to the twin brothers next.

Tranquilized as to the future, after his interview with Mr. Sebright, Oscar presented himself at his best during the time of which I am now writing. Lucilla's main reliance, in her days in the darkened room, was on what her lover could do to relieve and to encourage her. He never once failed her; his patience was perfect; his devotion was inexhaustible. It is sad to say so, in view of what happened afterward; but I only tell a necessary truth when I declare that he immensely strengthened his hold on her affections in those last days of her blindness, when his society was most precious to her. Ah, how fervently she used to talk of him when she and I were left together at night! Forgive me if I leave this part of the history of the courtship untold. I don't like to write of it—I don't like to think of it. Let us get on to something else.

Nugent comes next. I would give a great deal, poor as I am, to be able to leave him out. It is not to be done. I must write about that lost wretch, and you must read about him, whether we like it or not.

The days of Lucilla's imprisonment were also the days when my favorite disappointed me for the first time. He and his brother seemed to change places. It was Nugent now who appeared to disadvantage by comparison with Oscar. He surprised and grieved his brother by leaving Browndown. "All I can do for you, I have done," he said. "I can be of no further use for the present to anybody. Let me go. I am stagnating in this miserable place—I must and will have change." Oscar's entreaties, in Nugent's present frame of mind, failed to move him. Away he went one morning, without bidding anybody good-by. He had talked of being absent for a week—he remained away for a month. We heard of him leading a wild life among a vicious set of men. It was reported that a frantic restlessness possessed him which nobody could understand. He came back as suddenly as he had left us. His variable nature had swung round, in the interval, to the opposite extreme. He was full of repentance for his reckless conduct; he was in a state of depression which defied rousing; he despaired of himself and his future. Sometimes he talked of going back to America, and sometimes he threatened to close his career by enlisting as a private soldier. Would any other person, in my place, have seen which way these signs pointed? I doubt it, if that person's mind had been absorbed, as mine was, in watching Lucilla day by day. Even if I had been a suspicious woman by nature—which, thank God, I am not—my distrust must have lain dormant, in the all-subduing atmosphere of suspense hanging heavily on me morning, noon, and night in the darkened room.

So much, briefly, for the sayings and doings of the persons principally concerned in this narrative, during the six weeks which separate Part the First from Part the Second.

I begin again on the ninth of August.

This was the memorable day chosen by Herr Grosse for risking the experiment of removing the bandage, and permitting Lucilla to try her sight for the first time. Conceive for yourselves (don't ask me to describe) the excitement that raged in our obscure little circle, now that we were standing face to face with that grand Event in our lives which I promised to relate in the opening sentence of these pages.

I was the earliest riser at the rectory that morning. My excitable French blood was in a fever. I was irresistibly reminded of myself at a time long past—the time when my glorious Pratolungo and I, succumbing to Fate and tyrants, fled to England for safety: martyrs to that ungrateful Republic (long live the Republic!) for which I laid down my money and my husband his life.

I opened my window, and hailed the good omen of sunrise in a clear sky. Just as I was turning away again from the view, I saw a figure steal out from the shrubbery and appear on the lawn. The figure came nearer. I recognized Oscar.

"What in the world are you doing there, at this time in the morning?" I called out.

He lifted his finger to his lips, and came close under my window before he answered.

"Hush!" he said. "Don't let Lucilla hear you. Come down to me as soon as you can. I am waiting to speak to you."

When I joined him in the garden I saw directly that something had gone wrong. "Bad news from Browndown?" I asked.

"Nugent has disappointed me," he answered. "Do you remember the evening when you met me after my consultation with Mr. Sebright?"

"Perfectly."

"I told you that I meant to ask Nugent to leave Dimchurch on the day when Lucilla tried her sight for the first time."

"Well?"

"Well—he refuses to leave Dimchurch."

"Have you explained your motives to him?"

"Carefully, before I asked him to go. I told him how impossible it was to say what might happen. I reminded him that it might be of the utmost importance to me to preserve the impression now in Lucilla's mind—for a certain time only—after Lucilla could see. I promised, the moment she became reconciled to the sight of me, to recall him, and in his presence to tell her the truth. All that I said to him—and how do you think he answered me?"

"Did he positively refuse?"

"No. He walked away from me to the window, and considered a little. Then he turned round suddenly and said, 'What did you tell me was Mr. Sebright's opinion? Mr. Sebright thought she would be relieved instead of being terrified. In that case, what need is there for me to go away? You can acknowledge at once that she has seen your face, and not mine.' He put his hands in his pockets when he had said that (you know Nugent's downright way), and turned back to the window as if he had settled everything."

"What did you say, on your side?"

"I said, 'Suppose Mr. Sebright is wrong?' He only answered, 'Suppose Mr. Sebright is right?' I followed him to the window—I never heard him speak so sourly to me as he spoke at that moment. 'What is your objection to going away for a day or two?' I asked. 'My objection is soon stated,' he answered. 'I am sick of these everlasting complications. It is useless and cruel to carry on the deception any longer. Mr. Sebright's advice is the wise advice and the right advice. Let her see you as you are.' With that answer, he walked out of the room. Something has upset him—I can't imagine what it is. Do, pray, see what you can make of him! My only hope is in you."

I own I felt reluctant to interfere. Suddenly and strangely as Nugent had altered his point of view, it seemed to me undeniable that Nugent was right. At the same time, Oscar looked so disappointed and distressed that it was really impossible, on that day above all others, to pain him additionally by roundly saying No. I undertook to do what I could—and I inwardly hoped that circumstances would absolve me from the necessity of doing anything at all.

Circumstances failed to justify my selfish confidence in them.

I was out in the village after breakfast, on a domestic errand connected with the necessary culinary preparations for the reception of Herr Grosse, when I heard my name pronounced behind me, and, turning round, found myself face to face with Nugent.

"Has my brother been bothering you this morning," he asked, "before I was up?"

I instantly noticed a return in him, as he said that, to the same dogged, ungracious manner which had perplexed and displeased me at my last confidential interview with him in the rectory garden.

"Oscar has been speaking to me this morning," I replied.

"About me?"

"About you. You have distressed and disappointed him—"

"I know! I know! Oscar is worse than a child. I am beginning to lose all patience with him."

"I am sorry to hear you say that, Nugent. You have borne with him so kindly thus far —surely you can make allowance for him to-day. His whole future may depend on what happens in Lucilla's sitting-room a few hours hence."

"He is making a mountain out of a mole-hill —and so are you."

Those words were spoken bitterly, almost rudely. I answered sharply on my side.

"You are the last person living who has any right to say that. Oscar is in a false position toward Lucilla, with your knowledge and consent. In your brother's interests you agreed to the fraud that has been practiced on her. In your brother's interests, again, you are asked to leave Dimchurch. Why do you refuse?"

"I refuse because I have come round to your way of thinking. What did you say of Oscar and of me in the summer-house? You said we were taking a cruel advantage of Lucilla's blindness. You were right. It *was* cruel not to have told her the truth. I won't be a party to concealing the truth from her any longer! I refuse to persist in deceiving her—in meanly deceiving her—on the day when she recovers her sight!"

It is entirely beyond my power to describe the

tone in which he made that reply. I can only declare that it struck me dumb for the moment. I drew a step nearer to him. With vague misgivings in me, I looked him searchingly in the face. He looked back at me without shrinking.

"Well?" he asked, with a hard smile which defied me to put him in the wrong.

I could discover nothing in his face; I could only follow my instincts as a woman. Those instincts warned me to accept his explanation.

"I am to understand, then, that you have decided on staying here?" I said.

"Certainly!"

"What do you propose to do when Herr Grosse arrives, and we assemble in Lucilla's room?"

"I propose to be present among the rest of you at the most interesting moment of Lucilla's life."

"No! you don't propose that!"

"I do!"

"You have forgotten something, Mr. Nugent Dubourg."

"What is it, Madame Pratolungo?"

"You have forgotten that Lucilla believes the brother with the discolored face to be You, and the brother with the fair complexion to be Oscar. You have forgotten that the surgeon has expressly forbidden us to agitate her by entering into any explanations before he allows her to use her eyes. You have forgotten that the very deception which you have just positively refused to go on with will be, nevertheless, a deception continued, if you are present when Lucilla sees. Your own resolution pledges you not to enter the rectory doors until Lucilla has discovered the truth." In those words I closed the vise on him. I had got Mr. Nugent Dubourg!

He turned deadly pale. His eyes dropped before mine for the first time.

"Thank you for reminding me," he said. "I *had* forgotten."

He pronounced those submissive words in a suddenly lowered voice. Something in his tone, or something in the dropping of his eyes, set my heart beating quickly, with a certain vague expectation which I was unable to realize to myself.

"You agree with me," I said, "that you can not be one among us at the rectory? What will you do?"

"I will remain at Browndown," he answered.

I felt he was lying. Don't ask for my reasons: I have no reasons to give. When he said, "I will remain at Browndown," I felt he was lying.

"Why not do what Oscar asks of you?" I went on. "If you are absent, you may as well be in one place as in another. There's plenty of time still to leave Dimchurch."

He looked up as suddenly as he had looked down.

"Do you and Oscar think me a stock or a stone?" he burst out angrily.

"What do you mean?"

"Who are you indebted to for what is going to happen to-day?" he went on, more and more passionately. "You are indebted to Me. Who among you all stood alone in refusing to believe that she was blind for life! *I* did! Who brought the man here who has given her back her sight? *I* brought the man! And I am the one person who is to be left in ignorance of how it ends. The others are to be present: I am to be sent away. The others are to see it: I am to hear by post (if any of you think of writing to me) what she does, what she says, how she looks, at the first heavenly moment when she opens her eyes on the world." He flung up his hand in the air and burst out savagely with a bitter laugh. "I astonish you, don't I? I am claiming a position which I have no right to occupy. What interest can *I* feel in it? Oh God! what do *I* care about the woman to whom I have given a new life!" His voice broke into a sob at those last wild words. He tore at the breast of his coat as if he was suffocating, and turned and left me.

I stood rooted to the spot. In one breathless instant the truth broke on me like a revelation. At last I had penetrated the terrible secret. Nugent loved her.

My first impulse, when I recovered myself, hurried me at the top of my speed back to the rectory. For a moment or two I think I must really have lost my senses. I felt a frantic suspicion that he had gone into the house, and that he was making his way to Lucilla at that moment. When I found that all was quiet—when Zillah had satisfied me that no visitor had come near our side of the rectory—I calmed down a little, and went back to the garden to compose myself before I ventured into Lucilla's presence.

After a while I got over the first horror of it, and saw my own position plainly. There was not a living soul at Dimchurch in whom I could confide. Come what might of it, in this dreadful emergency, I must trust in myself alone.

I had just arrived at that startling conclusion; I had shed some bitter tears when I remembered how hardly I had judged poor Oscar on more than one occasion; I had decided that my favorite Nugent was the most hateful villain living, and that I would leave nothing undone that the craft of a woman could compass to drive him out of the place—when I was forced back to present necessities by the sound of Zillah's voice calling to me from the house. I went to her directly. The nurse had a message for me from her young mistress. My poor Lucilla was lonely and anxious: she was surprised at my leaving her; she insisted on seeing me immediately.

I took my first precaution against a surprise from Nugent, as I crossed the threshold of the door.

"Our dear child must not be disturbed by visitors to-day," I said to Zillah. "If Mr. Nugent Dubourg comes here and asks for her, don't tell Lucilla; tell *me*."

This said, I went upstairs and joined my darling in the darkened room.

CHAPTER THE THIRTY-FIFTH

LUCILLA TRIES HER SIGHT.

SHE was sitting alone in the dim light, with the bandage over her eyes, with her pretty hands crossed patiently on her lap. My heart swelled in me as I looked at her, and felt the horrid discovery that I had made still present in my mind. "Forgive me for leaving you," I said, in as steady a voice as I could command at the moment, and kissed her.

She instantly discovered my agitation, carefully as I thought I had concealed it.

"You are frightened too!" she exclaimed, taking my hands in hers.

"Frightened, my love?" I repeated. (I was perfectly stupefied; I really did not know what to say!)

"Yes. Now the time is so near I feel my courage failing me. I forbode all sorts of horrible things. Oh, when will it be over? What will Oscar look like when I see him?"

I answered the first question. Who could answer the second?

"Herr Grosse comes to us by the morning train," I said. "It will soon be over."

"Where is Oscar?"

"On his way here, I have no doubt."

"Describe him to me once more," she said,

eagerly. "For the last time before I see. His eyes, his hair, his complexion—everything!"

How I should have got through the painful task which she had innocently imposed on me, if I had attempted to perform it, I hardly like to think. To my infinite relief, I was interrupted at my first word by the opening of the door, and the sudden appearance of a family deputation in the room.

First, strutting with slow and solemn steps, with one hand laid pathetically on the breast of his clerical waistcoat, appeared Reverend Finch. After him came his wife, shorn of all her proper accompaniments, except the baby. Without her novel, without her jacket, petticoat, or shawl, without even the handkerchief which she was always losing—clothed, for the first time in my experience, in a complete gown —the metamorphosis of damp Mrs. Finch was complete. But for the baby I believe I should have taken her, in the dim light, for a stranger! She stood (apparently doubtful of her reception) hesitating in the doorway, and so hiding a third member of the deputation who appealed piteously to the general notice in a small voice which I knew well, and in a form of address familiar to me from past experience.

"Jicks wants to come in."

The rector took his hand from his waistcoat, and held it up in faint protest against the intrusion of the third member. Mrs. Finch moved mechanically into the room. Jicks appeared, hugging her disreputable doll, and showing signs of recent wandering in the white dust which dropped on the carpet from her frock and her shoes, as she advanced toward the place in which I was sitting. Arrived in front of me, she peered quaintly up at my face through the obscurity of the room, lifted her doll by the legs, hit me a smart rap with the head of it on my knee, and said:

"Jicks will sit here."

I rubbed my knee, and enthroned Jicks as ordered. At the same time Mr. Finch solemnly stalked up to his daughter, laid his hands on her head, raised his eyes to the ceiling, and said, in bass notes that rumbled with paternal emotion, "Bless you, my child!"

At the sound of her husband's magnificent voice Mrs. Finch became herself again. She said, meekly: "How d'ye do, Lucilla?" and sat down in a corner, and suckled the baby.

Mr. Finch set in for one of his harangues.

"My advice has been neglected, Lucilla. My paternal influence has been repudiated. My Moral Weight has been, so to speak, set aside. I don't complain. Understand me — I simply state sad facts." (Here he became aware of my existence.) "Good-morning, Madame Pratolungo; I hope I see you well?—There has been variance between us, Lucilla. I come, my child, with healing on my wings (healing being understood, for present purposes, as reconciliation)— I come and bring Mrs. Finch with me—don't speak, Mrs. Finch!—to offer my heartfelt wishes, my fervent prayers, on this the most eventful day in my daughter's life. No vulgar curiosity has turned my steps this way. No hint shall escape my lips touching any misgivings which I may still feel as to this purely worldly interference with the ways of an inscrutable Providence. I am here as parent and peacemaker. My wife accompanies me—don't speak, Mrs. Finch!—as step-parent and step-peacemaker. (You understand the distinction, Madame Pratolungo? Thank you. Good creature.) Shall I preach forgiveness of injuries from the pulpit and not practice that forgiveness at home? Can I remain, on this momentous occasion, at variance with my child? Lucilla! I forgive you. With full heart and tearful eyes, I forgive you. (You have never had any children, I believe, Madame Pratolungo? Ah! you cannot possibly understand this. Not your fault. Good creature, not your fault.) The kiss of peace, my child; the kiss of peace." He solemnly bent his bristly head and deposited the kiss of peace on Lucilla's forehead. He sighed superbly, and, in a burst of magnanimity, held out his hand next to *me*. "My Hand, Madame Pratolungo. Compose yourself. Don't cry. God bless you!" Mrs. Finch, deeply affected by her husband's noble conduct, began to sob hysterically. The baby, disarranged in his proceedings by the emotions of his mamma, set up a sympathetic scream. Mr. Finch crossed the room to them, with domestic healing on his wings. "This does you credit, Mrs. Finch; but, under the circumstances, it must not be continued. Control yourself, in consideration of the infant. Mysterious mechanism of Nature!" cried the rector, raising his prodigious voice over the louder and louder screeching of the baby. "Marvelous and beautiful sympathy which makes the maternal sustenance the conducting medium, as it were, of disturbance between mother and child. What problems confront us, what forces environ us, even in this mortal life! Nature! Maternity! Inscrutable Providence!"

"Inscrutable Providence" was the rector's fatal phrase—it always brought with it an interruption; and it brought one now. Before Mr. Finch (brimful of pathetic apostrophies) could burst into more exclamations, the door opened and Oscar walked into the room.

Lucilla instantly recognized his footsteps.

"Any signs, Oscar, of Herr Grosse?" she asked.

"Yes. His chaise has been seen on the road. He will be here directly."

Giving that answer, and passing by my chair to place himself on the other side of Lucilla, Oscar cast at me one imploring look—a look which said plainly: "Don't desert me when the time comes!" I nodded my head to show that I understood him and felt for him. He sat down in the vacant chair by Lucilla, and took her hand in silence. It was hard to say which of the two felt the position, at that trying moment, most painfully. I don't think I ever saw any sight so simply and irresistibly touching as the sight of these two poor young creatures sitting hand in hand, waiting the event which was to make the happiness or the misery of their future lives.

"Have you seen anything of your brother?" I asked, putting the question in as careless a tone as my devouring anxiety would allow me to assume.

"Nugent has gone to meet Herr Grosse."

Oscar's eyes once more encountered mine, as he replied in those terms; I saw again the imploring look more marked in them than ever. It was plain to him, as it was plain to me, that Nugent had gone to meet the German with the purpose of making Herr Grosse the innocent means of bringing him into the house.

Before I could speak again, Mr. Finch, recovering himself after the interruption which had silenced him, saw his opportunity of setting in for another harangue. Mrs. Finch had left off sobbing; the baby had left off screaming; the rest of us were silent and nervous. In a word, Mr. Finch's domestic congregation was entirely at Mr. Finch's mercy. He strutted up to Oscar's chair. Was he going to propose to read "Hamlet"? No! He was going to invoke a blessing on Oscar's head.

"On this interesting occasion," began the rector, in his pulpit tones, "now that we are all united in the same room, all animated by the same hope, I could wish, as pastor and parent (God bless you, Oscar; I look on you as a son. Mrs. Finch, follow my example, look on him as a son!)—I could wish, as pastor and parent, to say a few pious and consoling words—"

The door—the friendly, admirable, judicious door—stopped the coming sermon, in the nick of time, by opening again. Herr Grosse's squat figure and owlish spectacles appeared on the threshold. And behind him (exactly as I had anticipated) stood Nugent Dubourg.

Lucilla turned deadly pale; she had heard the door open; she knew by instinct that the surgeon had come. Oscar got up, stole behind my chair, and whispered to me: "For God's sake, get Nugent out of the room!" I gave him a reassuring squeeze of the hand, and, putting Jicks down on the floor, rose to welcome our good Grosse.

The child, as it happened, was beforehand with me. She and the illustrious oculist had met in the garden at one of the German's professional visits to Lucilla, and had taken an amazing fancy to each other. Herr Grosse never afterward appeared at the rectory without some unwholesome eatable thing in his pocket for Jicks; who gave him in return as many kisses as he might ask for, and further distinguished him as the only living creature whom she permitted to nurse the disreputable doll. Grasping this same doll now with both hands, and using it head-foremost as a kind of battering-ram, Jicks plunged in front of me, and butted with all her might at the surgeon's bandy-legs, insisting on a monopoly of his attention before he presumed to speak to any other person in the room. While he was lifting her to a level with his face, and talking to her in his wonderful broken English—while the rector and Mrs. Finch were making the necessary apologies for the child's conduct—Nugent came round from behind Herr Grosse, and drew me mysteriously into a corner of the room. As I followed him I saw the silent torture of anxiety expressed in Oscar's face as he stood by Lucilla's chair. It did me good; it strung up my resolution to the right pitch; it made me feel myself a match, and more than a match, for Nugent Dubourg.

"I am afraid I behaved in a very odd manner when we met in the village," he said. "The fact is, I am not at all well. I have been in a strange feverish state lately. I don't think the air of this place suits me." There he stopped, keeping his eyes steadily fixed on mine, trying to read my mind in my face.

"I am not surprised to hear you say that," I answered. "I have noticed that you have not been looking well lately."

My tone and manner (otherwise perfectly composed) expressed polite sympathy, and nothing more. I saw I puzzled him. He tried again.

"I hope I didn't say or do anything rude?" he went on.

"Oh, no!"

"I was excited—painfully excited. You are too kind to admit it. I am sure I owe you my apologies?"

"No, indeed! You are certainly excited, as you say. But we are all in the same state today. The occasion, Mr. Nugent, is your sufficient apology."

Not the slightest sign in my face of any sort
of suspicion of him rewarded the close and continued scrutiny with which he regarded me. I
saw in his perplexed expression the certain assurance that I was beating him at his own
weapons. He made a last effort to entrap me
into revealing that I suspected his secret—he
attempted, by irritating my quick temper, to
take me by surprise.

"You are, no doubt, astonished at seeing me
here," he resumed. "I have not forgotten that
I promised to remain at Browndown instead of
coming to the rectory. Don't be angry with me.
I am under medical orders which forbid me to
keep my promise."

"I don't understand you," I said, just as coolly
as ever.

"I will explain myself," he rejoined. "You
remember that we long since took Grosse into
our confidence on the subject of Oscar's position
toward Lucilla?"

"I am not likely to have forgotten it," I answered, "considering that it was I who first
warned your brother that Herr Grosse might do
terrible mischief by innocently letting out the
truth."

"Do you recollect how he took the warning
when we gave it to him?"

"Perfectly. He promised to be careful. But,
at the same time, he gruffly forbade us to involve
him in any more of our family troubles. He
said he was determined to preserve his professional freedom of action, without being hampered

by domestic difficulties which might concern *us*, but which did not concern *him*. Is my memory accurate enough to satisfy you?"

"Your memory is wonderful. You will now understand me when I tell you that Grosse asserts his professional freedom of action on this occasion. I had it from his own lips on our way here. He considers it very important that Lucilla should not be frightened at the moment when she tries her sight. Oscar's face is sure to startle her, if it is the first face she sees. Grosse has accordingly requested me to be present (as the only other young man in the room), and to place myself so that I shall be the first person who attracts her notice. Ask him yourself, Madame Pratolungo, if you don't believe me."

"Of course I believe you!" I answered. "It is useless to dispute the surgeon's orders at such a time as this."

With that I left him, showing just as much annoyance as an unsuspecting woman, in my position, might have naturally betrayed, and no more. Knowing, as I did, what was going on under the surface, I understood only too plainly what had happened. Nugent had caught at the opportunity which the surgeon had innocently offered to him as a means of misleading Lucilla at the moment, and (possibly) of taking some base advantage of her afterward. I trembled inwardly with rage and fear as I turned my back on him. Our one chance was to make sure of his absence, at the critical moment; and, cudgel my brains as I might, how to reach that end successfully was more than I could see.

When I returned to the other persons in the room, Oscar and Lucilla were still occupying the same positions. Mr. Finch had presented himself (at full length) to Herr Grosse. And Jicks was established on a stool in a corner, devouring a rampant horse, carved in a bilious-yellow German gingerbread, with a voracious relish wonderful and terrible to see.

"Ah, my goot Madame Pratolungo!" said Herr Grosse, stopping on his way to Lucilla to shake hands with me. "Have you made anodder lofely Mayonnaise? I have come on purpose with an empty stomachs, and a wolf's-appetite in fine order. Look at that little Imps," he went on, pointing to Jicks. "Ach Gott! I believe I am in lofe with her. I have sent all the ways to Germany for gingerbreads for Jick. Aha, you Jick! does it stick in your tooths! Is it nice-clammy-sweet?" He glared benevolently at the child through his spectacles, and tucked my hand sentimentally in the breast of his waist-coat. "Promise me a child like adorable Jick," he said, solemnly, "I will marry the first wife you bring me—nice womans, nasty womans, I don't care which. Soh! there is my domestic sentiments laid bare before you. Enough of that. Now for my pretty Feench! Come-begin-begin!"

He crossed the room to Lucilla, and called Nugent to follow him.

"Open the shutters," he said. "Light-light-light, and plenty of him, for my lofely Feench!"

Nugent opened the shutters, beginning with the lower window, and ending with the window at which Lucilla was sitting. Acting on this plan, he had only to wait where he was to place himself close by her—to be the first object she saw. He did it. The villain did it. I stepped forward, determined to interfere—and stopped, not knowing what to say or do. I could have beaten my own stupid brains out against the wall. There stood Nugent right before her, as the surgeon turned his patient toward the window. And not the ghost of an idea came to me!

The German stretched out his hairy hands, and took hold of the knot of the bandage to undo it.

Lucilla trembled from head to foot.

Herr Grosse hesitated—looked at her—let go of the bandage—and, lifting one of her hands, laid his fingers on her pulse.

In the moment of silence that followed I had one of my inspirations. The missing idea turned up in my brains at last.

"Soh!" cried Grosse, dropping her hand with a sudden outbreak of annoyance and surprise. "Who has been frightening my pretty Feench? Why these cold trembles? these sinking pulses? Some of you tell me—what does it mean?"

Here was my opportunity. I tried my idea on the spot.

"It means," I said, "that there are too many people in this room. We confuse her and frighten her. Take her into her bedroom, Herr Grosse; and only let the rest of us in when you think right—one at a time."

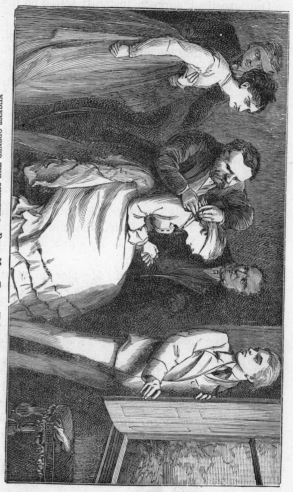

NUGENT OPENED THE SHUTTERS.—POOR MISS FINCH, Vol. XV., page 386.

Our excellent surgeon instantly seized on my idea, and made it his own.

"You are a phenix among womens," he said, paternally patting me on the shoulder. "Which is most perfectest, your advice or your Mayonnaise, I am at a loss to know." He turned to Lucilla, and raised her gently from her chair. "Come into your own rooms with me, my poor little Feench. I shall see if I dare take off your bandages to-day!"

Lucilla clasped her hands entreatingly.

"You promised!" she said. "Oh, Herr Grosse, you promised to let me use my eyes to-day!"

"Answer me this!" retorted the German. "Did I know, when I promised, that I should find you all shaky-pale, and white as my shirts when he comes back from the wash?"

"I am quite myself again," she pleaded, faintly. "I am quite fit to have the bandage taken off."

"What! you know better than I do? Which of us is surgeon-optic—you or me? No more of this. Come under my arms! Come into the odder rooms!"

He put her arm in his, and walked with her to the door. There her variable humor suddenly changed. She rallied on the instant. Her face flushed; her courage came back. To my horror, she snatched her arm away from the surgeon, and refused to leave the room.

"No!" she said. "I am quite composed again; I claim your promise. Examine me here. I must and will have my first look at Oscar in this room."

(I was afraid—literally afraid—to turn my eyes Oscar's way. I glanced at Nugent instead. There was a devilish smile on his face that it drove me nearly mad to see.)

"You must and weel?" repeated Grosse. "Now mind!" He took out his watch. "I give you one little minutes to think in. If you don't come with me in that time, you shall find it is I who must and weel. Now!"

"Why do you object to go into your own room?" I asked.

"Because I want everybody to see me," she answered. "How many of you are there here?"

"There are five of us. Mr. and Mrs. Finch, Mr. Nugent Dubourg, Oscar and myself."

"I wish there were five hundred of you, instead of five!" she burst out.

"Why?"

"Because you would see me pick out Oscar from all the rest the instant the bandage was off my eyes!"

Still holding to her own fatal conviction that the image in her mind of Oscar was the right one! For the second time, though I felt the longing in me to look at him, I shrank from doing it.

Herr Grosse put his watch back in his pocket.

"The minutes is past," he said. "Will you come into the odder rooms? Will you understand that I cannot properly examine you before all these peoples? Say, my lofely Feench—Yes? or No?"

"No!" she cried, obstinately, with a childish

stamp of her foot. "I insist on showing everybody that I can pick out Oscar the moment I open my eyes."

Herr Grosse buttoned his coat, set his owlish spectacles firmly on his nose, and took up his hat. "Goot-morning," he said. "I have nothing more to do with you or your eyes. Cure yourself, you little-spitfire-Feench. I am going back to London."

He opened the door. Even Lucilla was obliged to yield when the surgeon in attendance on her threatened to throw up the case.

"You brute!" she said, indignantly — and took his arm again.

Grosse indulged himself in his diabolical grin. "When you are able to use your eyes, my lofe, you will see that I am not such a brutes as I look." With those words he took her out.

We were left in the sitting-room to wait until the surgeon had decided whether he would or would not let Lucilla try her sight on that day.

While the others were, in their various ways, all suffering the same uneasy sense of expectation, I was as quiet in my mind as the baby now sleeping in his mother's arms. Thanks to Grosse's resolution to act on the hint that I had given to him, I had now made it impossible—even if the bandage was removed on that day—for Nugent to catch Lucilla's first look when she opened her eyes. Her betrothed husband might certainly, on such a special occasion as this, be admitted into her bed-chamber, in company with her father or with me. But the commonest sense of pro-

priety would dictate the closing of the door on
Nugent. In the sitting-room he must wait (if
he still persisted in remaining at the rectory)
until she was allowed to join him there. I privately resolved, having the control of the matter
now in my own hands, that this should not happen until Lucilla knew which of the twins was
Nugent and which was Oscar. A delicious inward glow of triumph diffused itself all through
me. I resisted the strong temptation that I felt
to discover how Nugent bore his defeat. If I
had yielded to it, he would have seen in my face
that I gloried in having outwitted him. I sat
down, the picture of innocence, in the nearest
chair, and crossed my hands on my lap, a composed and lady-like person, edifying to see.

The slow minutes followed each other—and
still we waited the event in silence. Even Mr.
Finch's tongue was, on this solitary occasion, a
tongue incapable of pronouncing a single word.
He sat by his wife at one end of the room. Oscar and I were at the other. Nugent stood by
himself at one of the windows, deep in his own
thoughts, plotting how he could pay me out.

Oscar was the first of the party who broke the
silence. After looking all round the room, he
suddenly addressed himself to me.

"Madame Pratolungo," he exclaimed, "what
has became of Jicks?"

I had completely forgotten the child. I too
looked round the room, and satisfied myself that
she had really disappeared. Mrs. Finch, observing our astonishment, timidly enlightened us.

The maternal eye had seen Jicks slip out of the room at Herr Grosse's heels. The child's object was plain enough. While there was any probability of the presence of more gingerbread in the surgeon's pocket, the wandering Arab of the family (as stealthy and as quick as a cat) was certain to keep within reach of her friend. Nobody who knew her could doubt that she had slipped into Lucilla's bed-chamber, under cover of Herr Grosse's ample coat-tails.

We had just accounted in this way for the mysterious absence of Jicks, when we heard the bed-chamber door opened, and the surgeon's voice calling for Zillah. In a minute more the nurse appeared, the bearer of a message from the next room.

We all surrounded her, with one and the same question to ask. What had Herr Grosse decided to do? The answer informed us that he had decided on forbidding Lucilla to try her eyes that day.

"Is she very much disappointed?" Oscar inquired, anxiously.

"I can hardly say, sir. She isn't like herself. I never knew Miss Lucilla so quiet when she was crossed in her wishes before. When the doctor called me into the room she said: 'Go in, Zillah, and tell them.' Those words, sir, and no more."

"Did she express no wish to see me?" I inquired.

"No, ma'am. I took the liberty of asking her if she wished to see you. Miss Lucilla shook her head, and sat herself down on the sofa and made the doctor sit by her. 'Leave us by ourselves.' Those were the last words she said to me before I came in here.''

Reverend Finch put the next question. The Pope of Dimchurch was himself again: the man of many words saw his chance of speaking once more.

"Good woman," said the rector, with ponderous politeness, "step this way. I wish to address an inquiry to you. Did Miss Finch make any remark, in your hearing, indicating a desire to be comforted by My Ministrations—as one bearing the double relation toward her of pastor and parent?"

"I didn't hear Miss Lucilla say anything to that effect, sir."

Mr. Finch waved his hand with a look of disgust, intimating that Zillah's audience was over. Nugent, upon that, came forward, and stopped her as she was leaving the room.

"Have you nothing more to tell us?" he asked.

"No, sir."

"Why don't they come back here? What are they doing in the other room?"

"They were doing what I mentioned just now, sir—they were sitting side by side on the sofa. Miss Lucilla was talking, and the doctor was listening to her. And Jicks," added Zillah, addressing herself confidentially to me, "was behind them, picking the doctor's pocket."

Oscar put in a word there—by no means in his most gracious manner.

"What was Miss Lucilla saying to the surgeon?"

"I don't know, sir."

"You don't know!"

"I couldn't hear, sir.   Miss Lucilla was speaking to him in a whisper."

After that there was no more to be said.
Zillah, disturbed over her domestic occupations,
and eager to get back to her kitchen, seized the
first chance of leaving the room; going out in
such a hurry that she forgot to close the door
after her. We all looked at each other. To
what conclusion did the nurse's strange answers point?   It was plainly impossible for
Oscar (no matter how quick his temper might
be) to feel jealous of a man of Grosse's age and
personal appearance.   Still, the prolonged interview between patient and surgeon—after the decision had been pronounced, and the trial of the
eyes definitely deferred to a future day—had a
strange appearance, to say the least of it.

Nugent returned to his place at the window—
puzzled, suspicious, deep in his own thoughts.
Reverend Finch, swelling with unspoken words,
rose portentously from his chair by his wife's
side.   Had he discovered another chance of inflicting his eloquence on us?   It was only too
evident that he had!   He looked at us with his
ominous smile.   He addressed us in his biggest
voice.

"My Christian friends—"

Nugent, unassailable by eloquence, persisted
in looking out of the window.   Oscar, insensible

to every earthly consideration except the one consideration of Lucilla, drew me aside unceremoniously out of the rector's hearing. Mr. Finch
resumed.

"My Christian friends, I could wish to say a
few appropriate words."

"Go to Lucilla," whispered Oscar, taking me
entreatingly by both hands. "*You* needn't stand
on ceremony with her. Do, do see what is going
on in the next room!"

Mr. Finch resumed.

"The occasion seems to call upon one in my
position for a little sustaining advice on Christian duty—I would say, the duty of being cheerful under disappointment."

Oscar persisted.

"Do me the greatest of all favors! Pray find
out what is keeping Lucilla with that man!"

Mr. Finch cleared his throat, and lifted his
right hand persuasively, by way of introduction
to his next sentence.

I answered Oscar in a whisper.

"I don't like intruding on them. Lucilla told
the nurse they were to be left by themselves."

Just as I said the words I became aware of a
sudden bump against me from behind. I turned,
and discovered Jicks with the battering-ram doll
preparing for a second plunge at me. She stopped
when she found that she had attracted my attention; and, taking hold of my dress, tried to pull
me out of the room.

"Remove that child!" cried the rector, exas-
perated by this new interruption.

The child pulled harder and harder at my dress. Something had apparently happened outside the sitting-room which had produced a strong impression on her. Her little round face was flushed; her bright blue eyes were wide open and staring. "Jicks wants to speak to you," she said, and pulled at me impatiently, harder than ever.

I stooped down, with the double purpose of obeying Mr. Finch's commands and of humoring the child's whim by carrying Jicks out of the room, when I was startled by a sound from the bedroom—the sound, loud and peremptory, of Lucilla's voice.

"Let me go!" she cried. "I am a woman— I won't be treated like a child."

There was a moment of silence, followed by the rustling sound of her dress approaching us along the corridor.

Grosse's voice, unmistakably angry and excited, became audible at the same time. "No! Come back! come back!"

The rustling sound came nearer and nearer.

Nugent and Mr. Finch moved together nearer to the door. Oscar caught me by the arm. He and I were on the left-hand side of the door; Nugent and the rector were on the right-hand side. It all happened with the suddenness of a flash of lightning. My heart stood still. I couldn't speak. I couldn't move.

The half-closed door of the sitting-room was burst wide open, roughly, violently, as if a man, not a woman, had been on the other side.

(The rector drew back; Nugent remained where he was.) Wildly groping her way with outstretched arms, as I had never seen her grope it in the time of her blindness, Lucilla staggered into the room. Merciful God! the bandage was off. The life, the new life of sight, was in her eyes. It transfigured her face. It irradiated her beauty with an awful and unearthly light. She saw! she saw!

For an instant she stopped at the door, swaying to and fro; giddy under the broad stare of daylight.

She looked at the rector, then at Mrs. Finch, who had followed her husband. She paused, bewildered, and put her hands over her eyes. She slightly changed her position; turned her head, as if to look at me; turned it back sharply toward the right-hand side of the door again; and threw up her arms in the air, with a burst of hysterical laughter. The laughter ended in a scream of triumph, which rang through the house. She rushed at Nugent Dubourg, so blindly incapable of measuring her distance that she struck against him violently, and nearly threw him down. "I know him! I know him!" she cried, and flung her arms round his neck. "Oh, Oscar! Oscar!" She clasped him to her with all her strength as the name passed her lips, and dropped her head on his bosom in an ecstasy of joy.

It was done before any of us had recovered the use of our senses. The whole horrible scene must have begun and ended in less than half a minute of time. The surgeon, who had run into the room after her, empty-handed, turned suddenly and left it again; coming back with the bandage, left forgotten in the bedroom. Grosse was the first among us to recover his presence of mind. He approached her in silence.

She heard him, before he could take her by surprise and slip the bandage over her eyes. The moment when I turned, horrorstruck, to look at Oscar was also the moment when she lifted her head from Nugent's bosom to look for the surgeon. Her eyes followed the direction taken by mine. They encountered Oscar's face. She saw the blue-black hue of it in full light.

A cry of terror escaped her: she started back, shuddering, and caught hold of Nugent's arm. Grosse motioned sternly to him to turn her face from the window, and lifted the bandage. She clutched at it with feverish eagerness as he held it up. "Put it on again!" she said, holding by Nugent with one hand, and lifting the other to point toward Oscar with a gesture of disgust. "Put it on again. I have seen too much already."

Grosse fastened the bandage over her eyes, and waited a little. She still held Nugent's arm. The sting of my indignation as I saw it roused me into doing something. I stepped forward to part them. Grosse stopped me. "No!" he said. "Don't make bad worse." I looked at Oscar for the second time. There he stood, as he had stood from the first moment

"I KNOW HIM! I KNOW HIM!" SHE CRIED.—POOR MISS FINCH, VOL. XV., page 397.

when she appeared at the door—his eyes staring wildly straight before him; his limbs set and fixed. I went to him and touched him. He seemed not to feel it. I spoke to him. I might as well have spoken to a man of stone.

Herr Grosse's voice drew my attention, for a moment, the other way.

"Come!" he said, trying to take Lucilla back into her own room.

She shook her head, and tightened her hold on Nugent's arm.

"*You* take me," she whispered, "as far as the door."

I again attempted to stop it, and again the German put me back.

"Not to-day!" he said, sternly. With that he made a sign to Nugent, and placed himself on Lucilla's other side. In silence the two men led her out of the room. The door closed on them. It was over.

CHAPTER THE THIRTY-SIXTH.

THE BROTHERS MEET.

A FAINT sound of crying found its way to my ears from the lower end of the room, and reminded me that the rector and his wife had been present among us. Feeble Mrs. Finch was lying back in her chair, weeping and wailing over what had happened. Her husband, with the baby in his arms, was trying to compose her. I ought, perhaps, to have offered my help; but, I own, poor Mrs. Finch's distress produced only a passing impression on me. My whole heart was with another person. I forgot the rector and his wife, and went back to Oscar.

This time he moved—he lifted his head when he saw me. Shall I ever forget the silent misery in that face, the dull, dreadful stare in those tearless eyes?

I took his hand. I felt for the poor, disfigured, rejected man as his mother might have felt for him. I gave him a mother's kiss. "Be comforted, Oscar," I said. "Trust me to set this right."

He drew a long, trembling breath, and pressed my hand gratefully. I attempted to speak to him again—he stopped me by looking suddenly toward the door.

"Is Nugent outside?" he asked, in a whisper.

I went into the corridor. It was empty. I looked into Lucilla's room. She and Grosse and the nurse were the only persons in it. I beckoned to Zillah to come out and speak to me. I asked for Nugent. He had left Lucilla abruptly at the bedroom door—he was out of the house. I inquired if it was known in what direction he had gone. Zillah had seen him in the field at the end of the garden, walking away rapidly, with his back to the village, and his face to the hills.

"Nugent has gone," I said, returning to Oscar.

"Add to your kindness to me," he answered. "Let *me* go too."

A quick fear crossed my mind that he might be bent on following his brother.

"Wait a little," I said, "and rest here."

He shook his head.

"I must be by myself," he said. After considering a little, he added a question. "Has Nugent gone to Browndown?"

"No. Nugent has been seen walking toward the hills."

He took my hand again. "Be merciful to me," he said. "Let me go."

"Home? To Browndown?"

"Yes."

"Let me go with you."

He shook his head. "Forgive me. You shall hear from me later in the day."

No tears; no flaming up of the quick temper that I knew so well! Nothing in his face, nothing in his voice, nothing in his manner, but a composure miserable to see—the composure of despair.

"At least let me accompany you to the gate," I said.

"God bless and reward you!" he answered. "Let me go."

With a gentle hand, and yet with a firmness which took me completely by surprise, he separated himself from me, and went out.

I could stand no longer—I dropped trembling into a chair. The conviction forced itself on me that there were worse complications, direr misfortunes, still to come. I was almost beside myself. I broke out vehemently with wild words spoken in my own language. Mrs. Finch recalled me to my senses. I saw her as in a dream, drying her tears, and looking at me in alarm. The rector approached, with profuse expressions of sympathy and offers of assistance. I wanted no comforting. I had served a hard apprenticeship to life; I had been well seasoned to trouble. "Thank you, sir," I said. "Look to Mrs. Finch." There was more air in the corridor. I went out again, to walk about, and get the better of it there.

A small object attracted my attention, crouched up on one of the window-seats. The small object was Jicks.

I suppose the child's instinct must have told her that something had gone wrong. She looked furtively sidewise at me round her doll: she had grave doubts of my intentions toward her. "Are you going to whack Jicks?" asked the curious little creature, shrinking into her corner. I sat down by her, and soon recovered my place in her confidence. She began to chatter again as fast as usual. I listened to her as I could have listened to no grown-up person at that moment. In some mysterious way that I cannot explain the child comforted me. Little by little I learned what she had wanted with me when she had attempted to drag me out of the room. She had seen all that had passed in the bed-chamber; and she had run out to take me back with her, and show me the wonderful sight of Lucilla with the bandage off her eyes. If I had been wise enough to listen to Jicks, I might have prevented the catastrophe that had happened. I might have met Lucilla in the corridor, and have forced her back into her own room and turned the key on her.

It was too late now to regret what had happened. "Jicks has been good," I said, patting my little friend on the head, with a heavy heart. The child listened, considered with herself gravely, got off the window-seat, and claimed her reward for being good, with that excellent brevity of speech which so eminently distinguished her: "Jicks will go out."

With those words, she shouldered her doll and walked off. The last I saw of her she was descending the stairs, as a workman descends a ladder, on her way to the garden—and from the garden (the first time the gate was opened) to the hills. If I could have gone out with her light heart, I would have joined Jicks.

I had hardly lost sight of the child before the door of Lucilla's room opened, and Herr Grosse appeared in the corridor.

"Soh!" he muttered, with a gesture of relief, "the very womans I was looking for. A nice mess-fix we are in now! I must stop with Feench. (I shall end in hating Feench!) Can you put me into a beds for the night?"

I assured him that he could easily sleep at the rectory. In answer to my inquiries after his patient, he gravely acknowledged that he was anxious about Lucilla. The varying and violent emotions which had shaken her (acting through her nervous system) might produce results which would imperil the recovery of her sight. Absolute repose was not simply necessary—it was now the only chance for her. For the next four-and-twenty hours he must keep watch over her eyes. At the end of that time—no earlier—he might be able to say whether the mischief done would be fatal to her sight or not. I asked how she had contrived to get her bandage off, and to make her fatal entrance into the sitting-room.

He shrugged his shoulders. "There are times," he said, cynically, "when every womans is a hussy, and every mans is a fool. This was one of the times."

It appeared, on further explanation, that my poor Lucilla had pleaded so earnestly (after the nurse had left the room) to be allowed to try her eyes, and had shown such ungovernable disappointment when he persisted in saying No, that he had yielded—not so much to her entreaties as to his own conviction that it would be less dangerous to humor her than to thwart her, with such a sensitive and irritable temperament as hers. He had first bargained, however, on his side, that she should remain in the bed-chamber, and be content, for that time, with using her sight on the objects round her in the room. She had promised all that he asked—and he had been foolish enough to trust to her promise. The bandage once off, she had instantly set every consideration at defiance, had torn herself out of his hands like a mad creature, and had rushed into the sitting-room before he could stop her.

The rest had followed as a matter of course. Feeble as it was at the first trial of it, her sense of sight was sufficiently restored to enable her to distinguish objects dimly. Of the three persons who had offered themselves to view on the right-hand side of the door, one (Mrs. Finch) was a woman; another (Mr. Finch) was a short, gray-headed, elderly man; the third (Nugent), in his height—which she could see—and in the color of his hair—which she could see—was the only one of the three who could possibly represent Oscar. The catastrophe that followed was (as things were) inevitable. Now that the harm was done, the one alternative left was to check the mischief at the point which it had already reached. Not the slightest hint at the terrible mistake that she had made must be suffered to reach her ears. If we any of us said one word about it, before he authorized us to do so, he would refuse to answer for the consequences, and would then and there throw up the case.

So, in his broken English, Herr Grosse explained what had happened, and issued his directions for our future conduct.

"No person is to go in to her," he said, in conclusion, "but you and goot Mrs. Zillahs. You two watch her, turn-about-turn-about. In a whiles she will sleep. For me, I go to smoke my tobaccos in the garden. Hear this, Madame Pratolungo. When Gott made the womens, he was sorry afterward for the poor mens—and he made tobaccos to comfort them."

Favoring me with this peculiar view of the

scheme of creation, Herr Grosse shook his shock head, and waddled away to the garden.

I softly opened the bedroom door and looked in—disappearing just in time to escape the rector and Mrs. Finch returning to their own side of the house.

Lucilla was lying on the sofa. She asked who it was in a drowsy voice—she was happily just sinking into slumber. Zillah occupied a chair near her. I was not wanted for the moment—and I was glad, for the first time in my experience at Dimchurch, to get out of the room again. By some contradiction in my character, which I am not able to explain, there was a certain hostile influence in the sympathy that I felt for Oscar, which estranged me, for the moment, from Lucilla. It was not her fault—and yet (I am ashamed to own it) I almost felt angry with her for reposing so comfortably, when I thought of the poor fellow, without a creature to say a kind word to him, alone at Browndown.

Out again in the corridor the question faced me: What was I to do next?

The loneliness of the house was insupportable; my anxiety about Oscar grew more than I could endure. I put on my hat, and went out.

Having no desire to interfere with Herr Grosse's enjoyment of his pipe, I made my way through the garden as quickly as possible, and found myself in the village again. My uneasiness on the subject of Oscar was matched by my angry desire to know what Nugent would do. Now, that he had worked the very mischief

which his brother had foreseen to be possible—
the very mischief which it had been Oscar's one
object to prevent in asking him to leave Dimchurch—would he take his departure? would he
rid us, at once and forever, of the sight of him?
The bare idea of the other alternative—I mean,
of his remaining in the place—shook me with
such an unutterable dread of what might happen next that my feet refused to support me. I
was obliged, just beyond the village, to sit down
by the roadside, and wait till my giddy head
steadied itself before I attempted to move again.

After a minute or two I heard footsteps coming along the road. My heart gave one great
leap in me. I thought it was Nugent.

A moment more brought the person in view.
It was only Mr. Gootheridge, of the village inn,
on his way home. He stopped and took off his hat.

"Tired, ma'am?" he said.

The uppermost idea in my mind found its way
somehow, ill as I was, to expression on my lips
—in the form of a question addressed to the
landlord.

"Do you happen to have seen anything of Mr.
Nugent Dubourg?" I asked.

"I saw him not five minutes since, ma'am?"

"Where?"

"Going into Browndown."

I started up as if I had been struck or shot.
Worthy Mr. Gootheridge stared. I wished him
good-day, and went on as fast as my feet would
take me, straight to Browndown. Had the
brothers met in the house? I turned cold at

the bare thought of it—but I still kept on.
There was an obstinate resolution in me to part
them, which served me in place of courage.
Account for it as you may, I was bold and
frightened both at the same time. At one moment I was fool enough to say to myself, "They
will kill me." At another, just as foolishly, I
found comfort in the opposite view. "Bah!
They are gentlemen; they can't hurt a woman!"

The servant was standing idling at the front-
door when I arrived in sight of the house. This,
in itself, was unusual. He was a hard-working,
well-trained man. On other occasions nobody
had ever seen him out of his proper place. He
advanced a few steps to meet me. I looked at
him carefully. Not the slightest appearance of
disturbance was visible in his face.

"Is Mr. Oscar at home?" I asked.

"I beg your pardon, ma'am. Mr. Oscar is at
home—but you can't see him. He and Mr. Nugent are together."

I rested my hand on the low wall in front of
the house, and made a desperate effort to put a
calm face on it.

"Surely Mr. Oscar will see *me?*" I said.

"I have Mr. Oscar's orders, ma'am, to wait at
the door, and tell everybody who comes to the
house (without exception) that he is engaged."

The house door was half open. I listened intently while the man was speaking. If they
had been at high words together, I must have
heard them, in the silence of the lonely hills all
round us. I heard nothing.

It was strange, it was inconceivable. At the same time it relieved me. There they were together, and no harm had come of it so far.

I left my card, and walked on a little past the corner of the house wall. As soon as I was out of the servant's sight, I turned back to the side of the building, and ventured as near as I durst to the window of the sitting-room. Their voices reached me, but not their words. On both sides the tones were low and confidential. Not a note of anger in either voice—listen for it as I might! I left the house again, breathless with amazement, and (so rapidly does a woman shift from one emotion to another) burning with curiosity.

After half an hour of aimless wandering in the valley, I returned to the rectory.

Lucilla was still sleeping. I took Zillah's place, and sent her into the kitchen. The landlady of the inn was there to help us with the dinner. But she was hardly equal, single-handed, to the superintendence of such dishes as we had to set before Herr Grosse. It was high time I relieved Zillah, if we were to pass successfully through the ordeal of the great surgeon's criticism as reviewer of all the sauces.

An hour more passed before Lucilla woke. I sent a messenger to Grosse, who appeared enveloped in a halo of tobacco, examined the patient's eyes, felt her pulse, ordered her wine and jelly, filled his monstrous pipe, and gruffly returned to his promenade in the garden.

The day wore on. Mr. Finch came to make inquiries, and then went back to his wife—

whom he described as "hysterically irresponsible," and in imminent need of another warm bath. He declined, in his most pathetic manner, to meet the German at dinner. "After what I have suffered, after what I have seen, these banquetings—I would say, these ticklings of the palate—are not to my taste. You mean well, Madame Pratolungo. (Good creature!) But I am not in heart for feasting. Simple fare, by my wife's couch; a few consoling words, in the character of pastor and husband, when the infant is quiet. So my day is laid out. I wish you well. I don't object to your little dinner. Good-day! good-day!"

A second examination of Lucilla's eyes brought us to the dinner hour.

At the sight of the table-cloth Herr Grosse's good humor returned. We two dined together alone—the German sending in selections of his own making from the dishes to Lucilla's room. So far, he said, she had escaped any serious injury. But he still insisted on keeping his patient perfectly quiet, and he refused to answer for anything until the night had passed. As for me, Oscar's continued silence weighed more and more heavily on my spirits. My past suspense in the darkened room with Lucilla seemed to be a mere trifle by comparison with the keener anxieties which I suffered now. I saw Grosse's eyes glaring discontentedly at me through his spectacles. He had good reason to look at me as he did: I had never before been so stupid and so disagreeable in all my life.

Toward the end of the dinner there came news from Browndown at last. The servant sent in a message by Zillah, begging me to see him for a moment outside the sitting-room door.

I made my excuses to my guest, and hurried out.

The instant I saw the servant's face my heart sank. Oscar's kindness had attached the man devotedly to his master. I saw his lips tremble, and his color come and go, when I looked at him.

"I have brought you a letter, ma'am."

He handed me a letter addressed to me in Oscar's handwriting.

"How is your master?" I asked.

"Not very well, ma'am, when I saw him last."

"When you saw him last?"

"I bring sad news, ma'am. There's a breaking up at Browndown."

"What do you mean? Where is Mr. Oscar?"

"Mr. Oscar has left Dimchurch."

CHAPTER THE THIRTY-SEVENTH.

THE BROTHERS CHANGE PLACES.

I VAINLY believed I had prepared myself for any misfortune that could fall on us. The man's last words dispelled my delusion. My gloomiest forebodings had never contemplated such a disaster as had now happened. I stood petrified, thinking of Lucilla, and looking helplessly at the servant. Try as I might, I was perfectly incapable of speaking to him.

He felt no such difficulty on his side. One of the strangest peculiarities in the humbler ranks of the English people is the sort of solemn relish which they have for talking of their own misfortunes. To be the objects of a calamity of any kind seems to raise them in their own estimations. With a dreary enjoyment of his miserable theme, the servant expatiated on his position as a man deprived of the best of masters; turned adrift again in the world to seek another service; hopeless of ever again finding himself in such a situation as he had lost. He roused me at last into speaking to him by sheer dint of irritating my nerves until I could endure him no longer.

"Has Mr. Oscar gone away alone?" I asked.

"Yes, ma'am, quite alone."

(What had become of Nugent? I was too much interested in Oscar to be able to put the question at that moment.)

"When did your master go?" I went on.

"Better than two hours since."

"Why didn't I hear of it before?"

"I had Mr. Oscar's orders not to tell you, ma'am, till this time in the evening."

Wretched as I was already, my spirits sank lower still when I heard that. The order given to the servant looked like a premeditated design not only to leave Dimchurch, but also to keep us in ignorance of his whereabouts afterward.

"Has Mr. Oscar gone to London?' I inquired.

"He hired Gootheridge's chaise, ma'am, to take him to Brighton. And he told me with his own lips that he had left Browndown never to come back. I know no more of it than that."

He had left Browndown never to come back! For Lucilla's sake, I declined to believe that. The servant was exaggerating, or the servant had misunderstood what had been said to him. The letter in my hand reminded me that I had perhaps needlessly questioned him on matters which his master had confided to my own knowledge only. Before I dismissed him for the night I made my deferred inquiry on the hateful subject of the other brother.

"Where is Mr. Nugent?"

"At Browndown."

"Do you mean to say that he is going to stay at Browndown?"

"I don't know, ma'am, for certain. I see no signs of his meaning to leave; and he has said nothing to that effect."

I had the greatest difficulty to keep myself from breaking out before the servant. My indignation almost choked me. The best way was to wish him good-night. I took the best way— only calling him back (as a measure of caution) to say one last word.

"Have you told anybody at the rectory of Mr. Oscar's departure?" I asked.

"No, ma'am."

"Say nothing about it, then, as you go out.

Thank you for bringing me the letter. Good-night."

Having thus provided against any whisper of what had happened reaching Lucilla's ears that evening, I turned to Herr Grosse to make my excuses, and to tell him (as I honestly could) that I was in sore need of being permitted to retire privately to my own room. I found my illustrious guest putting a plate over the final dish of the dinner, full of the tenderest anxiety to keep it warm on my account.

"Here is a lofely cheese-omelettes," said Grosse. "Two-thirds of him I have eaten my own self. The odder third I sweat with anxiety to keep warm for you. Sit down! sit down! Every moment he is getting cold."

"I am much obliged to you, Herr Grosse. I have just heard some miserable news—"

"Ach, Gott! don't tell it to me!" the wretch burst out, with a look of consternation. "No miserable news, I pray you, after such a dinner as I have eaten. Let me do my digestions! My goot-dear-creature, if you lofe me, let me do my digestions!"

"Will you excuse me, if I leave you to your digestion, and retire to my own room?"

He rose in a violent hurry, and opened the door for me.

"Yes! yes! From the deep bottoms of my heart I excuse you. Goot Madame Pratolungo, retire! retire!"

I had barely passed the threshold before the door was closed behind me. I heard the selfish old brute rub his hands, and chuckle over his success in shutting me and my sorrow both out of the room together.

Just as my hand was on my own door it occurred to me that I should do well to make sure of not being surprised by Lucilla over the reading of Oscar's letter. The truth is, that I shrank from reading it. In spite of my resolution to disbelieve the servant, the dread was now growing on me that the letter would confirm his statement, and would force it on me as the truth that Oscar had left us never to return. I retraced my steps, and entered Lucilla's room.

I could just see her, by the dim night-light burning in a corner to enable the surgeon or the nurse to find their way to her. She was alone in her favorite little wicker-work chair, with the doleful white bandage over her eyes—to all appearance quite content—busily knitting!

"Don't you feel lonely, Lucilla?"

She turned her head toward me, and answered in her gayest tones:

"Not in the least. I am quite happy as I am."

"Why is Zillah not with you?"

"I sent her away."

"You sent her away?"

"Yes! I couldn't enjoy myself thoroughly to-night unless I felt that I was quite alone. I have seen him, my dear—I have seen him! How could you possibly think I felt lonely? I am so inordinately happy that I am obliged to knit to keep myself quiet. If you say much more, I shall get up and dance—I know I shall! Where is Oscar? That odious Grosse—no! it is too bad to talk of the dear old man in that way, after he has given me back my sight. Still it *is* cruel of him to say that I am over-excited, and to forbid Oscar to come and see me to-night. Is Oscar with you, in the next room? Is he very much disappointed at being parted from me in this way? Say I am thinking of him—since I have seen him—with such new thoughts!"

"Oscar is not here to-night, my dear."

"No? then he is at Browndown, of course— with that poor, wretched, disfigured brother of his. I have got over my terror of Nugent's hideous face. I am even beginning (though I never liked him, as you know) to pity him, with such a dreadful complexion as that. Don't let us talk about it! Don't let us talk at all! I want to go on thinking of Oscar."

She resumed her knitting, and shut herself up luxuriously in her own happy thoughts. Knowing what I knew, it was nothing less than heart-breaking to see her and hear her. Afraid to trust myself to say another word, I softly closed the door, and charged Zillah (when her mistress rang her bell) to say for me that I was weary after the events of the day, and had gone to rest in my bedroom.

At last I was alone. At last I was at the end of my maneuvers to spare myself the miserable necessity of opening Oscar's letter. After first locking my door, I broke the seal, and read the lines which follow:

"KIND AND DEAR FRIEND—Forgive me: I am going to surprise and distress you. My letter thanks you gratefully, and bids you a last farewell.

"Summon all your indulgence for me. Read these lines to the end: they will tell you what happened after I left the rectory.

"Nothing had been seen of Nugent, when I reached this house. It was not till a quarter of an hour later that I heard his voice at the door, calling to me, and asking if I had come back. I answered, and he joined me in the sitting-room. Nugent's first words to me were these:

" 'Oscar, I have come to ask your pardon, and to bid you good-by.'

"I can give you no idea of the tone in which he said those words: it would have gone straight to your heart, as it went straight to mine. For the moment, I was not able to answer him. I could only offer him my hand. He sighed bitterly, and refused to take it.

" 'I have something still to tell you,' he said. 'Wait till you have heard it; and give me your hand afterward—if you can.'

"He even refused to take the chair to which I pointed. He distressed me by standing in my presence as if he was my inferior. He said—

"No! I have need of all my calmness and all my courage. It shakes both to recall what he said to me. I sat down to write this, intending to repeat to you everything that passed between us. Another of my weaknesses! another of my failures! The tears come into my eyes again when my mind attempts to dwell on the details. I can only tell you the result. My brother's confession may be summed up in three words. Prepare yourself to be startled; prepare yourself to be grieved.

"Nugent loves her.

"Think of this discovery, falling on me after I had seen my innocent Lucilla's arms round his neck—after my own eyes had shown me how she rejoiced over her first sight of *him;* how she shuddered at her first sight of *me?* Need I tell you what I suffered? No.

"Nugent held out his hand when he had done —as I had held out mine before he began.

"'The one atonement I can make to you and to her,' he said, 'is never to let either of you set eyes on me again. Shake hands, Oscar, and let me go.'

"If I had willed it so—so it might have ended. I willed it differently. It has ended differently. Can you guess how?"

I laid down the letter for a moment. It cut me with such keen regret—it fired me with such hot rage—that I was within a hair-breadth of tearing the rest of it up unread, and trampling it under my feet. I took a turn in the room. I dipped my handkerchief in water and bound it round my head. In a minute or two I was myself again—I could force my mind away from my poor Lucilla, and return to the letter. I proceeded thus:

"I can write calmly of what I have next to tell you. You shall hear what I have decided, and what I have done.

"I told Nugent to wait in the room while I went away and thought over what he had said to me by myself. He attempted to resist this. I insisted on his yielding. For the first time in our lives, we changed places. It was I who took the lead, and he who followed. I left him, and went out into the valley alone.

"The heavenly tranquillity, the comforting solitude, helped me. I saw my position and his in their true light. Before I got back I had decided (cost me what it might) on myself making the sacrifice to which my brother had offered to submit. For Lucilla's sake, and for Nugent's sake, I felt the certain assurance in my own mind that it was *my* duty, and not *his*, to go.

"Don't blame me; don't grieve for me. Read the rest. I want you to think of this with my thoughts—to feel about it as I feel at this moment.

"Bearing in mind what Nugent has confessed, and what I have myself seen, have I any right to hold Lucilla to her engagement? I am firmly persuaded that I have no right. After inspiring her with terror and disgust at the moment when her eyes first looked at me—after seeing her innocently happy in Nugent's arms—how, in God's name, can I claim her as mine? Our marriage has become an impossibility. For her own sake, I can not, I dare not, appeal to our engagement.

The wreck of *my* happiness is nothing. The wreck of *her* happiness would be a crime. I absolve her from her engagement. She is free.

"There is my duty toward Lucilla—as I see it.

"As to Nugent next. I owe it entirely to my brother (at the time of the Trial) that the honor of our family has been saved, and that I have escaped a shameful death on the scaffold. Is there any limit to the obligation that he has laid on me, after doing me such a service as this? There is no limit. The man who loves Lucilla and the brother who has saved my life are one. I am bound to leave him free—I do leave him free—to win Lucilla by open and loyal means, if he can. As soon as Herr Grosse considers that she is fit to bear the disclosure, let her be told of the error into which she has fallen (through my fault), let her read these lines— purposely written to meet her eye as well as yours—and let my brother tell her afterward what has passed to-night in this house between himself and me. She loves him now, believing him to be Oscar. Will she love him still, after she has learned to know him under his own name? The answer to that question rests with Time. If it is an answer in Nugent's favor, I have already arranged to set aside from my income a sufficient yearly sum to place my brother in a position to begin his married life. I wish to leave his genius free to assert itself, untrammeled by pecuniary cares. Possessing, as I do, far more than enough for my own simple wants, I can dedicate my spare money to no better and nobler use than this.

"There is my duty toward Nugent—as I see it.

"What I have decided on, you now know. What I have done can be told in two words. I have left Browndown forever. I have gone, to live or die (as God pleases) under the blow that has fallen on me, far away from you all.

"Perhaps, when years have passed, and when their children are growing up round them, I may see Lucilla again, and may take, as the hand of my sister, the hand of the beloved woman who might once have been my wife. This may happen, if I live. If I die, you will none of you hear of it. My death shall not cast its shadow of sadness on their lives. Forgive me, and forget me; and keep, as I keep, that first and noblest of all mortal hopes—the hope of the life to come.

"I inclose, when there is need for you to write to me, the address of my bankers in London. They will have their instructions. If you love me, if you pity me, abstain from attempting to shake my resolution. You may distress me— but you will never change me. Wait to write until Nugent has had the opportunity of pleading his own cause, and Lucilla has decided on her future life.

"Once more I thank you for the kindness which has borne with my weaknesses and my follies. God bless you—and good-by.   OSCAR."

Of the effect which the first reading of this letter produced on me I shall say nothing. Even at this distance of time, I shrink from reviving the memory of what I suffered alone in my room on that miserable night. Let it be enough if I tell you briefly at what decision I arrived.

I determined on doing two things. First, on going to London by the earliest train the next morning, and finding my way to Oscar by means of his bankers. Secondly, on taking measures for preventing the villain who had accepted the sacrifice of his brother's happiness from entering the rectory in my absence.

The one comfort I had that night was in feeling that, on these two points, my mind was made up. There was a stimulant in my sense of my own resolution which strengthened me to make my excuses to Lucilla without betraying the grief that tortured me when I found myself in her presence again. Before I went to my bed I had left her quiet and happy; I had arranged with Herr Grosse that he was still to keep his excitable patient secluded from visitors all through the next day; and I had secured as an ally to help me in preventing Nugent from entering the house no less a person than Reverend Finch himself. I saw him in his study overnight, and told him all that had happened; keeping one circumstance only concealed—namely, Oscar's insane determination to share his fortune with his infamous brother. I purposely left the rector to suppose that Oscar had left Lucilla free to receive the addresses of a man who had dissipated his fortune to the last farthing. Mr. Finch's harangue, when this prospect was brought within his range of contemplation, was something to be remembered, but not (on this occasion) to be reported —in mercy to the Church.

By the train of the next morning I left for London.

By the train of the same evening I returned alone to Dimchurch, having completely failed to achieve the purpose which had taken me to the metropolis.

Oscar had appeared at the bank as soon as the doors were opened in the morning; had drawn out some hundreds of pounds in circular notes; had told the bankers that they would be furnished with an address, at which they could write to him, in due course of time; and had departed for the Continent, without leaving a trace behind him.

I spent the day in making what arrangements I could for discovering him by the usual methods of inquiry pursued in such cases; and took the return train to the country, with my mind alternating between despair when I thought of Lucilla, and anger when I thought of the twin brothers. In the first bitterness of my disappointment, I was quite as indignant with Oscar as with Nugent. With all my heart I cursed the day which had brought the one and the other to Dimchurch.

As we lengthened our distance from London, flying smoothly by the tranquil woods and fields, my mind, with time to help it, began to recover its balance. Little by little the unexpected revelation of firmness and decision in Oscar's con-

duct—heartily as I still deplored and blamed
that conduct—began to have a new effect on my
mind. I now looked back, in amazement and
self-reproach, at my own superficial estimate of
the characters of the twin brothers.

Thinking it over uninterruptedly, with no one
in the carriage but myself, I arrived at a conclusion which strongly influenced my conduct in
guiding Lucilla through the troubles and perils
that were still to come.

Our physical constitutions have, as I take it,
more to do with the actions which determine
other people's opinions of us (as well as with the
course of our own lives) than we generally suppose. A man with delicately strung nerves says
and does things which often lead us to think
more meanly of him than he deserves. It is his
great misfortune constantly to present himself at
his worst. On the other hand, a man provided
with nerves vigorously constituted is provided
also with a constitutional health and hardihood
which express themselves brightly in his manners, and which lead to a mistaken impression
that his nature is what it appears to be on the
surface. Having good health, he has good spirits.
Having good spirits, he wins as an agreeable
companion on the persons with whom he comes
in contact—although he may be hiding all the
while, under an outer covering which is physically wholesome, an inner nature which is morally
foul. In the last of these two typical men I saw
reflected — Nugent. In the first — Oscar. All
that was feeblest and poorest in Oscar's nature

had shown itself on the surface in past times, to
the concealment of its stronger and its nobler
side.   There had been something hidden in this
supersensitive man, who had shrunk under all
the small trials of his life in our village, which
had proved firm enough, when the greatness of
the need called on it, to sustain the terrible disaster that had fallen on him.   The nearer I got
to the end of my journey the more certain I felt
that I was only now learning (bitterly as he had
disappointed me) to estimate Oscar's character
at its true value.   Inspired by this conviction,
I began already to face our hopeless prospects
boldly.   As long as I had life and strength to
help her, I determined that Lucilla should *not*
lose the man whose best qualities I had failed to
discover until he had made up his mind to turn
his back on her forever.

When I reached the rectory, I was informed
that Mr. Finch wished to speak to me.   My anxiety about Lucilla made me unwilling to submit
to any delay in seeing her.   I sent a message informing the rector that I would be with him in
a few minutes, and ran upstairs into Lucilla's
room.

"Has it been a very long day, my dear?" I
asked, when our first greetings were over.

"It has been a delightful day," she answered,
joyously.   "Grosse took me out for a walk before
he went back to London.   Can you guess where
our walk led us?"

A chilly sense of misgiving seized me.   I drew
back from her.   I looked at her lovely, happy

face without the slightest admiration of it—worse still, with downright distrust of it.

"Where did you go?" I asked.

"To Browndown, of course!"

An exclamation escaped me. ("Infamous Grosse!" spit out between my teeth, in my own language.) I could *not* help it. I should have died if I had repressed it—I was in such a rage.

Lucilla laughed. "There! there! It was my fault; I insisted on speaking to Oscar. As soon as I had my own way, I behaved perfectly. I never asked to have the bandage taken off; I was satisfied with only speaking to him. Dear old Grosse—he isn't half as hard on me as you and my father—was with us all the time. It has done me so much good. Don't be sulky about it, you darling Pratolungo? My 'surgeon-optic' sanctions my imprudence. I won't ask you to go with me to Browndown to-morrow; Oscar is coming to return my visit."

Those last words decided me. I had had a weary time of it since the morning; but (for me) the day was not at an end yet. I said to myself: "I will have it out with Mr. Nugent Dubourg before I go to my bed to-night!"

"Can you spare me for a little while?" I asked. "I must go to the other side of the house. Your father wishes to speak to me."

Lucilla started. "About what?" she inquired, eagerly.

"About business in London," I answered—and left her, before her curiosity could madden me (in the state I was in at that moment) with more questions.

I found the rector prepared to favor me with his usual flow of language. Fifty Mr. Finches could not have possessed themselves of my attention in the humor I was in at that moment. To the reverend gentleman's amazement, it was I who began—and not he.

"I have just left Lucilla, Mr. Finch. I know what has happened."

"Wait a minute, Madame Pratolungo! One thing is of the utmost importance to begin with. Do you thoroughly understand that *I* am, in no sense of the word, to blame—"

"Thoroughly," I interposed. "Of course they would not have gone to Browndown if you had consented to let Nugent Dubourg into the house."

"Stop!" said Mr. Finch, elevating his right hand. "My good creature, you are in a state of hysterical precipitation. I *will* be heard! I did more than refuse my consent. When the man Grosse—I insist on your composing yourself—when the man Grosse came and spoke to me about it, I did more, I say, infinitely more, than refuse my consent. You know my force of language. Don't be alarmed! I said: 'Sir! as pastor and parent, My Foot is down—'"

"I understand, Mr. Finch. Whatever you said to Herr Grosse was quite useless; he entirely ignored your personal point of view."

"Madame Pratolungo—"

"He found Lucilla dangerously agitated by

her separation from Oscar: he asserted what he calls his professional freedom of action."

"Madame Pratolungo—"

"You persisted in closing your doors to Nugent Dubourg. *He* persisted, on his side—and took Lucilla to Browndown."

Mr. Finch got on his feet, and asserted himself at the full pitch of his tremendous voice.

"Silence!" he shouted, with a smack of his open hand on the table at his side.

I didn't care. *I* shouted, *I* came down with a smack of my hand on the opposite side of the table.

"One question, sir, before I leave you," I said. "Since your daughter went to Browndown you have had many hours at your disposal. Have you seen Mr. Nugent Dubourg?"

The Pope of Dimchurch suddenly collapsed, in full fulmination of his domestic Bulls.

"Pardon me," he replied, adopting his most elaborately polite manner. "This requires considerable explanation."

I declined to wait for considerable explanation. "You have *not* seen him?" I said.

"I have *not* seen him," echoed Mr. Finch. "My position toward Nugent Dubourg is very remarkable, Madame Pratolungo. In my parental character, I should like to wring his neck. In my clerical character, I feel it incumbent on me to pause, and write to him. You feel the responsibility? You understand the distinction?"

I understood that he was afraid. Answering

him by an inclination of the head (I hate a coward!) I walked silently to the door.

Mr. Finch returned my bow with a look of helpless perplexity. "Are you going to leave me?" he inquired, blandly.

"I am going to Browndown."

If I had said that I was going to a place which the rector had frequent occasion to mention in the stronger passages of his sermons, Mr. Finch's face could hardly have shown more astonishment than it exhibited when I replied to him in those terms. He lifted his persuasive right hand; he opened his eloquent lips. Before the coming overflow of language could reach me I was out of the room, on my way to Browndown.

CHAPTER THE THIRTY-EIGHTH.

IS THERE NO EXCUSE FOR HIM?

OSCAR'S dismissed servant (left, during the usual month of warning, to take care of the house) opened the door to me when I knocked. Although the hour was already a late one in primitive Dimchurch, the man showed no signs of surprise at seeing me.

"Is Mr. Nugent Dubourg at home?"

"Yes, ma'am." He lowered his voice, and added: "I think Mr. Nugent expected to see you to-night."

Whether he intended it or not, the servant had done me a good turn—he had put me on my

"SILENCE!" HE SHOUTED.—POOR MISS FINCH, Vol. XV., page 429.

guard. Nugent Dubourg understood my character better than I had understood his. He had foreseen what would happen when I heard of Lucilla's visit, on my return to the rectory, and he had, no doubt, prepared himself accordingly. I was conscious of a certain nervous trembling (I own) as I followed the servant to the sitting-room. At the moment, however, when he opened the door, this ignoble sensation left me as suddenly as it had come. I felt myself Pratolungo's widow again when I entered the room.

A reading-lamp, with its shade down, was the only light on the table. Nugent Dubourg, comfortably reposing in an easy-chair, sat by the lamp, with a cigar in his mouth and a book in his hand. He put down the book on the table as he rose to receive me. Knowing by this time what sort of a man I had to deal with, I was determined not to let even the merest trifles escape me. It might have its use in helping me to understand him if I knew how he had been occupying his mind while he was expecting me to arrive. I looked at the book. It was "Rousseau's Confessions."

He advanced with his pleasant smile, and offered his hand as if nothing had happened to disturb our ordinary relations toward each other. I drew back a step, and looked at him.

"Won't you shake hands with me?" he asked.

"I will answer that directly," I said. "Where is your brother?"

"I don't know."

"When you *do* know, Mr. Nugent Dubourg,

and when you have brought your brother back to this house, I will take your hand—not before."

He bowed resignedly, with a little satirical shrug of his shoulders, and asked if he might offer me a chair.

I took a chair for myself, and placed it so that I might be opposite to him when he resumed his seat. He checked himself in the act of sitting down, and looked toward the open window.

"Shall I throw away my cigar?" he said.

"Not on my account. I have no objection to smoking."

"Thank you." He took his chair—keeping his face in the partial obscurity cast by the shade of the lamp. After smoking for a moment he spoke again, without turning to look at me. "May I ask what your object is in honoring me with this visit?"

"I have two objects. The first is to see that you leave Dimchurch to-morrow morning. The second is to restore your brother to happiness by uniting him to his promised wife."

He looked round at me quickly. His experience of my irritable temper had not prepared him for the perfect composure of voice and manner with which I answered his question. He looked back again from me to his cigar, and knocked off the ash at the tip of it (considering with himself) before he addressed his next words to me.

"We will come to the question of my leaving Dimchurch presently," he said. "Have you received a letter from Oscar?"

"Yes."

"Have you read it?"

"I have read it."

"Then you know that we understand each other?"

"I know that your brother has sacrificed himself, and that you have taken a base advantage of the sacrifice."

He started, and looked round at me once more. I saw that something in my language or in my tone of speaking had stung him.

"You have your privilege as a lady," he said. "Don't push it too far. What Oscar has done, he has done of his own free-will."

"What Oscar has done," I rejoined, "is lamentably foolish, cruelly wrong. Still, perverted as it is, there is something generous, something noble, in the motive which has led *him*. As for your conduct in this matter, I see nothing but what is mean, nothing but what is cowardly, in the motive which has led *you*."

He started to his feet, flung his cigar into the empty fireplace.

"Madame Pratolungo," he said, "I have not the honor of knowing anything of your family. I can't call a woman to account for insulting me. Do you happen to have any *man* related to you, in or out of England?"

"I happen to have what will do equally well on this occasion," I replied. "I have a hearty contempt for threats of all sorts, and a steady resolution in me to say what I think."

He walked to the door, and opened it.

"I decline to give you the opportunity of saying anything more," he rejoined. "I beg to leave you in possession of the room, and to wish you good-evening."

He opened the door. I had entered the house armed in my own mind with a last, desperate resolve, only to be communicated to him, or to anybody, in the final emergency and at the eleventh hour. The time had come for saying what I had hoped with my whole heart to have left unsaid.

I rose on my side, and stopped him as he was leaving the room.

"Return to your chair and your book," I said. "Our interview is at an end. In leaving the house I have one last word to say. You are wasting your time in remaining at Dimchurch."

"I am the best judge of that," he answered, making way for me to go out.

"Pardon me, you are not in a position to judge at all. You don't know what I mean to do as soon as I get back to the rectory."

He instantly changed his position, placing himself in the doorway so as to prevent me from leaving the room.

"What do you mean to do?" he asked, keeping his eyes attentively fixed on mine.

"I mean to force you to leave Dimchurch."

He laughed insolently. I went on as quietly as before. "You have personated your brother to Lucilla this morning," I said. "You have done that, Mr. Nugent Dubourg, for the last time."

"Have I? Who will prevent me from doing it again?"

"I will."

This time he took it seriously.

"You?" he said. "How are *you* to control me, if you please?"

"I can control you through Lucilla. When I get back to the rectory I can, and will, tell Lucilla the truth."

He started, and instantly recovered himself.

"You forget something, Madame Pratolungo. You forget what the surgeon in attendance on her has told us."

"I remember it perfectly. If we say or do anything to agitate his patient, in her present state, the surgeon refuses to answer for the consequences."

"Well?"

"Well—between the alternative of leaving you free to break both their hearts, and the alternative of setting the surgeon's warning at defiance— dreadful as the choice is, my choice is made. I tell you to your face, I would rather see Lucilla blind again than see her your wife."

His estimate of the strength of the position on his side had been necessarily based on one conviction—the conviction that Grosse's professional authority would tie my tongue. I had scattered his calculations to the winds. He turned so deadly pale that, dim as the light was, I could see the change in his face.

"I don't believe you!" he said.

"Present yourself at the rectory to-morrow," I answered, "and you will see. I have no more to say to you. Let me by."

You may suppose I was only trying to frighten him. I was doing nothing of the sort. Blame me or approve of me as you please I was expressing the resolution which I had in my mind when I spoke. Whether my courage would have held out through the walk from Browndown to the rectory—whether I should have shrunk from it when I actually found myself in Lucilla's presence—is more than I can venture to decide. All I say is that I did, in my desperation, positively mean doing it at the moment when I threatened to do it, and that Nugent Dubourg heard something in my voice which told him I was in earnest.

"You fiend!" he burst out, stepping close up to me, with a look of fury.

The whole passionate fervor of the love that the miserable wretch felt for her shook him from head to foot as his horror of me found its way to expression in those two words.

"Spare me your opinion of my character," I said. "I don't expect *you* to understand the motives of an honest woman. For the last time, let me by!"

Instead of letting me by, he locked the door, and put the key in his pocket. That done, he pointed to the chair that I had left.

"Sit down," he said, with a sudden sinking in his voice, which implied a sudden change in his temper. "Let me have a minute to myself."

I returned to my place. He took his own chair on the other side of the table, and covered his face with his hands. We waited a while in silence. I looked at him once or twice, as the minutes followed each other. The shaded lamplight glistened dimly on something between his fingers. I rose softly and stretched across the table to look closer. Tears! On my word of honor, tears forcing their way through his fingers, as he held them over his face! I had been on the point of speaking. I sat down again in silence.

"Say what you want of me. Tell me what you wish me to do."

Those were his first words. He spoke them without moving his hands; so quietly, so sadly, with such hopeless sorrow, such uncomplaining resignation in his voice, that I, who had entered that room hating him, rose again, and went round to his chair. I, who a minute ago, if I had had the strength, would have struck him down on the floor at my feet, laid my hand on his shoulder, pitying him from the bottom of my heart. That is what women are! There is a specimen of their sense, firmness, and self-control!

"Be just, Nugent," I said. "Be honorable. Be all that I once thought you. I want no more."

He dropped his arms on the table; his head fell on them, and he burst into a fit of crying. It was so like his brother that I could almost have fancied I, too, had mistaken one of them for the other. "Oscar over again," I thought to myself, "on the first day when I spoke to him in this very room!"

"Come!" I said, when he was quieter. "We

shall end in understanding each other and in respecting each other, after all."

He irritably shook my hand off his shoulder, and turned his face away from the light.

"Don't talk of understanding *me*," he said. "Your sympathy is for Oscar. He is the victim; he is the martyr; he has all your consideration and all your pity. I am a coward; I am a villain; I have no honor and no heart. Tread Me under foot like a reptile. *My* misery is only what I deserve! Compassion is thrown away—isn't it?—on such a scoundrel as I am!"

I was sorely puzzled how to answer him. All that he had said against himself I had thought of him in my own mind. And why not? He *had* behaved infamously; he *was* a fit object for righteous indignation. And yet—and yet—it is sometimes so very hard, however badly a man may have behaved, for women to hold out against forgiving him when they know that a woman is at the bottom of it!

"Whatever I may have thought of you," I said, "it is still in your power, Nugent, to win back my old regard for you."

"Is it?" he answered, scornfully. "I know better than that. You are not talking to Oscar now—you are talking to a man who has had some experience of women. I know how you all hold to your opinions because they *are* your opinions, without asking yourselves whether they are right or wrong. There are men who could understand me and pity me. No woman can do it. The best and cleverest among you don't know what love is—as a man feels it. It isn't the frenzy with You that it is with Us. It acknowledges restraints in a woman—it bursts through everything in a man. It robs him of his intelligence, his honor, his self-respect; it levels him with the brutes; it debases him into idiocy; it lashes him into madness. I tell you I am not accountable for my own actions. The kindest thing you could do for me would be to shut me up in a mad-house. The best thing I could do for myself would be to cut my throat. Oh yes! this is a shocking way of talking, isn't it? I ought to struggle against it, as you say. I ought to summon my self-control. Ha! ha! ha! Here is a clever woman—here is an experienced woman. And yet, though she has seen me in Lucilla's company hundreds of times, she has never once discovered the signs of a struggle in me! From the moment when I first saw that heavenly creature it has been one long fight against myeslf, one infernal torment of shame and remorse; and this clever friend of mine has observed so little and knows so little that she can only view my conduct in one light— it is the conduct of a coward and a villain!"

He got up, and took a turn in the room. I was—naturally, I think—a little irritated by his way of putting it. A man assuming to know more about love than a woman! Was there ever such a monstrous perversion of the truth as that? I appeal to the women!

"You ought to be the last person to blame me," I said. "I had too high an opinion of you to suspect what was going on. I will never make the same mistake again—I promise you that!"

He came back, and stood still in front of me, looking me hard in the face.

"Do you really mean to say you saw nothing to set you thinking on the day when I first met her?" he asked. "You were there in the room —didn't you see that she struck me dumb? Did you notice nothing suspicious at a later time? When I was suffering martyrdom, if I only looked at her, was there nothing to be seen in me which told its own tale?"

"I noticed that you were never at your ease with her," I replied. "But I liked you and trusted you, and I failed to understand it. That's all."

"Did you fail to understand everything that followed? Didn't I speak to her father? Didn't I try to hasten their marriage? Did I really conceal what I felt when you told me that the first thing which attracted her to Oscar was his voice, and when I remembered that my voice and his were exactly alike? When we first talked of his telling Lucilla of the discoloration of his face, did I not agree with you that he ought to put himself right with her, in his own interests? When she all but found it out for herself, whose influence was used to make him own it? Mine! What did I do when he tried to confess it, and failed to make her understand him? what did I do when she first committed the mistake of believing *me* to be the disfigured man?"

The audacity of that last question fairly took
away my breath. "You cruelly helped to de-
cieve her," I answered, indignantly. "You
basely encouraged your brother in his fatal
policy of silence."

He looked at me with an angry amazement
on his side which more than equaled the angry
amazement on mine.

"So much for the delicate perception of a woman!" he exclaimed; "so much for the wonderful tact which is the peculiar gift of the sex!
You can see no motive but a bad motive in my
sacrificing myself for Oscar's sake!"

I began to discern faintly that there might
have been another than a bad motive for his
conduct. But—well! I dare say I was wrong;
I resented the tone he was taking with me; I
would have owned I had made a mistake to anybody else in the world; I wouldn't own it to
him. There!

"Look back for one moment," he resumed, in
quieter and gentler tones. "See how hardly you
have judged me! I seized the opportunity—I
swear to you this is true—I seized the opportunity of making myself an object of horror to her
the moment I heard of the mistake that she had
made. Feeling in myself that I was growing
less and less capable of avoiding her, I caught at
the chance of making *her* avoid *me;* I did that,
and I did more: I entreated Oscar to let me
leave Dimchurch. He appealed to me, in the
name of our love for each other, to remain. I
couldn't resist him. Where do you see signs of

the conduct of a scoundrel in all this? Would a
scoundrel have betrayed himself to you a dozen
times over—as I did in that talk of ours in the
summer-house? I remember saying in so many
words I wished I had never come to Dimchurch.
What reason but one could there be for my saying that? How is it that you never even asked
me what I meant?"

"You forget," I interposed, "that I had no
opportunity of asking you. Lucilla interrupted
us, and diverted my attention to other things.
What do you mean by putting me on my defense
in this way?" I went on, more and more irritated by the tone he was taking with me. "What
right have you to judge my conduct?"

He looked at me with a kind of vacant
surprise.

"*Have* I been judging your conduct?" he asked.
"Yes!"

"Perhaps I was thinking, if you had seen my
infatuation in time, you might have checked it
in time. No!" he exclaimed, before I could answer him. "Nothing could have checked it—
nothing will cure it but my death. Let us try
to agree. I beg your pardon if I have offended
you. I am willing to take a just view of your
conduct. Will you take a just view of mine?"

I tried hard to take a just view. Though I
resented his manner of speaking to me, I nevertheless secretly felt for him, as I have confessed.
Still, I could not forget that he had attempted to
attract to himself Lucilla's first look on the day
when she tried her sight; that he had person-

ated his brother to Lucilla that very morning; that he had suffered his brother to go away heart-broken, a voluntary exile from all that he held dear. No! I could feel for him, but I could *not* take a just view of him. I sat down, and said nothing.

He returned to the question between us, treating me with the needful politeness when he spoke next. For all that, he alarmed me by what he now said, as he had not alarmed me yet.

"I repeat what I have already told you," he proceeded. "I am no longer accountable for what I do. If I know anything of myself, I believe it will be useless to trust me in the future. While I am capable of speaking the truth, let me tell it. Whatever happens at a later time, remember this—I have honestly made a clean breast of it to-night."

"Stop!" I cried. "I don't understand your reckless way of talking. Every man is accountable for what he does."

He checked me there by an impatient wave of his hand.

"Keep your opinion! I don't dispute it. You will see; you will see. Madame Pratolungo, the day when we had that private talk of ours in the rectory summer-house marks a memorable day in my calendar. My last honest struggle to be true to my poor Oscar ended with that day. The efforts I have made since then have been little better than mere outbreaks of despair. They have done nothing to help me against the passion that has become the one feeling and the one misery of my life. Don't talk of resistance. All resistance stops at a certain point. Since the time I have told you of, *my* resistance has reached its limits. You have heard how I struggled against temptation as long as I could resist it. I have only to tell you how I have yielded to it now."

The reckless, shameless composure with which he said that began to set me against him once more. The perpetual shifts and contradictions in him bewildered and irritated me. Quicksilver itself seemed to be less slippery to lay hold of than this man.

"Do you remember the day," he asked, "when Lucilla lost her temper, and received you so rudely at your visit to Browndown?"

I made a sign in the affirmative.

"You spoke, a little while since, of my personating Oscar to her. I personated him, on the occasion I have just mentioned, for the first time. You were present and heard me. Did you care to speculate on the motives which made me impose myself on her as my brother?"

"As well as I can remember," I answered, "I made the first guess that occurred to me. I thought you were indulging in a moment's mischievous amusement at Lucilla's expense."

"I was indulging in the passion that consumed me! I longed to feel the luxury of her touching me and being familiar with me, under the impression that I was Oscar. Worse even than that, I wanted to try how completely I could impose on her—how easily I might marry her, if I could only deceive you all, and take her away somewhere by herself. The devil was in possession of me. I don't know how it might have ended if Oscar had not come in, and if Lucilla had not burst out as she did. She distressed me—she frightened me—she gave me back again to my better self. I rushed, without stopping to prepare her, into the question of her restoration to sight, as the only way of diverting her mind from the vile advantage that I had taken of her blindness. That night, Madame Pratolungo, I suffered pangs of self-reproach and remorse which would even have satisfied *you*. At the very next opportunity that offered I made my atonement to Oscar. I supported his interests; I even put the words he was to say to Lucilla into his lips—''

''When?'' I broke in. ''Where? How?''

''When the two surgeons had left us. In Lucilla's sitting-room. In the heat of the discussion whether she should submit to the operation at once, or whether she should marry Oscar first, and let Grosse try his experiment on her eyes at a later time. If you recall our conversation, you will remember that I did all I could to persuade Lucilla to marry my brother before Grosse tried his experiment on her sight. Quite useless! You threw all the weight of your influence into the opposite scale. I failed. It made no difference. I had done what I had done in sheer despair; mere impulse—it didn't last. When the next temptation tried me I behaved like a scoundrel—as you say.''

"I have said nothing," I answered, shortly.

"Very well—as you *think*, then. Did you suspect me at last, when we met in the village yesterday? Surely even your eyes must have seen through me on that occasion?"

I answered silently by an inclination of my head. I had no wish to drift into another quarrel. Sorely as he was presuming on my endurance, I tried, in Lucilla's interests, to keep on friendly terms with him.

"You concealed it wonderfully well," he went on, "when I tried to find out whether you had or had not discovered me. You virtuous people are not bad hands at deception when it suits your interests to deceive. I needn't tell you what my temptation was yesterday. The first look of her eyes when they opened on the world, the first light of love and joy breaking on her heavenly face—what madness to expect me to let that look fall on another man, that light show itself to other eyes! No living being, adoring her as I adored her, would have acted otherwise than I did. I could have fallen down on my knees and worshiped Grosse when he innocently proposed to me to take the very place in the room which I was determined to occupy. You saw what I had in my mind. You did your best—and did it admirably—to defeat me. Oh, you pattern people, you can be as shifty with your resources, when a cunning trick is to be played, as the worst of us. You saw how it ended. Fortune stood my friend at the eleventh hour; fortune can shine, like the sun, on the just and the unjust! *I* had the first look of her eyes! *I* felt the first light of love and joy in her face falling on *me!* *I* have had her arms round me, and her bosom on mine—"

I could endure it no longer.

"Open the door!" I said. "I am ashamed to be sitting in the same room with you!"

"I don't wonder at it," he answered. "You may well be ashamed of me. I am ashamed of myself."

There was nothing cynical in his tone, nothing insolent in his manner. The same man who had just gloried, in that abominable way, in his victory over innocence and misfortune, now spoke and looked like a man who was honestly ashamed of himself. If I could only have felt convinced that he was mocking me or playing the hypocrite with me, I should have known what to do. But I say again—impossible as it seems—he was, beyond all doubt, genuinely penitent for what he had said the instant after he had said it! With all my experience of humanity, and all my practice in dealing with strange characters, I stopped midway between Nugent and the locked door, thoroughly puzzled.

"Do you believe me?" he asked.

"I don't understand you," I answered.

He took the key of the door out of his pocket, and put it on the table, close to the chair from which I had just risen.

"I lose my head when I talk of her or think of her," he went on. "I would give everything I possess not to have said what I said just now.

No language you can use is too strong to condemn it. The words burst out of me. If Lucilla herself had been present, I couldn't have controlled them. Go, if you like. I have no right to keep you here after behaving as I have done. There is the key, at your service. Only think first, before you leave me. You had something to propose when you came in. You might influence me—you might shame me into behaving like an honorable man. Do as you please. It rests with you."

Which was I—a good Christian, or a contemptible fool? I went back once more to my chair, and determined to give him a last chance.

"That's kind," he said. "You encourage me; you show me that I am worth trying again. I had a generous impulse in this room yesterday. It might have been something better than an impulse, if I had not had another temptation set straight in my way."

"What temptation?" I asked.

"Oscar's letter has told you; Oscar himself put the temptation in my way. You must have seen it."

"I saw nothing of the sort."

"Doesn't he tell you that I offered to leave Dimchurch forever? I meant it. I saw the misery in the poor fellow's face when Grosse and I were leading Lucilla out of the room. With my whole heart I meant it. If he had taken my hand, and had said Good-by, I should have gone. He wouldn't take my hand. He insisted on thinking it over by himself. He came back resolved to make the sacrifice on his side—"

"Why did you accept the sacrifice?"

"Because he tempted me."

"Tempted you?"

"Yes. What else can you call it, when he offered to leave me free to plead my own cause with Lucilla? What else can you call it, when he showed me a future life, which was a life with Lucilla? Poor, dear, generous fellow, he tempted me to stay when he ought to have encouraged me to go. How could I resist him? Blame the passion that has got me body and soul; don't blame *me!*"

I looked at the book on the table—the book that he had been reading when I entered the room. These sophistical confidences of his were nothing but Rousseau at second hand. Good! If he talked false Rousseau, nothing was left for me but to talk genuine Pratolungo. I let myself go—I was just in the humor for it.

"How can a clever man like you impose on yourself in that way?" I said. "Your future with Lucilla! You have no future with Lucilla which is not shocking to think of. Suppose— you shall never do it as long as I live—suppose you married her? Good Heavens! what a miserable life it would be for both of you! You love your brother. Do you think you could ever really know a moment's peace, with one reflection perpetually forcing itself on your mind? 'I have cheated Oscar out of the woman whom he loved; I have wasted his life; I have broken his heart.' You couldn't look at her, you couldn't speak to her, you couldn't touch her, without feeling it all imbittered by that horrible reproach. And she? What sort of wife would she make you when she knew how you had got her? I don't know which of the two she would hate most—you or herself. Not a man would pass her in the street who would not rouse the thought in her, 'I wonder whether *he* has ever done anything as base as what my husband has done.' Not a married woman of her acquaintance but would make her sick at heart with envy and regret. 'Whatever faults he may have, your husband hasn't won you as my husband won me.' You happy? Your married life endurable? Come! I have saved a few pounds since I have been with Lucilla: I will lay you every farthing I possess you two would be separated by mutual consent before you had been six months man and wife. *Now*, which will you do—will you start for the Continent or stay here? Will you bring Oscar back, like an honorable man, or let him go, and disgrace yourself forever?"

His eyes sparkled; his color rose. He sprang to his feet, and unlocked the door. What was he going to do? To start for the Continent, or to turn me out of the house?

He called to the servant.

"James!"

"Yes, sir?"

"Make the house fast when Madame Pratolungo and I have left it. I am not coming back again."

"Sir!"

"Pack my portmanteau, and send it after me to-morrow, to Nagle's Hotel, London."

He closed the door again and came back to me.

"You refused to take my hand when you came in!" he said. "Will you take it now? I leave Browndown when you leave it; and I won't come back again till I bring Oscar with me."

"Both hands!" I exclaimed—and took him by both hands. I could say nothing more. I could only wonder whether I was waking or sleeping; fit to be put into an asylum, or fit to go at large?

"Come!" he said. "I will see you as far as the rectory gate."

"You can't go to-night," I answered. "The last train has left hours since."

"I can. I can walk to Brighton, and get a bed there, and leave for London to-morrow morning. Nothing will induce me to pass another night at Browndown. Stop! One question before I put the lamp out."

"What is it?"

"Did you do anything toward tracing Oscar when you were in London to-day?"

"I went to a lawyer, and made what arrangements with him I could."

"Here is my pocketbook. Write me down his name and address."

I wrote them. He extinguished the lamp, and led me into the passage. The servant was standing there, bewildered. "Good-night, James. I am going to bring your master back to Browndown." With that explanation, he took up his hat and stick, and gave me his arm. The moment after, we were out in the dark valley, on our way to the village.

On the walk back to the rectory he talked with a feverish volubility and excitement. Avoiding the slightest reference to the subject discussed at our strange and stormy interview, he returned, with tenfold confidence in himself, to his old boastful assertion of the great things he was going to do as a painter. The mission which called him to reconcile Humanity and Nature; the superb scale on which he proposed to interpret sympathetic scenery for the benefit of suffering mankind; the prime necessity of understanding him, not as a mere painter, but as Grand Consoler in Art—I had it all over again, by way of satisfying my mind as to his prospects and occupations in his future life. It was only when we stopped at the rectory gate that he referred to what had passed between us—and even then he only touched on the subject in the briefest possible way.

"Well?" he said. "Have I won back your old regard for me? Do you believe there is a fine side to be found in the nature of Nugent Dubourg? Man is a compound animal. You are a woman in ten thousand. Give me a kiss."

He kissed me, foreign fashion, on both cheeks.

"Now for Oscar!" he shouted, cheerfully. He waved his hat and disappeared in the darkness. I stood at the gate till the last rapid pitpat of his feet died away in the silence of the night.

An indescribable depression seized on my spirits. I began to doubt him again the instant I was alone.

"Is there a time coming," I asked myself, "when all that I have done to-night must be done over again?"

I opened the rectory gate. Mr. Finch intercepted me before I could get round to our side of the house. He held up before me, in solemn triumph, a manuscript of many pages.

"My Letter," he said. "A letter of Christian remonstrance to Nugent Dubourg."

"Nugent Dubourg has left Dimchurch."

With that reply, I told the rector in as few words as possible how my visit to Browndown had ended.

Mr. Finch looked at his letter. All those pages of eloquence written for nothing? No! In the nature of things *that* could not possibly be. "You have done very well, Madame Pratolungo," he remarked, in his most patronizing manner. "Very well indeed, all things considered. *But*, I don't think I shall act wisely if I destroy this." He carefully locked up his manuscript, and turned to me again with a mysterious smile. "I venture to think," said Mr. Finch, with mock humility, "My Letter will be wanted. Don't let me discourage you about Nugent Dubourg. Only let me say: Is he to be trusted?"

It was said by a fool; it would never have been said at all if he had not written his wonderful letter. Still it echoed with a painful fidelity the misgiving secretly present at that moment in my own mind; and, more yet, it echoed the misgiving in Nugent's mind—the doubt of himself which his own lips had confessed to me in so many words. I wished the rector good-night, and went upstairs.

Lucilla was in bed and asleep when I softly opened her door.

After looking for a while at her lovely, peaceful face, I was obliged to turn away. It was time I left the bedside, when the sight of her only made my spirits sink lower and lower. As I cast my last look at her before I closed the door, Mr. Finch's ominous question forced itself on me again. In spite of myself, I said to myself: "Is he to be trusted?"

CHAPTER THE THIRTY-NINTH

SHE LEARNS TO SEE.

With the new morning certain reflections found their way into my mind which were not of the most welcome sort. There was one serious element of embarrassment in my position toward Lucilla which had not discovered itself to me when Nugent and I parted at the rectory gate.

Browndown was now empty. In the absence of both the brothers, what was I to say to Lucilla when the false Oscar failed to pay her his promised visit that day?

In what a labyrinth of lies had the first fatal

suppression of the truth involved us all! One deception after another had been forced on us; one disaster after another had followed retributively as the result—and, now that I was left to deal single-handed with the hard necessities of our position, no choice seemed left to me but to go on deceiving Lucilla still! I was weary of it and ashamed of it. At breakfast-time I evaded all further discussion of the subject after I had first ascertained that Lucilla did not expect her visitor before the afternoon. For some time after breakfast I kept her at the piano. When she wearied of music, and began to talk of Oscar once more, I put on my hat, and set forth on a domestic errand (of the kind usually intrusted to Zillah), solely for the purpose of keeping out of the way, and putting off to the last moment the hateful necessity of telling more lies. The weather stood my friend. It threatened to rain; and Lucilla, on that account, refrained from proposing to accompany me.

My errand took me to a farmhouse on the road which led to Brighton. After settling my business I prolonged my walk, though the rain was already beginning to fall. I had nothing on me that would spoil; and, in my present frame of mind, a wet gown was a preferable alternative to returning to the rectory.

After I had walked about a mile further on, the solitude of the road was enlivened by the appearance of an open carriage approaching me from the direction of Brighton. The hood was up to protect the person inside from the rain.

The person looked out as I passed, and stopped
the carriage in a voice which I instantly recognized as the voice of Grosse.   Our gallant oculist
insisted (in the state of the weather) on my instantly taking shelter by his side, and returning
with him to the house.

"This is an unexpected pleasure," I said.   "I
thought you had arranged not to see Lucilla
again till the end of the week."

Grosse's eyes glared at me through his spectacles with a dignity and gravity worthy of Mr.
Finch himself.

"Shall I tell you something?" he said.   "You
see sitting at your side a lost surgeon-optic.   I
shall die soon.   Put on my tombs, if you please,
The malady which killed this German mans was
—Lofely Feench.   When I am away from her
—gif me your sympathies: I so much want it—
I sweat with anxiousness for young miss.   Your
damn-mess-fix about those two brodders is a sort
of perpetual blisters on my mind.   Instead of
snoring peaceably all night in my nice big English bedt, I roll wide awake on my pillows,
fidgeting for Feench.   I am here to-day before
my time.   For what?   For to try her eyes, you
think?   Goot madam, you think wrong!   It is
not her eyes which troubles me.   Her eyes will
do.   It is You—and the odders at your rectory-
place.   You make me nervous-anxious about my
patients.   I am afraid some of you will let the
mess-fix of those brodder-twins find its way to
her pretty ears, and turn her poor little mind
topsy-turvies when I am not near to see to it

in time. Will you let her be comfortable-easy
for two months more? Ach Gott! if I could
only be certain-sure of *that*, I might leave those
weak new eyes of hers to cure themselves, and
go my ways back to London again."

I had intended to remonstrate with him pretty
sharply for taking Lucilla to Browndown. After
what he had now said it was useless to attempt
anything of that sort—and doubly useless to
hope that he would let me extricate myself from
my difficulties by letting me tell her the truth.

"Of course you are the best judge," I said.
"But you little know what these precautions of
yours cost the unfortunate people who are left
to carry them out."

He took me up sharply at those words.

"You shall see for your own self," he said, "if
it is not worth the cost. If her eyes satisfy me,
Feench shall learn to see to-day. You shall stand
by, you obstinate womans, and judge if it is goot
to add shock and agitation to the exhaustions and
irritabilities and bedevilments of all sorts which
our poor miss must suffer in learning to see, after
being blind for all her life. No more of it now
till we get to the rectory-place." By way of
changing the subject for the present, he put a
question to me which I felt it necessary to answer with some caution. "How is my nice boys?
—my bright-clever Nugent?" he asked.

"Very well."

There I stopped, not feeling at all sure of the
ground I was treading on.

"Mind this!" Grosse went on. "My bright-

boy-Nugent keeps her comfortable-easy. My
bright-boy-Nugent is worth all the rest of you
togedder. I insist on his making his visits to
young miss at the rectory-place, in spite of that
windy-talky-puff-bag-Feench-father of hers. I
say positively — Nugent shall come into the
house."

There was no help for it now. I was obliged
to tell him that Nugent had left Browndown,
and that I was the person who had sent him
away.

For a moment I was really in doubt whether
the skilled hand of the great surgeon would not
be ignobly employed in boxing my ears. No
perversion of spelling can possibly report the
complicated German-English jargon in which
his fury poured itself out on my devoted head.

Let it be enough to say that he declared Nugent's abominable personation of his brother to
be vitally important—so long as Oscar was absent—to his successful treatment of the sensitive
and excitable patient whom we had placed under
his care. I vainly assured him that Nugent's
object in leaving Dimchurch was to set matters
right again in bringing his brother back. Grosse
flatly declined to allow himself to be influenced
by any speculative consideration of that sort.
He said (and swore) that my meddling had raised
a serious obstacle in his way, and that nothing
but his own tender regard for Lucilla prevented
him from turning "the coachmans back," and
leaving us henceforth to shift for ourselves.

When we reached the rectory gate he had

cooled a little. As we crossed the garden he reminded me that I stood pledged to be present when the bandage was taken off.

"Now mind!" he said. "You are going to see if it is goot or bad to tell her that she has had those nice white arms of hers round the wrong brodder. You are going to tell me afterward if you dare to say to her, in plain English words, 'Blue-Face is the man.' "

We found Lucilla in the sitting-room. Grosse briefly informed her that he had nothing particular to occupy him in London, and that he had advanced the date of his visit on that account. "You want something to do, my lofe, on this soaky-rainy day. Show Papa-Grosse what you can do with your eyes, now you have got them back again." With those words he unfastened the bandage, and, taking her by the chin, examined her eyes—first without his magnifying glass; then with it.

"Am I going on well?" she asked, anxiously.

"Famous-well! You go on (as my goot friends say in America) first-class. Now use your eyes for yourself. Gif one lofing look to Grosse first. Then—see! see! see!"

There was no mistaking the tone in which he spoke to her. He was not only satisfied about her eyes — he was triumphant. "Soh!" he grunted, turning to me. "Why is Mr. Sebrights not here to look at this?"

I eagerly approached Lucilla. There was still a little dimness left in her eyes. I noticed also that they moved to and fro restlessly, and (at times) wildly. But, oh, the bright change in her! the new life of beauty which the new sense .had bestowed on her already! Her smile, always charming, now caught light from her eyes, and spread its gentle fascination over all her face. It was impossible not to long to kiss her. I advanced to congratulate, to embrace her. Grosse stepped forward, and checked me.

"No," he said. "Walk your ways to the odder end of the rooms, and let us see if *she* can go to *you*."

Like all other people knowing no more of the subject than I knew, I had no idea of the pitiably helpless manner in which the restored sense of sight struggles to assert itself in persons who have been blind for life. In such cases the effort of the eyes that are first learning to see is like the effort of the limbs when a child is first learn- ing to walk. But for Grosse's odd way of tak- ing it, the scene which I was now to witness would have been painful in the last degree. My poor Lucilla—instead of filling me with joy, as I had anticipated—would, I really believe, have wrung my heart, and have made me burst out crying.

"Now!" said Grosse, laying one hand on Lu- cilla's arm, while he pointed to me with the other. "There she stands. Can you go to her?"

"Of course I can!"

"I lay you a bet-wager you can *not*. Ten thausand pounds to six pennies. Done-done. Now try!"

She answered by a little gesture of defiance, and took three hasty steps forward. Bewildered and frightened, she stopped suddenly, at the third step, before she had advanced half the way from her end of the room to mine.

"I saw her here," she said, pointing down to the spot on which she was standing, and appealing piteously to Grosse. "I see her now, and I don't know where she is! She is so near, I feel as if she touched my eyes—and yet" (she advanced another step and clutched with her hands at the empty air)—"and yet I can't get near enough to take hold of her. Oh! what does it mean? what does it mean?"

"It means—pay me my six pennies!" said Grosse. "The wager-bet is mine!"

She resented his laughing at her with an obstinate shake of her head, and an angry knitting of her pretty eyebrows.

"Wait a little," she said. "You shan't win quite so easily as that. I will get to her yet!"

She came straight to me in a moment—just as easily as I could have gone to her myself if I had tried.

"Another wager-bet!" cried Grosse, still standing behind her and calling to me. "Twenty thausand pounds this time to a four-pennies-bit. *She has shut her eyes to get to you.* Hey?"

It was true—she had blindfolded herself! With her eyes closed she could measure to a hair-breadth the distance which, with her eyes opened, she was perfectly incompetent to calculate! Detected by both of us, she sat down, poor dear,

with a sigh of despair. "Was it worth while,"
she said to me sadly, "to go through the operation for *this?*"

Grosse joined us at our end of the room.

"All in goot time," he said. "Patience, and
these helpless eyes of yours will learn. Soh! I
shall begin to teach them now. You have got
your own notions—hey?—about this colors and
that? When you were blind did you think what
would be your favorite colors if you could see?
You did? Which colors is it? Tell me. Come."

"White first," she answered. "Then scarlet."

Grosse paused and considered.

"White I understand," he said. "White is
the fancy of a young girls. But why scarlets?
Could you see scarlets when you were blind?"

"Almost," she answered, "if it was bright
enough. I used to feel something pass before
my eyes when scarlet was shown to me."

"In these cataracts-cases it is constantly scarlets that they almost see," muttered Grosse to
himself. "There must be reason for this—and
I must find him." He went on with his questions to Lucilla. "And the colors you hate most
—which is *he?*"

"Black."

Grosse nodded his head approvingly. "I
thought so," he said. "It is always black that
they hate. For this also there must be reason
—and I must find *him.*"

Having expressed that resolution, he approached the writing-table, and took a sheet
of paper out of the case, and a circular pen-

"I WILL GET TO HER YET!"—Poor Miss Finch, Vol. XV., page 463.

wiper of scarlet cloth out of the inkstand.
After that he looked about him, waddled back
to the other end of the room, and fetched the
black felt hat in which he had traveled from
London. He ranged the hat, the paper, and
the pen-wiper in a row. Before he could put
his next question to her she pointed to the hat
with a gesture of disapproval.

"Take it away," she said. "I don't like that."

Grosse stopped me before I could speak.

"Wait a little," he whispered in my ear. "It
is not quite so wonderful as you think. These
blind peoples, when they first see, have all alike
the same hatred of anything what is dark."
He turned to Lucilla. "Say," he asked, "is
your favorite colors among these things here?"

She passed by the hat in contempt; looked at
the pen-wiper, and put it down; looked at the
sheet of paper, and put it down; hesitated—and
again shut her eyes.

"No!" cried Grosse. "I won't have it! How
dare you blind yourself in the presence of Me?
What! I give you back your sights, and you go
shut your eyes. Open them—or I will put you
in the corner like a naughty girls. Your favorite
colors? Now, now, now!"

She opened her eyes (very unwillingly), and
looked once more at the pen-wiper and the paper.

"I see nothing as bright as my favorite colors
here," she said.

Grosse held up the sheet of paper, and pressed
the question without mercy.

"What! Is white whiter than this?"

"Fifty thousand times whiter than that!"

"Goot. Now mind! This paper is white." (He snatched her handkerchief out of her apron-pocket.) "This handkerchief is white too; whitest of the white, both of them. First lesson, my lofe! Here in my hands is your favorite colors, in the time when you were blind."

"*Those!*" she exclaimed, pointing to the paper and the handkerchief, with a look of blank disappointment as he dropped them on the table. She turned over the pen-wiper and the hat, and looked round at me. Grosse, waiting to try another experiment, left it to me to answer. The result in both cases was the same as in the cases of the sheet of paper and the handkerchief. Scarlet was not half as red—black not one-hundredth part as black—as her imagination had figured them to her in the days when she was blind. Still as to this last color—as to black—she could feel some little encouragement. It had affected her disagreeably (just as poor Oscar's face had affected her), though she had not actually known it for the color that she disliked. She made an effort, poor child, to assert herself against her merciless surgeon-teacher. "I didn't know it was black," she said; "but I hated the sight of it, for all that."

She tried, as she spoke, to toss the hat onto a chair standing close by her, and threw it instead high above the back of the chair, against the wall, at least six feet away from the object at which she had aimed. "I am a helpless fool!" she burst out, her face flushing crimson with mortification. "Don't let Oscar see me! I can't bear the thought of making myself ridiculous before *him!* He is coming here," she added, turning to me entreatingly. "Manage to make some excuse for his not seeing me till later in the day."

I promised to find the excuse—all the more readily, that I now saw an unexpected chance of reconciling her in some degree (so long as she was learning to see) to the blank produced in her life by Oscar's absence.

She addressed herself again to Grosse.

"Go on!" she said, impatiently. "Teach me to be something better than an idiot—or put the bandage on and blind me again. My eyes are of no use to me! Do you hear?" she cried, furiously, taking him by his broad shoulders and shaking him with all her might—"my eyes are of no use to me!"

"Now! now! now!" cried Grosse. "If you don't keep your tempers, you little spitfire, I will teach you nothing." He took up the sheet of paper and the pen-wiper; and, forcing her to sit down, placed them together before her, in her lap.

"Do you know one thing?" he went on. "Do you know what is meant by an objects which is square? Do you know what is meant by an objects which is round?"

Instead of answering him, she appealed indignantly to my opinion.

"Is it not monstrous," she asked, "to hear him put such a question to me as that? Do I know round from square? Oh, how cruelly humiliating! Don't tell Oscar! don't tell Oscar!"

"If you know," persisted Grosse, "you can tell me. Look at those two things in your lap. Are they both round or both square? or is one round and the odder square? Look now, and tell me."

She looked—and said nothing.

"Well?" continued Grosse.

"You put me out, standing there staring at me through your horrid spectacles!" she said, irritably. "Don't look at me, and I will tell you directly."

Grosse turned his head my way, with his diabolical grin; and signed to me to keep watch on her in his place.

The instant his back was turned she shut her eyes, and ran over the paper and the pen-wiper with the tips of her fingers!

"One is round, and one is square," she answered, cunningly, opening her eyes again, just in time to bear critical inspection when Grosse turned round toward her once more.

He took the paper and the pen-wiper out of her hands; and (thoroughly understanding the trick she had played him) changed them for a bronze saucer and a book. "Which is round and which is square of these?" he asked, holding them up before her.

She looked first at one, and then at the other

—plainly incapable (with only her eyes to help her) of answering the question.

"I put you out—don't I?" said Grosse. "You can't shut your eyes, my lofely Feench, while I am looking—can you?"

She turned red, then pale again. I began to be afraid she would burst out crying. Grosse managed her to perfection. The tact of this rough, ugly, eccentric old man was the most perfect tact I have ever met with.

"Shut your eyes," he said, soothingly. "It is the right ways to learn. Shut your eyes, and take them in your hands, and tell me which is round and which is square in that way first."

She told him directly.

"Goot! now open your eyes, and see for yourself it is the saucers you have got in your right hand, and the books you have got in your left. You see? Goot again? Put them back on the table now. What shall we do next?"

"May I try if I can write?" she asked, eagerly. "I do so want to see if I can write with my eyes instead of my finger!"

"No! Ten thausand times no! I forbid reading; I forbid writing, yet. Come with me to the window. How do these most troublesome eyes of yours do at a distance?"

While we had been trying our experiment with Lucilla the weather had brightened again. The clouds were parting; the sun was coming out; the bright gaps of blue in the sky were widening every moment; the shadows were traveling grandly over the windy slopes of the hills. Lu-

cilla lifted her hands in speechless admiration as
the German threw open the window, and placed
her face to face with the view.

"Oh!" she exclaimed, "don't speak to me!
don't touch me!—let me enjoy it! There is
no disappointment *here*. I have never thought,
I have never dreamed, of anything half so beautiful as *this!*"

Grosse looked at me, and silently pointed to
her. She had turned pale—she was trembling
in every limb, overwhelmed by her own ecstatic
sense of the glory of the sky and the beauty of
the earth, as they now met her view for the first
time. I penetrated the surgeon's object in di-
recting my attention to her. "See" (he meant
to say,) "what a delicately organized creature
we have to deal with! Is it possible to be too
careful in handling such a sensitive temperament as that?" Understanding him only too
well, I also trembled when I thought of the
future. Everything now depended on Nugent.
And Nugent's own lips had told me that he
could not depend on himself!

It was a relief to me when Grosse interrupted
her.

She pleaded hard to be allowed to stay at the
window a little longer. He refused to allow it.
Upon that she flew instantly into the opposite
extreme. "I am in my own room, and I am
my own mistress," she said, angrily; "I insist
on having my own way." Grosse was ready
with his answer.

"Take your own ways; fatigue those weak

new eyes of yours, and to-morrow, when you try to look out of window, you will not be able to see at all.'' This reply terrified her into instant submission. She assisted in replacing the bandage with her own hands. "May I go away to my own room?" she asked, with the simplicity of a child. "I have seen such beautiful sights —and I do so want to think of them by myself.''

The medical adviser instantly granted the patient's request. Any proceeding which tended to compose her was a proceeding of which he highly approved.

"If Oscar comes,'' she whispered, as she passed me on her way to the door, "mind I hear of it, and mind you don't tell him of the mistakes I have made.'' She paused for a moment, thinking. "I don't understand myself,'' she said. "I never was so happy in my life. And yet I feel almost ready to cry!'' She turned toward Grosse. "Come here, papa. You have been very good to me to-day. I will give you a kiss.'' She laid her hands lightly on his shoulders, kissed his lined and wrinkled cheek, gave me a little squeeze round the waist—and left us. Grosse turned sharply to the window, and used his huge silk handkerchief for a purpose to which (I suspect) it had not been put for many a long year past.

CHAPTER THE FORTIETH.

TRACES OF NUGENT.

"Madame Pratolungo!"

"Herr Grosse?"

He put his handkerchief back into his pocket, and turned to me from the window with his face composed again, and his tea-caddy snuff-box in his hand.

"Now you have seen for your own self," he said, with an emphatic rap on the box, "do you dare tell that sweet girls which of them it is that has gone his ways and left her forever?"

It is not easy to find a limit to the obstinacy of women—when men expect them to acknowledge themselves to have been wrong. After what I had seen, I no more dared tell her than he did. I was only too obstinate to acknowledge it to him—just yet.

"Mind this!" he went on. "Whether you shake her with frights, or whether you heat her with rages, or whether you wound her with griefs —it all goes straight the same to those weak new eyes of hers. They are so weak and so new that I must ask once more for my bedt here to-night, for to see to-morrow if I have not already tried them too much. Now, for the last time of asking, have you got the abominable courage in you to tell her the truth?"

He had found my limit at last. I was obliged

to own (heartily as I disliked doing it) that there was, for the present, no choice left but mercifully to conceal the truth. Having gone this length, I next attempted to consult him as to the safest manner in which I could account to Lucilla for Oscar's absence. He refused (as a man) to recognize the slightest necessity for giving me (as a woman) any advice on a question of evasions and excuses. "I have not lived all my years in the world without learning something," he said. "When it comes to walking upon eggshells and telling fips, the womens have nothing to learn from the mens.—Will you take a little stroll-walk with me in the garden? I have one odder thing to say to you; and I am hungry and thirsty both togedder—for This."

He produced "This" in the form of his pipe. We left the room at once for our stroll in the garden.

Having solaced himself with his first mouthful of tobacco-smoke, he startled me by announcing that he meant to remove Lucilla forthwith from Dimchurch to the sea-side. In doing this he was actuated by two motives—first, the medical motive of strengthening her constitution; second, the personal motive of preserving her from making painful discoveries by placing her out of reach of the gossip of the rectory and the village. Grosse had the lowest opinion of Mr. Finch and his household. His dislike and distrust of the rector, in particular, knew no bounds: he characterized the Pope of Dimchurch as an Ape with a long tongue and a man-and-monkey capacity for doing mischief. Ramsgate was the watering-place which he had fixed on. It was at a safe distance from Dimchurch; and it was near enough to London to enable him to visit Lucilla frequently. The one thing needed was my co-operation in the new plan. If I was at liberty to take charge of Lucilla, he would speak to the Ape with the long tongue; and we might start for Ramsgate before the end of the week.

Was there anything to prevent me from carrying out the arrangement proposed?

There was nothing to prevent me. My one other anxiety apart from Lucilla—anxiety about good Papa—had now, for some time, been happily set at rest. Letter after letter from my sister in France brought me always the same cheering news. My ever green parent had at last discovered that he was no longer in the first bloom of his youth. He had resigned to his juniors, with pathetic expressions of regret, the making of love and the fighting of duels. Ravaged by past passions, this dear innocent had now found a refuge from swords, pistols, and the sex, in collecting butterflies and playing on the guitar. I was free wholly to devote myself to Lucilla, and I honestly rejoiced in the prospect before me. Alone with her, and away from the rectory (where there was always danger of gossip reaching her ears), I could rely on myself to protect her from harm in the present, and to preserve her for Oscar in the future. With all my heart I agreed to the arrangements as Grosse proposed them. When we parted in the garden, he went round to the rector's side of the house to announce (in his medical capacity) the decision at which he had arrived; while I, on my side, went back to Lucilla to make the best excuses that I could invent for Oscar, and to prepare her for our speedy removal from Dimchurch.

"Gone, without coming to say good-by! Gone, without even writing to me!"

There was the first impression I produced on her, when I had done my best to account harmlessly for Oscar's absence. I had, as I thought, taken the shortest and simplest way out of the difficulty by merely inverting the truth. In other words, by telling her that Nugent had got into some serious embarrassment abroad, and that Oscar had been called away at a moment's notice to follow him and help him. It was in vain that I reminded her of Oscar's well-known horror of leave-takings of all kinds; in vain that I represented the urgency of the matter as leaving him no alternative but to confide his excuses and his farewells to me; in vain I promised for him that he would write to her at the first opportunity. She listened, without conviction. The more perseveringly I tried to account for it, the more perseveringly she dwelt on Oscar's unaccountable disregard of her claims on his consideration for her. As for our journey to Ramsgate, it was impossible to interest her in the subject. I gave it up in despair.

"Surely Oscar has left some address at which I can write to him?" she said.

I could only answer that he was not sure enough of his movements to be able to do that before he went away.

"It is more provoking than you think," she went on. "I believe Oscar is afraid to bring his unfortunate brother into my presence. The blue face startled me when I saw it, I know. But I have quite got over that. I feel none of the absurd terror of the poor man which I felt when I was blind. Now that I have seen for myself what he is really like, I can feel for him. I wanted to tell Oscar this—I wanted to say that he might bring his brother to live with us if he liked—I wanted to prevent (just what has happened) his going away from *me* when he wishes to see his brother. You are using me very hardly among you; and I have some reason to complain of it."

While she was talking in this mortifying manner, I felt some consolation nevertheless. Oscar's disfigured complexion would not be the terrible obstacle in the way of his restoration to Lucilla that I had feared. All the comfort which this reflection could give I wanted badly enough. There was no open hostility toward me on Lucilla's part, but there was a coolness which I found more distressing to bear than hostility itself.

I breakfasted in bed the next morning, and only rose toward noon—just in time to say goodby to Grosse before he returned to London. He was in high good spirits about his patient. Her eyes were the better instead of the worse for the exertion to which he had subjected them on the previous day. The bracing air of Ramsgate was all that was wanting to complete the success of the operation. Mr. Finch had started objections, all turning on the question of expense. But with a daughter who was her own mistress, and who had her own fortune, his objections mattered nothing. By the next day, or the day after at latest, we were to start for Ramsgate. I promised to write to our good surgeon as soon as we were established; and he engaged, on his side, to visit us immediately after. "Let her use her eyes for two goot hours every day," said Grosse, at parting. "She may do what she likes with them, except that she must not peep into books or take up pens, till I come to you at Ramsgate. It is most wonderful-beautiful to see how those new eyes of hers do get along. When I next meet goot Mr. Sebrights—hey! how I shall cock-crow over that spick-span-respectable man!"

I felt a little nervous as to how the day would pass, when the German left me alone with Lucilla.

To my amazement, she not only met me with the needful excuses for her behavior on the previous day, but showed herself to be perfectly resigned to the temporary loss of Oscar's society. It was she (not I) who remarked that he could not have chosen a better time for being away from her than the humiliating time when she was learning to distinguish between round and square. It was she (not I) who welcomed the little journey to Ramsgate as a pleasant change in her dull life which would help to reconcile her to Oscar's absence. In brief, if she had actually received a letter from Oscar, relieving her of all anxiety about him, her words and looks could hardly have offered a completer contrast than they now showed to her words and looks of the previous day.

If I had noticed no other alteration in her than this welcome change for the better, my record of the day would have ended here as the record of unmixed happiness.

But, I grieve to say, I have something unpleasant to add. While she was making her excuses to me, and speaking in the sensible and satisfactory terms which I have just repeated, I noticed a curious underlying embarrassment in her manner, entirely unlike any previous embarrassment which had ever intruded itself between us. And, stranger still, on the first occasion when Zillah came into the room while I was in it, I observed that Lucilla's embarrassment was reflected (when the old woman spoke to me) in the face and manner of Lucilla's nurse.

But one conclusion could possibly follow from what I saw: they were both concealing something from me, and they were both more or less ashamed of what they were doing.

Somewhere—not very far back in these pages—I have said of myself that I am not by nature a woman who is easily ready to suspect others. On this very account, when I find suspicion absolutely forced on me—as it was now—I am apt to fly into the opposite extreme. In the present case, I fixed on the person to suspect—all the more readily from having been slow to suspect him in by-gone days. "In some way or other," I said to myself, "Nugent Dubourg is at the bottom of this."

Was he communicating with her privately, in the name and in the character of Oscar?

The bare idea of it hurried me headlong into letting her know that I had noticed the change in her.

"Lucilla!" I said. "Has anything happened?"

"What do you mean?" she asked, coldly.

"I fancy I see some change—" I began.

"I don't understand you," she answered, walking away from me as she spoke.

I said no more. If our intimacy had been less close and less affectionate, I might have openly avowed to her what was passing in my mind. But how could I say to Lucilla: You are deceiving me? It would have been the end of our sisterhood—the end of our friendship. When confidence is withdrawn between two people who love each other, everything is withdrawn. They are on the footing of strangers from that moment, and must stand on ceremony. Delicate minds will understand why I accepted the check she had administered to me, and said no more.

I went into the village alone. Managing matters so as to excite no surprise, I contrived to have a little gossip about Nugent with Gootheridge at the inn, and with the servant at Browndown. If Nugent had returned secretly to Dimchurch, one of these two men, in our little village, must almost certainly have seen him. Neither of them had seen him.

I inferred from this that he had not tried to communicate with her personally. Had he attempted it (more cunningly and more safely) by letter?

I went back to the rectory. It was close on the hour which I had appointed with Lucilla—now that the responsibility rested on my shoulders—for allowing her to use her eyes. On taking off the bandage I noticed a circumstance which confirmed the conclusion at which I had already arrived. Her eyes deliberately avoided looking into mine. Suppressing as well as I could the pain which this new discovery caused me, I repeated Grosse's words prohibiting her from attempting to look into a book or to use a pen until he had seen her again.

"There is no need for him to forbid me to do that," she said.

"Have you attempted it already?" I inquired.

"I looked into a little book of engravings," she answered. "But I could distinguish nothing. The lines all mingled together and swam before my eyes."

"Have you tried to write?" I asked next. (I was ashamed of myself for laying that trap for her—although the serious necessity of discovering whether she was privately in correspondence with Nugent might surely have excused it.)

"No," she replied. "I have not tried to write."

She changed color when she made that answer.

It is necessary to own that, in putting my ques-

tion, I was too much excited to call to mind what
I should have remembered in a calmer state.
There was no necessity for her trying to use her
eyes—even if she was really carrying on a correspondence which she wished to keep secret from
me. Zillah had been in the habit of reading her
letters to her before I appeared at the rectory;
and she could write short notes (as I have already
mentioned) by feeling her way on the paper with
her finger. Besides, having learned to read by
touch (that is to say, with raised characters),
just as she had learned to write, even if her eyes
had been sufficiently recovered to enable her to
distinguish small objects, nothing but practice
could have enabled her to use them for purposes
of correspondence.

These considerations, though they did not strike
me at the time, occurred to me later in the day,
and altered my opinion to a certain extent. I
now interpreted the change of color which I had
noticed in her as the outward sign of suspicion
on her side—suspicion that I had a motive of my
own in interrogating her. For the rest, my doubts
of Nugent remained unmoved. Try as I might,
I could not divest my mind of the idea that he
was playing me false, and that in one way or
another he had contrived not only to communicate with Lucilla, but to persuade her to keep me
in ignorance of what he had done.

I deferred to the next day any attempt at making further discoveries.

The last thing at night, I had a momentary
impulse to question Zillah. Reflection soon

checked it. My experience of the nurse's character told me that she would take refuge in flat denial—and would then inform her mistress of what had happened. I knew enough of Lucilla to know (after what had already passed between us) that a quarrel with me would follow. Things were bad enough already, without making them worse in that way. When the morning came, I resolved to keep a watchful eye on the village post-office, and on the movements of the nurse.

When the morning came, there was a letter for me from abroad.

The address was in the handwriting of one of my sisters. We usually wrote to each other at intervals of a fortnight or three weeks. This letter had followed its predecessor after an interval of less than one week. What did it mean? Good news or bad?

I opened the letter.

It inclosed a telegram announcing that my poor dear father was lying dangerously wounded at Marseilles. My sisters had already gone to him; they implored me to follow them without one moment of needless delay. Is it necessary to tell the story of this horrible calamity? Of course it begins with a woman and an elopement. Of course it ends with a young man and a duel. Have I not told you already?—Papa was so susceptible; Papa was so brave. Oh, dear, dear! the old story over again. You have an English proverb: "What is bred in the bone—" et cetera, et cetera. Let us drop the veil. I mean, let us end the chapter.

CHAPTER THE FORTY-FIRST.

A HARD TIME FOR MADAME PRATOLUNGO.

OUGHT I to have been prepared for the calamity which had now fallen on my sisters and myself? If I had looked my own experience of my poor father fairly in the face, would it not have been plain to me that the habits of a life were not likely to be altered at the end of a life? Surely, if I had exerted my intelligence, I might have foreseen that the longer his reformation lasted, the nearer he was to a relapse, and the more obviously probable it became that he would fail to fulfill the hopeful expectations which I had cherished of his conduct in the future? I grant it all. But where are the pattern people who can exert their intelligence, when their intelligence points to one conclusion and their interests to another? Ah, my dear ladies and gentlemen, there is such a fine, strong foundation of stupidity at the bottom of our common humanity —if we only knew it!

I could feel no hesitation—as soon as I had recovered myself—about what it was my duty to do. My duty was to leave Dimchurch in time to catch the fast mail-train from London to the Continent, at eight o'clock that night.

And leave Lucilla?

Yes! not even Lucilla's interests—dearly as I

loved her, alarmed as I felt about her—were as
sacred as the interests which called me to my
father's bedside. I had some hours to spare before it would be necessary for me to leave her.
All I could do was to employ those hours in taking the strictest precautions I could think of to
protect her in my absence. I could not be long
parted from her. One way or the other, the
miserable doubt whether my father would live
or die would, at his age, soon be over.

I sent for her to see me in my room, and
showed her my letter.

She was honestly grieved when she read it.
For a moment—when she spoke her few words
of sympathy—the painful constraint in her manner toward me passed away. It returned again
when I announced my intention of starting for
France that day, and expressed the regret I felt
at being obliged to defer our visit to Ramsgate
for the present. She not only answered re-
strainedly (forming, as I fancied, some thought
at the moment in her own mind)—she left me
with a commonplace excuse. "You must have
much to think of in this sad affliction: I won't
intrude on you any longer. If you want me,
you know where to find me." With no more
than those words, she walked out of the room.

I never remember, at any other time, such a
sense of helplessness and confusion as came over
me when she had closed the door. I set to work
to pack up the few things I wanted for the journey, feeling instinctively that if I did not occupy
myself in doing something, I should break down

altogether. Accustomed, in all the other emergencies of my life, to decide rapidly, I was not even clear enough in my mind to see the facts as they were. As to resolving on anything, I was about as capable of doing that as the baby in Mrs. Finch's arms.

The effort of packing aided me to rally a little —but did no more toward restoring me to my customary tone of mind.

I sat down helplessly, when I had done, feeling the serious necessity of clearing matters up between Lucilla and myself before I went away, and still as ignorant as ever how to do it. To my indescribable disgust, I actually felt tears beginning to find their way into my eyes! I had just enough of Pratolungo's widow left in me to feel heartily ashamed of myself. Past vicissitudes and dangers, in the days of my republican life with my husband, had made me a sturdy walker—with a gypsy relish (like my little Jicks) for the open air. I snatched up my hat and went out to see what exercise would do for me.

I tried the garden. No! the garden was (for some inscrutable reason) not big enough. I had still some hours to spare. I tried the hills next.

Turning toward the left, and passing the church, I heard through the open windows the *boom-boom* of Reverend Finch's voice catechising the village children. Thank Heaven, he was out of my way, at any rate! I mounted the hills, hurrying on as fast as I could. The air and the movement cleared my mind. After more than an hour of hard walking, I returned to the rectory, feeling like my old self again.

Perhaps there were some dregs of irresolution still left in me. Or perhaps there was some enervating influence in my affliction, which made me feel more sensitively than ever the change in the relations between Lucilla and myself. Having, by this time, resolved to come to a plain explanation, before I left her unprotected at the rectory, I shrank, even yet, from confronting a possible repulse by speaking to her personally. Taking a leaf out of poor Oscar's book, I wrote what I wanted to say to her in a note.

I rang the bell—once, twice. Nobody answered it.

I went to the kitchen. Zillah was not there. I knocked at the door of her bedroom. There was no answer; the bedroom was empty when I looked in. Awkward as it would be, I found myself obliged either to give my note to Lucilla with my own hand, or to decide on speaking to her, after all.

I could *not* prevail on myself to speak to her. So I went to her room with my note and knocked at the door.

Here again there was no reply. I knocked once more—with the same result. I looked in. There was no one in the room. On the little table at the foot of the bed there lay a letter addressed to me. The writing was in Zillah's hand. But Lucilla had written her name in the corner, in the usual way, to show that she had dictated the letter to her nurse. A load was lifted off my heart as I took it up. The same idea (I concluded) had occurred to her which had occurred to me. She too had shrunk from the embarrassment of a personal explanation. She too had written—and was keeping out of the way until her letter had spoken for her, and had united us again as friends before I left the house.

With these pleasant anticipations I opened the letter. Judge what I felt when I found what it really contained.

"DEAR MADAME PRATOLUNGO—You will agree with me that it is very important, after what Herr Grosse has said about the recovery of my sight, that my visit to Ramsgate should not be delayed. As you are unable, through circumstances which I sincerely regret, to accompany me to the sea-side, I have determined to go to London to my aunt, Miss Batchford, and to ask her to be my companion instead of you. I have had experience enough of her sincere affection for me to be quite sure that she will gladly take the charge of me off your hands. As no time is to be lost, I start for London without waiting for your return from your walk to wish you good-by. You so thoroughly understand the necessity of dispensing with formal farewells, in cases of emergency, that I am sure you will not feel offended at my taking leave of you in this way. With best wishes for your father's recovery, believe me,

"Yours very truly,
"LUCILLA.

"P.S.—You need be under no apprehension about me. Zillah goes with me as far as London; and I shall communicate with Herr Grosse when I arrive at my aunt's house."

But for one sentence in it I should most assuredly have answered this cruel letter by instantly resigning my situation as Lucilla's companion.

The sentence to which I refer contained the words which cast in my teeth the excuses that I had made for Oscar's absence. The sarcastic reference to my recent connection with a case of emergency, and to my experience of the necessity of dispensing with formal farewells, removed my last lingering doubts of Nugent's treachery. I now felt not suspicion only, but positive conviction that he had communicated with her in his brother's name, and that he had contrived (by some means at which it was impossible for me to guess) so to work on Lucilla's mind—so to excite that indwelling distrust which her blindness had rooted in her character—as to destroy her confidence in me for the time being.

Arriving at this conclusion, I could still feel compassionately and generously toward Lucilla. Far from blaming my poor deluded sister-friend for her cruel departure and her yet crueler letter, I laid the whole fault on the shoulders of Nugent. Full as my mind was of my own troubles, I could still think of the danger that threatened Lucilla, and of the wrong that Oscar had suffered. I could still feel the old glow of my resolution

to bring them together again, and still remember
(and determined to pay) the debt I owed to
Nugent Dubourg.

In the turn things had taken, and with the
short time still at my disposal, what was I to do
next? Assuming that Miss Batchford would accompany her niece to Ramsgate, how could I put
the necessary obstacle in Nugent's way, if he
attempted to communicate with Lucilla at the
sea-side, in my absence?

It was impossible for me to decide this, unless
I first knew whether Miss Batchford, as a member of the family, was to be confidentially informed of the sad position in which Oscar and
Lucilla now stood toward each other.

The person to consult in this difficulty was the
rector. As head of the household, and in my
absence, the responsibility evidently rested with
Reverend Finch.

I went round at once to the other side of the
house. If Mr. Finch had returned to the rectory, after the catechising was over, well and
good. If not, I should be obliged to inquire in
the village, and seek him at the cottages of his
parishioners. His magnificent voice relieved me
from all anxiety on this head. The *boom boom*
which I had last heard in the church, I now
heard again in the study.

When I entered the room Mr. Finch was on
his legs, highly excited, haranguing Mrs. Finch
and the baby, ensconced as usual in a corner.
My appearance on the scene diverted his flow of
language, for the moment, so that it all poured

itself out on my unlucky self. (If you recollect that the rector and Lucilla's aunt had been, from time immemorial, on the worst of terms, you will be prepared for what is coming. If you have forgotten this, look back at my sixth chapter and refresh your memory.)

"The very person I was going to send for!" said the Pope of Dimchurch. "Don't excite Mrs. Finch! Don't speak to Mrs. Finch! You shall hear why directly. Address yourself exclusively to Me. Be calm, Madame Pratolungo! you don't know what has happened. I am here to tell you."

I ventured to stop him, mentioning that Lucilla's letter had informed me of his daughter's sudden departure for her aunt's house. Mr. Finch waved away my answer with his hand, as something too infinitely unimportant to be worthy of a moment's notice.

"Yes! yes! yes!" he said. "You have a superficial acquaintance with the facts. But you are far from being aware of what my daughter's sudden removal of herself from my roof really means. Now don't be frightened, Madame Pratolungo! and don't excite Mrs. Finch!—How are you, my dear? how is the child? Both well. Thanks to an overruling Providence, both well. —Now, Madame Pratolungo, attend to this. My daughter's flight—I say flight advisedly: it is nothing less—my daughter's flight from my house means (I entreat you to be calm!)—means ANOTHER BLOW dealt at me by the family of my first wife. Dealt at me," repeated Mr.

Finch, heating himself with the recollection of his old feud with the Batchfords—"dealt at me by Miss Batchford (by Lucilla's aunt, Madame Pratolungo) through my unoffending second wife and my innocent child.—Are you sure you are well, my dear? are you sure the infant is well? Thank Providence!—Concentrate your attention, Madame Pratolungo! Your attention is wandering. Prompted by Miss Batchford, my daughter has left my roof. Ramsgate is a mere excuse. And how has she left it? Not only without first seeing Me—I am Nobody!—but without showing the slightest sympathy for Mrs. Finch's maternal situation. Attired in her traveling costume, my daughter precipitately entered (or to use my wife's graphic expression, '*bounced into*') the nursery, while Mrs. Finch was administering maternal sustenance to the infant. Under circumstances which might have touched the heart of a bandit or a savage, my unnatural daughter (remind me, Mrs. Finch; we will have a little Shakespeare to-night; I will read 'King Lear')—my unnatural daughter announced without one word of preparation that a domestic affliction would prevent you from accompanying her to Ramsgate. Grieved, dear Madame Pratolungo, to hear it. Cast your burden on Providence.—Bear up, Mrs. Finch; bear up.—Having startled my wife with this harrowing news, my daughter next shocked her by declaring that she was going to leave her father's roof without waiting to bid her father good-by. The catching of a train, you will observe, was (no doubt at Miss Batchford's instigation) of more importance than the parental embrace or the pastoral blessing. Leaving a message of apology for Me, my heartless child (I use Mrs. Finch's graphic language again—you have fair, very fair powers of expression, Mrs. Finch) — my heartless child 'bounced out' of the nursery to catch her train; having, for all she knew or cared, administered a shock to my wife which might have soured the fountain of maternal sustenance at its source. *There* is where the Blow falls, Madame Pratolungo! How do I know that acid disturbance is not being communicated at this moment, instead of wholesome nourishment, between mother and child?—I shall prepare you an alkaline draught, Mrs. Finch, to be taken after meals. Don't speak; don't move! Give me your pulse.—I hold Miss Batchford accountable, Madame Pratolungo, for whatever happens—my daughter is a mere instrument in the hands of my first wife's family.—Give me your pulse, Mrs. Finch. I don't like your pulse. Come upstairs directly. A recumbent position and another warm bath—under Providence, Madame Pratolungo!—may parry the Blow.—Would you kindly open the door, and pick up Mrs. Finch's handkerchief? Never mind the novel—the handkerchief.''

I seized my first opportunity of speaking again, while Mr. Finch was conducting his wife (with his arm round her waist) to the door—putting the question which I had been waiting to ask in this cautious form:

"Do you propose to communicate, sir, either with your daughter or with Miss Batchford, while Lucilla is away from the rectory? My object in venturing to ask—"

Before I could state my object Mr. Finch turned round (turning Mrs. Finch with him) and surveyed me from head to foot with a look of indignant astonishment.

"Is it possible you can see this double Wreck," said Mr. Finch, indicating his wife and child, "and suppose that I would communicate, or sanction communication of any sort, with the persons who are responsible for it? My dear! can you account for Madame Pratolungo's extraordinary question? Am I to understand (do *you* understand) that Madame Pratolungo is insulting me?"

It was useless to try to explain myself. It was useless for Mrs. Finch (who had made several abortive efforts to put in a word or two on her own part) to attempt to pacify her husband. All the poor damp lady could do was to beg me to write to her from foreign parts. "I'm sorry you're in trouble; and I should really be glad to hear from you." Mrs. Finch had barely time to say those kind words before the rector, in a voice of thunder, desired me to look at "that double Wreck, and respect *it* if I did not respect *him*" —and with that walked himself, his wife, and his baby out of the room.

Having gained the object which had brought me into the study, I made no attempt to detain him. The little sense the man possessed at the

best of times was completely upset by the shock
which Lucilla's abrupt departure had inflicted
on his high opinion of his own importance.
That he would end in being reconciled to his
daughter—before her next subscription to the
household expenses fell due—was a matter of
downright certainty. But, until that time came,
I felt equally sure that he would vindicate his
outraged dignity by declining to hold any communication, in person or in writing, with Ramsgate. During the short term of my absence from
England Miss Batchford would be left as ignorant of her niece's perilous position between the
twin brothers as Lucilla herself. To know this
was to have gained the information that I
wanted. Nothing was left but to set my brains
to work at once and act on it.

How was I to act on it?

On the spur of the moment I could see but one
way. If Grosse pronounced Lucilla's recovery
to be complete before I returned from abroad,
the best thing I could do would be to place Miss
Batchford in a position to reveal the truth in my
place, without running any risk of a premature
discovery—in other words, without letting the
old lady into the secret before the time arrived
at which it could be safely divulged.

This apparently intricate difficulty was easily
overcome by writing two letters (before I went
away) instead of one.

The first letter I addressed to Lucilla. Without any reference to her behavior to me, I stated,
in the fullest detail and with all needful delicacy,

her position between Oscar and Nugent; and referred her for proof of the truth of my assertions to her relatives at the rectory. "I leave it entirely to your discretion" (I added) "to write me an answer or not. Put the warning which I now give you to the proof; and if you wonder why it has been so long delayed, apply to Herr Grosse, on whom the whole responsibility rests." There I ended; being resolved, after the wrong that Lucilla had inflicted on me, to leave my justification to facts. I confess I was too deeply wounded by her conduct—though I *did* lay all the blame of it on Nugent—to care to say a word in my own defense.

This letter sealed, I wrote next to Lucilla's aunt.

It was not an easy matter to address Miss Batchford. The contempt with which she regarded Mr. Finch's opinions in politics and religion was more than matched by the strong aversion which she felt for my republican opinions. I have already mentioned, far back in these pages, that a dispute on politics between the Tory old lady and myself ended in a quarrel between us which closed the doors of her house on me from that time forth. Knowing this, I ventured on writing to her nevertheless, because I also knew Miss Batchford to be (apart from her furious prejudices) a gentlewoman in the best sense of the word; devotedly attached to her niece, and quite as capable, when that devotion was appealed to, of doing justice to me (apart from *my* furious prejudice) as I was of

doing justice to her. Writing in a tone of unaffected respect, and appealing to her forbearance to encourage mine, I requested her to hand
my letter to Lucilla on the day when the surgeon reported that all further necessity for his
attendance had ceased. In the interval before
this happened, I entreated Miss Batchford, in
her niece's interests, to consider my letter as a
strictly private communication; adding that my
sufficient reason for venturing to make this condition would be found in my letter to Lucilla,
which I authorized her aunt to read as soon as
the time had arrived for opening it.

By this means I had, as I firmly believed,
taken the only possible way of preventing Nugent Dubourg from doing any serious mischief
in my absence.

Whatever his uncontrolled infatuation for Lucilla might lead him to do next, he could proceed to no serious extremities until Grosse pronounced her recovery to be complete. On the
day when Grosse did that, she would receive my
letter, and would discover for herself the abominable deception which had been practiced on
her. As to attempting to find Nugent, no idea
of doing this entered my mind. Wherever he
might be, at home or abroad, it would be equally
useless to appeal to his honor again. It would
be degrading myself to speak to him or to trust
him. To expose him to Lucilla the moment it
became possible was the one thing to be done.

I was ready with my letters, one inclosed in
the other, when good Mr. Gootheridge (with

whom I had arranged previously) called to drive me to Brighton in his light cart. The chaise which he had for hire had been already used to make the same journey by Lucilla and the nurse, and had not yet been returned to the inn. I reached my train before the hour of starting, and arrived in London with a sufficient margin of time to spare.

Resolved to make sure that no possible mischance could occur, I drove to Miss Batchford's house, and saw the cabman give my letter into the servant's hands.

It was a bitter moment when I found myself pulling down my veil in the fear that Lucilla might be at the window and see me! Nobody was visible but the man who answered the door. If pen, ink and paper had been within my reach at the moment, I think I should have written to her on my own account, after all. As it was, I could only forgive her the injury she had done me. From the bottom of my heart I forgave her, and longed for the blessed time which should unite us again. In the meanwhile, having done everything that I could to guard and help her, I was now free to give to Oscar all the thoughts that I could spare from my poor, misguided father.

Being bound for the Continent, I determined (though the chances were a hundred to one against me) to do all that I could, in my painful position, to discover the place of Oscar's retreat. The weary hours of suspense at my father's bedside would be lightened to me, if I could feel that the search for the lost man was being carried on at my instigation, and that from day to day there was a bare possibility of my hearing of him, if there was no more.

The office of the lawyer whom I had consulted during my previous visit to London lay in my way to the terminus. I drove there next, and was fortunate enough to find him still at business.

No tidings had been heard from Oscar. The lawyer, however, proved to be useful by giving me a letter of introduction to a person at Marseilles accustomed to conduct difficult confidential inquiries, and having agents whom he could employ in all the great cities of Europe. A man of Oscar's startling personal appearance would be surely more or less easy to trace, if the right machinery to do it could be only set at work. My savings would suffice for this purpose to a certain extent—and to that extent I resolved that they should be used when I reached my journey's end.

It was a troubled sea on the Channel passage that night. I remained on deck, accepting any inconvenience rather than descend into the atmosphere of the cabin. As I looked out to sea on one side and on the other, the dark waste of the tossing waters seemed to be the fit and dreary type of the dark prospect that was before me. On the trackless path that we were plowing a faint, misty moonlight shed its doubtful ray, like the doubtful light of hope faintly flickering on my mind when I thought of the coming time!

CHAPTER THE FORTY-SECOND.

THE STORY OF LUCILLA: TOLD BY HERSELF.

In my description of what Lucilla said and did on the occasion when the surgeon was teaching her to use her sight, it will be remembered that she is represented as having been particularly anxious to be allowed to try how she could write.

The motive at the bottom of this was the motive which is always at the bottom of a woman's conduct when she loves. Her one ambition is to present herself to advantage, even in the most trifling matters, before the man on whom her heart is fixed. Lucilla's one ambition with Oscar was this and no more.

Conscious that her handwriting — thus far, painfully and incompletely guided by her sense of touch—must present itself in sadly unfavorable contrast to the handwriting of other women who could see, she persisted in petitioning Grosse to permit her to learn to "write with her eyes instead of her finger," until she fairly wearied out the worthy German's power of resistance. The rapid improvement in her sight after her removal to the sea-side justified him (as I was afterward informed) in letting her have her way. Little by little, using her eyes for a longer and longer time on each succeeding day, she mastered the serious difficulty of teaching herself to write by sight instead of by touch. Beginning with lines in copy-books, she got on to writing easy words to dictation. From that, again, she advanced to writing notes; and from writing notes to keeping a journal—this last at the suggestion of her aunt, who had lived in the days before penny postage, when people kept journals and wrote long letters: in short, when people had time to think of themselves, and, more wonderful still, to write about it too.

Lucilla's Journal at Ramsgate lies before me as I trace these lines.

I had planned at first to make use of it, so as to continue the course of my narrative without a check, still writing in my own person, as I have written thus far, and as I propose to write again when I re-appear on the scene.

But on thinking over it once more, and after reading the Journal again, it strikes me as the wiser proceeding to let Lucilla tell the story of her life at Ramsgate herself, adding notes of my own occasionally where they appear to be required. Variety, freshness, and reality—1 believe I shall secure them all three by following this plan. Why is History in general (1 know there are brilliant exceptions to the rule) such dull reading? Because it is the narrative of events written at second-hand. Now I will be anything else you please except dull. You may say I have been dull already? As I am an honest woman, I don't agree with you. There are some people who bring dull minds to their reading, and then blame the writer for it. I say no more.

Consider it arranged, then. During my absence on the Continent Lucilla shall tell the story of events at Ramsgate. (And I will sprinkle a few notes over it here and there, signed P.)

LUCILLA'S JOURNAL.

East Cliff, Ramsgate, August 28.—A fortnight to-day since my aunt and I arrived at this place. I sent Zillah back to the rectory from London. Her rheumatic infirmities trouble her tenfold, poor old soul, in the moist air of the sea-side.

How has my writing got on for the last week? I am becoming a little better satisfied with it. I use my pen more easily; my hand is less like the hand of a backward child than it was. I shall be able to write as well as other ladies do when I am Oscar's wife.

[*Note.*— She is easily satisfied, poor dear. Her improved handwriting is sadly crooked. Some of the letters embrace each other at close quarters like dear frends, and some start asunder like bitter enemies. This is not to reflect on Lucilla, but to excuse myself if I make any mistakes in transcribing the Journal. Now let her go on.—P.]

Oscar's wife! When shall I be Oscar's wife? I have not so much as seen him yet. Something

—I am afraid a difficulty with his brother—still keeps him on the Continent. The tone in which he writes continues to have a certain reserve in it which disquiets and puzzles me. Am I quite as happy as I expected to be when I recovered my sight? Not yet!

It is not Oscar's fault if I am out of spirits every now and then. It is my own fault. I have offended my father; and I sometimes fear I have not acted justly toward Madame Pratolungo. These things vex me.

It seems to be my fate to be always misunderstood. My sudden flight from the rectory meant no disrespect to my father. I left as I did because I was incapable of facing the woman whom I had once dearly loved—thinking of her as I think now. It is so unendurable to feel that your confidence is lost in a person whom you once trusted without limit, and to go on meeting that person every hour in the day with a smooth face, as if nothing had happened! The impulse to escape more meetings (when I discovered that she had left the house for a walk) was irresistible. I should do it again, if I was in the same position again. I have hinted at this in writing to my father; telling him that something unpleasant had happened between Madame Pratolungo and me, and that I went away so suddenly on that account alone. No use! He has not answered my letter. I have written since to my stepmother. Mrs. Finch's reply has informed me of the unjust manner in which he speaks of my aunt. Without the slightest reason for it, he is even more deeply offended with Miss Batch-ford than he is with me!

Sad as this estrangement is, there is one con-solation, so far as I am concerned: it will not last. My father and I are sure, sooner or later, to come to an understanding together. When I return to the rectory I shall make my peace with him, and we shall get on again as smoothly as ever.

But how will it end between Madame Prato-lungo and me?

She has not answered the letter I wrote to her. (I begin to wish I had never written it, or at least some of it—the latter part of it, I mean.) I have heard absolutely nothing of her since she has been abroad. I don't know when she will return, or if she will ever return, to live at Dim-church again. Oh, what would I not give to have this dreadful mystery cleared up! to know whether I ought to fall down on my knees before her and beg her pardon, or whether I ought to count among the saddest days of my life the day which brought that woman to live with me as companion and friend?

Have I acted rashly, or have I acted wisely?

There is the question which always comes to me and torments me when I wake in the night. Let me look again (for the fiftieth time at least) at Oscar's letter.

[*Note.*—I copy the letter. Other eyes than hers ought to see it in this place. It is Nugent, of course, who here writes in Oscar's character and in Oscar's name. You will observe that his good resolutions, when he left me, held out as far as Paris, and then gave way, as follows.—P.]

"MY OWN DEAREST—I have reached Paris, and have found my first opportunity of writing to you since I left Browndown. Madame Pratolungo has no doubt told you that a sudden necessity has called me to my brother. I have not yet reached the place at which I am to meet him. Before I meet him, let me tell you what the necessity which parted us really is. Madame Pratolungo no longer possesses my confidence. When you have read on a little further, she will no longer possess yours.

"Alas, my love, I must amaze you, shock you, grieve you—I who would lay down my life for your happiness! Let me write it in the fewest words. I have made a terrible discovery. Lucilla, you have trusted Madame Pratolungo as your friend. Trust her no longer. She is your enemy, and mine!

"I suspected her some time since. My worst suspicions have been confirmed.

"Long ere this I ought to have told you what I tell you now. But I shrink from distressing you. To see a sad look on your dear face breaks my heart. It is only when I am away from you —when I fear the consequences if you are not warned of your danger—that I can summon the courage to tear off the mask from that woman's false face, and show her to you as she really is. It is impossible for me to enter into details in the space of a letter; I reserve all particulars until we meet again, and until I can produce what you have a right to ask for—proof that I am speaking the truth.

"In the meanwhile, I beg you to look back into your own thoughts, to recall your own words, on the day when Madame Pratolungo offended you in the rectory garden. On that occasion the truth escaped the Frenchwoman's lips—and she knew it!

"Do you remember what you said after she had followed you to Browndown?—I mean after she had declared that you would have fallen in love with my brother if you had met him first, and after Nugent (at her instigation, no doubt) had taken advantage of your blindness to make you believe that you were speaking to *me*. When you were smarting under the insult, and when you had found out the trick, what did you say?

"You said these—or nearly these—words:

"'She hated you from the first, Oscar—she took up with your brother directly he came here. Don't marry me at Dimchurch! Find out some place that they don't know of! They are both in a conspiracy together against you and against me. Take care of them! take care of them!'

"Lucilla, I echo your own words to you! I return the warning — the prophetic warning— which you unconsciously gave me in that past time. I am afraid my unhappy brother loves you—and I know for certain that Madame Pratolungo feels the interest in *him* which she has never felt in *me.* What you said, I say. They are in a conspiracy together against us. Take care of them! take care of them!

"When we meet again I shall be prepared to defeat the conspiracy. Till that time comes, as you value your happiness and mine, don't let Madame Pratolungo suspect that you have discovered her. It is she, I firmly believe, who is to blame. I am going to my brother—as you will now understand—with an object far different to the object which I put forward as an excuse to your false friend. Fear no dispute between Nugent and me. I know him. I firmly believe that I shall find that he has been tempted and misled. I answer—now that no evil influences are at work on him—for his acting like an honorable man, and deserving your pardon and mine. The excuse I have made to Madame Pratolungo will prevent her from interfering between us. That was my one object in making it.

"Keep me correctly informed of your movements and of hers. I inclose an address to which you can write with the certainty that your letters will be forwarded.

"On my side, I promise to write constantly. Once more, don't trust a living creature about you with the secret which this letter reveals! Expect me back at the earliest possible moment to free you—with a husband's authority—from the woman who has so cruelly deceived us.

"Yours, with the truest affection, the fondest love, OSCAR."

[*Note.*—It is quite needless for me to dwell here on the devilish cunning—I can use no other phrase—which inspired this abominable letter. Look back to the twenty-seventh and twenty-eighth chapters, and you will see how skillfully what I said in a moment of foolish irritation, and what Lucilla said when she too had lost her temper, is turned to account to poison her mind against me.   We are made innocently to supply our enemy with the foundation on which he builds his plot.   For the rest, the letter explains itself.   Nugent still persists in personating his brother.   He guesses easily at the excuse I should make to Lucilla for his absence; and he gets over the difficulty of appearing to have confided his errand to a woman whom he distrusts by declaring that he felt it necessary to deceive me as to what the nature of that errand really was.   As the Journal proceeds you will see how dexterously he works the machinery which his letter has set in motion.   All I need add here, in the way of explanation, is that the delay in his arrival at Ramsgate, of which Lucilla complains, was caused by nothing but his own hesitation.   His sense of honor—as I know from discoveries made at a later time—was not entirely lost yet.   The lower he sank the harder his better nature struggled to raise him.   Nothing, positively nothing, but his own remorse need have kept him at Paris (it is needless to say that he never stirred further, and never discovered the place of his brother's retreat) after Lucilla had informed him by letter that I had gone abroad, and that she was at

Ramsgate with her aunt. I have done: let Lucilla go on again.—P.]

I have read Oscar's letter once more.

He is the soul of honor; he is incapable of deceiving me. I remember saying what he tells me I said, and thinking it too—for the moment only—when I was beside myself with rage. Still, may it not be possible that appearances have misled Oscar? Oh, Madame Pratolungo! I had such a high opinion of you, I loved you so dearly —*can* you have been unworthy of the admiration and affection that you once inspired in me?

I quite agree with Oscar that his brother is not to blame. It is sad and shocking that Mr. Nugent Dubourg should have allowed himself to fall in love with me. But I cannot help pitying him. Poor disfigured man, I hope he will get a good wife! How he must have suffered!

It is impossible to endure any longer my present state of suspense. Oscar must and shall satisfy me about Madame Pratolungo—with his own lips. I shall write to him by this post, and insist on his coming to Ramsgate.

August 29.—I wrote to him yesterday, to the address in Paris. My letter will be delivered to-morrow. Where is he? when will he get it?

[*Note.*—That innocent letter did its fatal mischief. It ended the struggle against himself which had kept Nugent Dubourg in Paris. On the morning when he received it he started for England. Here is the entry in Lucilla's Journal.—P.]

August 31.—A telegram for me at breakfast-time. I am too happy to keep my hand steady; I am writing horribly. It doesn't matter: nothing matters but my telegram. (Oh, what a noble creature the man was who invented telegrams!) Oscar is on his way to Ramsgate!

CHAPTER THE FORTY-THIRD.

LUCILLA'S JOURNAL, CONTINUED.

September 1.—I am composed enough to return to my Journal, and to let my mind dwell a little on all that I have thought and felt since Oscar has been here.

Now that I have lost Madame Pratolungo, I have no friend with whom I can talk over my little secrets. My aunt is all that is kind and good to me; but with a person so much older than I am—who has lived in such a different world from my world, and whose ideas seem to be so far away from mine—how can I talk about my follies and extravagances, and expect sympathy in return! My one confidential friend is my Journal—I can only talk about myself *to* myself, in these pages. My position feels sometimes like a very lonely one. I saw two girls telling all their secrets to each other on the sands to-day—and I am afraid I envied them.

Well, my dear Journal, how did I feel—after longing for Oscar—when Oscar came to me?

It is dreadful to own it; but my book locks up,

and my book can be trusted with the truth. I felt ready to cry—I was so unexpectedly, so horribly, disappointed.

No. "Disappointed" is not the word. I can't find the word. There was a moment—I hardly dare write it: it seems so atrociously wicked—there was a moment when I almost wished myself blind again.

He took me in his arms; he held my hand in his. In the time when I was blind, how I should have felt it! how the delicious *tingle* would have run through me when he touched me! Nothing of the kind happened now. He might have been Oscar's brother for all the effect he produced on me. I have myself taken his hand since, and shut my eyes to try and renew my blindness, and put myself back completely as I was in the old time. The same result still. Nothing, nothing, nothing!

Is it that he is a little restrained with me, on his side? He certainly is! I felt it the moment he came into the room—I have felt it ever since.

No: it is not that. In the old time, when we were only beginning to love each other, he was restrained with me. But it made no difference then. I was not the insensible creature in those days that I have become since.

I can only account for it in one way. The restoration of my sight has made a new creature of me. I have gained a sense—I am no longer the same woman. This great change must have had some influence over me that I never suspected until Oscar came here. Can the loss of my sense

of feeling be the price that I have paid for the
recovery of my sense of sight?

When Grosse comes next I shall put that question to him.

In the meanwhile, I have had a second disappointment. He is not nearly so beautiful as I
thought he was when I was blind.

On the day when my bandage was taken off
for the first time I could only see indistinctly.
When I ran into the room at the rectory, I
guessed it was Oscar rather than knew it was
Oscar. My father's gray head and Mrs. Finch's
woman's dress would, no doubt, have helped
anybody in my place to fix, as I did, on the right
man. But this is all different now. I can see
his features in detail, and the result is (though
I won't own it to any of them) that I find my
idea of him in the days of my blindness—oh, so
unlike the reality! The one thing that is *not* a
disappointment to me is his voice. When he
cannot see me I close my eyes and let my ears
feel the old charm again—so far.

And this is what I have gained by submitting
to the operation, and enduring my imprisonment
in the darkened room!

What am I writing? I ought to be ashamed
of myself! Is it nothing to have had all the
beauty of land and sea, all the glory of cloud
and sunshine, revealed to me? Is it nothing to
be able to look at my fellow-creatures—to see
the bright faces of children smile at me when I
speak to them? Enough of myself! I am unhappy and ungrateful when I think of myself.

Let me write about Oscar.

My aunt approves of him. She thinks him handsome, and says he has the manners of a gentleman. This last is high praise from Miss Batchford. She despises the present generation of young men. "In my time," she said the other day, "I used to see young gentlemen. I only see young animals now — well-fed, well-washed, well-dressed; riding animals, rowing animals, betting animals—nothing more."

Oscar, on his side, seems to like Miss Batchford on better acquaintance. When I first presented him to her, he rather surprised me by changing color and looking very uneasy. He is almost distressingly nervous, on certain occasions. I suppose my aunt's grand manner daunted him.

[*Note.*—I really must break in here. Her aunt's "grand manner" makes me sick. It is nothing (between ourselves) but a hook-nose and a stiff pair of stays. What daunted Nugent Dubourg, when he first found himself in the old lady's presence, was the fear of discovery. He would, no doubt, have learned from his brother that Oscar and Miss Batchford had never met. You will see, if you look back, that it was, in the nature of things, impossible they should have met. But is it equally clear that Nugent could find out beforehand that Miss Batchford had been left in ignorance of what had happened at Dimchurch? He could do nothing of the sort—he could feel no assurance of his security from exposure, until he had tried the ground in his own proper person first. The risk here was certainly serious enough to make even Nugent Dubourg feel uneasy. And Lucilla talks of her aunt's "grand manner!" Poor innocent! I leave her to go on.—P.]

As soon as my aunt left us together, the first words I said to Oscar referred (of course) to his letter about Madame Pratolungo.

He made a little sign of entreaty, and looked distressed.

"Why should we spoil the pleasure of our first meeting by talking of her?" he said. "It is so inexpressibly painful to you and to me. Let us return to it in a day or two. Not now, Lucilla —not now!"

His brother was the next subject in my mind. I was not at all sure how he would take my speaking about it. I risked a question, however, for all that. He made another sign of entreaty, and looked distressed again.

"My brother and I understand each other, Lucilla. He will remain abroad for the present. Shall we drop that subject, too? Let me hear your own news—I want to know what is going on at the rectory. I have heard nothing since you wrote me word that you were here with your aunt, and that Madame Pratolungo had gone abroad to her father. Is Mr. Finch well? Is he coming to Ramsgate to see you?"

I was unwilling to tell him of the misunderstanding at home.

"I have not heard from my father since I have been here," I said. "Now you have come back, I can write and announce your return, and get all the news from the rectory."

He looked at me rather strangely—in a way which led me to fear that he saw some objection to my writing to my father.

"I suppose you would like Mr. Finch to come here?" he said; and then stopped suddenly and looked at me again.

"There is very little chance of his coming here," I answered.

Oscar seemed to be wonderfully interested about my father. "Very little chance?" he repeated. "Why?"

I was obliged to refer to the family quarrel—still, however, saying nothing of the unjust manner in which my father had spoken of my aunt.

"As long as I am with Miss Batchford," I said, "it is useless to hope that my father will come here. They are on bad terms; and I am afraid there is no prospect, at present, of their being friends again. Do you object to my writing home to say you have come to Ramsgate?" I asked.

"I!" he exclaimed, looking the picture of astonishment. "What could possibly make you think that? Write by all means—and leave a little space for me. I will add a few lines to your letter."

It is impossible to say how his answer relieved me. It was quite plain that I had stupidly misinterpreted him. Oh, my new eyes! my new eyes! shall I ever be able to depend on you as I could once depend on my touch?

[*Note.*—I must intrude myself again. I shall burst with indignation, while I am copying the Journal, if I don't relieve my mind at certain places in it. Remark, before you go any further, how skillfully Nugent contrives to ascertain his exact position at Ramsgate, and see with what a fatal unanimity all the chances of his personating Oscar, without discovery, declare themselves in his favor! Miss Batchford, as you have seen, is entirely at his mercy. She not only knows nothing herself, but she operates as a check on Mr. Finch, who would otherwise have joined his daughter at Ramsgate, and have instantly exposed the conspiracy. On every side of him Nugent is, to all appearance, safe. I am away in one direction. Oscar is away in another. Mrs. Finch is anchored immovably in her nursery. Zillah has been sent back from London to the rectory. The Dimchurch doctor (who attended Oscar, and who might have proved an awkward witness) is settled in India, as you will see, if you refer to the twenty-second chapter. The London doctor with whom he consulted has long since ceased to have any relations with his former patient. As for Herr Grosse, if *he* appears on the scene, he can be trusted to shut his eyes professionally to all that is going on, and to let matters take their course in the only interest he recognizes—the interest of Lucilla's health. There is literally no obstacle in Nugent's way; and no sort of protection for Lucilla, except in the faithful instinct which persists in warning her that this is the wrong man —though it speaks in an unknown tongue. Will she end in understanding the warning before it is too late? My friend, this note is intended to relieve my mind—not yours. All *you* have to do is to read on. Here is the Journal. I won't stand another moment in your way.—P.]

September 2.—A rainy day. Very little said that is worth recording between Oscar and me.

My aunt, whose spirits are always affected by bad weather, kept me a long time in her sitting-room, amusing herself by making me exercise my sight. Oscar was present by special invitation, and assisted the old lady in setting this new seeing-sense of mine all sorts of tasks. He tried hard to prevail on me to let him see my writing. I refused. It is improving as fast as it can; but it is not good enough yet.

I notice here what a dreadfully difficult thing it is to get back—in such a case as mine—to the exercise of one's sight.

We have a cat and a dog in the house. Would it be credited, if I was telling it to the world instead of telling it to my Journal, that I actually mistook one for the other to-day?—after seeing so well, too, as I do now, and being able to write with so few false strokes in making my letters! It is nevertheless true that I did mistake the two animals; having trusted to nothing but my memory to inform my eyes which was which, instead of helping my memory by my touch. I have now set this right. I caught up puss, and shut my eyes (oh, that habit! when shall I get over it?) and felt her soft fur (so different from a dog's hair!), and opened my eyes again, and associated the feel of it forever afterward with the sight of a cat.

To-day's experience has also informed me that I make slow progress in teaching myself to judge correctly of distances.

In spite of this drawback, however, there is nothing I enjoy so much in using my sight as looking at a great wide prospect of any kind— provided I am not asked to judge how far or how near objects may be. It seems like escaping out of prison to look (after having been shut up in my blindness) at the long curve of the beach, and the bold promontory of the pier, and the grand sweep of the sea beyond—all visible from our windows. The moment my aunt begins to question me about distances she makes a toil of my pleasure. It is worse still when I am asked about the relative sizes of ships and boats. When I see nothing but a boat I fancy it larger than it is. When I see the boat in comparison with a ship, and then look back at the boat, I instantly go to the other extreme, and fancy it smaller than it is. The setting this right still vexes me almost as keenly as my stupidity vexed me some time since when I saw my first horse and cart from an upper window and took it for a dog drawing a wheelbarrow! Let me add in my own defense that both horse and cart were figured

at least five times their proper size in my blind
fancy—which makes my mistake, I think, not
so very stupid, after all.

Well, I amused my aunt. And what effect
did I produce on Oscar?

If I could trust my eyes, I should say I produced exactly the contrary effect on *him*—I
made him melancholy. But I don't trust my
eyes. They must be deceiving me when they
tell me that he looked, in my company, a mop-
ing, anxious, miserable man.

Or is it that he sees and feels something
changed in Me? I could scream with vexation
and rage against myself. Here is *my* Oscar—
and yet he is not the Oscar I knew when I was
blind. Contradictory as it seems, I used to understand how he looked at me when I was unable
to see it. Now that I *can* see it, I ask myself,
Is this really love that is looking at me in his
eyes? or is it something else? How should I
know? I knew when I had only my own fancy
to tell me. But now, try as I may, I cannot
make the old fancy and the new sight to serve
me in harmony both together. I am afraid he
sees that I don't understand him. Oh, dear!
dear! why did I not meet my good old Grosse,
and become the new creature that he has made
me before I met Oscar? I should have had no
blind memories and prepossessions to get over
then. I shall become used to my new self, I
hope, and believe, with time—and that will accustom me to my new impressions of Oscar—and
so it may all come right in the end. It is all

wrong enough now. He put his arm round me
and gave me a little tender squeeze, while we
were following Miss Batchford down to the
dining - room this afternoon. Nothing in me
answered to it. I should have felt it all over
me a few months since.

Here is a tear on the paper. What a fool I
am? Why can't I write about something else?

I sent my second letter to my father to-day,
telling him of Oscar's return from abroad, and
taking no notice of his not having replied to my
first letter. The only way to manage my father
is not to take notice, and to let him come right
by himself. I showed Oscar my letter, with a
space left at the end for his postscript. While
he was writing it he asked me to get something
which happened to be upstairs in my room. When
I came back he had sealed the envelope, forget-
ing to show me his postscript. It was not worth
while to open the letter again; he told me what
he had written, and that did just as well.

[*Note.*—I must trouble you with a copy of
what Nugent really did write. It shows why
he sent her out of the room, and closed the envelope before she could come back. The postscript is also worthy of notice, in this respect—
that it plays a part in a page of my narrative
which is still to come.

Thus Nugent writes, in Oscar's name and
character, to the rector of Dimchurch. (He would
find the imitation of his brother's handwriting
no obstacle in his way. A close similarity of

handwritings was—as I have, I think, already
mentioned—one among the other striking points
of resemblance between the twins.)

"DEAR MR. FINCH—Lucilla's letter will have
told you that I have come to my senses, and that
I am again paying my addresses to her as her
affianced husband. My principal object in adding these lines is to propose that we should forget the past, and go on again as if nothing had
happened.

"Nugent has behaved nobly. He absolves me
from the engagements toward him into which I
so rashly entered at our last interview before I
left Browndown. Most generously and amply
he has redeemed his pledge to Madame Pratolungo to discover the place of my retreat and to
restore me to Lucilla. For the present he remains abroad.

"If you favor me with a reply to this, I must
warn you to be careful how you write; for Lucilla is sure to ask to see your letter. Remember
that she only supposes me to have returned to
her after a brief absence from England, caused
by a necessity for joining my brother on the
Continent. It will be also desirable to say nothing on the subject of my unfortunate peculiarity
of complexion. I have made it all right with
Lucilla, and she is getting accustomed to me.
Still, the subject is a sore one, and the less it is
referred to the better. Truly yours, OSCAR."

Unless I add a word of explanation here, you
will hardly appreciate the extraordinary skillful-

ness with which the deception is continued by means of this postscript.

Written in Oscar's character (and representing Nugent as having done all that he had promised me to do), it designedly omits the customary courtesy of Oscar's style. The object of this is to offend Mr. Finch—with what end in view you will presently see. The rector was the last man in existence to dispense with the necessary apologies and expressions of regret from a man engaged to his daughter, who had left her as Oscar had left her—no matter how the circumstances might appear to excuse him. The curt, off-hand postscript signed "Oscar" was the very thing to exasperate the wound already inflicted on Mr. Finch's self-esteem, and to render it at least probable that he would reconsider his intention of himself performing the marriage ceremony. In the event of his refusal, what would happen? A stranger, entirely ignorant of which was Nugent and which was Oscar, would officiate in his place. Do you see it now?

But even the cleverest people are not always capable of providing for every emergency. The completest plot generally has its weak place.

The postscript, as you have seen, was a little masterpiece. But it nevertheless exposed the writer to a danger, which (as the Journal will tell you) he only appreciated at its true value when it was too late to alter his mind. Finding himself forced, for the sake of appearances, to permit Lucilla to inform her father of his arrival at Ramsgate, he was now obliged to run the risk of having that important piece of domestic news communicated—either by Mr. Finch or by his wife—to no less a person than myself. You will remember that worthy Mrs. Finch, when we parted at the rectory, had asked me to write to her while I was abroad—and you will see, after the hint I have given you, that clever Mr. Nugent is beginning already to walk upon delicate ground. I say no more: Lucilla's turn now.—P.]

September 3.—Oscar has (I suppose) forgotten something which he ought to have included in his postscript to my letter.

More than two hours after I had sent it to the post he asked if the letter had gone. For the moment he looked annoyed when I said, Yes. But he soon recovered himself. It mattered nothing (he said); he could easily write again. "Talking of letters," he added, "do you expect Madame Pratolungo to write to you?" (This time it was he who referred to her!) I told him that there was not much chance, after what had passed on her side and on mine, of her writing to me—and then tried to put some of those questions about her which he had once already requested me not to press yet. For the second time he entreated me to defer the discussion of that unpleasant subject for the present—and yet, with a curious inconsistency, he made another inquiry relating to the subject in the same breath.

"Do you think she is likely to be in corre-

spondence with your father or your step-mother
while she is out of England?" he asked.

"I should doubt her writing to my father," I
said. "But she might correspond with Mrs.
Finch."

He considered a little, and then turned the talk
to the topic of our residence at Ramsgate next.

"How long do you stay here?" he inquired.

"It depends on Herr Grosse," I answered. "I
will ask him when he comes next."

He turned away to the window—suddenly, as
if he was a little put out.

"Are you tired of Ramsgate already?" I
asked.

He came back to me and took my hand—my
cold, insensible hand, that won't feel his touch
as it ought!

"Let me be your husband, Lucilla," he whispered; "and I will live at Ramsgate if you like
—for your sake."

Although there was everything to please me in
those words, there was something that startled
me—I cannot describe it—in his look and manner when he said them. I made no answer at
the moment. He went on.

"Why should we not be married at once?" he
asked. "We are both of age. We have only
ourselves to think of."

[*Note.*—Alter his words as follows: "Why
should we not be married before Madame Pratolungo can hear of my arrival at Ramsgate?" and
you will rightly interpret his motives. The sit-

uation is now fast reaching its climax of peril. Nugent's one chance is to persuade Lucilla to marry him before any discoveries can reach my ears, and before Grosse considers her sufficiently recovered to leave Ramsgate.—P.]

"You forget," I answered, more surprised than ever; "we have my father to think of. It was always arranged that he was to marry us at Dimchurch."

Oscar smiled—not at all the charming smile I used to imagine when I was blind!

"We shall wait a long time, I am afraid," he said, "if we wait until your father marries us."

"What do you mean?" I asked.

"When we enter on the painful subject of Madame Pratolungo," he replied, "I will tell you. In the meantime, do you think Mr. Finch will answer your letter?"

"I hope so."

"Do you think he will answer my postscript?"

"I am sure he will!"

The same unpleasant smile showed itself again in his face. He abruptly dropped the conversation, and went to play *piquet* with my aunt.

All this happened yesterday evening. I went to bed, sadly dissatisfied with somebody. Was it with Oscar? or with myself? or with both? I fancy with both.

To-day we went out together for a walk on the cliffs. What a delight it was to move through the fresh briny air, and see the lovely sights on every side of me! Oscar enjoyed it too. All through the first part of our walk he was charming, and I was more in love with him than ever. On our return a little incident occurred which altered him for the worse, and which made my spirits sink again.

It happened in this way.

I proposed returning by the sands. Ramsgate is still crowded with visitors; and the animated scene on the beach in the later part of the day has attractions for me, after my blind life, which it does not (I dare say) possess for people who have always enjoyed the use of their eyes. Oscar, who has a nervous horror of crowds, and who shrinks from contact with people not so refined as himself, was surprised at my wishing to mix with what he called "the mob on the sands." However, he said he would go if I particularly wished it. I did particularly wish it. So we went.

There were chairs on the beach. We hired two, and sat down to look about us.

All sorts of diversions were going on. Monkeys, organs, girls on stilts, a conjurer, and a troop of negro minstrels were all at work to amuse the visitors. I thought the varied color and bustling enjoyment of the crowd, with the bright blue sea beyond and the glorious sunshine overhead, quite delightful—I declare I felt as if two eyes were not half enough to see with! A nice old lady, sitting near, entered into conversation with me, hospitably offering me biscuits and sherry out of her own bag. Oscar, to my disappointment, looked quite disgusted with all of us. He thought my nice old lady vulgar, and he called the company on the beach "a herd of snobs." While he was still muttering under his breath about the "mixture of low people," he suddenly cast a side-look at some person or thing —I could not at the moment tell which—and, rising, placed himself so as to intercept my view of the promenade on the sands immediately before me. I happened to have noticed, at the same moment, a lady approaching us in a dress of a peculiar color; and I pulled Oscar on one side, to look at her as she passed in front of me. "Why do you get in my way?" I asked. Before he could answer the question the lady passed, with two lovely children, and with a tall man at her side. My eyes, looking first at the lady and the children, found their way next to the gentleman—and saw, repeated in his face, the same black-blue complexion which had startled me in the face of Oscar's brother when I first opened my eyes at the rectory! For the moment I felt startled again—more, as I believe, by the unexpected repetition of the blue face in the face of a stranger than by the ugliness of the complexion itself. At any rate, I was composed enough to admire the lady's dress and the beauty of the children before they had passed beyond my range of view. Oscar spoke to me, while I was looking at them, in a tone of reproach, for which, as I thought, there was no occasion and no excuse.

"I tried to spare you," he said. "You have yourself to thank, if that man has frightened you."

"He has *not* frightened me," I answered—sharply enough.

Oscar looked at me very attentively, and sat down again without saying a word more.

The good-humored old woman on my other side, who had seen and heard all that had passed, began to talk of the gentleman with the discolored face, and of the lady and the children who accompanied him. He was a retired Indian officer, she said. The lady was his wife, and the two beautiful children were his own children. "It seems a pity that such a handsome man should be disfigured in that way," my new acquaintance remarked. "But still it don't matter much, after all. There he is, as you see, with a fine woman for a wife, and with two lovely children. I know the landlady of the house where they lodge—and a happier family you couldn't lay your hand on in all England. That is my friend's account of them. Even a blue face don't seem such a dreadful misfortune, when you look at it in that light—does it, miss?"

I entirely agreed with the old lady. Our talk seemed, for some incomprehensible reason, to irritate Oscar. He got up again impatiently, and looked at his watch.

"Your aunt will be wondering what has become of us," he said. "Surely you have had enough of the mob on the sands by this time!"

I had not had enough of it, and I should have been quite content to have made one of the mob for some time longer. But I saw that Oscar would be seriously vexed if I persisted in keeping my place. So I took leave of my nice old lady, and left the pleasant sands—not very willingly.

He said nothing more until we had threaded our way out of the crowd. Then he returned, without any reason for it that I could discover, to the subject of the Indian officer, and to the remembrance which the stranger's complexion must have awakened in me of his brother's face.

"I don't understand your telling me you were not frightened when you saw that man," he said. "You were terribly frightened by my brother when you first saw him."

"I was terribly frightened by my own imagination *before* I saw him," I answered. "*After* I saw him I soon got over it."

"So you say," he rejoined.

There is something excessively provoking—at least to me—in being told to my face that I have said something which is not worthy of belief. It was not a very becoming act on my part (after what he had told me in his letter about his brother's infatuation) to mention his brother. I ought not to have done it. I did it, for all that.

"I say what I mean," I replied. "Before I knew what you told me about your brother I was going to propose to you, for your sake and for his, that he should live with us after we were married."

Oscar suddenly stopped. He had given me his arm to lead me through the crowd—he dropped it now.

"You say that because you are angry with me!" he said.

I denied being angry with him; I declared once more that I was only speaking the truth.

"You really mean," he went on, "that you could have lived comfortably with my brother's blue face before you every hour of the day?"

"Quite comfortably—if he would have been *my* brother too."

Oscar pointed to the house in which my aunt and I are living—within a few yards of the place on which we stood.

"You are close at home," he said, speaking in an odd, muffled voice, with his eyes on the ground. "I want a longer walk. We shall meet at dinner-time."

He left me—without looking up, and without saying a word more.

Jealous of his brother! There is something unnatural, something degrading, in such jealousy as that. I am ashamed of myself for thinking it of him. And yet what else could his conduct mean?

[*Note*.—It is for me to answer that question. Give the miserable wretch his due. His conduct meant, in one plain word—remorse. The only excuse left that he could make to his own conscience for the infamous part which he was playing was this—that his brother's personal disfigurement presented a fatal obstacle in the way of his brother's marriage. And now Lucilla's own words, Lucilla's own actions, had told him that

Oscar's face was no obstacle to her seeing Oscar perpetually in the familiar intercourse of domestic life. The torture of self-reproach which this discovery inflicted on him drove him out of her presence. His own lips would have betrayed him if he had spoken a word more to her at that moment. This is no speculation of mine. I know what I am now writing to be the truth. —P.]

It is night again. I am in my bedroom—too nervous and too anxious to go to rest yet. Let me employ myself in finishing this private record of the events of the day.

Oscar came a little before dinner-time, haggard and pale, and so absent in mind that he hardly seemed to know what he was talking about. No explanations passed between us. He asked my pardon for the hard things he had said, and the ill-temper he had shown earlier in the day. I readily accepted his excuses, and did my best to conceal the uneasiness which his vacant, preoccupied manner caused me. All the time he was speaking to me he was plainly thinking of something else—he was more unlike the Oscar of my blind remembrances than ever. It was the old voice talking in a new way: I can only describe it to myself in those terms.

As for his manner, I know it used to be always more or less quiet and retiring in the old days; but was it ever so hopelessly subdued and depressed as I have seen it to-day? Useless to ask! In the bygone time I was not able to see it. My past judgment of him and my present judgment of him have been arrived at by such totally different means that it seems useless to compare them. Oh, how I miss Madame Pratolungo! What a relief, what a consolation it would have been to have said all this to her, and to have heard what she thought of it in return!

There is, however, a chance of my finding my way out of some of my perplexities, at any rate —if I can only wait till to-morrow.

Oscar seems to have made up his mind at last to enter into the explanations which he has hitherto withheld from me. He has asked me to give him a private interview in the morning. The circumstances which led to his making this request have highly excited my curiosity. Something is evidently going on under the surface, in which my interests are concerned—and possibly Oscar's interests too.

It all came about in this way.

On returning to the house after Oscar had left me, I found that a letter from Grosse had arrived by the afternoon post. My dear old surgeon wrote to say that he was coming to see me— and added in a postscript that he would arrive the next day at luncheon-time. Past experience told me that this meant a demand on my aunt's housekeeping for all the good things that it could produce. (Ah, dear! I thought of Madame Pratolungo and the Mayonnaise. Will those times never come again?) Well—at dinner I announced Grosse's visit, adding significantly, "at luncheon-time."

My aunt looked up from her plate with a little start—not interested, as I was prepared to hear, in the serious question of luncheon, but in the opinion which my medical adviser was likely to give of the state of my health.

"I am anxious to hear what Mr. Grosse says about you to-morrow," the old lady began. "I shall insist on his giving me a far more complete report of you than he gave last time. The recovery of your sight appears to me, my dear, to be quite complete."

"Do you want me to be cured, aunt, because you want to get away?" I asked. "Are you weary of Ramsgate?"

Miss Batchford's quick temper flashed at me out of Miss Batchford's bright old eyes.

"I am weary of keeping a letter of yours," she burst out, with a look of disgust.

"A letter of mine!" I exclaimed.

"Yes. A letter which is only to be given to you when Mr. Grosse pronounces that you are quite yourself again."

Oscar—who had not taken the slightest interest in the conversation thus far—suddenly stopped, with his fork halfway to his mouth, changed color, and looked eagerly at my aunt.

"What letter?" I asked. "Who gave it to you? Why am I not to see it until I am quite myself again?"

Miss Batchford obstinately shook her head three times in answer to those three questions.

"I hate secrets and mysteries," she said, impatiently. "This is a secret and a mystery—and I long to have done with it. That is all. I have said too much already. I shall say no more."

All my entreaties were of no avail. My aunt's quick temper had evidently led her into committing an imprudence of some sort. Having done that, she was now provokingly determined not to make bad worse. Nothing that I could say would induce her to open her lips on the subject of the mysterious letter. "Wait till Mr. Grosse comes to-morrow." That was the only reply I could get.

As for Oscar, this little incident appeared to have an effect on him which added immensely to the curiosity that my aunt had roused in me.

He listened with breathless attention while I was trying to induce Miss Batchford to answer my questions. When I gave it up he pushed away his plate and ate no more. On the other hand (though generally the most temperate of men), he drank a great deal of wine, both at dinner and after. In the evening he made so many mistakes in playing cards with my aunt that she dismissed him from the game in disgrace. He sat in a corner for the rest of the time, pretending to listen while I was playing the piano—really lost to me and my music; buried, fathoms deep, in some uneasy thoughts of his own.

When he took his leave he whispered these words in my ear, anxiously pressing my hand while he spoke:

"I must see you alone to-morrow, before Grosse comes. Can you manage it?"

"Yes."

"When?"

"At the stairs on the cliff at eleven o'clock."

On that he left me. But one question has pursued me ever since. Does Oscar know the writer of the mysterious letter? I firmly believe he does. To-morrow will prove whether I am right or wrong. How I long for to-morrow to come!

CHAPTER THE FORTY-FOURTH.

LUCILLA'S JOURNAL, CONTINUED.

September 4.—I mark this day as one of the saddest days of my life. Oscar has shown Madame Pratolungo to me in her true colors. He has reasoned out this miserable matter with a plainness which it is impossible for me to resist. I have thrown away my love and my confidence on a false woman: there is no sense of honor, no feeling of gratitude or of delicacy, in her nature. And I once thought her—it sickens me to recall it! I will see her no more.

[*Note.*—Did it ever occur to you to be obliged to copy out, with your own hand, this sort of opinion of your own character? I can recommend the sensation produced as something quite new, and the temptation to add a line or two

on your own account to be as nearly as possible
beyond mortal resistance.—P.]

Oscar and I met at the stairs at eleven o'clock,
as we had arranged.

He took me to the west pier. At that hour of
the morning (excepting a few sailors who paid
no heed to us) the place was a solitude. It was
one of the loveliest days of the season. When
we were tired of pacing to and fro we could
sit down under the mellow sunshine and enjoy
the balmy sea air. In that pure light, with all
those lovely colors about us, there was something,
to my mind, horribly and shamefully out of place
in the talk that engrossed us—talk that still
turned, hour after hour, on nothing but plots and
lies, cruelty, ingratitude, and deceit!

I managed to ask my first question so as to
make him enter on the subject at once, without
wasting time in phrases to prepare me for what
was to come.

"When my aunt mentioned that letter at dinner yesterday," I said, "I fancied that you knew
something about it. Was I right?"

"Very nearly right," he answered. "I can't
say I knew anything about it. I only suspected
that it was the production of an enemy of yours
and mine."

"Not Madame Pratolungo."

"Yes! Madame Pratolungo."

I disagreed with him at the outset. Madame
Pratolungo and my aunt had quarreled about
politics. Any correspondence between them—a

confidential correspondence especially—seemed to be one of the most unlikely things that could take place. I asked Oscar if he could guess what the letter contained, and why it was not to be given to me until Grosse reported that I was quite cured.

"I can't guess at the contents—I can only guess at the object of the letter," he said.

"What is it?"

"The object which she has had in view from the first—to place every possible obstacle in the way of my marrying you."

"What interest can she have in doing that?"

"My brother's interest."

"Forgive me, Oscar. I cannot believe it of her."

We were walking while these words were passing between us. When I said that, he stopped and looked at me very earnestly.

"You believed it of her when you answered my letter," he said.

I admitted that.

"I believed your letter," I replied; "and I shared your opinion of her as long as she was in the same house with me. Her presence fed my anger and my horror of her in some way that I can't account for. Now she has left me—now I have time to think—there is something in her absence that pleads for her, and tortures me with doubts if I have done right. I can't explain it —I don't understand it. I only know that so it is."

He still looked at me more and more attentively. "Your good opinion of her must have been very firmly rooted, to assert itself in this obstinate manner," he said. "What can she have done to deserve it?"

If I had looked back through all my old recollections of her, and had recalled them one by one, it would only have ended in making me cry. And yet I felt that I ought to stand up for her as long as I could. I managed to meet the difficulty in this way.

"I will tell you what she did," I said, "after I received your letter. Fortunately for me, she was not very well that morning, and she breakfasted in bed. I had plenty of time to compose myself, and to caution Zillah (who read your letter to me), before we met for the first time that day. On the previous day I had felt hurt and offended with the manner in which she accounted for your absence from Browndown. I thought she was not treating me with the same confidence which I should have placed in her, if our positions had been reversed. When I next saw her, having your warning in my mind, I made my excuses, and said what I thought she would expect me to say under the circumstances. In my excitement and my wretchedness, I dare say I overacted my part. At any rate, I roused the suspicion in her that something was wrong. She not only asked me if anything had happened—she went the length of saying, in so many words, that she thought she saw a change in me. I stopped it there by declaring that I did not understand her. She must have seen

that I was not telling the truth—she must have
known as well as I knew that I was concealing
something from her. For all that, not one word
more escaped her lips. A proud delicacy—I saw
it as plainly in her face as I now see you—a
proud delicacy silenced her: she looked wounded
and hurt. I have been thinking of that look
since I have been here. I have asked myself
(what did not occur to me at the time) if a false
woman, who knew herself to be guilty, would
have behaved in that way? Surely a false woman would have set her wits against mine, and
have tried to lead me into betraying to her what
discoveries I had really made? Oscar! that delicate silence, that wounded look, *will* plead for
her when I think of her in her absence. I can
not feel as satisfied as I once did that she is the
abominable creature you declare her to be. I
know you are incapable of deceiving me—I
know you believe what you say. But is it not
possible that appearances have misled you?
Can you really be sure that you have not
made some dreadful mistake?"

Without answering me, he suddenly stopped
at a seat under the stone parapet of the pier, and
signed to me to sit down by him. I obeyed.
Instead of looking at me, he kept his head turned
away, looking out over the sea. I could not make
him out. He perplexed—he almost alarmed me.

"Have I offended you?" I asked.

He turned toward me again as abruptly as he
had turned away. His eyes wandered; bis face
was pale.

"You are a good, generous creature," he said, in a confused, hasty way. "Let us talk of something else."

"No!" I answered. "I am too deeply interested in knowing the truth to talk of anything else."

His color changed again at that. His face flushed; he gave a heavy sigh as one does sometimes when one is making a great effort.

"You *will* have it?" he said.

"I *will* have it."

He rose again. The nearer he was to telling me all that he had kept concealed from me thus far, the harder it seemed to be to him to say the first words.

"Do you mind walking on again?" he asked.

I silently rose on my side, and put my arm in his. We walked on slowly toward the end of the pier. Arrived there, he stood still, and spoke those first hard words — looking out over the broad blue waters: not looking at me.

"I won't ask you to take anything for granted on my assertion only," he began. "The woman's own words, the woman's own actions, shall prove her guilty. How I first came to suspect her—how I afterward found my suspicions confirmed—I refrain from telling you, for this reason, that I am determined not to use my influence to shape your views to mine. Carry your memory back to the time I have already mentioned in my letter—the time when she betrayed herself to you in the rectory garden. Is it true that she said you would have fallen in love with my brother, if you had met him first, instead of me?"

"It is true that she said it," I answered: "at a moment," I added, "when her temper had got the better of her, and when mine had got the better of me."

"Advance the hour a little," he went on—"to the time when she followed you to Browndown. Was she still out of temper when she made her excuses to you?"

"No."

"Did she interfere when Nugent took advantage of your blindness to make you believe you were talking to me?"

"No."

"Was she out of temper then?"

I still defended her. "She might well have been angry," I said. "She had made her excuses to me in the kindest manner, and I had received them with the most unpardonable rudeness."

My defense produced no effect on him. He summed it up coolly so far. "She compared me disadvantageously with my brother, and she allowed my brother to personate me, in speaking to you, without interfering to stop it. In both these cases her temper excuses and accounts for her conduct. Very good. We may, or may not, differ so far. Before we go further let us, if we can, agree on one unanswerable fact. Which of us two brothers was her favorite from the first?"

About *that* there could be no doubt. I admitted at once that Nugent was her favorite. And more than this, I remembered accusing her myself of never having done justice to Oscar from the first. (*Note.*—See the sixteenth chapter, and Madame Pratolungo's remark, warning you that you would hear of this circumstance again. —P.)

Oscar went on:

"Bear that in mind," he said. "And now let us get to the time when we were assembled in your sitting-room, to discuss the subject of the operation on your eyes. The question before us, as I remember it, was this. Were you to marry me before the operation, or were you to keep me waiting until the operation had been performed, and the cure was complete? How did Madame Pratolungo decide on that occasion? She decided against my interests; she encouraged you to delay our marriage."

I persisted in defending her. "She did that out of sympathy with me," I said.

He surprised me by again accepting my view of the matter without attempting to dispute it.

"We will say she did it out of sympathy with you," he proceeded. "Whatever her motives might be, the result was the same. My marriage to you was indefinitely put off, and Madame Pratolungo voted for that delay."

"And your brother," I added, "took the other side, and tried to persuade me to marry you first. How can you reconcile that with what you have told me—"

He interposed before I could say more. "Don't

bring my brother into the inquiry," he said. "My brother at that time could still behave like an honorable man, and sacrifice his own feelings to his duty to me. Let us strictly confine ourselves, for the present, to what Madame Pratolungo said and did. And let us advance again to a few minutes later on the same day, when our little domestic debate had ended. My brother was the first to go. Then you retired, and left Madame Pratolungo and me alone in the room. Do you remember?"

I remembered perfectly.

"You had bitterly disappointed me," I said. "You had shown no sympathy with my eagerness to be restored to the blessing of sight. You made objections and started difficulties. I recollect speaking to you with some of the bitterness that I felt—blaming you for not believing in my future as I believed in it, and hoping as I hoped —and then leaving you and locking myself up in my own room."

In those terms I satisfied him that my memory of the events of that day was as clear as his own. He listened without making any remark, and went on when I had done.

"Madame Pratolungo shared your hard opinion of me on that occasion," he proceeded; "and expressed it in infinitely stronger terms. She betrayed herself to *you* in the rectory garden. She betrayed herself to *me* after you had left us together in the sitting-room. Her hasty temper again, beyond all doubt! I quite agree with you. What she said to me in your absence she would never have said if she had been mistress of herself."

I began to feel a little startled. "How is it that you now tell me of this for the first time?" I said. "Were you afraid of distressing me?"

"I was afraid of losing you," he answered.

Hitherto I had kept my arm in his. I drew it out now. If his reply meant anything, it meant that he had once thought me capable of breaking faith with him. He saw that I was hurt.

"Remember," he said, "that I had unhappily offended you that day, and that you have not heard yet what Madame Pratolungo had the audacity to say to me under those circumstances."

"What did she say to you?"

"This: 'It would have been a happier prospect for Lucilla if she had been going to marry your brother, instead of marrying you.' I repeat literally: those were the words."

I could no more believe it of her than I could have believed it of myself.

"Are you really sure?" I asked him. "*Can* she have said anything so cruel to you as that?"

Instead of answering me, he took his pocket-book from the breast-pocket of his coat, searched in it, and produced a morsel of folded and crumpled paper. He opened the paper, and showed me some writing inside.

"Is that my writing?" he asked.

It was his writing. I had seen enough of his

letters since the recovery of my sight to feel sure
of that.

"Read it," he said, "and judge for yourself."

[*Note.*—You have made your acquaintance
with this letter already, in my thirty-second
chapter. I had said those foolish words to Oscar (as you will find in my record of the time),
under the influence of a natural indignation,
which any other woman with a spark of spirit
in her would have felt in my place. Instead of
personally remonstrating with me, Oscar had (as
usual) gone home, and written me a letter of ex-
postulation. Having, on my side, had time to
cool, and feeling the absurdity of our exchang-
ing letters when we were within a few minutes'
walk of each other, I had gone straight to Browndown on receiving the letter, first crumpling it
up and (as I supposed) throwing it into the fire.
After personally setting myself right with Oscar,
I had returned to the rectory, and had there heard
that Nugent had been to see me in my absence,
had waited a little while alone in the sitting-
room, and had gone away again. When I tell
you that the letter which he was now showing
to Lucilla was that same letter of Oscar's, which
I had (as I believed) destroyed, you will understand that I had thrown it into the fender instead
of into the fire, and that I failed to see it in the
fender on my return simply because Nugent had
seen it first, and had taken it away with him.
These particulars are described in greater detail
in the chapter to which I have referred, the let-

ter itself being there inserted at full length.
However, I will save you the trouble of looking back—I know how you hate trouble!—by
transcribing literally what I find before me in
the Journal. The original letter is pasted on
the page: I will copy it from the page for the
second time. Am I not good to you? What
author by profession would do as much for you
as this? I am afraid I am praising myself! Let
Lucilla proceed.—P.]

I took the letter from him and read it. At
my request, he has permitted me to keep it. The
letter is my justification for thinking of Madame
Pratolungo as I now think of her. I place it
here before I write another line in my Journal.

"MADAME PRATOLUNGO—You have distressed
and pained me more than I can say. There are
faults, and serious ones, on my side, I know. I
heartily beg your pardon for anything that I may
have said or done to offend you. I cannot submit to your hard verdict on me. If you knew
how I adore Lucilla, you would make allowances for me—you would understand me better
than you do. I cannot get your last cruel words
out of my ears. I cannot meet you again without some explanation of them. You stabbed me
to the heart when you said this evening that it
would be a happier prospect for Lucilla if she
had been going to marry my brother instead of
marrying me. I hope you did not really mean
that? Will you please write and tell me whether
you did or not?   OSCAR."

My first proceeding after reading those lines was, of course, to put my arm again in his, and to draw him as close to me as close could be. My second proceeding followed in due time. I asked, naturally, for Madame Pratolungo's answer to that most affectionate and most touching letter.

"I have no answer to show you," he said.

"You have lost it?" I asked.

"I never had it."

"What do you mean?"

"Madame Pratolungo never answered my letter."

I made him repeat that—once, twice. Was it not incredible that such an appeal could be made to any woman not utterly depraved, and be left unnoticed? Twice he reiterated the same answer. Twice he declared on his honor that not a line of reply had been returned to him. She *was*, then, utterly depraved? No! there was a last excuse left that justice and friendship might still make for her. I made it.

"There is but one explanation of her conduct," I said. "She never received the letter. Where did you send it to?"

"To the rectory."

"Who took it?"

"My own servant."

"He may have lost it on the way, and have been afraid to tell you. Or the servant at the rectory may have forgotten to deliver it."

Oscar shook his head. "Quite impossible! I know Madame Pratolungo received the letter."

"How?"

"I found it crumpled up in a corner inside the fender in *your sitting-room at the rectory.*"

"Had it been opened?"

"It had been opened. She had received it; she had read it; and she had not thrown quite far enough to throw it into the fire. Now, Lucilla! Is Madame Pratolungo an injured woman? and am I a man who has slandered her?"

There was another public seat a few paces distant from us. I could stand no longer—I went away by myself and sat down. A dull sensation possessed me. I could neither speak nor cry. There I sat in silence; slowly wringing my hands in my lap, and feeling the last ties that still bound me to the once-loved friend of former days falling away one after the other, and leaving us parted for life.

He followed me, and stood over me—he summed her up in stern, quiet tones, which carried conviction into my mind, and made me feel ashamed of myself for having ever regretted her.

"Look back for the last time, Lucilla, at what this woman has said and done. You will find that the idea of your marrying Nugent is, under one form or another, always present to her mind. Present alike when she forgets herself and speaks in a rage, or when she reflects and acts with a purpose. At one time she tells you that you would have fallen in love with my brother if you had seen him first. At another time she stands by while my brother is personating me to you, and never interferes to stop it. On a third occasion she sees that you are offended with me, and triumphs so cruelly in seeing it that she tells me to my face your prospect would have been a much happier one if you had been engaged to marry my brother instead of me. She is asked in writing, civilly and kindly asked, to explain what she means by those abominable words. She has had time to reflect since she spoke them; and what does she do? Does she answer me? No! she contemptuously tosses my letter into the fireplace. Add to these plain facts what you yourself have observed. Nugent has all her admiration; Nugent is her favorite: from the first she has always disliked and wronged *me*. Add to this, again, that Nugent (as I know for certain) privately confessed to her that he was himself in love with you. Look at all these circumstances, and what plain conclusion follows? I ask you once more—Is Madame Pratolungo a slandered woman? or am I right in warning you to beware of her?"

What could I do but own that he was right? It was due to him and due to me to close my heart to her from that moment. Oscar sat down by me and took my hand.

"After my experience of her in the past," he went on, softly, "can you wonder that I dread what she may do in the future? Has no such thing ever happened as the parting of true lovers by treachery which has secretly undermined their confidence in each other? Is Madame Pratolungo not clever enough and unscrupulous enough to undermine *our* confidence, and to turn against us, to the wickedest purpose, the influence which she already possesses at the rectory? How do we know that she is not in communication with my brother at this moment?"

I stopped him there—I could not endure it. "You have seen your brother," I said. "You have told me that you and he understand each other. What have you to dread after that?"

"I have to dread Madame Pratolungo's influence and my brother's infatuation for you," he answered. "The promises which he has honestly made to me are promises which I cannot depend on when my back is turned, and when Madame Pratolungo may be with him in my absence. Something under the surface is going on already! I don't like that mysterious letter, which is only to be shown to you on certain conditions. I don't like your father's silence. He has had time to answer your letter. Has he done it? He has had time to answer my postscript. Has he done it?"

Those were awkward questions. He had certainly left both our letters unanswered—thus far. Still, the next post might bring his reply. I persisted in taking this view, and I said so to Oscar. He persisted just as obstinately on his side.

"Suppose we go on to the end of the week," he said, "and still no letter from your father comes for you or for me? Will you admit *then* that his silence is suspicious?"

"I will admit that his silence shows a sad want of proper consideration for *you*," I replied.

"And there you will stop? You won't see (what I see) the influence of Madame Pratolungo making itself felt at the rectory, and poisoning your father's mind against our marriage?"

He was pressing me rather hardly. I did my best, however, to tell him honestly what was passing in my mind.

"I can see," I said, "that Madame Pratolungo has behaved most cruelly to you. And I believe, after what you have told me, that she would rejoice if I broke my engagement, and married your brother. But I can *not* understand that she is mad enough to be actually plotting to make me do it. Nobody knows better than she does how faithfully I love you, and how hopeless it would be to attempt to make me marry another man. Would the stupidest woman living, who looked at you two brothers (knowing what she knows), be stupid enough to do what you suspect Madame Pratolungo of doing?"

I thought this unanswerable. He had his reply to it ready, for all that.

"If you had seen more of the world, Lucilla," he said, "you would know that a true love like yours is a mystery to a woman like Madame Pratolungo. She doesn't believe in it—she doesn't understand it. She knows herself to be capable of breaking any engagement, if the circumstances encouraged her, and she estimates your fidelity

by her knowledge of her own nature. There is
nothing in her experience of you, or in her knowledge of my brother's disfigurement, to discourage
such a woman from scheming to part us. She
has seen for herself—what you have already told
me—that you have got over your first aversion
to him. She knows that women as charming as
you are have, over and over again, married men
far more personally repulsive than my brother.
Lucilla! something which is not to be outargued,
and not to be contradicted, tells me that her return to England will be fatal to my hopes, if
that return finds you and me with no closer tie
between us than the tie that binds us now. Are
these fanciful apprehensions unworthy of a man?
My darling, worthy or not worthy, you ought to
make allowances for them. They are apprehensions inspired by my love for You!"

Under those circumstances, I could make every
allowance for him—and I said so. He moved
nearer to me, and put his arm round me.

"Are we not engaged to each other to be man
and wife?" he whispered.

"Yes."

"Are we not both of age, and both free to do
as we like?"

"Yes."

"Would you relieve me from the anxieties
under which I am suffering if you could?"

"You know I would."

"You *can* relieve me."

"How?"

"By giving me a husband's claim to you, Lucilla—by consenting to marry me in London in a fortnight's time."

I started back and looked at him in amazement. For the moment I was incapable of answering in any other way than that.

"I ask you to do nothing unworthy of you," he said. "I have spoken to a relative of mine living near London — a married lady — whose house is open to you in the interval before our wedding-day. In a fortnight from the time when I get the License we can be married. Write home by all means to prevent them from feeling anxious about you. Tell them that you are safe and happy, and under responsible and respectable care—but say no more. As long as it is possible for Madame Pratolungo to make mischief between us, conceal the place in which you are living. The instant we are married reveal everything. Let all your friends, let all the world, know that we are man and wife!"

His arm trembled round me; his face flushed deep; his eyes devoured me. Some women, in my place, might have been offended; others might have been flattered. As for me—I can trust the secret to these pages—I was frightened.

"Is it an elopement that you are proposing to me?" I asked.

"An elopement!" he repeated: "between two engaged people who have only themselves to think of!"

"I have my father to think of, and my aunt to think of," I said. "You are proposing to me to run away from them, and to keep in hiding from them."

"I am asking you to pay a fortnight's visit at the house of a married lady, and to keep the knowledge of that visit from the ears of the worst enemy you have until you have become my wife," he answered. "Is there anything so very terrible in my request that you should turn pale at it, and look at me in that frightened way? Have I not courted you with your father's consent? Am I not your promised husband? Are we not free to decide for ourselves? There is literally no reason—if it could be done —why we should not be married to-morrow. And you still hesitate? Lucilla! Lucilla! you force me to own the doubt that has made me miserable ever since I have been here. Are you indeed as changed toward me as you seem? Do you really no longer love me as you once loved me in the days that are gone?"

He rose and walked away a few paces, leaning over the parapet with his head in his hands.

I sat alone, not knowing what to say or do. The uneasy sense in me that he had reason to complain of my treating him coldly was not to be dismissed from my mind by any effort that I could make. He had no right to expect me to take the step which he had proposed—there were objections to it which any woman would have felt in my place. Still, though I was satisfied of this, there was an obstinate something in me which would take his part. It could not have been my conscience surely which said to me: "There was a time when his entreaties would have prevailed on you; there was a time when you would not have hesitated as you are hesitating now?"

Whatever the influence was, it moved me to rise from my seat and join him at the parapet.

"You cannot expect me to decide on such a serious matter as this at once," I said. "Will you give me a little time to think?"

"You are your own mistress," he rejoined, bitterly. "Why ask me to give you time? You take any time you please; you can do as you like."

"Give me till the end of the week," I went on. "Let me be sure that my father persists in not answering either your letter or mine. Though I *am* my own mistress, nothing but his silence can justify me in going away secretly, and being married to you by a stranger. Don't press me, Oscar. It isn't very long to the end of the week."

Something seemed to startle him—something in my voice perhaps which told him that I was really distressed. He looked round at me quickly and caught me with the tears in my eyes.

"Don't cry, for God's sake!" he said. "It shall be as you wish. Take your time. We will say no more about it till the end of the week."

He kissed me in a hurried, startled way, and gave me his arm to walk back.

"Grosse is coming to-day," he continued. "He mustn't see you looking as you are look-

ing now. You must rest and compose yourself.
Come home.''

I went back with him, feeling—oh, so sad and
sore at heart! My last faint hope of a renewal
of my once pleasant intimacy with Madame
Pratolungo was at an end. She stood revealed
to me now as a woman whom I ought never to
have known—a woman with whom I could never
again exchange a friendly word. I had lost the
companion with whom I had once been so happy;
and I had pained and disappointed Oscar. My
life has never looked so wretched and so worth-
less to me as it looked to-day on the pier at
Ramsgate.

He left me at the door, with a gentle, encouraging pressure of my hand.

"I will call again, later," he said, "and hear
what Grosse's report of you is, before he goes
back to London. Rest, Lucilla—rest and compose yourself!''

A heavy footstep sounded suddenly behind us
as he spoke. We both turned round. Time had
slipped by more rapidly than we had thought.
There stood Herr Grosse, just arrived on foot
from the railway station.

His first look at me seemed to startle and disappoint him. His eyes stared into mine through
his spectacles, with an expression of surprise and
anxiety which I had never seen in them before.
Then he turned his head and looked at Oscar
with a sudden change—a change unpleasantly
suggestive (to my fancy) of anger or distrust.
Not a word fell from his lips. Oscar was left

to break the awkward silence. He spoke to
Grosse.

"I won't disturb you and your patient now,"
he said. "I will come back in an hour's time."

"No! you will come in along with me, if you
please. I have something, my young gentle-
mans, that I may want to say to you." He
spoke with a frown on his bushy eyebrows, and
pointed in a very peremptory manner to the
house door.

Oscar rang the bell. At the same moment my
aunt, hearing us outside, appeared on the bal-
cony above the door.

"Good-morning, Mr. Grosse," she said. "I
hope you find Lucilla looking her best. Only
yesterday I expressed my opinion that she was
quite well again."

Grosse took off his hat sulkily to my aunt and
looked back again at me—looked so hard and
so long that he began to confuse me.

"Your aunt's opinions is not my opinions," he
growled, close at my ear. "I don't like the looks
of you, miss. Go in!"

The servant was waiting for us at the open
door. I went in without making any answer.
Grosse waited to see Oscar enter the house before
him. Oscar's face darkened as he joined me in
the hall. He looked half angry, half confused.
Grosse pushed himself roughly between us, and
gave me his arm. I went upstairs with him,
wondering what it all meant.

CHAPTER THE FORTY-FIFTH.

LUCILLA'S JOURNAL, CONCLUDED.

September 4 (*continued*). — Arrived in the drawing-room, Grosse placed me in a chair near the window. He leaned forward, and looked at me close; he drew back, and looked at me from a distance; he took out his magnifying-glass, and had a long stare through it at my eyes; he felt my pulse, dropped my wrist as if it disgusted him, and, turning to the window, looked out in grim silence, without taking the slightest notice of any one in the room.

My aunt was the first person who spoke under these discouraging circumstances.

"Mr. Grosse!" she said, sharply. "Have you nothing to tell me about your patient to-day? Do you find Lucilla—"

He turned suddenly round from the window, and interrupted Miss Batchford without the slightest ceremony.

"I find her gone back, back, back!" he growled, getting louder and louder at each repetition of the word. "When I sent her here, I said—'Keep her comfortable-easy.' You have *not* kept her comfortable - easy. Something has turned her poor little mind topsy - turvies. What is it? Who is it?" He looked fiercely backward and forward between Oscar and my aunt—then turned

my way, and putting his heavy hands on my
shoulders, looked down at me with an odd angry
kind of pity in his face. "My childs is melan-
cholic; my childs is ill," he went on. "Where
is our goot-dear Pratolungo? What did you tell
me about her, my little-lofe, when I last saw
you? You said she had gone aways to see her
Papa. Send a telegrams and say I want Pratolungo here."

At the repetition of Madame Pratolungo's
name Miss Batchford rose to her feet, and stood
(apparently) several inches higher than usual.

"Am I to understand, sir," inquired the old
lady, "that your extraordinary language is intended to cast a reproach on my conduct toward
my niece?"

"You are to understand this, madam. In the
face of the goot sea airs, miss your niece is fretting herself ill. I sent her to this place for to
get a rosy face, for to put on a firm flesh. How
do I find her? She has got nothing, she has put
on nothing—she is emphatically flabby-pale. In
this fine airs, she can be flabby-pale but for one
reason. She is fretting herself about something
or anodder. Is fretting herself goot for her eyes?
Ho-damn-damn! it is as bad for her eyes as bad
can be. If you can do no better than this, take
her aways back again. You are wasting your
moneys in this lodgment here."

My aunt addressed herself to me in her grandest manner.

"You will understand, Lucilla, that it is impossible for me to notice such language as this

in any other way than by leaving the room. If you can bring Mr. Grosse to his senses, inform him that I will receive his apologies and explanations in writing." Pronouncing these lofty words with her severest emphasis, Miss Batchford rose another inch, and sailed majestically out of the room.

Grosse took no notice of the offended lady; he only put his hands in his pockets, and looked out of window once more. As the door closed, Oscar left the corner in which he had seated himself, not overgraciously, when we entered the room.

"Am I wanted here?" he asked.

Grosse was on the point of answering the question even less amiably than it had been put—when I stopped him by a look. "I want to speak to you," I whispered in his ear. He nodded, and, turning sharply to Oscar, put this question to him:

"Are you living in the house?"

"I am staying at the hotel at the corner."

"Go to the hotel, and wait there till I come to you."

Greatly to my surprise, Oscar submitted to be treated in this peremptory manner. He took his leave of me silently, and left the room. Grosse drew a chair close to mine, and sat down by me in a comforting, confidential, fatherly way.

"Now, my goot-girls," he said. "What have you been fretting yourself about since I was last in this house? Open it all, if you please, to Papa Grosse. Come-begin-begin!"

I suppose he had exhausted his ill-temper on my aunt and Oscar. He said those words more than kindly—almost tenderly. His fierce eyes seemed to soften behind his spectacles: he took my hand and patted it to encourage me.

There are some things written in these pages of mine which it was, of course, impossible for me to confide to him. With those necessary reservations—and without entering on the painful subject of my altered relations with Madame Pratolungo—I owned quite frankly how sadly changed I felt myself to be toward Oscar, and how much less happy I was with him, in consequence of the change. "I am not ill as you suppose," I explained. "I am only disappointed in myself, and a little downhearted when I think of the future." Having opened it to him in this way, I thought it time to put the question which I had determined to ask when I next saw him.

"The restoration of my sight," I said, "has made a new being of me. In gaining the sense of seeing, have I lost the sense of feeling which I had when I was blind? I want to know if it will come back when I have got used to the novelty of my position? I want to know if I shall ever enjoy Oscar's society again, as I used to enjoy it in the old days before you cured me— the happy days, Papa Grosse, when I was an object of pity, and when all the people spoke of me as Poor Miss Finch?"

I had more to say—but at this place, Grosse (without meaning it, I am sure) suddenly stopped me. To my amazement, he let go of my hand,

and turned his face away sharply, as if he resented my looking at him. His big head sank
on his breast. He lifted his great hairy hands,
shook them mournfully, and let them fall on his
knees. This strange behavior, and the still stranger silence which accompanied it, made me so
uneasy that I insisted on his explaining himself.
"What is the matter with you?" I said. "Why
don't you answer me?"

He roused himself with a start, and put his
arm round me with a wonderful gentleness for
a man who was so rough at other times.

"It is nothing, my pretty lofe," he said. "I
am out of sort, as you call it. Your English
climate sometimes gives your English blue-
devil to foreign mens like me. I have got him
now—an English blue-devil in a German inside.
Soh! I shall go and walk him out, and come
back empty-cheerful, and see you again." He
rose, after this curious explanation, and attempted some sort of answer—a very odd one
—to the question which I had asked of him.
"As to that odder thing," he went on, "yes-
indeed-yes. You have hit your nail on his
head. It is, as you say, your seeings which
has got in the way of your feelings. When
your seeings-feelings has got used to one anodder, your seeings will stay where he is, your
feelings will come back to where they was; one
will balance the odder; you will feel as you did;
you will see as you didn't, all at the same times,
all jolly-nice again as before. You have my
opinions. Now let me walk out my blue-devil.

I swear to come back again with a new inside. By-by-my-Feench-good-by."

Saying all this in a violent hurry, as if he was eager to get away, he gave me a kiss on the forehead, snatched up his shabby hat, and ran out of the room.

What did it mean?

Does he persist in thinking me seriously ill? I am too weary to puzzle my brains in the effort to understand my dear old surgeon. It is one o'clock in the morning; and I have still to write the story of all that happened later in the day. My eyes are beginning to ache; and, strange to say, I have hardly been able to see the last two or three lines I have written. They look as if the ink was fading from them. If Grosse knew what I am about at this moment! His last words to me, when he went back to his patients in London, were—"No more readings! no more writings till I come again!" It is all very well to talk in that way. I have got so used to my Journal that I can't do without it. Nevertheless I must stop now—for the best of reasons. Though I have got three lighted candles on my table, I really cannot see to write any more.

To bed! to bed!

[Note.—I have purposely abstained from interrupting Lucilla's Journal until my extracts from it reached this place. Here the writer pauses and gives me a chance, and here there are matters that must be mentioned of which she had personally no knowledge at the time.

You have seen how her faithful instinct still tries to reveal to my poor darling the cruel deception that is being practiced on her, and still tries in vain. In spite of herself she shrinks from the man who is tempting her to go away with him, though he pleads in the character of her betrothed husband. In spite of herself she detects the weak places in the case which Nugent has made out against me—the absence of sufficient motive for the conduct of which he accuses me, and the utter improbability of my plotting and intriguing (without anything to gain by it) to make her marry the man who was not the man of her choice. She feels these hesitations and difficulties. But what they really signify it is morally impossible for her to guess.

Thus far, no doubt, her strange and touching position has been plainly revealed to you. But can I feel quite so sure that you understand how seriously she has been affected by the anxiety, disappointment, and suspense which have combined together to torture her at this critical interval in her life.

I doubt it, for the sufficient reason that you have only had her Journal to enlighten you, and that her Journal shows she does not understand it herself. As things are, it seems to be time for me to step on the stage, and to discover to you plainly what her surgeon really thought of her by telling you what passed between Grosse and Nugent when the German presented himself at the hotel.

I am writing now (as a matter of course) from

information given to me, at an after-period, by
the persons themselves. As to particulars, the
accounts vary. As to results, they both agree.
The discovery that Nugent was at Ramsgate
necessarily took Grosse by surprise. With his
previous knowledge, however, of the situation
of affairs at Dimchurch, he could be at no loss
to understand in what character Nugent had presented himself to Lucilla; and he could certainly
not fail to understand—after what he had seen
and what she had herself told him—that the
deception was, under present circumstances, producing the worst possible effect on her mind.
Arriving at this conclusion, he was not a man
to hesitate about the duty that lay before him.
When he entered the room at the hotel in which
Nugent was waiting for him, he announced the
object of his visit in these four plain words, as
follows:

"Pack up and go!"

Nugent coolly offered him a chair, and asked
what he meant.

Grosse refused the chair, but consented to explain himself in terms variously reported by the
two parties. Combining the statements, and
translating Grosse (in this grave matter) into
plain English, I find that the German must have
expressed himself in these or nearly in these
words:

"As a professional man, Mr. Nugent, I invariably refuse to enter into domestic considerations connected with my patients with which I
have nothing to do. In the case of Miss Finch,

my business is not with your family complications. My business is to secure the recovery of
the young lady's sight. If I find her health improving, I don't inqurie how or why. No matter what private and personal frauds you may be
practicing upon her, I have nothing to say to
them—more, I am ready to take advantage of
them myself—so long as their influence is directly beneficial in keeping her morally and
physically in the condition in which I wish
her to be. But the instant I discover that this
domestic conspiracy of yours—this personation
of your brother, which once quieted and comforted her—is unfavorably affecting her health
of body and peace of mind, I interfere between
you in the character of her medical attendant,
and stop it on medical grounds. You are producing in my patient a conflict of feeling which,
in a nervous temperament like hers, cannot go
on without serious injury to her health. And
serious injury to her health means serious injury
to her eyes. I won't have that—I tell you plainly to pack up and go. I meddle with nothing
else. After what you have yourself seen, I leave
you to decide whether you will restore your brother to Miss Finch or not. All I say is, Go.
Make any excuse you like, but go before you
have done more mischief. You shake your
head! Is that a sign that you refuse? Take
a day to think before you make up your mind.
I have patients in London to whom I am obliged
to go back. But the day after to-morrow I shall
return to Ramsgate. If I find you still here, I

shall tell Miss Finch you are no more Oscar Dubourg than I am. In her present state, I see less
danger in giving her even that serious shock than
in leaving her to the slow torment of mind which
you are inflicting by your continued presence in
this place. My last word is said. I go back by
the next train in an hour's time. Good-morning,
Mr. Nugent. If you are a wise man, you will
meet me at the station."

After this the accounts vary. Nugent's statement asserts that he accompanied Grosse on his
way back to Miss Batchford's lodging, arguing
the matter with him, and only leaving him at
the door of the house. Grosse's statement, on
the other hand, makes no allusion to this. The
disagreement between them is, however, of no
consequence here. It is admitted, on either side,
that the result of the interview was the same.
When Grosse took the train for London, Nugent
Dubourg was not at the station. The next entry
in the Journal shows that he remained that day
and night, at least, at Ramsgate.

You now know, from the narrative of the surgeon's own proceedings, how seriously he thought
of his patient's case, and how firmly he did his
duty as an honorable man. Having given you
this necessary information, I again retire, and
leave Lucilla to take up the next link in the
chain of events.—P.]

September 5. *Six o'clock in the morning.*—
A few hours of restless, broken sleep, disturbed
by horrid dreams, and waking over and over

again with startings that seemed to shake me from head to foot. I can bear it no longer. The sun is rising. I have got up—and here I am at the writing-table, trying to finish the long story of yesterday, still uncompleted in my Journal.

I have just been looking at the view from my window, and I notice one thing which has struck me. The mist this morning is the thickest mist I have yet seen here.

The sea view is almost invisible, it is so dim and dull. Even the objects about me in my room are nothing like so plain as usual. The mist is stealing in, no doubt, through my open window. It gets between me and my paper, and obliges me to bend down close over the page to see what I am about. When the sun is higher, things will be clear again. In the meantime I must do as well as I can.

Grosse came back after his walk as mysterious as ever.

He was quite peremptory in ordering me not to overtask my eyes—forbidding reading and writing, as I have already mentioned. But when I asked for his reasons, he had, for the first time in my experience of him, no reasons to give. I have the less scruple about disobeying him on that account. Still I am a little uneasy, I confess, when I think of his strange behavior yesterday. He looked at me, in the oddest way, as if he saw something in my face which he had never seen before. Twice he took his leave, and twice he returned, doubtful whether he would not remain at Ramsgate, and let his patients in London take care of themselves. His extraordinary indecision was put an end to at last by the arrival of a telegram which had followed him from London—an urgent message, I suppose, from one of the patients. He went away in a bad temper and a violent hurry, and told me, at the door, to expect him back on the sixth.

When Oscar came, later, there was another surprise for me.

Like Grosse, he was not himself—he too behaved strangely! First, he was so cold and so silent that I thought he was offended. Then he went straight to the other extreme, and became so loudly talkative, so obstreperously cheerful, that my aunt asked me privately whether I did not suspect (as she did) that he had been taking too much wine. It ended in his trying to sing to my accompaniment on the piano, and in his breaking down. He walked away to the other end of the room without explanation or apology.

When I followed him there, a little while after, he had a look that indescribably distressed me—a look as if he had been crying. Toward the end of the evening my aunt fell asleep over her book, and gave us a chance of speaking to each other in a little second room which opens out of the drawing-room in this house. It was I who took the chance—not he. He was so incomprehensibly unwilling to go into the room and speak to me that I had to do a very unladylike thing; I mean that I had to take his arm and lead him in myself, and entreat him (in a whisper) to tell me what was the matter with him.

"Only the old complaint," he answered.

I made him sit down by me on a little old-fashioned couch that just held two.

"What do you mean by the old complaint?" I asked.

"Oh! you know!"

"I *don't* know."

"You would know if you really loved me."

"Oscar! it is a shame to say that. It is a shame to doubt that I love you!"

"Is it? Ever since I have been here I have doubted that you loved me. It is getting to be an old complaint of mine now. I still suffer a little sometimes. Don't notice it!"

He was so cruel and so unjust that I got up to leave him without saying a word more. But, oh! he looked so forlorn and so submissive—sitting with his head down, and his hands crossed listlessly over his knees—that I could not find it in my heart to treat him harshly. Was I wrong? I don't know! I have no idea how to manage men—and no Madame Pratolungo now to teach me. Right or wrong, it ended in my sitting down by him again in the place which I had just left.

"You ought to beg my pardon," I said, "for thinking of me as you think, and talking to me as you talk."

"I do beg your pardon," he answered, humbly. "I am sorry if I have offended you."

How could I resist that? I put my hand on

his shoulder, and tried to make him lift up his head and look at me.

"You will always believe in me in the future?" I went on. "Promise me that."

"I can promise to try, Lucilla. As things are now, I can promise no more."

"As things are now? You are speaking in riddles to-night. Explain yourself."

"I explained myself this morning on the pier."

Surely this was hard on me—after he had promised to give me till the end of the week to consider his proposal! I took my hand off his shoulder. He, who never used to displease or disappoint me when I was blind, had displeased and disappointed me for the second time in a few minutes!

"Do you wish to force me?" I asked. "After telling me this morning that you would give me time to reflect?"

He rose, on his side, languidly and mechanically, like a man who neither knew nor cared what he was doing.

"Force you?" he repeated. "Did I say that? I don't know what I am talking about; I don't know what I am doing. You are right and I am wrong. I am a miserable wretch, Lucilla—I am utterly unworthy of you. It would be better for you if you never saw me again!" He paused, and, taking me by both hands, looked earnestly and sadly into my face. "Good-night, my dear!" he said, and suddenly dropped my hands, and turned away to go out.

I stopped him.

"Going already?" I said. "It is not late yet."

"It is best for me to go."

"Why?"

"I am in wretched spirits. It is better for me to be by myself."

"Don't say that! It sounds like a reproach to *me*."

"On the contrary, it is all my fault. Goodnight!"

I refused to say good-night; I refused to let him go. His wanting to go was in itself a reproach to me. He had never done it before. I asked him to sit down again.

He shook his head.

"For ten minutes!"

He shook his head again.

"For five minutes!"

Instead of answering, he gently lifted a long lock of my hair which hung at the side of my neck. (My head, I should add, had been dressed that evening on the old-fashioned plan by my aunt's maid—to please my aunt.)

"If I stay five minutes longer," he said, "I shall ask for something."

"For what?"

"You have beautiful hair, Lucilla."

"You can't want a lock of my hair, surely?"

"Why not?"

"I gave you a keepsake of that sort—ages ago. Have you forgotten it?"

[*Note.*—The keepsake had, of course, been given to the true Oscar, and was then, as it is

now, still in his possession. Notice, when he
recovers himself, how quickly the false Oscar
infers this, and how cleverly he founds his excuse upon it.—P.]

His face flushed deep, his eyes dropped before
mine. I could see that he was ashamed of himself; I could only conclude that he *had* forgotten
it! A morsel of *his* hair was, at that moment,
in a locket which I wore round my neck. I had
more reason, I think, to doubt him than he had
to doubt me. I was so mortified that I stepped
aside, and made way for him to go out.

"You wish to go away," I said; "I won't
keep you any longer."

It was his turn now to plead with *me*.

"Suppose I have been deprived of your keepsake?" he said. "Suppose somebody whom I
would rather not mention has taken it away
from me?"

I instantly understood him. His miserable
brother had taken it. My work-basket was
close by. I cut off a lock of my hair, and tied
it at each end with a morsel of my favorite light
blue ribbon.

"Are we friends again, Oscar?" was all I
said as I put it into his hand.

He caught me in his arms in a kind of frenzy
—holding me to him so violently that he hurt
me; kissing me so fiercely that he frightened
me. Before I had recovered breath enough to
speak to him he had released me, and had gone
out in such headlong haste that he knocked down

a little round table with books on it, and awoke my aunt.

The old lady called for me in her most formidable voice, and showed me the family temper in its sourest aspect. Grosse had gone back to London without making any apology to her, and Oscar had knocked down her books. The indignation aroused by these two outrages called loudly for a victim—and (no one else being near at the moment) selected Me. Miss Batchford discovered for the first time that she had undertaken too much in undertaking to take the sole charge of her niece at Ramsgate.

"I decline to assume the entire responsibility," said my aunt. "At my age, the entire responsibility is too much for me. I shall write to your father, Lucilla. I always did, and always shall, detest him, as you know. His views on politics and religion are (in a clergyman) simply detestable. Still he *is* your father; and it is a duty on my part, after what that rude foreigner has said about your health, to offer to restore you to your father's roof—or, at least, to obtain your father's sanction to your continuing to remain under my care. This course, in either case, you will observe, relieves me from the entire responsibility. I am doing nothing to compromise my position. My position is quite plain to me. I should have formally accepted your father's hospitality on the occasion of your wedding, if I had been well enough, and if the wedding had taken place. It follows as a matter of course that I may formally report to your father what the medical opinion is of your health. However brutally it may have been given, it *is* a medical opinion—and as such I am bound to communicate it."

Knowing but too well how bitterly my aunt's aversion to him is reciprocated by my father, I did my best to combat Miss Batchford's resolution, without making matters worse by telling her what my motives really were. With some difficulty I prevailed on her to defer the proposed report of me for a day or two—and we parted for the night (the old lady's fits of temper are soon over) as good friends as usual.

This little episode in the history of the evening diverted my mind for the time from Oscar's strange conduct yesterday evening. But once up here by myself in my own room, I have been thinking of it, or dreaming of it (such horrid dreams!—I cannot write them down!), almost incessantly from that time to this. When we meet again to-day, how will he look? what will he say?

He was right yesterday. I *am* cold to him; there *is* some change in me toward him which I don't understand myself. My conscience accuses me now I am alone—and yet, God knows, it is not my fault.

Poor Oscar! Poor Me!

I have never longed to see him, since we met at this place, as I long now. He sometimes comes to breakfast. Will he come to breakfast to-day?

Oh, how my eyes ache! and how obstinately

the mist stops in the room! Suppose I close the window, and go back to bed again for a little while?

Nine o'clock.—The maid came in half an hour since and awoke me. She went to open the window as usual. I stopped her.

"Is the mist gone?" I asked.

The girl started. "What mist, miss?"

"Haven't you seen it?"

"No, miss."

"What time did you get up?"

"At seven, miss."

At seven I was still writing in my Journal, and the mist was still over everything in the room. Persons in the lower ranks of life are curiously unobservant of the aspects of Nature. I never (in the days of my blindness) got any information from servants or laborers about the views round Dimchurch. They seemed to have no eyes for anything beyond the range of the kitchen or the plowed field. I got out of bed, and took the maid myself to the window, and opened it.

"There!" I said. "It is not quite so thick as it was some hours since. But there is the mist as plain as can be!"

The girl looked backward and forward in a state of bewilderment between me and the view.

"Miss?" she repeated. "Begging your pardon, miss, it's a beautiful clear morning—as I see it."

"Clear?" I repeated, on my side.

"Yes, miss."

"Do you mean to tell me it's clear over the sea?"

"The sea is a beautiful blue, miss. Far and near you can see the ships."

"Where are the ships?"

She pointed out of the window to a certain spot.

"There are two of them, miss. A big ship with three masts. And a little ship, just behind, with one."

I looked along her finger, and strained my eyes to see. All I could make out was a dim, grayish mist, with something like a little spot or blur on it at the place which the maid's finger indicated as the position occupied by the two ships.

The idea struck me for the first time that the dimness which I had attributed to the mist was, in plain truth, the dimness in my own eyes. For the moment I was a little startled. I left the window, and made the best excuse that I could to the girl. As soon as it was possible to dismiss her I sent her away, and bathed my eyes with one of Grosse's lotions, and then tried them again in writing this entry. To my relief, I can see to write better than I did earlier in the morning. Still I have had a warning to pay a little more attention to Grosse's directions than I have hitherto done. Is it possible that he saw something in the state of my eyes which he was afraid to tell me of? Nonsense! Grosse is not the sort of man who shrinks from speaking out. I have fatigued my eyes—that is all. Let me shut up my book and go downstairs to breakfast.

Ten o'clock.—For a moment I open my Journal.

Something has happened which I must positively set down in this history of my life. I am so vexed and so angry! The maid (wretched, chattering fool) has told my aunt what passed between us this morning at my window. Miss Batchford has taken the alarm, and has insisted on writing not only to Grosse, but to my father. In the present imbittered state of my father's feeling against my aunt, he will either leave her letter unanswered, or he will offend her by an angry reply. In either case I shall be the sufferer: my aunt's sense of injury—which cannot address itself to my father—will find a convenient object to assail in *me.* I shall never hear the last of it. Being already nervous and dispirited, the prospect of finding myself involved in a new family quarrel quite daunts me. I feel ungratefully inclined to run away from Miss Batchford when I think of it!

No signs of Oscar; and no news of Oscar—yet.

Twelve o'clock.—But one trial more was wanted to make my life here quite unendurable. The trial has come.

A letter from Oscar (sent by messenger from his hotel) has just been placed in my hands. It informs me that he has decided on leaving Ramsgate by the next train. The next train starts in forty minutes. Good God! what am I to do?

My eyes are burning. I know it does them
harm to cry. How can I help crying? It is all
over between us if I let Oscar go away alone—
his letter as good as tells me so. Oh, why have I
behaved so coldly to him? I ought to make any
sacrifice of my own feelings to atone for it. And
yet there is an obstinate something in me that
shrinks. What am I to do? what am I to do?

I must drop the pen, and try if I can think.
My eyes completely fail me. I can write no
more.

[*Note.*—I copy the letter to which Lucilla
refers.

Nugent's own assertion is that he wrote it in
a moment of remorse, to give her an opportunity
of breaking the engagement by which she innocently supposed herself to be held to him. He
declared that he honestly believed the letter
would offend her when he wrote it. The other
interpretation of the document is that, finding
himself obliged to leave Ramsgate—under penalty (if he remained) of being exposed by Grosse
as an impostor when the surgeon visited his patient on the next day—Nugent seized the opportunity of making his absence the means of working on Lucilla's feelings so as to persuade her to
accompany him to London. Don't ask me which
of these two conclusions I favor. For reasons
which you will understand when you have come
to the end of my narrative, I would rather not
express my opinion either one way or the other.
Read the letter, and decide for yourselves:

"MY DARLING—After a sleepless night I have decided on leaving Ramsgate by the next train that starts after you receive these lines. Last night's experience has satisfied me that my presence here (after what I said to you on the pier) only distresses you. Some influence that is too strong for you to resist has changed your heart toward me. When the time comes for you to determine whether you will be my wife on the conditions that I have proposed, I see but too plainly that you will say No. Let me make it less hard for you, my love, to do that by leaving you to write the word, instead of saying it to me. If you wish for your freedom, cost me what it may, I will absolve you from your engagement. I love you too dearly to blame you. My address in London is on the other leaf. Farewell!   OSCAR."

The address given on the blank leaf is at a hotel.

A few lines more in the Journal follow the lines last quoted in this place. Except a word or two here and there, it is impossible any longer to decipher the writing. The mischief done to her eyes by her reckless use of them, by her fits of crying, by her disturbed nights, by the long-continued strain on her of agitation and suspense, has evidently justified the worst of those unacknowledged forebodings which Grosse felt when he saw her. The last lines of the Journal are, as writing, actually inferior to her worst writing in the days when she was blind.

However, the course which she ended in taking on receipt of the letter which you have just read is sufficiently indicated by a note of Nugent's writing, left at Miss Batchford's residence at Ramsgate by a porter from the railway. After-events make it necessary to preserve this note also. It runs thus:

"MADAM—I write, by Lucilla's wish, to beg that you will not be anxious on discovering that your niece has left Ramsgate. She accompanies me, at my express request, to the house of a married lady who is a relative of mine, and under whose care she will remain until the time arrives for our marriage. The reasons which have led to her taking this step, and which oblige her to keep her new place of residence concealed for the present, will be frankly stated to you and to her father on the day when we are man and wife. In the meantime Lucilla begs that you will excuse her abrupt departure, and that you will be so good as to send this letter on to her father. Both you and he will, I hope, remember that she is of an age to act for herself, and that she is only hastening her marriage with a man to whom she has long been engaged with the sanction and approval of her family.—Believe me, madam, your faithful servant,

"OSCAR DUBOURG."

This letter was delivered at luncheon-time—almost at the moment when the servant had announced to her mistress that Miss Finch was nowhere to be found, and that her traveling-bag had disappeared from her room. The London train had then started. Miss Batchford, having no right to interfere, decided—after consultation with a friend—on at once traveling to Dimchurch and placing the matter in Mr. Finch's hands.—P.]

MADAME PRATOLUNGO'S NARRATIVE RESUMED

CHAPTER THE FORTY-SIXTH.

THE ITALIAN STEAMER.

LUCILLA'S Journal has told you all that Lucilla can tell. Permit me to re-appear in these pages. Shall I say, with your favorite English clown, re-appearing every year in your barbarous English pantomime, "Here I am again: how do you do"? No—I had better leave that out. Your clown is one of your national institutions. With this mysterious source of British amusement let no foreign person presume to trifle!

I arrived at Marseilles, as well as I can remember, on the fifteenth of August.

You cannot be expected to feel my interest in good Papa. I will pass over this venerable victim of the amiable delusions of the heart as rapidly as respect and affection will permit. The duel (I hope you remember the duel?) had been fought with pistols, and the bullet had not been extracted when I joined my sisters at the suffer-

er's bedside. He was delirious and did not know
me. Two days later, the removal of the bullet
was accomplished by the surgeon in attendance.
For a time he improved after this. Then there
was a relapse. It was only on the first of September that we were permitted to hope that he
might still be spared to us.

On that day I was composed enough to think
again of Lucilla, and to remember Mrs. Finch's
polite request to me that I would write to her
from Marseilles.

I wrote briefly, telling the damp lady of the
rectory (only at greater length) what I have told
here. My main motive in doing this was, I confess, to obtain, through Mrs. Finch, some news
of Lucilla. After posting the letter I attended
to another duty which I had neglected while my
father was in danger of death. I went to the
person to whom my lawyer had recommended
me, to institute that search for Oscar which I
had determined to set on foot when I left London. The person was connected with the police,
in the capacity (as nearly as I can express it in
English) of a sort of private superintendent—not
officially recognized, but secretly trusted, for all
that.

When he heard of the time that had elapsed
without any discovery of the slightest trace of
the fugitive, he looked grave, and declared, honestly enough, that he doubted if he could reward
my confidence in him by proving himself to be
of the slightest service to me. Seeing, however,
that I was earnestly bent on making some sort

of effort, he put a last question to me in these
terms:

"You have not described the gentleman yet.
Is there, by lucky chance, anything remarkable
in his personal appearance?"

"There is something very remarkable, sir," I
answered.

"Describe it exactly, ma'am, if you please."

I described Oscar's complexion. My excellent
superintendent showed encouraging signs of interest as he listened. He was a most elegantly
dressed gentleman, with the gracious manners of
a prince. It was quite a privilege to be allowed
to talk to him.

"If the missing man has passed through
France," he said, "with such a remarkable
face as that, there is a fair chance of finding
him. I will set preliminary inquiries going at
the railway station, at the steam-packet office,
and at the port. You shall hear the result to-
morrow."

I went back to good Papa's bedside—satisfied,
so far.

The next day my superintendent honored me
by a visit.

"Any news, sir?" I asked.

"News already, ma'am. The clerk at the
steam-packet office perfectly well remembers
selling a ticket to a stranger with a terrible
blue face. Unhappily, his memory is not equally
good as to other matters. He cannot accurately
call to mind either the name of the stranger or
the place for which the stranger embarked. We

know that he must either have gone to some port in Italy or to some port in the East. And, thus far, we know no more.''

"What are we to do next?'' I inquired.

"I propose—with your permission—sending personal descriptions of the gentleman, by telegraph, to the different ports in Italy first. If nothing is heard of him in reply, we will try the ports in the East next. That is the course which I have the honor of submitting to your consideration. Do you approve of it?''

I cordially approved of it, and waited for the results with all the patience that I could command.

The next day passed, and nothing happened. My unhappy father got on very slowly. The vile woman who had caused the disaster (and who had run off with his antagonist) was perpetually in his mind, disturbing him and keeping him back. Why is a destroying wretch of this sort, a pitiless, treacherous, devouring monster in female form, allowed to be out of prison? You shut up in a cage a poor tigress, who only eats you when she is hungry and can't provide for her dear little children in any other way, and you let the other and far more dangerous beast of the two range at large under protection of the law! Ah, it is easy to see that the men make the laws. Never mind. The women are coming to the front. Wait a little. The tigresses on two legs will have a bad time of it when *we* get into Parliament.

On the fourth of the month the superintendent

wrote to me. More news of the lost Oscar already!

The blue man had disembarked at Genoa, and had been traced to the station of the railway running to Turin. More inquiries had been, thereupon, sent by telegraph to Turin. In the meantime, and in the possible event of the missing person returning to England by way of Marseilles, experienced men, provided with a personal description of him, would be posted at various public places, to pass in review all travelers arriving either by land or sea, and to report to me if the right traveler appeared. Once more my princely superintendent submitted this course to my consideration, and waited for my approval— and got it, with my admiration thrown in as part of the bargain.

The days passed—and good Papa still vacillated between better and worse.

My sisters broke down, poor souls, under their anxieties. It all fell as usual on my shoulders. Day by day my prospect of returning to England seemed to grow more and more remote. Not a line of reply reached me from Mrs. Finch. This in itself fidgeted and disturbed me. Lucilla was now hardly ever out of my thoughts. Over and over again my anxiety urged me to run the risk, and write to her. But the same obstacle always raised itself in my way. After what had happened between us, it was impossible for me to write to her directly without first restoring myself to my former place in her estimation. And I could only do this by entering into particulars which, for all I knew to the contrary, it might still be cruel and dangerous to reveal.

As for writing to Miss Batchford, I had already tried the old lady's patience in that way before leaving England. If I tried it again, with no better excuse for a second intrusion than my own anxieties might suggest, the chances were that this uncompromising royalist would throw my letter into the fire, and treat her republican correspondent with contemptuous silence. Grosse was the third and last person from whom I might hope to obtain information. But—shall I confess it?—I did not know what Lucilla might have told him of the estrangement between us, and my pride (remember, if you please, that I am a poverty-stricken foreigner) revolted at the idea of exposing myself to a possible repulse.

However, by the eleventh of the month I began to feel my suspense so keenly, and to suffer under such painful doubts of what Nugent might be doing in my absence, that I resolved at all hazards on writing to Grosse. It was at least possible, as I calculated—and the Journal will show you that I calculated right—that Lucilla had only told him of my melancholy errand at Marseilles, and had mentioned nothing more. I had just opened my desk when our surgeon in attendance entered the room, and announced the joyful intelligence that he could answer at last for the recovery of good Papa.

"Can I go back to England?" I asked, eagerly.

"Not immediately. You are his favorite nurse —you must gradually accustom him to the idea

of your going away. If you do anything sudden
you may cause a relapse."

"I will do nothing sudden. Only tell me when
it will be safe—absolutely safe—for me to go?"

"Say in a week."

"On the eighteenth?"

"On the eighteenth."

I shut up my writing-desk. Within a few
days I might now hope to be in England as soon
as I could receive Grosse's answer at Marseilles.
Under these circumstances, it would be better
to wait until I could make my inquiries, safely
and independently, in my own proper person.
Comparison of dates will show that if I *had* written to the German oculist, it would have been
too late. It was now the eleventh, and Lucilla
had left Ramsgate with Nugent on the fifth.

All this time but one small morsel of news rewarded our inquiries after Oscar—and even that
small morsel seemed to me to be unworthy of
belief.

It was said that he had been seen at a military
hospital—the hospital of Alessandria, in Pied-
mont, I think—acting, under the surgeons, as
attendant on the badly wounded men who had
survived the famous campaign of France and
Italy against Austria. (Bear in mind, if you
please, that I am writing of the year eighteen
hundred and fifty-nine, and that the peace of
Villafranca was only signed in the July of that
year.) Occupation as hospital man-nurse was,
to my mind, occupation so utterly at variance
with Oscar's temperament and character that I

persisted in considering the intelligence thus received of him to be on the face of it false.

On the seventeenth of the month I had got my passport regulated, and had packed up the greater part of my baggage in anticipation of my journey back to England on the next day.

Carefully as I had tried to accustom his mind to the idea, my poor father remained so immovably reluctant to let me leave him that I was obliged to consent to a sort of compromise. I promised, when the business which took me to England was settled, to return again to Marseilles, and to travel back with him to his home in Paris as soon as he was fit to be moved. On this condition I gained permission to go. Poor as I was, I infinitely preferred charging my slender purse with the expenses of the double journey to remaining any longer in ignorance of what was going on at Ramsgate—or at Dimchurch, as the case might be. Now that my mind was free from anxiety about my father—I don't know which tormented me most—my eagerness to set myself right with my sister friend, or my vague dread of the mischief which Nugent might have done while my back was turned. Over and over again I asked myself whether Miss Batchford had or had not shown my letter to Lucilla. Over and over again I wondered whether it had been my happy privilege to reveal Nugent under his true aspect, and to preserve Lucilla for Oscar, after all.

Toward the afternoon, on the seventeenth, I went out alone to get a breath of fresh air, and a look at the shop windows. I don't care who or what she may be—high or low, handsome or ugly, young or old—it always relieves a woman's mind to look at the shop windows.

I had not been five minutes out before I met my princely superintendent.

"Any news for me to-day?" I asked.

"Not yet."

"Not yet?" I repeated. "You expect news, then?"

"We expect an Italian steamship to arrive in port before the evening," said the superintendent. "Who knows what may happen?"

He bowed and left me. I felt no great elation on contemplating the barren prospect which his last words had placed before me. So many steamers had arrived at Marseilles without bringing any news of the missing man that I attached very little importance to the arrival of the Italian ship. However, I had nothing to do—I wanted a walk—and I thought I might as well stroll down to the port and see the vessel come in.

The vessel was just entering the harbor by the time I got to the landing-stage.

I found our man employed to investigate travelers arriving by sea punctually at his post. His influence broke through the vexatious French rules and regulations which forbid all freedom of public movement within official limits, and procured me a place in the room at the custom-house through which the passengers by the steamer would be obliged to pass. I accepted his polite attention, simply because I was glad to sit down and rest in a quiet place after my walk—not even the shadow of an idea that anything would come of my visit to the harbor being in my mind at the time.

After a long interval the passengers began to stream into the room. Looking languidly enough at the first half-dozen strangers who came in, I felt myself touched on the shoulder from behind. There was our man, in a state of indescribable excitement, entreating me to compose myself!

Being perfectly composed already, I stared at him, and asked: "Why?"

"He is here!" cried the man. "Look!"

He pointed to the passengers still crowding into the room. I looked, and, instantly losing my head, started up with a cry that turned everybody's eyes on me. Yes! there was the poor, dear discolored face—there was Oscar himself, thunderstruck, on his side, at the sight of Me!

I snatched the key of his portmanteau out of his hand, and gave it to our man, who undertook to submit it to the custom-house examination, and to bring it to my lodging afterward. Holding Oscar fast by the arm, I pushed my way through the crowd in the room, got outside, and hailed a cab at the dock-gates. The people about, noticing my agitation, said to each other, compassionately: "It's the blue man's mother!" Idiots! They might have seen, I think, that I was only old enough to be his sister.

Once sheltered in the vehicle, I could draw my breath again, and reward him for all the

anxiety he had caused me by giving him a kiss.
I might have given him a thousand kisses.
Amazement made him a perfectly passive creature in my hands. He only repeated, faintly,
over and over again: "What does it mean? what
does it mean?"

"It means that you have friends, you wretch,
who are fools enough to be too fond of you to
give you up!" I said. "I am one of the fools.
You will come to England with me to-morrow,
and see for yourself if Lucilla is not another."

That reference to Lucilla restored him to the
possession of his senses. He began to ask the
questions that naturally occurred to him under
the circumstances. Having plenty of questions
in reserve, on my side, I told him briefly enough
what had brought me to Marseilles, and what I
had done during my residence in that city toward discovering the place of his retreat.

When he asked me next—after a momentary
struggle with himself—what I could tell him of
Nugent and Lucilla, it is not to be denied that I
hesitated before I answered him. A moment's
consideration, however, was enough to decide
me on speaking out, for this plain reason, that
a moment's consideration reminded me of the
troubles and annoyances which had already be-
fallen us as the result of concealing the truth. I
told Oscar honestly all that I have related here
—starting from my night interview with Nugent
at Browndown, and ending with my precaution-
ary measures for the protection of Lucilla while
she was living under the care of her aunt.

I was greatly interested in watching the effect which these disclosures produced on Oscar.

My observation led me to form two conclusions. First conclusion, that time and absence had not produced the slightest change in the love which the poor fellow bore to Lucilla. Second conclusion, that nothing but absolute proof would induce him to agree in my unfavorable opinion of his brother's character. It was in vain I declared that Nugent had quitted England pledged to find him, and had left it to me (as the event had now proved) to make the discovery. He owned readily that he had seen nothing and heard nothing of Nugent. Nevertheless, his confidence in his brother remained unshaken. "Nugent is the soul of honor," he repeated again and again, with a side-look at me which suggested that my frankly avowed opinion of his brother had hurt and offended him.

I had barely time to notice this before we reached my lodgings. He appeared to be unwilling to follow me into the house.

"I suppose you have some proof to support what you have said of Nugent," he resumed, stopping in the courtyard. "Have you written to England since you have been here? and have you had a reply?"

"I have written to Mrs. Finch," I answered; "and I have not had a word in reply."

"Have you written to no one else?"

I explained to him the position in which I stood toward Miss Batchford, and the hesitation which I had felt about writing to Grosse. The smoldering resentment against me that had been in him ever since I had spoken of his brother and of Lucilla flamed up at last.

"I entirely disagree with you," he broke out, angrily. "You are wronging Lucilla and wronging Nugent. Lucilla is incapable of saying anything against you to Grosse, and Nugent is equally incapable of misleading her as you suppose. What horrible ingratitude you attribute to one of them—and what horrible baseness to the other! I have listened to you as patiently as I can; and I feel sincerely obliged by the interest which you have shown in me—but I cannot remain in your company any longer. Madame Pratolungo, your suspicions are inhuman! You have not brought forward a shadow of proof in support of them. I will send here for my luggage, if you will allow me, and I will start for England by the next train. After what you have said, I can't rest till I have found out the truth for myself."

This was my reward for all the trouble that I had taken to discover Oscar Dubourg! Never mind the money I had spent—I am not rich enough to care about money—only consider the trouble. If I had been a man, I do really think I should have knocked him down. Being only a woman, I dropped him a low courtesy, and stung him with my tongue.

"As you please, sir," I said. "I have done my best to serve you—and you quarrel with me and leave me in return. Go! You are not the first fool who has quarreled with his best friend."

Either the words or the courtesy—or both together—brought him to his senses. He made me an apology, which I received. And he looked excessively foolish, which put me in an excellent humor again. "You stupid boy," I said, taking his arm and leading him to the stairs. "When we first met at Dimchurch did you find me a suspicious woman or an inhuman woman? Answer me that!"

He answered frankly enough.

"I found you all that was kind and good. Still, it is surely only natural to want *some* confirmation—" He checked himself there, and reverted abruptly to my letter to Mrs. Finch. The silence of the rector's wife evidently alarmed him. "How long is it since you wrote?" he inquired.

"As long ago as the first of this month," I replied.

He fell into thought. We ascended the next flight of stairs in silence. At the landing he stopped me, and spoke again. My unanswered letter was still uppermost in his mind.

"Mrs. Finch loses everything that *can* be lost," he said. "Is it not likely—with her habits—that when she had written her answer, and wanted your letter to look at to put the address on it, your letter was like her handkerchief, or her novel, or anything else—not to be found?"

So far, no doubt, this was quite in Mrs. Finch's character. I could see that, but my mind was too much preoccupied to draw the inference that followed. Oscar's next words enlightened me.

"Have you tried the Poste-Restante?" he asked.

What could I possibly have been thinking of? Of course she had lost my letter. Of course the whole house would be upset in looking for it, and the rector would silence the uproar by ordering his wife to try the Poste-Restante. How strangely we had changed places! Instead of my clear head thinking for Oscar, here was Oscar's clear head thinking for Me. Is my stupidity quite incredible? Remember, if you please, what a weight of trouble and anxiety had lain on my mind while I was at Marseilles. Can one think of everything while one is afflicted as I was? Not even such a clever person as You can do that. If, as the saying is, "Homer sometimes nods"—why not Madame Pratolungo?

"I never thought of the Poste-Restante," I said to Oscar. "If you don't mind going back a little way, shall we inquire at once?"

He was perfectly willing. We went downstairs again, and out into the street. On our way to the post-office I seized my first opportunity of making Oscar give me some account of himself.

"I have satisfied your curiosity to the best of my ability," I said, as we walked arm-in-arm through the streets. "Now suppose you satisfy mine. A report of your having been seen in a military hospital in Italy is the only report of you which has reached me here. Of course it is not true?"

"It is perfectly true."

"You, in a hospital, nursing wounded sol-
diers!"

"That is exactly what I have been doing."

No words could express my astonishment. I
could only stop and look at him.

"Was that the occupation which you had in
view when you left England?" I asked.

"I had no object in leaving England but the
object which I mentioned in my letter to you.
After what had happened, I owed it to Lucilla
and I owed it to Nugent to go. I left England
without caring where I went. The train to Lyons happened to be the first train that started on
my arrival at Paris. I took the first train. At
Lyons I saw by chance an account in a French
newspaper of the sufferings of some of the badly
wounded men left still uncured after the bat-
tle of Solferino. I felt an impulse, in my own
wretchedness, to help these other sufferers in *their*
misery. On every other side of it my life was
wasted. The one worthy use to which I could
put it was to employ myself in doing good; and
here was good to be done. I managed to get the
necessary letters of introduction at Turin. With
the help of these I made myself of some use (under
the regular surgeons and dressers) in nursing the
poor mutilated, crippled men; and I have helped
a little afterward, from my own resources, in
starting them comfortably in new ways of life."

In those manly and simple words he told me
his story.

Once more I felt, what I had felt already, that
there were hidden reserves of strength in the char-

acter of this innocent young fellow which had utterly escaped my superficial observation of him.
In choosing his vocation, he was, no doubt, only
following the conventional modern course in such
cases.   Despair has its fashions as well as dress.
Ancient despair (especially of Oscar's sort) used
to turn soldier, or go into a monastery.   Modern despair turns nurse, binds up wounds, gives
physic, and gets cured or not in that useful but
nasty way.   Oscar had certainly struck out nothing new for himself: he had only followed the
fashion.   Still, it implied, as I thought, both
courage and resolution to have conquered the
obstacles which he must have overcome, and
to have held steadily on his course after he had
once entered it.   Having begun by quarreling
with him, I was in a fair way to end by respecting him.   Surely this man was worth preserving for Lucilla, after all!

"May I ask where you were going when we
met at the port?" I continued.   "Have you left
Italy because there were no more wounded sol-
diers to be cured?"

"There was no more work for me at the hospital to which I was attached," he said.   "And
there were certain obstacles in my way, as a
stranger and a Protestant, among the poor and
afflicted population outside the hospital.   I might
have overcome those obstacles, with little trouble,
among a people so essentially good-tempered and
courteous as the Italians, if I had tried.   But it
occurred to me that my first duty was to my own
countrymen.   The misery crying for relief in

London is misery not paralleled in any city of Italy. When you met me I was on my way to London to place my services at the disposal of any clergyman in a poor neighborhood who would accept such help as I can offer him." He paused a little—hesitated—and added, in lower tones: "That was one of my objects in returning to England. It is only honest to own to you that I had another motive besides."

"A motive connected with your brother and with Lucilla?" I suggested.

"Yes. Don't misinterpret me. I am not returning to England to retract what I said to Nugent. I still leave him free to plead his own cause with Lucilla in his own person. I am still resolved not to distress myself and distress them by returning to Dimchurch. But I have a longing that nothing can subdue to know how it has ended between them. Don't ask me to say more than that! In spite of the time that has passed, it breaks my heart to talk of Lucilla. I had looked forward to a meeting with you in London, and to hearing what I longed to hear from your lips. Judge for yourself what my hopes were when I first saw your face; and forgive me if I felt my disappointment bitterly when I found that you had really [no news to tell, and when you spoke of Nugent as you did." He stopped, and pressed my arm earnestly. "Suppose I am right about Mrs. Finch's letter?" he added. "Suppose it should really be waiting for you at the post?"

"Well?"

"The letter may contain the news which I most want to hear."

I checked him there. "I am not sure of that," I answered, "I don't know what news you most want to hear."

I said those words with a purpose. What was the news he was longing for? In spite of what he had said, my woman's observation answered, News that Lucilla is still a single woman. My object in speaking as I had just spoken was to tempt him into a reply which might confirm me in this opinion. He evaded the reply. Was that confirmation in itself? Yes—as I think!

"Will you tell me what there is in the letter?" he asked, passing, as you see, entirely over what I had just said to him.

"Yes, if you wish it," I answered, not over-well pleased with his want of confidence in me.

"No matter what the letter contains?" he went on, evidently doubting me.

I said Yes, again—that one word and no more.

"I suppose it would be asking too much," he persisted, "to ask you to let me read the letter myself?"

My temper, as you are well aware by this time, is not the temper of a saint. I drew my arm smartly out of his arm, and I surveyed him with what poor Pratolungo used to call "my Roman look."

"Mr. Oscar Dubourg! say, in plain words, that you distrust me."

He protested, of course, that he did nothing of the kind—without producing the slightest effect

on me.   Just run over in your mind the insults,
worries, and anxieties which had assailed me as
the reward for my friendly interest in this man's
welfare.   Or, if that is too great an effort, be so
good as to remember that Lucilla's farewell letter to me at Dimchurch was now followed by the
equally ungracious expression of Oscar's distrust
—and this at a time when I had had serious trials
of my own to sustain at my father's bedside.   I
think you will admit that a sweeter temper than
mine might have not unnaturally turned a little
sour under present circumstances.

I answered not a word to Oscar's protesta-
tions—I only searched vehemently in the pocket
of my dress.

"Here," I said, opening my card-case, "is
my address in this place; and here," I went
on, producing the document, "is my passport,
if they want it."

I forced the card and the passport into his
hands.   He took them in helpless astonishment.

"What am I to do with these?" he asked.

"Take them to the Poste-Restante.   If there is
a letter for me with the Dimchurch post-mark, I
authorize you to open it.   Read it before it comes
into my hands—and then perhaps you will be
satisfied."

He declared that he would do nothing of the
sort, and tried to force my documents back into
my own possession.

"Please yourself," I said.   "I have done with
you and your affairs.   Mrs. Finch's letter is of

no earthly consequence to me. If it *is* at the Poste-Restante, I shall not trouble myself to ask for it. What concern have I with news about Lucilla? What does it matter to *me* whether she is married no not? I am going back to my father and my sisters. Decide for yourself whether you want Mrs. Finch's letter or not."

That settled it. He went his way with my documents to the post-office; and I went mine back to the lodging.

Arrived in my room, I still held to the resolution which I had expressed to Oscar in the street. Why should I leave my poor old father to go back to England, and mix myself up in Lucilla's affairs? After the manner in which she had taken her leave of me, had I any reasonable prospect of being civilly received? Oscar was on his way back to England—let Oscar manage his own affairs; let them all three (Oscar, Nugent, Lucilla) fight it out together among themselves. What had I, Pratolungo's widow, to do with this trumpery family entanglement? Nothing! It was a warm day for the time of year—Pratolungo's widow, like a wise woman, determined to make herself comfortable. She unlocked her packed box; she loosened her stays; she put on her dressing-gown; she took a turn in the room —and, if you had come across her at that moment, I wouldn't have stood in *your* shoes for something, I can tell you!

(What do you think of my consistency by this time? How often have I changed my mind about Lucilla and Oscar? Reckon it up from

the time when I left Dimchurch. What a picture of perpetual self-contradiction I present—and
how improbable it is that I should act in this
illogical way! *You* never alter your mind under
the influence of your temper or your circumstances. No: you are what they call a consistent character. And I? Oh, I am only a human being—and I feel painfully conscious that
I have no business to be in a book.)

In about half an hour's time, the servant appeared with a little paper parcel for me. It had
been left by a stranger with an English accent
and a terrible face. He had announced his intention of calling a little later. The servant, a
bouncing fat wench, trembled as she repeated the
message, and asked if there was anything amiss
between me and the man with the terrible face.

I opened the parcel. It contained my passport,
and, sure enough, the letter from Mrs. Finch.

Had he opened it? Yes! He had not been
able to resist the temptation to read it. And
more, he had written a line or two on it in
pencil, thus: "As soon as I am fit to see you,
I will implore your pardon. I dare not trust
myself in your presence yet. Read the letter,
and you will understand why."

I opened the letter.

It was dated the fifth of September. I ran
over the first few sentences carelessly enough.
Thanks for my letter—congratulations on my father's prospect of recovery—information about
baby's gums and the rector's last sermon —
more information about somebody else, which

Mrs. Finch felt quite sure would interest and delight me. What!!! "Mr. Oscar Dubourg has come back, and is now with Lucilla at Ramsgate."

I crumpled the letter up in my hand. Nugent had justified my worst anticipations of what he would do in my absence. What did the true Mr. Oscar Dubourg, reading that sentence at Marseilles, think of his brother now? We are all mortal—we are all wicked. It is monstrous, but it is true. I had a moment's triumph.

The wicked moment gone, I was good again—that is to say, I was ashamed of myself.

I smoothed out the letter, and looked eagerly for news of Lucilla's health. If the news was favorable, my letter committed to Miss Batchford's care must have been shown to Lucilla by this time, must have exposed Nugent's abominable personation of his brother, and must have thus preserved her for Oscar. In that case, all would be well again (and my darling herself would own it)—thanks to Me!

After telling me the news from Ramsgate, Mrs. Finch began to drift into what you call Twaddle. She had just discovered (exactly as Oscar had supposed) that she had lost my letter. She would keep her own letter back until the next day on the chance of finding it; if she failed she must try Poste-Restante, at the suggestion (not of Mr. Finch—there I was wrong) —at the suggestion of Zillah, who had relatives in foreign parts, and had tried Poste-Restante in her case too. So Mrs. Finch driveled mildly on,

in her large, loose, untidy handwriting, to the
bottom of the third page.

I turned over. The handwriting suddenly
grew untidier than ever; two great blots defaced
the paper; the style became feebly hysterical.
Good Heavens! what did I read when I made it
out at last? See for yourselves; here are the
words:

"Some hours have passed—it is just tea-time
—oh, my dear friend, I can hardly hold the pen,
I tremble so—would you believe it, Miss Batchford has arrived at the rectory—she brings the
dreadful news that Lucilla has eloped with
Oscar—we don't know why—we don't know
where, except that they have gone away together privately—a letter from Oscar tells Miss
Batchford as much as that, and no more—oh,
pray come back as soon as you can—Mr. Finch
washes his hands of it—and Miss Batchford has
left the house again in a fury with him—I am
in a dreadful agitation, and I have given it, Mr.
Finch says, to baby, who is screaming black in
the face. Yours affectionately,
                          "AMELIA FINCH."

All the rages I had ever been in before in my
life were as nothing compared with the rage that
devoured me when I had read that fourth page
of Mrs. Finch's letter. Nugent had got the better of me and my precautions! Nugent had
robbed his brother of Lucilla, in the vilest manner, with perfect impunity! I cast all feminine

restraints to the winds. I sat down with my
legs anyhow, like a man. I rammed my hands
into the pockets of my dressing-gown. Did I
cry? A word in your ear—and let it go no further. I swore.

How long the fit lasted I don't know. I only
remember that I was disturbed by a knock at
my door.

I flung open the door in a fury, and confronted
Oscar on the threshold.

There was a look in his face that instantly
quieted me. There was a tone in his voice that
brought the tears suddenly into my eyes.

"I must leave for England in two hours," he
said. "Will you forgive me, and go with me?"

Only those words! And yet—if you had seen
him, if you had heard him, as he spoke them—
you would have been ready to go to the ends of
the earth with him, as I was; and you would
have told him so, as I did.

In two hours more we were in the train on our
way to England.

CHAPTER THE FORTY-SEVENTH.

ON THE WAY TO THE END.—FIRST STAGE.

You will perhaps expect me to give some account of how Oscar bore the discovery of his
brother's conduct.

I find it by no means easy to do this. Oscar
baffled me.

The first words of any importance which he addressed to me were spoken on our way to the station. Rousing himself from his own thoughts, he said, very earnestly:

"I want to know what conclusion you have drawn from Mrs. Finch's letter."

Naturally enough, under the circumstances, I tried to avoid answering him. He was not to be put off in that way.

"You will do me a favor," he went on, "if you will reply to my question. The letter has bred in me such a vile suspicion of my dear, good brother, who never deceived me in his life, that I would rather believe I am out of my mind than believe in my own interpretation of it. Do *you* infer from what Mrs. Finch writes that Nugent has presented himself to Lucilla under my name? Do *you* believe that he has persuaded her to leave her friends under the impression that she has yielded to My entreaties, and trusted herself to My care?"

There was no avoiding it. I answered in the fewest and the plainest words, "That is what your brother has done."

I saw a change pass over him when I made the reply.

"That is what my brother has done," he repeated. "After all that I sacrificed to him— after all that I trusted to his honor when I left England." He paused and considered a little. "What does such a man deserve?" he went on, speaking to himself in a low, threatening tone that startled me.

"He deserves," I said, "what he will get when we reach England. You have only to show yourself to make him repent his wickedness to the last day of his life. Are exposure and defeat not punishment enough for such a man as Nugent?" I stopped and waited for his answer.

He turned his face away from me, and said no more until we arrived at the station. There he drew me aside for a moment out of hearing of the strangers about us.

"Why should I take you away from your father?" he asked, abruptly. "I am behaving very selfishly—and I only see it now."

"Make your mind easy," I said. "If I had not met you to-day, I should have gone to England to-morrow for Lucilla's sake."

"But now you *have* met me," he persisted, "why shouldn't I spare you the journey? I could write and tell you everything, without putting you to this fatigue and expense."

"If you say a word more," I answered, "I shall think you have some reason of your own for wishing to go to England by yourself."

He cast one quick, suspicious look at me, and led the way back to the booking-office without uttering another word. I was not at all satisfied with him. I thought his conduct very strange.

In silence we took our tickets; in silence we got into the railway carriage. I attempted to say something encouraging when we started. "Don't notice me," was all he replied. "You will be doing me a kindness if you will let me

bear it by myself." In my former experience
of him he had talked his way out of all his other
troubles—he had clamorously demanded the expression of my sympathy with him. In this
greatest trouble he was like another being; I
hardly knew him again. Were the hidden reserves in his nature (stirred up by another serious call on them) showing themselves once more
on the surface as they had shown themselves already on the fatal first day when Lucilla tried
her sight? In that way I accounted for the mere
superficial change in him at the time. What
was actually going on below the surface it defied my ingenuity even to guess. Perhaps 1
shall best describe the sort of vague apprehension which he aroused in me—after what had
passed between us at the station—by saying that
I would not for worlds have allowed him to go
to England by himself.

Left as I now was to my own resources, I occupied the first hours of the journey in considering what course it would be safest and best for
us to take on reaching England.

I decided, in the first place, that we ought to
go straight to Dimchurch. If any tidings had
been obtained of Lucilla, they would be sure to
have received them at the rectory. Our route,
after reaching Paris, must be, therefore, by way
of Dieppe; thence across the channel to Newhaven, near Brighton, and so to Dimchurch.

In the second place—assuming it to be always
possible that we might see Lucilla at the rectory
—the risk of abruptly presenting Oscar to her in

his own proper person might, for all I knew to the contrary, be a very serious one. It would relieve us, as I thought, of a grave responsibility, if we warned Grosse of our arrival, and so enabled him to be present, if he thought it necessary, in the interest of Lucilla's health. I put this view (as also my plan for returning by way of Dieppe) to Oscar. He briefly consented to everything—he ungraciously left it all to me.

Accordingly, on our arrival at Lyons, having some time for refreshment at our disposal before we went on, I telegraphed to Mr. Finch at the rectory, and to Grosse in London, informing them (as well as I could calculate it) that, if we were lucky in catching trains and steamboats, Oscar and I might be at Dimchurch in good time on the next night—that is to say, on the night of the eighteenth. In any case, they were to expect us at the earliest possible moment.

These difficulties disposed of, and a little store of refreshment for the night packed in my basket, we re-entered the train for our long journey to Paris.

Among the new passengers who joined us at Lyons was a gentleman whose face was English, and whose dress was the dress of a clergyman. For the first time in my life I hailed the appearance of a priest with a feeling of relief. The reason was this. From the moment when I had read Mrs. Finch's letter until now a horrid doubt, which a priest was just the man to solve, had laid its leaden weight on my mind—and, I firmly believe, on Oscar's mind as well. Had time enough passed since Lucilla had left Ramsgate to allow of Nugent's marrying her under his brother's name?

As the train rolled out of the station, I, the enemy of priests, began to make myself agreeable to *this* priest. He was young and shy, but I conquered him. Just as the other travelers were beginning (with the exception of Oscar) to compose themselves to sleep, I put my case to the clergyman. "A and B, sir, lady and gentleman, both of age, leave one town in England, and go to another town, on the fifth of this month—how soon, if you please, can they be lawfully married after that?"

"I presume you mean in church?" said the young clergyman.

"In church, of course." (To that extent I believed I might answer for Lucilla without any fear of making a mistake.)

"They may be married by License," said the clergyman—"providing one of them continues to reside in that other town to which they traveled on the fifth—on the twenty-first, or (possibly) even the twentieth of this month."

"Not before?"

"Certainly not before."

It was then the night of the seventeenth. I gave my companion's hand a little squeeze in the dark. Here was a glimpse of encouragement to cheer us on the journey. Before the marriage could take place we should be in England. "We have time before us," I whispered to Oscar. "We will save Lucilla yet."

"Shall we find Lucilla?" was all he whispered back.

I had forgotten that serious difficulty. No answer to Oscar's question could possibly present itself until we reached the rectory. Between this and then, there was nothing for it but to keep patience and to keep hope.

I refrain from encumbering this part of my narrative with any detailed account of the little accidents, lucky and unlucky, which alternately hastened or retarded our journey home. Let me only say that before midnight on the eighteenth Oscar and I drove up to the rectory gate.

Mr. Finch himself came out to receive us, with a lamp in his hand. He lifted his eyes (and his lamp) devotionally to the sky when he saw Oscar. The two first words he said were:

"Inscrutable Providence!"

"Have you found Lucilla?" I asked.

Mr. Finch—with his whole attention fixed on Oscar—wrung my hand mechanically, and said I was a "good creature," much as he might have patted and spoken to Oscar's companion, if that companion had been a dog. I almost wished myself that animal for the moment—I should have had the privilege of biting Mr. Finch. Oscar impatiently repeated my question; the rector at the time officiously assisting him to descend from the carriage, and leaving me to get out as I could.

"Did you hear Madame Pratolungo?" Oscar asked. "Is Lucilla found?"

"Dear Oscar, we hope to find her, now you have come."

That answer revealed to me the secret of Mr. Finch's extraordinary politeness to his young friend. The last chance, as things were, of preventing Lucilla's marriage to a man who had squandered away every farthing of his money was the chance of Oscar's arrival in England before the ceremony could take place. The measure of Oscar's importance to Mr. Finch was now, more literally than ever, the measure of Oscar's fortune.

I asked for news of Grosse as we went in. The rector actually found some comparatively high notes in his prodigious voice to express his amazement at my audacity in speaking to him of anybody but Oscar.

"Oh dear, dear me!" cried Mr. Finch, impatiently conceding to me one precious moment of his attention. "Don't bother about Grosse! Grosse is ill in London. There is a note for you from Grosse.—Take care of the doorstep, dear Oscar," he went on, in his deepest and gravest bass notes. "Mrs. Finch is so anxious to see you. We have both looked forward to your arrival with such eager hope—such impatient affection, so to speak. Let me put down your hat. Ah! how you must have suffered! Share my trust in an all-wise Providence, and meet this trial with cheerful submission as I do. All is not lost yet. Bear up! bear up!" He threw open the parlor door. "Mrs. Finch! compose yourself. Our dear adopted son! Our afflicted Oscar!"

Is it necessary to say what Mrs. Finch was
about, and how Mrs. Finch looked?

There were the three unchangeable institutions—the novel, the baby, and the lost pocket-
handkerchief! There was the gaudy jacket over
the long trailing dressing-gown—and the damp
lady inside them, damp as ever! Receiving
Oscar with a mouth drawn down at the corners, and a head that shook sadly in sympathy
with him, Mrs. Finch's face underwent a most
extraordinary transformation when she turned
my way next. To my astonishment, her dim
eyes actually sparkled; a broad smile of irrepressible contentment showed itself cunningly to
me, in place of the dismal expression which had
welcomed Oscar. Holding up the baby in triumph, the lady of the rectory whispered these
words in my ear:

"What do you think he has done since you
have been away?"

"I really don't know," I answered.

"He has cut two teeth! Put your finger in
and feel."

Others might bewail the family misfortune.
The family triumph filled the secret mind of
Mrs. Finch, to the exclusion of every other
earthly consideration. I put my finger in as
instructed, and got instantly bitten by the ferocious baby. But for a new outburst of the rector's voice at the moment, Mrs. Finch (if I am
any judge of physiognomy) must have certainly
relieved herself by a scream of delight. As it
was, she opened her mouth; and (having lost

her handkerchief, as already stated) retired into a corner, and gagged herself with the baby.

In the meantime Mr. Finch had produced from a cupboard near the fire-place two letters. The first he threw down impatiently on the table. "Oh, dear, dear! what a nuisance other people's letters are!" The second he handled with extraordinary care, offering it to Oscar with a heavy sigh, and with eyes that turned up martyr-like to the ceiling. "Rouse yourself and read it," said Mr. Finch, in his most pathetic pulpit tones. "I would have spared you, Oscar, if I could. All our hopes depend, dear boy, on what you can say to guide us when you have read those lines."

Oscar took the inclosure out of the envelope— ran over the first words—glanced at the signature—and, with a look of mingled rage and horror, threw the letter on the floor.

"Don't ask me to read it!" he cried, in the first burst of passion which had escaped him yet. "If I read it, I shall kill him when we meet." He dropped into a chair and hid his face in his hands. "Oh, Nugent! Nugent! Nugent!" he moaned to himself with a cry that was dreadful to hear.

It was no time for standing on ceremony. I picked up the letter and looked at it without asking leave. It proved to be the letter from Nugent (already inserted at the close of Lucilla's Journal) informing Miss Batchford of her niece's flight from Ramsgate, and signed in Oscar's name. The only words which it is necessary to repeat here are these: "She accompanies me, at my express request, to the house of a married lady who is a relative of mine, and under whose care she will remain until the time arrives for our marriage."

Those lines instantly lightened my heart of the burden that had oppressed it on the journey. Nugent's married relative was Oscar's married relative too. Oscar had only to tell us where the lady lived—and Lucilla would be found.

I stopped Mr. Finch in the act of maddening Oscar by administering pastoral consolation to him.

"Leave it to me," I said, showing him the letter. "I know what you want."

The rector stared at me indignantly. I turned to Mrs. Finch.

"We have had a weary journey," I went on. "Oscar is not so well used to traveling as I am. Where is his room?"

Mrs. Finch rose to show the way. Her husband opened his lips to interfere.

"Leave it to me," I repeated. "I understand him, and you don't."

For once in his life the Pope of Dimchurch was reduced to silence. His amazement at my audacity defied even *his* powers of expression. I took Oscar's arm, and said, "You are worn out. Go to your room. I will make you something warm and bring it up to you myself in a few minutes." He neither looked at me nor answered me—he yielded silently, and followed Mrs. Finch. I took from the sideboard—on

which supper was waiting—the materials I
wanted, set the kettle boiling, made my reno-
vating mixture, and advanced to the door with
it—followed from first to last, move where I
might, by the staring and scandalized eyes of
Mr. Finch. The moment in which I opened the
door was also the moment in which the rector
recovered himself. "Permit me to inquire, Madame Pratolungo," he said, with his loftiest emphasis, "in what capacity are You here?"

"In the capacity of Oscar's friend," I answered. "You will get rid of us both to-morrow." I banged the door behind me, and went
upstairs. If I had been Mr. Finch's wife, I believe I should have ended in making quite an
agreeable man of him.

Mrs. Finch met me in the passage on the first
floor, and pointed out Oscar's room. I found
him walking backward and forward restlessly.
The first words he said alluded to his brother's
letter. I had arranged not to disturb him by
any reference to that painful matter until the
next morning, and I tried to change the topic.
It was useless. There was an anxiety in his
mind which was not to be dismissed at will.
He insisted on my instantly setting that anxiety
at rest.

"I don't want to see the letter," he said. "I
only want to know all that it says about Lucilla."

"All that it says may be summed up in this.
Lucilla is perfectly safe."

He caught me by the arm, and looked me
searchingly in the face.

"Where?" he asked. "With *him?*"

"With a married lady who is a relative of his."

He dropped my arm, and considered for a moment.

"My cousin at Sydenham!" he exclaimed.

"Do you know the house?"

"Perfectly well."

"We will go there to-morrow. Let that content you for to-night. Get to rest."

I gave him my hand. He took it mechanically—absorbed in his own thoughts.

"Didn't I say something foolish downstairs?" he asked, putting the question suddenly, with an odd, suspicious look at me.

"You were quite worn out," I said, consolingly. "Nobody noticed it."

"You are sure of that?"

"Quite sure. Good-night."

I left the room, feeling much as I had felt at the station at Marseilles. I was not satisfied with him. I thought his conduct very strange.

On returning to the parlor I found nobody there but Mrs. Finch. The rector's offended dignity had left the rector no honorable alternative but to withdraw to his own room. I ate my supper in peace; and Mrs. Finch (rocking the cradle with her foot) chattered away to her heart's content about all that had happened in my absence.

I gathered, here and there, from what she said, some particulars worth mentioning.

The new disagreement between Mr. Finch and
Miss Batchford, which had driven the old lady
out of the rectory almost as soon as she set foot
in it, had originated in Mr. Finch's exasperating
composure when he heard of his daughter's flight.
He supposed, of course, that Lucilla had left
Ramsgate with Oscar—whose signed settlements
on his future wife were safe in Mr. Finch's possession. It was only when Miss Batchford had
communicated with Grosse, and when the discovery followed which revealed the penniless
Nugent as the man who had eloped with Lucilla, that Mr. Finch's parental anxiety (seeing
no money likely to come of it) became roused
to action. He, Miss Batchford, and Grosse had
all, in their various ways, done their best to
trace the fugitives, and had all alike been baffled
by the impossibility of discovering the residence
of the lady mentioned in Nugent's letter. My
telegram, announcing my return to England with
Oscar, had inspired them with their first hope of
being able to interfere, and stop the marriage before it was too late.

The occurrence of Grosse's name in Mrs.
Finch's rambling narrative recalled to my memory what the rector had told me at the garden
gate. I had not yet received the letter which
the German had sent to wait my arrival at Dimchurch. After a short search we found it—where
it had been contemptuously thrown by Mr. Finch
—on the parlor table.

A few lines comprised the whole letter. Grosse
informed me that he had so fretted himself about

Lucilla that he had been attacked by a "visita-
tion of gouts." It was impossible to move his
"foots" without instantly plunging into the torture of the infernal regions. "If it is you, my
goot dear, who are going to find her," he concluded, "come to me first in London. I have
something most dismal-serious to say to you
about our poor little Feench's eyes."

No words can tell how that last sentence startled
and grieved me. Mrs. Finch increased my anxiety and alarm by repeating what she had heard
Miss Batchford say, during her brief visit to the
rectory, on the subject of Lucilla's sight. Grosse
had been seriously dissatisfied with the state of
his patient's eyes when he had seen them as long
ago as the fourth of the month; and on the morning of the next day the servant had reported Lucilla as being hardly able to distinguish objects
in the view from the window of her room. Later
on the same day she had secretly left Ramsgate;
and Grosse's letter proved that she had not been
near her surgical attendant since.

Weary as I was after the journey, this miserable news kept me waking long after I had
gone to my bed. The next morning I was up
with the servants—impatient to start for London
by the first train.

CHAPTER THE FORTY-EIGHTH.

ON THE WAY TO THE END.—SECOND STAGE.

EARLY riser as I was, I found that Oscar had risen earlier still. He had left the rectory, and had disturbed Mr. Gootheridge's morning slumbers by an application at the inn for the key of Browndown.

On his return to the rectory he merely said that he had been to see after various things belonging to him which were still left in the empty house. His look and manner as he gave us this brief explanation were, to my mind, more unsatisfactory than ever. I made no remark; and, observing that his loose traveling coat was bottoned awry over the breast, I set it right for him. My hand, as I did this, touched his breast pocket. He started back directly, as if there was something in the pocket which he did not wish me to feel. Was it something he had brought from Browndown?

We got away—encumbered by Mr. Finch, who insisted on attaching himself to Óscar—by the first express train, which took us straight to London. Comparison of time-tables, on reaching the terminus, showed that I had leisure to spare for a brief visit to Grosse before we again took the railway back to Sydenham. Having decided not to mention the bad news about Lucilla's eyes to Oscar until I had seen the German first, I made the best excuse that suggested itself, and drove away, leaving the two gentlemen in the waiting-room at the station.

I found Grosse confined to his easy-chair, with his gouty foot enveloped in cool cabbage leaves. Between pain and anxiety, his eyes were wilder, his broken English was more grotesque, than ever. When I appeared at the door of his room and said good-morning—in the frenzy of his impatience he shook his fist at me.

"Good-morning go-damn!" he roared out. "Where? where? where is Feench?"

I told him where we believed Lucilla to be. Grosse turned his head, and shook his fist at a bottle on the chimney-piece next.

"Get that bottles on the chimney," he said. "And the eye-baths by the side of him. Don't stop with your talky-talky-chatterations here. Go! Save her eyes! Look! You do this. You throw her head back—soh!" He illustrated the position so forcibly with his own head that he shook his gouty foot, and screamed with the pain of it. He went on nevertheless, glaring frightfully through his spectacles, gnashing his mustache fiercely between his teeth. "Throw her head back. Fill the eye-baths; turn him upsides-down over her open eyes. Drown them turn-turn-about in my mixtures. Drown them, I say, one - down - todder - come - on, and if she screech never mind it. Then bring her to me. For the lofe of Gott, bring her to me. If you tie her hands and foots, bring her to me. What is the womans stopping for? Go! go! go!"

"I want to ask you a question about Oscar," I said, "before I go."

He seized the pillow which supported his head —evidently intending to expedite my departure by throwing it at me. I produced the railway time-table as the best defensive weapon at my command. "Look at it for yourself," I said, "and you will see that I must wait at the station, if I don't wait here."

With some difficulty I satisfied him that it was impossible to leave London for Sydenham before a certain hour, and that I had at least ten minutes to spare, which might be just as well passed in consulting him. He closed his glaring eyes, and laid his head back on the chair, thoroughly exhausted with his own outbreak of excitement. "No matter how things goes," he said, "a womans must wag her tongue. Goot. Wag yours."

"I am placed in a very difficult position," I began. "Oscar is going with me to Lucilla. I shall, of course, take care, in the first place, that he and Nugent do not meet, unless I am present at the interview. But I am not equally sure of what I ought to do in the case of Lucilla. Must I keep them apart until I have first prepared her to see Oscar?"

"Let her see the devil himself if you like," growled Grosse, "so long as you bring her here afterwards-directly to me. You will do the bettermost thing if you prepare Oscar. *She* wants no preparations! She is enough disappointed in him as it is!"

"Disappointed in him?" I repeated. "I don't understand you."

He settled himself wearily in his chair, and referred, in a softened and saddened tone, to that private conversation of his with Lucilla, at Ramsgate, which has already been reported in the Journal. I was now informed, for the first time, of those changes in her sensations and in her ways of thinking which had so keenly vexed and mortified her. I heard of the ominous absence of the old thrill of pleasure when Nugent took her hand on meeting her at the seaside—I heard how bitterly his personal appearance had disappointed her (when she had seen his features in detail) by comparison with the charming ideal picture which she had formed of her lover in the days of her blindness: those happier days, as she had called them, when she was Poor Miss Finch.

"Surely," I said, "all the old feelings will come back to her when she sees Oscar?"

"They will never come back to her—no, not if she sees fifty Oscars!"

He was beginning to frighten me, or to irritate me—I can hardly say which. I only know that I persisted in disputing with him. "When she sees the true man," I went on, "do you mean to say she will feel the same disappointment—"

I could get no further than that. He cut me short there, without ceremony.

"You foolish womans!" he interposed, "she will feel more than the same. I have told you already it was one enormous disappointments to her when she saw the handsome brodder with the fair complexions. Ask your own self what will it be when she sees the ugly brodder with the blue face. I tell you this!—she will think your true man the worst impostor of the two."

There I indignantly contradicted him.

"His face *may* be a disappointment to her," I said; "I own that. But there it will end. Her hand will tell her, when he takes it, that there is no impostor deceiving her this time."

"Her hand will tell her nothing—no more than yours. I had not so much hard hearts in me as to say that to *her* when she asked me. I say it to *you*. Hold your tongue and listen. All those thrill-tingles that she once had when he touched her belong to anodder time—the time gone-by, when her sight was in her fingers and not in her eyes. With those fine-superfine-feelings of the days when she was blind she pays now for her grand new privilege of opening her eyes on the world. (And worth the price too!) Do you understand yet? It is a sort of swop-bargain between Nature and this poor girls of ours. I take away your eyes—I give you your fine touch. I give you your eyes—I take away your fine touch. Soh! that is plain. You see now?"

I was too mortified and too miserable to answer him. Through all our later troubles I had looked forward so confidently to Oscar's reappearance as the one sufficient condition on which Lucilla's happiness would be certainly restored! What had become of my anticipations now? I sat silent, staring in stupid depression at the pattern of the carpet. Grosse took out his watch.

"Your ten-minutes-time has counted himself out," he said.

I neither moved nor heeded him. His ferocious eyes began to flame again behind his monstrous spectacles.

"Go-be-off-with-you!" he shouted at me as if I was deaf. "Her eyes! her eyes!. While you stop chatterboxing here, her eyes are in danger. What with her frettings and her cryings and her damn-nonsense-lofe-business, I swear you my solemn oath her sight was in danger when I saw her a whole fortnight gone-by. Do you want my big pillow to fly bang at your head? You don't want him. Be-off-away with you, then, or you will have him in one-two-three time! Be-off-away—and bring her back to me before night!"

I returned to the railway. Of all the women whom I passed in the crowded streets, I doubt if one had a heavier heart in her bosom that morning than mine.

To make matters worse still, my traveling companions (one in the refreshment-room, and one pacing the platform) received my account of my interview with Grosse in a manner which seriously disappointed and discouraged me. Mr. Finch's inhuman conceit treated my melancholy news of his daughter as a species of complimentary tribute to his own foresight. "You remember, Madame Pratolungo, I took high ground in this matter from the first. I protested against

the proceedings of the man Grosse as involving
a purely worldly interference with the ways of
an inscrutable Providence. With what effect?
My paternal influence was repudiated; my Moral
Weight was, so to speak, set aside. And now
you see the result. Take it to heart, dear friend.
May it be a warning to you!" He sighed with
ponderous complacency, and turned from me to
the girl behind the counter. "I will take another cup of tea."

Oscar's reception of me, when I found him on
the platform, and told him next of Lucilla's
critical state, was more than discouraging. It
is no exaggeration to say that he alarmed me.

"Another item in the debt I owe to Nugent!"
he said. Not a word of sympathy, not a word
of sorrow. That vindictive answer, and nothing
more.

We started for Sydenham.

From time to time I looked at Oscar sitting
opposite to me, to see if any change appeared in
him as we drew nearer and nearer to the place
in which Lucilla was now living. No! Still
the same ominous silence, the same unnatural
self-repression possessed him. Except the momentary outbreak when Mr. Finch had placed
Nugent's letter in his hand on the previous evening, not the faintest token of what was really
going on in his mind had escaped him since we
had left Marseilles. He, who could weep over
all his others grief as easily and as spontaneously
as a woman, had not shed a tear since the fatal
day when he had discovered that his brother had

played him false—that brother who had been the
god of his idolatry, the sacred object of his gratitude and love! When a man of Oscar's temperament becomes frozen up for days together in his
own thoughts—when he keeps his own counsel
—when he asks for no sympathy, and utters no
complaint—the sign is a serious one. There are
hidden forces gathering in him which will burst
their way to the surface—for good or for evil—
with an irresistible result. Watching Oscar attentively behind my veil, I felt the certain assurance that the part he would take in the terrible
conflict of interests now awaiting us would be a
part which I should remember to the latest day
of my life.

We reached Sydenham, and went to the nearest hotel.

On the railway—with other travelers in the
carriage—it had been impossible to consult on
the safest method of approaching Lucilla in the
first instance. That serious question now pressed
for instant decision. We sat down to consult on
it in the room which we had hired at the hotel.

CHAPTER THE FORTY-NINTH.

ON THE WAY TO THE END.—THIRD STAGE.

On former occasions of doubt or difficulty it
had always been Oscar's habit to follow the
opinions of others. On this occasion he was

the first to speak, and to assert an opinion of his own.

"It seems needless to waste time in discussing our different views," he said. "There is only one thing to be done. I am the person principally concerned in this matter. Wait here, while I go to the house."

He spoke without any of his usual hesitation, and took up his hat without looking either at Mr. Finch or at me. I felt more and more convinced that the influence which Nugent's vile breach of confidence had exerted over Oscar's mind was an influence which had made a dangerous man of him. Resolved to prevent him from leaving us, I insisted on his returning to his chair, and hearing what I had to say. At the same moment Mr. Finch rose, and placed himself between Oscar and the door. Seeing this, I thought it might be wise if I kept my interference in reserve, and allowed the rector to speak first.

"Wait a moment, Oscar," said Mr. Finch, gravely. "You are forgetting Me."

Oscar waited doggedly, hat in hand.

Mr. Finch paused, evidently considering what words he should use before he spoke again. His respect for Oscar's pecuniary position was great; but his respect for himself—especially at the present crisis—was, if possible, greater still. In deference to the first sentiment he was as polite, and in deference to the second he was as positive, in phrasing his remonstrance, as a man could be.

"Permit me to remind you, dear Oscar, that my claim to interfere, as Lucilla's father, is at least equal to yours," proceeded the rector. "In the hour of my daughter's need it is my parental duty to be present. If you go to your cousin's house, my position imperatively requires that I should go, too."

Oscar's reception of this proposal confirmed the grave apprehensions with which he had inspired me. He flatly refused to have Mr. Finch for a companion.

"Excuse me," he answered shortly. "I wish to go to the house alone."

"Permit me to ask your reason," said the rector, still preserving his conciliatory manner.

"I wish to see my brother in private," Oscar replied, with his eyes on the ground.

Mr. Finch, still restraining himself, but still not moving from the door, looked at me. I hastened to interfere before there was any serious disagreement between them.

"I venture to think," I said, "that you are both wrong. Whether one of you goes or both of you go, the result will be the same. The chances are a hundred to one against your being admitted into the house."

They both turned on me together and asked what I meant.

"You can't force your way in," I said. "You must do one of two things. You must either give your names to the servant at the door, or you must withhold your names. If you give them, you warn Nugent of what is coming—and he is not the man to let you into the house under those circumstances. If you take the other way, and keep your names concealed, you present yourselves as strangers. Is Nugent likely to be accessible to strangers? Would Lucilla, in her present position, consent to receive two men who are unknown to her? Take my word for it— you will not only gain nothing if you go to the house—you will actually make it more difficult to communicate with Lucilla than it is already."

There was a moment's silence. Both the men felt that my objections were not easy to answer. Once more Oscar took the lead.

"Do *you* propose to go?" he asked.

"No," I answered. "I propose to send a letter to Lucilla. A letter will find its way to her."

This again was unanswerable. Oscar inquired next what the purport of the letter was to be. I replied "that I proposed to ask her to grant me a private interview—nothing more."

"Suppose Lucilla refuses?" said Mr. Finch.

"She will not refuse," I rejoined. "There was a little misunderstanding between us—I admit—at the time when I went abroad. I mean to refer frankly to that misundertsanding as my reason for writing. I shall put your daughter on her honor to give me an opportunity of setting things right btween us. If I summon Lucilla to do an act of justice, I believe she will not refuse me."

(This, let me add in parenthesis, was the plan of action which I had formed on the way to Sydenham. I had only waited to mention it

until 1 had heard what the two men proposed
to do first.)

Oscar, standing hat in hand, glanced at Mr.
Finch (also hat in hand), keeping obstinately
near the door. If he persisted in carrying out
his purpose of going alone to his cousin's house,
the rector's face and manner expressed, with the
politest plainness, the intention of following him.
Oscar was placed between a clergyman and a
woman both equally determined to have their
own way. Under those circumstances, there
was no alternative—unless he wished to produce a public scandal—but to yield, or appear
to yield, to one or the other of us. He selected me.

"If you succeed in seeing her," he asked,
"what do you mean to do?"

"I mean either to bring her back with me
here to her father and to you, or to make an appointment with her to see you both where she is
now living," I replied.

Oscar—after another look at the immovable
rector—rang the bell, and ordered writing materials.

"One more question," he said. "Assuming
that Lucilla receives you at the house, do you
intend to see—" He stopped; his eyes shrank
from meeting mine. "Do you intend to see anybody else?" he resumed: still evading the plain
utterance of his brother's name.

"I intend to see nobody but Lucilla," I said.
"It is no business of mine to interfere between
you and your brother." (Heaven forgive me for
speaking in that way to him while I had the

firm resolution to interfere between them in my mind all the time!)

"Write your letter," he said, "on condition that I see the reply."

"It is needless, I presume, for me to make the same stipulation?" added the rector. "In my parental capacity—"

I recognized his parental capacity before he could say any more. "You shall both see the reply," I said, and sat down to my letter—writing merely what I had told them I should write:

"DEAR LUCILLA—I have just returned from the Continent. For the sake of justice, and for the sake of old times, let me see you immediately— without mentioning our appointment to anybody. I pledge myself to satisfy you in five minutes that I have never been unworthy of your affection and your confidence. The bearer waits for your reply."

I handed those lines to the two gentlemen to read. Mr. Finch made no remark—he was palpably dissatisfied at the secondary position which he occupied. Oscar said: "I see no objection to the letter. I will do nothing until I have read the answer." With those words, he dictated to me his cousin's address. I gave the letter myself to one of the servants at the hotel.

"Is it far from here?" I asked.

"Barely ten minutes' walk, ma'am."

"You understand that you are to wait for an answer?"

"Yes, ma'am."

He went out. As well as I can remember, an interval of at least half an hour passed before his return. You will form some idea of the terrible oppression of suspense that now laid its slowly torturing weight on all three of us, when I tell you that not one word was spoken in the room from the time when the servant went out to the time when the servant came in again.

When the man returned he had a letter in his hand!

My fingers shook so that I could hardly open it. Before I had read a word the sight of the writing struck a sudden chill through me. The body of the note was written by the hand of a stranger! And the signature at the end was traced in the large, straggling, childish characters which I remembered so well when Lucilla had written her first letter to Oscar in the days when she was blind!

The note was expressed in these strange words: "I cannot receive you here; but I can, and will, come to you at your hotel if you will wait for me. I am not able to appoint a time. I can only promise to watch for my first opportunity, and to take advantage of it instantly—for your sake and for mine."

But one interpretation could be placed on such language as this. Lucilla was not a free agent. Both Oscar and the rector were now obliged to acknowledge that my view of the case had been the correct one. If it was impossible for me to be received into the house, how doubly impossible would it be for the men to gain admission! Oscar, after reading the note, withdrew to the further end of the room, keeping his thoughts to himself. Mr. Finch decided on stepping out of his secondary position by forthwith taking a course of his own. "Am I to infer," he began, "that it is really useless for me to attempt to see my own child?"

"Her letter speaks for itself," I replied. "If you attempt to see her, you will probably be the means of preventing your daughter from coming here."

"In my parental capacity," continued Mr. Finch, "it is impossible for me to remain passive. As a brother clergyman, I have, I conceive, a claim on the rector of this parish. It is quite likely that notice may have been already given of this fraudulent marriage. In that case, it is not only my duty to myself and my child— it is my duty to the Church, to confer with my reverend colleague. I go to confer with him." He strutted to the door, and added: "If Lucilla arrives in my absence, I invest you with my authority, Madame Pratolungo, to detain her until my return." With that parting charge to me, he walked out.

I looked at Oscar. He came slowly toward me from the other end of the room.

"You will wait here, of course?" he said.

"Of course. And you?"

"I shall go out for a little while."

"For any particular purpose?"

"No. To get through the time. I am weary of waiting."

I felt positively assured, from the manner in which he answered me, that he was going—now he had got rid of Mr. Finch—straight to his cousin's house.

"You forget," I said, "that Lucilla may come here while you are out. Your presence in the room, or in the room next to this, may be of the greatest importance, when I tell her what your brother has done. Suppose she refuses to believe me? What am I to do if I have not got you to appeal to? In your own interest, as well as in Lucilla's, I request you to remain here with me till she comes."

Putting it on that ground only, I waited to see what he would do. After a certain hesitation, he answered, with a sullen assumption of in-difference: "Just as you please!" and walked away again toward the other end of the room. As he turned his back on me I heard him say to himself: "It's only waiting a little longer!"

"Waiting for what?" I asked.

He looked round at me over his shoulder.

"Patience for the present!" he answered. "You will hear soon enough." For the moment I said no more to him. The tone in which he had replied warned me that it would be use-less.

After an interval — how long an interval I cannot well say—I heard the sound of women's dresses in the passage outside.

The instant after there was a knock at the door.

I signed to Oscar to open a second door, close

by him at the lower end of the room, and (for the moment at least) to keep out of sight. Then I answered the knock, and said as steadily as I could: "Come in."

A woman unknown to me entered, dressed like a respectable servant. She came in leading Lucilla by the hand. My first look at my darling told me the horrible truth. As I had seen her in the corridor at the rectory on the first day when we met, so I now saw her once more. Again the sightless eyes turned on me, insensibly reflecting the light that fell on them. Blind! O God! after a few brief weeks of sight, blind again!

In that miserable discovery I forgot everything else. I flew to her, and caught her in my arms. I cast one look at her pale, wasted face, and burst out crying on her bosom.

She held my head gently with one hand, and waited with the patience of an angel until that first outbreak of my grief had exhausted itself. "Don't cry about my blindness," said the soft, sweet voice that I knew so well. "The days when I had my sight have been the unhappiest days of my life. If I look as if I had been fretting, don't think it is about my eyes." She paused, and sighed bitterly. "I may tell *you*," she went on, in a whisper. "It's a relief, it's a consolation, to tell *you*. I am fretting about my marriage."

Those words roused me. I lifted my head and kissed her. "I have come back to comfort you," I said; "and I have behaved like a fool."

She smiled faintly. "How like you," she exclaimed, "to say that!" She tapped my cheek with her fingers in the old familiar way. The repetition of that little trifling action almost broke my heart. I nearly choked myself in forcing back the stupid, cowardly, useless tears that tried to burst from me again. "Come!" she said. "No more crying. Let us sit down and talk as if we were at Dimchurch."

I took her to the sofa; we sat side by side. She put her arm round my waist and laid her head on my shoulder. Again the faint smile flickered like a dying light on her lovely face, wan and wasted, yet still beautiful — still the Virgin's face in Raphael's picture. "We are a strange pair," she said, with a momentary flash of her old irresistible humor. "You are my bitterest enemy, and you burst out crying over me the moment we meet. I have been shockingly treated by you, and I have got my arm round your waist and my head on your shoulder, and I wouldn't let go of you for the world!" Her face saddened again; her voice suddenly altered its tone. "Tell me," she went on, "how it is that appearances were so terribly against you? Oscar satisfied me, at Ramsgate, that I ought to give you up, that I ought never to see you again. I took his view—there is no denying it, my dear —I agreed with him in detesting you, for a little while. But when the blindness came back, I could keep it up no longer. Little by little, as the light died out, my heart *would* turn to you again. When I heard your letter read, when I knew that you were near me, it was just like the old times; I was mad to see you. And here I am—satisfied, before you explain it to me, that you have been the victim of some terrible mistake."

I tried, in grateful acknowledgment of those generous words, to enter on my justification there and then. It was impossible. I could think of nothing, I could speak of nothing, but the dreadful discovery of her blindness.

"Give me a few minutes," I said, "and you shall hear it all. I can't talk of myself yet; I can only talk of you. Oh, Lucilla, why did you keep away from Grosse? Come with me to him to-day. Let him try what he can do. At once, my love—before it is too late."

"It *is* too late," she said. "I have been to another oculist—a stranger. He said what Mr. Sebright said: he doubted if there was ever any chance for me; he thought the operation ought never to have been performed."

"Why did you go to a stranger?" I asked. "Why did you give up Grosse?"

"You must ask Oscar," she answered. "It was at his desire that I kept away from Grosse."

Hearing this, I penetrated for myself the motive which had actuated Nugent, as I afterward found it set forth in the Journal. If he had let Lucilla go to Grosse, our good German might have noticed that her position was preying on her mind, and might have seen his reasons for exposing the deception that Nugent was practicing on her. For the rest, I still persisted in entreating Lucilla to go back with me to our old friend.

"Remember our conversation on this very subject," she rejoined, shaking her head decisively. "I mean at the time when the operation was going to be performed. I told you I was used to being blind. I said I only wanted to recover my sight to see Oscar. And when I did see him —what happened? The disappointment was so dreadful, I wished myself blind again. Don't start! don't cry out as if you were shocked! I mean what I say. You people who can see attach such an absurd importance to your eyes! Don't you recollect my saying that when we last talked about it?"

I recollected perfectly. She had said those words. She had declared that she had never honestly envied any of us the use of our eyes. She had even reviled our eyes; comparing them contemptuously with *her* touch; deriding them as deceivers who were constantly leading us wrong. I acknowledged all this, without being in the least reconciled to the catastrophe that had happened. If she would only have listened to me, I should still have gone on obstinately pleading with her. But she flatly refused to listen. "We have very little time to spare," she said. "Let us talk of something more interesting before I am obliged to leave you."

"Obliged to leave me?" I repeated. "Are you not your own mistress?" Her face clouded over; her manner became embarrassed.

"I cannot honestly tell you that I am a prisoner," she answered. "I can only say I am watched. When Oscar is away from me, Oscar's cousin—a sly, suspicious, false woman— always contrives to put herself in his place. I heard her say to her husband that she believed I should break my marriage engagement unless I was closely looked after. I don't know what

I should do but for one of the servants in the house, who is an excellent creature, who sympathizes with me and helps me—" She stopped, and lifted her head inquiringly. "Where *is* the servant?" she asked.

I had forgotten the woman who had brought her into the room. She must have delicately left us together after leading Lucilla in. When I looked up she was not to be seen.

"The servant is, no doubt, waiting downstairs," I said. "Go on."

"But for that good creature," Lucilla resumed, "I should never have got here. She brought me your letter, and read it to me, and wrote my reply. I arranged with her to slip out at the first opportunity. One chance was in our favor—we had only the cousin to keep an eye on us. Oscar was not in the house."

She suddenly checked herself at the last word. A slight sound at the lower end of the room, which had passed unnoticed by me, had caught her delicate ear. "What is that noise?" she asked. "Anybody in the room with us?"

I looked up once more. While she was talking of the false Oscar, the true Oscar was standing listening to her at the other end of the room.

When he discovered that I was looking at him, he entreated me by a gesture not to betray his presence. He had evidently heard what we had been saying to each other before I detected him, for he touched his eyes, and lifted his hands pityingly in allusion to Lucilla's blindness. Whatever his mood might be, that melancholy discovery must surely have affected him—Lucilla's influence over him now *could* only be an influence for good? I signed to him to remain, and told Lucilla that there was nothing to be alarmed about. She went on.

"Oscar went to London early this morning," she said. "Can you guess what he has gone for?

He has gone to get the Marriage License—he has given notice of the marriage at the church! My last hope is in your. In spite of everything that I can say to him, he has fixed the day for the twenty-first—in two days more! I have done all I could to put it off; I have insisted on every possible delay. Oh, if you knew—'' Her rising agitation stifled her utterance for the moment. "I mustn't waste the precious minutes; I must get back before Oscar returns,'' she went on, rallying again. "Oh, my old friend, you are never at a loss; you always know what to do! Find me some way of putting off my marriage. Suggest something which will take them by surprise, and force them to give me time!''

I looked toward the lower end of the room. Listening in breathless interest, Oscar had noiselessly advanced half-way toward us. At a sign from me he checked himself and came no further.

"Do you really mean, Lucilla, that you no longer love him?'' I said.

"I can tell you nothing about it,'' she answered, "except that some dreadful change has come over me. While I had my sight I could partly account for it—I believed that the new sense had made a new being of me. But now I have lost my sight again—now I am once more what I have been all my life—still the same horrible insensibility possesses me. I have so little feeling for him that I sometimes find it hard to persuade myself that he really *is* Oscar. You know how I used to adore him; you know how enchanted I should once have been to marry him. Think of what I must suffer, feeling toward him as I feel now!''

I looked up again. Oscar had stolen nearer; I could see his face plainly. The good influence of Lucilla was beginning to do its good work! I saw the tears rising in his eyes; I saw love and pity taking the place of hatred and revenge. The Oscar of my old recollections was standing before me once more!

"I don't want to go away," Lucilla went on; "I don't want to leave him. All I ask for is a little more time. Time *must* help me to get back again to my old self. My blind days have been the days of my whole life. Can a few weeks of sight have deprived me of the feelings which have been growing in me for years? I won't believe it! I can find my way about the house; I can tell things by my touch; I can do all that I did in my blindness, just as well as ever, now I am blind again. The feeling for *him* will come back to me like the rest. Only give me time! only give me time!"

At the last word she started to her feet in sudden alarm. "There *is* some one in the room," she said. "Some one who is crying! Who is it?"

Oscar was close to us. The tears were falling fast over his cheeks; the one faint, sobbing breath which had escaped him had caught my ear as well as Lucilla's. I took his hand in one of my hands, and I took Lucilla's hand in the other. For good or for evil, the result rested with God's mercy. The time had come.

"Who is it?" Lucilla repeated, impatiently.

"Try if you can tell, my love, without asking me."

With those words, I put her hand in Oscar's hand, and stood close, watching her face.

For one awful moment, when she first felt the familiar touch, the blood left her cheeks. Her blind eyes dilated fearfully. She stood petrified. Then, with a long, low cry—a cry of breathless rapture—she flung her arms passionately round his neck. The life flowed back into her face; her lovely smile just trembled on her parted lips; her breath came faint and quick and fluttering. In soft tones of ecstasy, with her lips on his cheek, she murmured the delicious words:

"Oh, Oscar! I know you once more!"

CHAPTER THE FIFTIETH.

THE END OF THE JOURNEY.

A LITTLE interval of time elapsed.

Her first exquisite sense of the recognition by touch had passed away. Her mind had recovered its balance. She separated herself from Oscar, and turned to me, with the one inevitable question which I knew must follow the joining of their hands.

"What does it mean?"

The exposure of Nugent's perfidy; the revelation of the fatal secret of Oscar's face; and last, not least the defense of my own conduct toward her, were all comprehended in the answer for which that question called. As carefully, as delicately, as mercifully as I could, I disclosed to her the whole truth. How the shock affected her, she did not tell me at the time, and has never told me since. With her hand in Oscar's hand, with her face hidden on Oscar's breast, she listened; not once interrupting me, from first to last, by so much as a single word. Now and then I saw her tremble; now and then I heard her sigh heavily. That was all. It was only when I had ended—it was only after a long interval, during which Oscar and I watched her in speechless anxiety—that she slowly lifted her head and broke the silence.

"Thank God," we heard her say to herself, fervently—"thank God, I am blind!"

Those were her last words. They filled me with horror. I cried out to her to recall them.

She quietly laid her head back on Oscar's breast.

"Why should I recall them?" she asked. "Do

you think. I wish to see him disfigured as he is
now? No! I wish to see him—and I *do* see
him!—as my fancy drew his picture in the first
days of our love. My blindness is my blessing.
It has given me back my old delightful sensation
when I touch him; it keeps my own beloved image of him—the one image I care for—un-
changed and unchangeable. You *will* persist
in thinking that my happiness depends on my
sight. I look back with horror at what I suffered when I had my sight—my one effort is to
forget that miserable time. Oh, how little you
know of me! Oh, what a loss it would be to me
if I saw him as you see him! Try to understand
me, and you won't talk of my affliction—you
will talk of my gain."

"Your gain!" I repeated. "What have you
gained?"

"Happiness," she answered. "My life lives
in my love. And my love lives in my blindness."

There was the story of her whole existence—
told in two words!

If you had seen her radiant face as she raised
it again in the excitement of speaking—if you
had remembered (as I remembered) what her
surgeon had said of the penalty which she must
inevitably pay for the recovery of her sight—
how would you have answered her? It is barely
possible, perhaps, that you might have done
what I did. That is to say, you might have
modestly admitted that she knew what the conditions of her happiness were better than you—
and you might not have answered her at all!

I left Oscar and Lucilla to talk together, and
took a turn in the room, considering with myself
what we were to do next.

It was not easy to say. The barren information which I had received from my darling was

all the information that I possessed. Nugent
had unflinchingly carried his cruel deception to
its end. He had falsely given notice of his marriage at the church in his brother's name, and
he was now in London falsely obtaining his Marriage License in his brother's name also. So
much I knew of his proceedings, and no more.

While I was still pondering Lucilla cut the
Gordian knot.

"Why are we stopping here?" she asked.
"Let us go—and never return to this hateful
place again!"

As she rose to her feet we were startled by a
soft knock at the door.

I answered the knock. The woman who had
brought Lucilla to the hotel appeared once more.
She seemed to be afraid to venture far from the
door. Standing just inside the room, she looked
nervously at Lucilla, and said, "Can I speak to
you, miss?"

"You can say anything you like before this
lady and gentleman," Lucilla answered. "What
is it?"

"I'm afraid we have been followed, miss."

"Followed! By whom?"

"By the lady's-maid. I saw her, a little
while since, looking up at the hotel, and then
she went back in a hurry on the way to the
house—and that's not the worst of it, miss."

"What else has happened?"

"We have made a mistake about the railway," said the woman. "There's a train from
London that we didn't notice in the time-table.
They tell me downstairs it came in more than a
quarter of an hour ago. Please to come back,
miss, or I fear we shall be found out."

"You can go back at once, Jane," said Lucilla.

"By myself?"

"Yes. Thank you for bringing me here—here
I remain."

She had barely taken her seat again between Oscar and me before the door was softly opened from the outside. A long, thin, nervous hand stole in through the opening, took the servant by the arm, and drew her out into the passage. In her place, a man entered the room with his hat on. The man was Nugent Dubourg.

He stopped where the servant had stopped. He looked at Lucilla; he looked at his brother; he looked at me.

Not a word fell from him. There he stood, fronting the friend whom he had calumniated, and the brother whom he had betrayed. There he stood—with his eyes fixed on Lucilla, sitting between us—knowing that it was all over; knowing that the woman for whom he had degraded himself was a woman parted from him forever. There he stood, in the hell of his own making, and devoured his torture in silence.

On his brother's appearance, Oscar had risen, and had put his arm round Lucilla. He now advanced a step toward Nugent, still holding to him his betrothed wife.

I followed him, eagerly watching his face. There was no fear in me now of what he might do. Lucilla's blessed influence had found, and cast out, the lurking demon that had been hidden in him. With a mind attentive but not alarmed, I waited to see how he would meet the emergency that confronted him.

"Nugent!" he said very quietly.

Nugent's head drooped—he made no answer. Lucilla, hearing Oscar pronounce the name, instantly understood what had happened. She shuddered with horror. Oscar gently placed her in my arms, and advanced again alone toward his brother. His face expressed the struggle in him of some subtly mingling influences of love and anguish, of sorrow and shame. He recalled to me in the strangest manner my past

experience of him when he had first trusted me
with the story of the Trial, and when he had
told me that Nugent was the good angel of his
life.

He went up to the place at which his brother
was standing. In the simple, boyish way so
familiar to me in the bygone time, he laid his
hand on his brother's arm.

"Nugent!" he said. "Are you the same
dear, good brother who saved me from dying
on the scaffold, and who cheered my hard life
afterward? Are you' the same bright, clever,
noble fellow that I was always so fond of and
so proud of?"

He paused, and removed his brother's hat.
With careful, caressing hand, he parted his
brother's ruffled hair over his forehead. Nugent's head sank lower. His face was distorted,
his hands were clinched, in the dumb agony of
remembrance which that tender voice and that
kind hand had set loose in him. Oscar gave
him time to recover himself: Oscar spoke next
to me.

"You know Nugent?" he said. "You remember, when we first met, my telling you that
Nugent was an angel? You saw for yourself,
when he came to Dimchurch, how kindly he
helped me; how faithfully he kept my secrets;
what a true friend he was? Look at him—and
you will feel, as I do, that we have misunderstood and misinterpreted him in some monstrous
way." He turned again to Nugent. "I daren't
tell you," he went on, "what I have heard about
you, and what I have believed about you, and
what vile unbrotherly thoughts I have had of
being revenged on you. Thank God, they are
gone! My dear fellow, I look back at them—
now I see you—as I might look back at a horrible dream. How *can* I see you, Nugent, and
believe that you have been false to me? You, a

villain who has tried to rob poor Me of the only woman in the world who cares for me! You, so handsome and so popular, who may marry any woman you like! It can't be. You have drifted innocently into some false position without knowing it. Defend yourself! No. Let *me* defend you. You shan't humble yourself to anybody. Tell me how you have really acted toward Lucilla and toward me, and leave it to your brother to set you right with everybody. Come, Nugent! lift up your head—and tell me what I shall say."

Nugent lifted his head, and looked at Oscar.

Ghastly as his face was, I saw something in his eyes, when he first fixed them on his brother, which again reminded me of past days—the days when he had joined us at Dimchurch, and when he used to talk of "poor Oscar" in the tender, light-hearted way that first won me. I thought once more of the memorable night interview between us at Browndown, when Oscar had left England. Again I called to mind the signs which had told of the nobler nature of the man pleading with him. Again I remembered the remorse which had moved him to tears—the effort he had made in my presence to atone for past misdoing, and to struggle for the last time against the guilty passion that possessed him. Was the nature which could feel that remorse utterly depraved? Was the man who had made that effort—the last of the many that had gone before it—irredeemably bad? "Wait!" I whispered to Lucilla, trembling and weeping in my arms. "He will deserve our sympathy; he will win our pardon and our pity yet!"

"Come!" Oscar repeated. "Tell me what I shall say."

Nugent drew from his pocket a sheet of paper with writing on it.

"Say," he answered, "that I gave notice of

your marriage at the church here—and that I
went to London and got you *this.*"

He handed the sheet of paper to his brother.
It was the Marriage License, taken out in his
brother's name.

"Be happy, Oscar," he added. "*You* deserve it."

He threw one arm in his old, easy, protecting
way round his brother. His hand, as it did this,
touched the breast pocket of Oscar's coat. Before
it was possible to stop him, his dexterous fingers
had opened the pocket, and had taken from it a
little toy pistol, with a chased silver handle of
Oscar's own workmanship.

"Was this for me?" he asked, with a faint
smile. "My poor boy! you could never have
done it, could you?" He kissed Oscar's dark
cheek, and put the pistol into his own pocket.
"The handle is your own work," he said. "I
shall take it as your present to me. Return to
Browndown when you are married. I am going
to travel again. You shall hear from me before
I leave England. God bless you, Oscar. Good-
by."

He put his brother back from him with a firm
and gentle hand. I attempted to advance with
Lucilla, and speak to him. Something in his
face—looking at me out of his mournful eyes,
calm, stern, and superhuman, like a look of doom
—warned me back from him, and filled me with
the foreboding that I should see him no more.
He walked to the door and opened it—turned—
and, fixing his farewell look on Lucilla, saluted
us silently with a bend of his head. The door
closed on him softly. In a few minutes only
from the time when he had entered the room
he had left us again—and left us forever.

We looked at each other—we could not speak.
The void that he had left behind him was dreary
and dreadful. I was the first who moved. In

silence I led Lucilla back to our seat on the sofa, and beckoned to Oscar to go to her in my place.

This done, I left them—and went out to meet Lucilla's father on his return to the hotel. I wished to prevent him from disturbing them. After what had happened, it was good for them to be alone.

EPILOGUE.

MADAME PRATOLUNGO'S LAST WORDS.

TWELVE years have passed since the events happened which it has been the business of these pages to relate. I am at my desk, looking idly at all the leaves of writing which my pen has filled, and asking myself if there is more yet to add before I have done.

There is more—not much.

Oscar and Lucilla claim me first. Two days after they were restored to each other at Sydenham they were married at the church in that place. It was a dull wedding. Nobody was in spirits but Mr. Finch. We parted in London. The bride and bridegroom returned to Browndown. The rector remained in town for a day or two visiting some friends. I went back to my father, to accompany him, as I had promised, on his journey from Marseilles to Paris.

As well as I remember, I remained a fortnight abroad. In the course of that time I received kind letters from Browndown. One of them announced that Oscar had heard from his brother.

Nugent's letter was not a long one. It was dated at Liverpool, and it announced his embarkation for America in two hours' time. He had heard of a new expedition to the Arctic regions—then fitting out in the United States—

with the object of discovering the open polar sea supposed to be situated between Spitzbergen and Nova Zembla. It had instantly struck him that this expedition offered an entirely new field of study to a landscape painter in search of the sublimest aspects of Nature. He had decided on volunteering to join the Arctic explorers, and he had already raised the necessary money for his outfit by the sale of the only valuables he possessed — his jewelry and his books. If he wanted more, he engaged to apply to Oscar. In any case, he promised to write again before the expedition sailed. And so, for the present only, he would bid his brother and sister affectionately farewell.—When I afterward looked at the letter myself, I found nothing in it which referred in the slightest degree to the past, or which hinted at the state of the writer's own health and spirits.

I returned to our remote Southdown village, and occupied the room which Lucilla had herself prepared for me at Browndown.

I found the married pair as tranquil and as happy in their union as a man and woman could be. The absent Nugent dwelt a little sadly in their minds at times, I suspect, as well as in mine. It was perhaps on this account that Lucilla appeared to me to be quieter than she used to be in her maiden days. However, my presence did something toward restoring her to her old spirits, and Grosse's speedy arrival exerted its enlivening influence in support of mine.

As soon as the gout would let him get on his feet he presented himself with his instruments at Browndown, eager for another experiment on Lucilla's eyes. "If my operations had failed," he said, "I should not have plagued you no more. But my operations has not failed: it is you who have failed to take care of your nice new eyes when I gave them to you." In those terms he endeavored to persuade her to let him attempt

another operation. She steadily refused to submit to it, and the discussion that followed roused
her famously.

More than once afterward Grosse tried to make
her change her mind. He tried in vain. The
disputes between the two made the house ring
again. Lucilla found all her old gayety in refut-
ing the grotesque arguments and persuasions of
our worthy German. To me—when I once or
twice attempted to shake her resolution—she replied in another way, merely repeating the words
she had said to me at Sydenham, "My life lives
in my love. And my love lives in my blindness." It is only right to add that Mr. Sebright,
and another competent authority, consulted with
him, declared unhesitatingly that she was right.
Under any circumstances, Mr. Sebright was of
opinion that the success of Grosse's operation
could never have been more than temporary.
His colleague, after examining Lucilla's eyes
at a later period, entirely agreed with him.
Which was in the right—these two or Grosse
—who can say? As blind Lucilla, you first
knew her. As blind Lucilla, you see the last
of her now. If you feel inclined to regret this,
remember that the one thing essential was the
thing she possessed. Her life was a happy one.
Bear this in mind—and don't forget that your
conditions of happiness need not necessarily be
her conditions also.

In the time I am now writing of, the second
letter from Nugent arrived. It was written the
evening before he sailed for the polar seas. One
line in it touched us deeply. "Who knows
whether I shall ever see England again? If
a boy is born to you, Oscar, call him by my
name—for my sake."

Inclosed in this letter was a private communication from Nugent addressed to me. It was
the confession to which I have alluded in my

notes attached to Lucilla's Journal.   These words
only were added at the end: "You now know
everything.   Forgive me—if you can.   I have
not escaped without suffering: remember that."
After making use of the narrative, as you already
know, I have burned it all, except those last
lines.

At distant intervals we heard twice of the ex-
ploring-ship from whaling-vessels.   Then there
was a long, dreary interval without news of any
sort.   Then a dreadful report that the expedition
was lost.   Then the confirmation of the report—
a lapse of a whole year, and no tidings of the
missing men.

They were well provided with supplies of all
kinds, and there was a general hope that they
might be holding out.   A new expedition was
sent—and sent vainly—in search of them over-
land.   Rewards were offered to whaling vessels
to find them, and were never earned.   We were
mourning for Nugent; we were a melancholy
household.   Two more years passed before the
fate of the lost expedition was discovered.   A
ship in the whale trade, driven out of her course,
fell in with a wrecked and dismantled vessel lost
in the ice.   Let the last sentences of the captain's
report tell the story:

"The wreck was drifting along a channel of
open water when we first saw it.   Before long
it was brought up by an iceberg.   I got into my
boat with some of my sailors, and we rowed to
the vessel.

"Not a man was to be seen on the deck, which
was covered with snow.   We hailed, and got no
reply.   I looked in through one of the circular
glazed portholes astern and saw dimly the figure
of a man seated at a table.   I knocked on the
thick glass, but he never moved.   We got on
deck, and opened the cabin hatchway, and went
below.   The man I had seen was before us, at

the end of the cabin. I led the way, and spoke
to him. He made no answer. I looked closer,
and touched one of his hands which lay on the
table. To my horror and astonishment, he was
a frozen corpse.

"On the table before him was the last entry in
the ship's log:

" 'Seventeen days since we have been shut up
in the ice! Our fire went out yesterday. The
captain tried to light it again, and has failed.
The surgeon and two seamen died of cold this
morning. The rest of us must soon follow. If
we are ever discovered, I beg the person who
finds me to send this—'

"There the hand that held the pen had dropped
into the writer's lap. The left hand still lay on
the table. Between the frozen fingers we found
a long lock of a woman's hair tied at each end
with a blue ribbon. The open eyes of the corpse
were still fixed on the lock of hair.

"The name of this man was found in his pocket-
book. It was Nugent Dubourg. I publish the
name in my report, in case it may meet the eyes
of his friends.

"Examination of the rest of the vessel, and
comparison of dates with the date of the log-book,
showed that the officers and crew had been dead
for more than two years. The positions in which
we found the frozen men, and the names where
it was possible to discover them, are here set forth
as follows" . . .

That "lock of a woman's hair" is now in Lucilla's possession. It will be buried with her, at
her own request, when she dies. Ah, poor Nugent! Are we not all sinners? Remember the
best of him, and forget the worst, as we do.

I still linger over my writing—reluctant to
leave it, if the truth must be told. But what
more is there to say? I hear Oscar hammering

away at his chasing, and whistling blithely over his work. In another room Lucilla is teaching the piano to her little girl. On my table is a letter from Mrs. Finch, dated from one of our distant colonies—over which Mr. Finch (who has risen gloriously in the world) presides pastorally as bishop. He harangues the "natives" to his heart's content: and the wonderful natives like it. "Jicks" is in her element among the aboriginal members of her father's congregation: there are fears that the wandering Arab of the Finch family will end in marrying "a chief." Mrs. Finch—I don't expect you to believe this— is anticipating another confinement.

Lucilla's eldest boy—called Nugent—has just come in, and stands by my desk. He lifts his bright blue eyes up to mine; his round, rosy face expresses strong disapproval of what I am doing. "Aunty," he says, "you have written enough. Come and play."

The boy is right. I must put away my manuscript and leave you. My excellent spirits are a little dashed at parting. I wonder whether you are sorry too? I shall never know! Well, I have many blessings to comfort me on closing my relations with you. I have kind souls who love me; and—observe this!—I stand on my political principles as firmly as ever. The world is getting converted to my way of thinking: the Pratolungo programme, my friends, is coming to the front with giant steps. Long live the Republic! Farewell.